JACK COMES BACK

TALES OF THE ETERNAL DOG

ALEC ROWELL

Copyright © 2022 by Alec Rowell

JACK COMES BACK: Tales of the Eternal Dog
Volumes 1-4

STONE DOG, Volume 1
IRON DOG, Volume 2
GOLD DOG, Volume 3
STEEL DOG, Volume 4

Cover design by GETCOVERS.com
Internal illustrations by KAMVANC@instagram

All rights reserved, including the right to reproduce this book or portions thereof in any form whatsoever.

All characters in this book are fictitious. Any resemblance to persons living or dead is coincidental.

First SOUND VOLUMES edition 2022
First U.S. edition 2022, Ingram Edition

SOUND VOLUMES LLC
Cascadia

www.soundvolumes.com

ISBN 0-9728919-0-0
JACK COMES BACK: Tales of the Eternal Dog, Volumes 1-4 (Print: SV01)

Printed in the United States of America

CONTENTS

STONE DOG

1. Bites Back	3
Bites Back and the Death-Claw	9
The Bardo of Bites Back	15
2. INTERLUDE: White Sides Follows Two Legs	25
3. Dyak: Dog of the People	28
Dyak and the Body Eaters	37
Bardo of Dyak	67

IRON DOG

1. Tekhe: Daughter of Anubis	75
The Ka of Tekhe	84
2. In the Sleeve of Fu Hao	92
3. The Castoff: A Dog of Rome	102
GLOSSARY for The Castoff	228

GOLD DOG

1. INUJIKI-NO-KAMI	251
2. Lionhunters of Bam-i-yan	265
3. Healing Arts	301
4. INTERLUDE: From the Royal Pocket	327
5. Jackanapes in Heaven	345

STEEL DOG

1. A Yaqui Dog	357
2. Tickle 'em Jock	384
3. Heroes of Passchendaele	402
4. Star Lost	415
5. This is My Yard	427

6. The Long Contract 452
7. Pureland Bardo of the Eternal Dog 468

Dedication 475
Acknowledgments 477
About the Author 479

STONE DOG

Tales of the Eternal Dog, V. 1

ALEC ROWELL

1

BITES BACK

72,000 BCE — somewhere in south-central Asia, one year after the eruption of the Lake Toba supervolcano

BITES BACK'S legs twitched as he slept. He was young, jumping on the backs of his littermates, hunting flowers and grass. His mother, Stone Eyes, was strong. There was no white in the dark fur of her muzzle. His father Fast Paw was still alive, brown and gray like Bites Back. Meat was everywhere and the family ran just to eat the air and feel their legs stretch.

This was before the great light dimmed, before the gray death leaves fell for so long. When the family was many.

Nearby, running hoof sounds of a Tall Runner roused Bites Back from sleep. His head rolled to where his mother had slept. But Stone Eyes was not there. She had not risen after the last light. The family sang long over the dead mother. Now they had no mother.

Bites Back yipped and woke the others. They all smelled the Tall Runner and they jumped and danced after it. Broken Tail was father of the family since Fast Paw fell. He ran first, but Bites Back was close behind.

The family had been running now for most of light. The meat they chased was tired. Flower Nose ran at Bites Back's side. She alone could be mother now. Her scent mixed with the warm smell of the meat that ran from them as he breathed the best air, the air of running. His legs scissored in, overlapping and then stretching out.

Ahead, Broken Tail moved to close-and-kill pace. The meat must be slowing. Grey death leaves were all over the ground. They piled around the dead trees where water from the sky did not wash them away but mounded them in mush piles. The family stayed away from these, even though they could hear Little Crunchy Meat living in them.

The Little Crunchy Meat was all that lived well now.

The trees ended before the hill. Broken Tail slipped on the rise above. No, he hadn't slipped; he had stopped. Strange behavior when meat was so close. The family could not afford to lose a whole light's run after meat.

Bites Back ran to the father's side, risking a snarl. Below them—a long rush away—their meat lay on its side, hooves kicking in the air. There also, tall and thin with a long stick on its front paw, a Two-Legs stood next to their meat. Another Two-Legs crouched at its neck, eating the family's kill.

Next to him, Bites Back felt the heat from Broken Tail, heard his heart and his panting as his own. He smelled the same breath and felt the same heart from Flower Nose and the others who stood behind. This kill might be the last they could make. The family had to have this meat.

Bites Back lowered his muzzle, turned toward Broken Tail, and whined. Broken Tail stood stiff and still, watching the Two-Legs. He growled low.

Sometimes, when the family made a new kill and the Long-tooths came, the family left the kill. The Longtooths liked the meat of dogs, too, and none could fight the Longtooths and win.

But these were not Longtooths, they were Two-Legs. Slow, soft-pawed, flat-tooth Two-Legs. Even now there were more dogs in the family than there were Two-Legs here, and if they did not take this meat they would all die weak like Stone Eyes. Better to lose a family member fighting Two-Legs than to lose all the family by running away.

A low growl crept up from deep in his belly. This was *their* kill, *their* meat. Bites Back looked quickly at the father again. Bites Back's growl warmed him. It made him feel larger than Broken Tail, as big as a Longtooth.

He looked down at the Two-Legs. The Two-Legs with the stick bared its teeth at the family, at Bites Back. It raised one of its extra legs that did not touch the ground and shook the stick in the paw at the end of that leg.

Bites Back's growl changed to the sound of attack as he

charged down the slope at the Two-Legs. It moved forward, lowering the stick and pointing it at him. Bites Back turned sharply and jumped instead on the Two-Legs that crouched by the family's meat. Jaws wide, he landed on this thief. Aiming for its neck, he missed and his teeth sliced into its shoulder. It made a loud noise and shook hard. His bite was not a kill, so Bites Back released. He fell on the other side of the dead Tall Runner.

The family followed him down the hill and attacked the Two-Legs.

The Two-Legs Bites Back had bitten rose to run. Mud Paw and Little Eyes bit its legs, but did not take it down. The other Two-Legs backed away, waving its stick. Jumps High, Grey Head, and Crooked Leg circled, searching for weakness.

Bites Back looked up at the hill. Broken Tail and Flower Nose stood there, watching the Two-Legs and the rest of the family. The Two-Legs had taken the family's kill. And the father did not fight. Bites Back raised his voice in a sharp song of anger.

Flower Nose ran down to join the family. Broken Tail stayed above, watching.

Nearby were sounds of pain. Mud Paw and Little Eyes were back from their chase; their Two-Legs was dead or it had gotten away. Only the Two-Legs with the stick now faced the family. It stopped moving its stick and turned to run. Slipping in from behind, Crooked Leg grabbed its paw, the top paw that didn't have the stick. The smell of the blood from the Two-Legs mixed with the scent from their kill and with the blood on Crooked Leg's back. Bites Back's belly shrank in crazy hunger.

Turning more quickly than Bites Back had seen a Two-Legs move before, it struck Crooked Leg with the end of its stick.

The stick went through Crooked Leg's neck as if it was water. Crooked Leg made the sounds of death and fell.

The family stopped their attacks. They knew death. Death was what they brought to others. Too often it found them. But the family had never seen a death like this. What kind of stick could do this? Forgotten in shock, the Two-Legs and its kill-stick slid away.

Flower Nose, who was Crooked Leg's littermate, began the song, and then the rest of the family joined. They sang of Crooked Leg's heart; they sang of how he danced when the Little Crunchy Meat flew up from the water, trying but never catching them in his mouth. They sang of him as a hunter—he had never been a good hunter because his leg left him always at the back, but he had powerful jaws and sometimes broke bones so the little ones could lick the marrow inside. They sang of him as a warm body in the cold of the nights after the gray death leaves fell from the sky. And Flower Nose sang of him as her littermate. Her song was loudest and strongest.

Before Flower Nose finished her song, Broken Tail ran down the hill, walked over to the kill, and dipped his muzzle into it. He was looking for the heart, always his favorite portion.

Muzzle wet with strange blood, Bites Back's legs stiffened. A growl grew in him, a growl he did not know he started. It filled him. Made him larger. Made him powerful.

With no other warning, he jumped on Broken Tail.

But Broken Tail was no Two-Legs. He had been father of the family since Bites Back ran in his first kill. Not long after that, Bites Back had challenged him—half in play, but half not. The fight had not taken long. Broken Tail had not bothered to bring blood as he stood over the young and foolish Bites Back. Since that time, Bites Back smelled his old defeat whenever he smelled Broken Tail.

He did not smell his defeat now. He felt only his anger. Anger at the Two-Legs, at Broken Tail. And he smelled fear all around him. Fear of finding no meat—of the family dying. The anger in his belly burned. Broken Tail had failed the family.

Broken Tail jumped aside as Bites Back came down on him. He had expected the attack. He bent low and grabbed Bites Back's front leg in his mouth, crushing down to cripple and shatter the small bones.

This would end the fight. Bites Back would die if he could no longer follow the hunt. But the growl in his belly was so large that Bites Back hardly felt Broken Tail's attack. While the older dog bore down on his leg, Bites Back took all of Broken Tail's neck in his own mouth and closed his jaws, jaws powered by the growl that shook his belly and his world and made him as strong as any dog had ever been.

Broken Tail released Bites Back's leg before the bones broke. The father's body tensed. All four of his legs extended straight and hard, and a sound came from him. This sound was not the song of death; it was a whimper. Not the whimper of a pup, or of an old dog, or of one in season asking another to mate, but a whimper that no dog ever wanted to make or that any of the family ever wanted to hear. Broken Tail would never run for the kill again.

He lay on his side, legs stiff and trembling. His sounds of pain continued, but grew softer.

Broken Tail could not turn his head, but his eyes moved enough to look into Bites Back's. His eyes, always dark like the earth, looked lighter now, like Bites Back's heavy fur or the gray death that had come from the sky and covered everything. Bites Back did not see anger in those eyes, the anger that he had felt toward Broken Tail. All he could see was himself looking back, as when he looked in the still water.

Bites Back leaned his head down and licked under Broken Tail's jaw.

Mud Paw, Broken Tail's youngest pup, began the song of death. One by one, the family joined. Except for Bites Back. He was father of the family now. He must keep the family safe.

BITES BACK AND THE DEATH-CLAW

BITES BACK KNEW the giant Death-Claw slept through the cold time in these hill dens. Warmth was returning and its smell was dusty and weak. Its paw prints, so like those of the family but much bigger and wider, were dry. And the family needed more warmth than the hard ground and dead trees could give them.

Flower Nose and their year-pups vanished from sight in the darkness of the hill den. The scents of the family and the smells of tree roots washed out the old musk of Death-Claw. Yet the odor of that killer remained.

Bites Back's gray fur bristled.

It came.

Bites Back stood nearest the opening. All the family was behind him, deeper in the den.

Like the family, but not like—with its short muzzle, standing on two legs tall and wide as a tree, but running faster than Bites Back when it dropped to four feet. He must fight long enough for the rest of the family to get out. No dogs could fight the Death-Claw and win. Maybe before the dark days when the family was many. Maybe.

The Death-Claw closed on him for its kill. Its eyes roved into the shadows. It looked for many kills today. Should he jump for those eyes, so far above his head? Then he would die too fast to help the family.

Bites Back had seen the Longtooths fight the Death-Claw. They ran up its back like a hill and drove their teeth down into its neck. That attack had not killed the Death-Claw, but it had run away and it did not kill the Longtooth's family.

He was not as big or strong as a Longtooth. He was not as quick, either, no one of the family was. But he was quicker than the Death-Claw.

He would fight like the Longtooth.

As fast as a tree could fall Bites Back knew this, before the rest of the family understood the Death-Claw had returned to its den. The Death-Claw would kill them all. Bites Back barked the warning that meant great danger—the bark meaning LONGTOOTH or DEATH-CLAW or flows of the HOT YELLOW DEATH that swallows everything—danger that meant RUN TOGETHER, FAR AND FAST.

Then he turned to face his own death.

It was as big as all the family together. With a head as large as Bites Back, it stood so tall that he wondered if he could make the jump to its back. Snuffling and drooling confidence, it rushed him, sure of this kill, sure of its next kill and the next. The Death-Claw could eat many dogs.

Bites Back heard the family rising behind him. He heard them running out of the den. He could not look back to see. He stood firm as the Death-Claw charged.

At the last instant before it smashed into him—almost too late—he plunged forward at the Death-Claw's feet, dipped his head and slashed the giant's paws, opening a small gash in the dense fur. Its blood tasted sharp like old fat.

The Death-Claw bellowed a sound that shook the air in the den and hurt Bites Back's ears.

Fast as falling water, the creature turned to strike him.

One touch of that paw would break him. Then he would be

down and the Death-Claw could eat him when it wanted and go on to kill more of the family.

He did not jump back—a glancing blow could be as deadly as a solid one. Instead, Bites Back splayed his legs out flat against the ground, as if he were playing with a pup.

The huge talons of the Death-Claw's paw brushed the fur of Bites Back's neck.

In the rock den behind, only Short Ears and Dirty Paw were still inside, waiting and watching.

Jaws bore down on him from above, jaws wide enough to take and crush his body in a bite. If he rose to run, he would rise into those jaws.

Fighting like a pup had worked once. Bites Back lowered his head and rolled—faster than he'd ever rolled as a pup in the green grass.

The rock den was at the top of a rise, so with a turn of his body Bites Back was rolling quickly downwards. There were many stones, but better the bites of these sharp stones than the Death-Claw's teeth.

The tall dark shape stared down from the den's entrance, hesitating. *Maybe the Death-Claw had never fought a pup?*

But Bites Back knew he was not safe. The Death-Claw was as fast as any foe the family fought. He could not outrun it unless he had a long lead. That was how the family kept from being eaten by the Death-Claw. They smelled its dark angry scent before it knew they were close and they stayed far enough away so that the Death-Claw could not use its quick short runs to catch them. Only the Tall Gray Dogs could match the family in a long run.

The giant roared again and charged down the hill. Bites Back had only time to stand. This would be his death. But the family was out of the cave now; there was Dirty Paw—first in, last out—running out behind the others.

As death raced down on him from above, Bites Back readied himself to spring in its face. Before he was crushed or eaten, he would bite the Death-Claw, maybe on its nose. Bites Back snarled and his growl was fierce. It gave him strength, though he did not frighten the Death-Claw. He bared his teeth and looked straight into the monster's eyes. They were dark and empty, not like the eyes of his family.

Looming on its back legs, it blotted out the darkness of the sky with the darkness of its body. Bites Back tensed to make his leap toward those jaws. But before his paws left the dirt, a flash of white streaked across the Death-Claw. With another deafening noise of pain and surprise, the monster fell forward, missing Bites Back by a paw's breadth.

Behind the stumbling Death-Claw appeared the bright head of White Sides, tongue lolling out the side of his mouth. Seeing Bites Back slash the Death-Claw's paw, White Sides had done the same.

The Death-Claw bellowed. Before it scrambled to its feet, Bites Back turned and ran—along the face of the rise and away from the rock den, away from the Death-Claw, away from his family. He would not run his fastest; he must be sure the Death-Claw followed.

He heard White Sides, too. Running after him.

Even now with sure death behind, running filled his nose with clean air, sharpened his eyes, cleared his ears, and centered his mind. He did not think of the Death-Claw behind him. He thought of the family. Someday, White Sides would be father of the family. White Sides, last whelp of their mother Stone Eyes, was the largest pup and now the largest dog Bites Back knew. Tall as one of the Giant Dog families, who hunted the Shaggy Walking Hills. Bites Back had wondered once if White Sides would kill him, if he became father. This did not matter now. White Sides was a swift hunter and powerful protector.

Bites Back's ears laid back against his head as he ran. This fight was wrong. Who would be father if he and White Sides both became meat for the Death-Claw? There were no others as strong, and meat was so hard to find.

Bites Back smelled White Sides and he smelled his own fear and he smelled the anger of the Death-Claw, already gaining on them. These smells brought him the sight of Broken Tail's dying. He saw himself in the old father's eyes. He felt the growl that he felt in his belly that day. Another scent he did not understand covered him. Something wrong. He tasted the hard dirt taste of Two-Legs blood.

The roar of the Death-Claw's anger was louder. Bites Back twisted his head around. White Sides was a bright blur hurtling toward him in the gloom, lined by the darker black that grew larger behind him. Soon that dark would close on White Sides.

Bites Back saw that this is what White Sides did in great danger. The family would be safe and would find meat with White Sides. Bites Back knew what he must do.

He wheeled to his right, against the cliff face—back toward White Sides and the Death-Claw. His spirit filled his legs as he climbed the dirt and stone until he was higher than his height, then higher than the Death-Claw, which was almost upon the dogs now. Bites Back leapt from the cliff wall down onto the broad bristling back.

It was slicker and rounder than he'd expected. His paws slipped even though he tried to dig his claws into the Death-Claw's pelt. Using his front teeth, he gripped tufts of fur—stiff fur that didn't come out as he bit it—and pulled himself toward its shoulders. When he neared the neck, he looked down at White Sides, who stood gaping below. The Death-Claw had stopped and was shaking now.

Bites Back risked falling and barked at White Sides. RUN! DEATH AND DANGER! I AM FATHER! RUN!

He tried to find the other dog's eyes, but the wide furry hump he rode twisted like the tops of the trees when the strong air blew. When he looked again, White Sides was gone.

The monster's twitching and bucking stopped.

Bites Back stood up straight on the Death-Claw's back and looked over the ground below. The little light shone above the trees, stark and open against the darkness. The family sang on such nights. Bites Back could see them down by the running water, far enough away to keep from being eaten by the Death-Claw. He could even see the flash of White Sides moving toward them. He would be a strong father.

Bites Back had not joined the family in song since the time when Flower Nose, his mate, had sung for Crooked Leg, who had been killed when the Two-Legs struck a stick through his neck. Something wrong had happened then; it left a smell on him that he could not rub out. Now, as he saw his family run to safety, that wrongness lifted and the white of the little light rang in his eyes. This clear emptiness filled his heart and his song leapt to meet the brightness in the air above. He sang the song his family sang to the little light when it rose in the darkness. He sang the song of death, for he was soon to be the Death-Claw's meat.

Running in the valley below, Flower Nose stopped when she heard the quick high yips and stuttering moan that was the song of the little light in the darkness. The family stood around her and listened. The father sang to them from above. Then the yips ended and the air wavered with the long wails of the song of death.

They did not understand why the Death-Claw let the father sing.

As Bites Back's voice soared, Flower Nose and then the whole family sang with him. Their voices climbed together, as one fell in song, another rose. White Sides, panting, plunged into the middle, his voice so strong that Flower Nose almost missed the final cry that rolled down from the hill above.

THE BARDO OF BITES BACK

BELOW HIM, Bites Back saw the Death-Claw's teeth close on Bites Back's own neck. The light from this watching hit his eyes like stones. It was like falling onto the water that was hard and colder than water. It felt as if he was bitten in the belly. But it bit him everywhere.

The Death-Claw carried Bites Back's body into the stone den.

Now his sight was above the family. They sang, but he did not hear them.

The great light shone overhead—as it had not for so long. He stood alone on grass. The wind blew, but his fur did not move.

He was neither hot nor cold. He was not hungry and he was not thirsty. When he'd stood on the Death-Claw and sang his death song, he was thirsty. Now he was dead.

He missed the family. He missed the hunt and the tearing of the meat after a kill.

But he was dead now. He could not eat. He would not hunt.

Sighing, Bites Back sat on the grass and closed his eyes.

. . .

FAMILIAR SOUNDS and scents filled the air. His fur flattened and his tail curled. He opened his eyes.

It was the time of the hunt with Broken Tail, when the family met the Two-Legs. He stood next to himself, next to his family. He saw himself and his family. They walked around him. They walked through him. Bites Back smelled the blood of Crooked Leg and Broken Tail on the ground. He smelled Flower Nose and all the others. He saw them, but he did not feel their touch. The fur on his neck bristled and he growled.

Mud Paw and the family sang of Broken Tail, who had just fallen. He saw himself trot away from the family.

He shut his eyes and whimpered like a pup. This was the wrongness and he would not see it.

He whined and held his eyes closed. For many breaths, all Bites Back could hear was his own moan. All he saw was blackness. He smelled the family's kill, the gray death leaves falling from the sky, the fresh blood and death scent of Crooked Leg, and—strongest of all—he tasted the blood of the Two-Legs he had chased and killed after he fought Broken Tail. The Two-Legs that had hit the stick through Crooked Leg.

Though he did not open his eyes, the dead Bites Back saw and smelled and touched as the Bites Back of *that* time—meat and blood of a wounded paw and a wounded leg. The Two-Legs had not gone far.

It fell to the ground on its back. Its eyes and smell and body told Bites Back this one no longer threatened the family. But the anger and growl of his fight with Broken Tail still filled him. Blood covered his mouth and eyes as he opened the Two-Legs throat.

He stood next to the Two-Legs and it sang its death song. With dying strength, it rolled on its side and looked at Bites Back. Its eyes were the dark color of stones in the running water, the color of Broken Tail's eyes. Blood pulsed slowly from its throat. Then the Two-Legs did something Bites Back did not understand. It reached out its paw and touched the fur on Bites

Back's neck. The touch of the Two-Legs paw on his fur was soft like the tongue of Bites Back's mother.

He stood over the dead Two-Legs, panting hard. Then Bites Back turned and walked away. His anger was gone. The smell of this kill was wrong. His heart did not beat as if he had made a kill. He had not killed the Two-Legs for meat. Bites Back would not feed on the dead Two-Legs. He walked back to Flower Nose, Mud Paw, and the rest of the family—legs and tail heavy, ears pressed against his head. They were feeding on the Tall Runner that was their kill. There was no light in Broken Tail's eyes or in Crooked Leg's. They were dead. The Little Crunchy Meat would feed on them, leaving only white bone. The smell of the blood of the Two-Legs clung to him, dulling the scent of his family and their kill.

Flower Nose looked at him. Bites Back held his broad tail down, just above his haunches and did not meet her eyes. She licked his muzzle, taking off some of the blood of the Two-Legs. And that blood did not make her hungry. She did not rise to hunt for it. Bites Back's ears pressed hard against his skull.

Though his belly was empty, he did not eat the Tall Runner meat. He waited until all the family gorged, then he led them away from this place, running from the bodies of Crooked Leg, Broken Tail, and the Two-Legs.

Dead Bites Back's smell and sight and sound blurred.

The memory of his family, buzzing sounds of the Little Crunchy Meat in his ears, the smell of nothing, no feel of air or earth: these things became gray light that covered Bites Back's eyes and ears and nose and fur.

He ran into the gray.

He did not tire. He ran as the light passed to dark. He could not eat or drink. He could not hunt. But he could run. His tongue fell from the side of his mouth as he ran, but his tongue was not dry and the air did not taste of anything.

Paths of light rose in the darkness above him. Light the color of water, a bright path the color of fresh blood, and a wide path the color of the little light in the darkness.

These paths shone on grass in a plain around a great dog, a dog of brightness, a dog of light that stood before Bites Back. He looked at this dog and Bite's Back's head bent down and turned to the side. His fur fanned in fear and he shrank away. Though he stood close, Bites Back knew he saw and heard only part of this strange dog.

The smell of the dog filled Bites Back's nose until he could not see or hear—only ride the scent. The *smell*! It was the smell of the grass and flowers and mud when he was a pup, before the gray death leaves fell, when there was always enough meat. It was the smell of his mother, Stone Eyes, and the smell of his mate, Flower Nose, and the smell of his family, when they were marked by him and a thousand other markings. The truth of smell washed all fear from Bites Back.

A walk of grass led to the dog of light and beyond. Bites Back walked this walk, past the great dog. It led to a flat, open run with a stone den at the far end.

Flower Nose, White Sides, Mud Paw—all of his family—walked in front of the den. He saw them; he smelled them as he ran.

And he smelled something else.

A Longtooth stalked over the top of the stone den. Why did his family not smell the Longtooth? He barked MORTAL DANGER. He ran and barked, but he drew no closer, and his family did not hear him. He whined.

As the Longtooth leapt from the top of the stone den, his throat tightened and he could not bark. *Was this what it was to be dead?*

Dead Bites Back's breath, his smell, his ears, and his eyes were covered as by a heavy fall of water from the sky. He trembled and shook away this covering.

His eyes and nose opened then on the same path, the same grass, the same stone den.

His family was gone. In front of the den were Two-Legs. They looked and smelled like all the Two-Legs he had met. Except there were young Two-Legs here, too. Bending their bottom legs on the ground, they sat like Two-Legs around a little part of the hot yellow death and they did not move away from it.

His legs straightened as he watched the Two-Legs family. He smelled that day with Broken Tail, the day the Two-Legs took his family's kill. He smelled the wrong thing that happened then. He raised his head into the bright overhead and sang, a deep howl of wrongness that could not be undone.

Over the stone den where the Two-Legs family sat, a Longtooth crept. Bites Back barked—as he'd tried to bark when he saw the Longtooth about to attack *his* family. The Two-Legs must not smell the Longtooth, either. He barked WARNING, but his paws held fast to the hillside. The Longtooth jumped from the top of the den. Before it reached the smallest of the Two-Legs, Dead Bites Back's smell and sight blurred again. His eyes failed him, but his nostrils held the scent of the young Two-Legs, and his heart did not forget the Longtooth's killing leap onto the little one who sat by the hot yellow death—a Two-Legs no larger than a pup.

Emptiness filled his nostrils and his eyes and his ears. He was no longer the Bites Back that ran with his family. He was again the dead Bites Back. The scents of the dog of light were lost in the air that was behind him now.

The ground changed again. The grass was darker; it looked like the grass of the land of his family.

His paws moved. He walked. He ran.

Bites Back swiveled his head as he ran. There were trees behind him now.

Eyes forward again, trees were on both sides. Branches grew above, drooping closer and closer.

He turned to run back the way he came, but the trees behind left no place to go.

Sticks sprouted up as he turned. Bites Back tried to jump

over or through them, but the branches grew too close together and were too strong. He fell back from his last jump, and the blackness of a night without the little light came over him.

BITES BACK DID NOT KNOW whether he opened his eyes or whether the light returned. He stood, surrounded by a stick den that had grown around him. It was only big enough for him to stand or lie down. Beyond this den, stony ground stretched out on every side.

There was no grass. But there were piles of bones.

He raised his nose into the air. Some bones were fresh. They were from many beasts, including dogs. And Two-Legs.

There was another smell Bites Back did not know. The sharp scent made his belly tighten and the fur on his back rise.

The light was brighter, too. But it was not the great light from above. It was a blood light that shone on everything.

Danger! Danger! Run! Run! dogs called to him with loud sharp barks. Bites Back turned. A short walk behind him was another stick den. Crooked Leg was in this pen, telling him to beware. To escape.

Bites Back barked recognition but the other dog kept signaling danger as if he did not hear Bites Back.

Bites Back saw many stick dens beyond Crooked Leg. Neither his nose nor his eyes could tell if these dens held others of the family.

Many dogs barked and howled in desperation and anger. Bites Back turned his head, seeking, smelling. The blood light grew stronger. There, only a quick run away, a creature beyond all his fears stalked toward Crooked Leg.

Its body was the body of the Death-Claw, but without fur and wider. It walked on its back legs—like a Two-Legs. And it had a head like a Two-Legs. This head was bigger than it should be. And all of this monster was the color of old blood. The fur on top of its Two-Legs head, its hairless hide: all was the color of dry blood. Its teeth—as long and sharp as a Longtooth—plunged down to its chin. Even these teeth were the color of old blood.

But its body and head and teeth were not what changed the growl in Bites Back's throat to a whimper. This creature had many heads: the head of a Longtooth next to its Two-Legs head. And the head of a Death-Claw. And on its body were too many legs and paws. In some paws were pointed sticks like the one that killed Crooked Leg. In others were the skulls of dogs and things Bites Back did not know, but that made him afraid.

Around and behind the heads of this animal hung the hot yellow death that eats trees and grass and animals. But the yellow death did not eat this monster. The yellow death shone behind it as it moved toward Crooked Leg, but the yellow death did not harm the creature's heads.

Bites Back barked his challenge. Bites Back had not stopped Crooked Legs' other death. He would stop this death.

I AM BITES BACK! He barked.

I CHALLENGE YOU, GREAT DANGER ANIMAL! I CHALLENGE YOU! FIGHT ME! FIGHT BITES BACK!

But the monster with the heads of Two-Legs, Longtooth, and Death-Claw did not look at Bites Back. It did not take his challenges, no matter how often and how loudly he made them.

It stopped before Crooked Leg. With a sweep of a paw, it shattered the stick den to pieces. With another paw it snatched Crooked Leg and held the yowling dog up, high as a tree, listening to Crooked Leg's sounds of fear. Drinking the dog's death fear.

Then, as slowly as it had stalked up to the stick den, it lowered the struggling dog into its wide, blood-colored Two-Legs mouth.

Bites Back threw himself again and again at the sticks that held him in. He barked challenges at the Two-Legs monster. Its jaws closed on Crooked Leg, but its blood eyes stared at Bites

Back. Crooked Legs' blood dripped from the long teeth that plunged down below the Two-Legs' chin.

Eyes fixed on Bites Back, it rushed forward. The monster raised a great paw and smashed it down, splintering Bites Back's stick den.

Bites Back was ready. He had seen this move when it took Crooked Leg. He leapt for the Two-Legs monster's throat.

But it moved quickly, so Bites Back struck its chest, driving it back. Off-balance, the monster staggered, tripping on a stone.

As they fell together, Bites Back closed his jaws on the top of one of the beast's legs. And as they fell the Two-Legs monster changed. It was smaller and smaller. The heads of the Death-Claw and the Longtooth went away, as did the hot yellow death that followed behind it. It lost all but its top and bottom legs.

When Bites Back and the Two-Legs monster struck the ground together, it became a Two-Legs—the Two-Legs Bites Back had killed before. And the leg Bites Back held in his teeth was now the leg with the paw that had touched him so gently.

Bites Back's jaw slacked open. He stood up by the Two-Legs. Its leg fell, dead, out of his mouth. This paw would not touch Bites Back again. The Two-Legs throat was open, blood pumping slowly out, even though Bites Back had not found its throat.

Dead Bites Back stepped away from the Two-Legs. He fell again into a world of darkness.

IN THAT BLACKNESS, Bites Back smelled Longtooth and Death-Claw. He smelled Two-Legs. He smelled the hot yellow death that swallows all it touches and he smelled the strange sharp scent that was the monster that took Crooked Leg in its mouth. His tail curled between his legs and fear filled him.

The wrongness he had made when he killed the Two-Legs returned like the stink of meat dead too long. His belly shrank and his ears lay flat against his head. He was like a pup when the mother pushes him away from her food. He smelled the water he made when he rolled on his back after Broken Tail beat him in his first foolish challenge. He no longer felt like the father of his family. He no longer felt like Bites Back.

Bites Back lay cold and small and afraid, muzzle on paws.

He lay long and longer like this, nose dry, haunches tight, panting fast.

Then a small scent slid in around the thick odors of the wrongness and the many-headed monster. He smelled Flower Nose and their litters. He smelled their pups playing, and the soft grass they played on. He smelled the flowers and the waters he had played in when he was young, before the gray death leaves fell. He saw Crooked Leg rolling down hills and prancing proudly like a pup, tail in the sky even when he was hurt and hungry. He saw Broken Tail panting, his tongue lolling to the side of his mouth as he watched Crooked Leg. He saw—he felt—he smelled his battle with the Death-Claw. He felt his heart when he heard White Sides bite the Death-Claw. He heard himself sing his song of death. It was his song, the song of Bites Back.

He would not lie down for this monster, even if it was more terrible than the Longtooth or the Death-Claw. He stood, stiff legged, and raised his voice in the short sharp barks of challenge.

A NEW SCENT grew in Bites Back's nose. It was the smell of the dog of light. It was the smell of the Two-Legs, the smell of Bites Back, and the scents of Two-Legs and Bites Back mixed with all the smells that first came to him from this dog.

Blinking at the brightness that now covered the gray, Bites Back saw the bright dog before him again. It stood on a stone, surrounded by the colored paths of light.

The great dog stared at Bites Back for many breaths. Its eyes were dark and light together. Bites Back could not tell what this dog would do or what it wanted. But Bites Back was not afraid. His tail did not curl beneath him, even when he smelled again the blood of the Two-Legs and the wrongness.

The harder Bites Back looked at this great dog of light, the harder it was to see. The smell of it was fading, too. Now he was not sure he saw the Great Dog at all. Its smell was faint. All smells and sounds emptied from him.

Bites Back's eyes burned. He shook his head and blinked. He opened his eyes and saw again the stone dens. The little Two-Legs stared up in fear at the Longtooth as the killer leaped down. Bites Back growled. The bush of his tail fanned. His legs stiffened.

I will make the Longtooth fear my song. I will lick the blood from the neck of the Longtooth. The little Two-Legs will not fear when I sing my song. I will empty my stomach of the wrongness I made.

Jumping in front of the little Two-Legs, his sight cleared; his voice was certain

I AM BITES BACK! I SING ON THE DEATH-CLAW! FEAR MAKES MY SONG STRONGER! I AM BITES BACK!

2

INTERLUDE: WHITE SIDES FOLLOWS TWO LEGS

FOUR WINTERS after the death of Bites Back

WHITE SIDES STOOD at the top of the grassy knob. Below him, the little running water moved across the ground. Grey humps rose up farther away: the stick dens of the Two-Legs.

The air filled with warmth as the great light climbed above the low edge of his sight. The family rose. Thorn Tail and another pup yipped.

White Sides ignored the yips, but turned his head at the sound of a low snarl from his mate, Sharp Paw.

In front of the mother, Thorn Tail's dark head lay on his paws. Jumper—his littermate—bounced away from mother and brother, whimpering and holding one leg up in surprised pain.

The rest of the family was awake, even old Flower Nose, who slept much now, whether the air was warm or cold.

There were more in the family than when White Sides had been a pup, when Bites Back—who sang to the Death-Claw—had been the father. Besides Thorn Tail and Jumper, Long Paw, Hard Tooth, and White Tail still lived from Sharp Paw's last litter. The fur on White Sides' back smoothed, his tail rose and the tip of it curled back. The family grew strong with their pups.

Turning back, he looked down again, across the water at the Two-Legs living place.

A Two-Legs walked out from between the stick dens. It moved even more slowly than Two-Legs usually moved, and it held something large in its top two paws. How did Two-Legs walk without falling over?

It walked toward the water and then dropped what it held, making a small mound. Many other mounds already shaped the ground.

The Two-Legs returned to its stick dens.

White Sides trotted back to the family. Sharp Paw's bright eyes met his. She shook her head and then her whole body, and stepped in to walk by his side. Mud Nose bowed to him and licked White Sides lightly under his chin. Mud Nose could not run and kill as he had done when White Sides was young, but his nose was still the best in the family. The old dog fell in and walked behind White Sides and his mate.

Flower Nose sat on a wide stone, warmed by the great light. Jumper ran up and tripped over her tail. Chasing him, not far behind, stumbled Thorn Tail and Hard Tooth.

White Sides walked slowly up to Flower Nose. He leaned over and licked her ears. She lowered her muzzle, now whiter than White Sides' fur, and closed her eyes.

As the littermates played around the old one, White Sides and Sharp Paw turned and ran, Mud Nose following as best he could.

Pausing to smell and look when they reached the rise, they pelted down the hill, waded through the running water, and came to the place of the Two-Legs mounds.

The smell of Two-Legs was everywhere. Mud Nose whined at the fuzzy scent—mostly like meat killers, but different. White Sides did not turn and snarl at Mud Nose; the fur on his back rose, too, at this scent.

But there were other, more promising smells all around them: faint smells of the little Tree Runners that were hard to catch, sweet light scents of the soft Grass Jumpers, old tangy smells of Tall Runner meat, the sharp scent of long, thin Grass Wigglers. White Sides felt the water slide from his open jaws; he saw it drip from Mud Nose's mouth. There was much meat here, enough for all the family.

Sharp Paw ran forward and buried her nose in the mound White Sides had seen the Two-Legs drop. She pried up the edge of the mound and the smell of fresh-killed meat—the chewy meat of a Flat-Tailed Tree-Biter—filled White Sides' nostrils.

He and Mud Nose trotted over as Sharp Paw scratched at the mound. White Sides bent down and pulled out the dead Tree-Biter. A big one. With much meat.

Smell of fresh kill struck full on his tongue and White Sides ripped and gobbled a bite of the juicy Tree-Biter. Why had the Two-Legs wasted this meat?

After White Sides grabbed this meat, Sharp Paw moved on to another mound. White Sides raised his head. Mud Nose pranced toward him with the crooked leg of a brown-furred Grass Jumper caught between his jaws. Sharp Paw pulled most of another Jumper from her new mound.

Air breathed through the leaves of the white trees that grew around the Two-Legs mounds. The clear smell of the little running water poured over the Two-Legs scent on the mounds as White Sides, Sharp Paw, and Mud Nose returned to the family with their prizes.

3

DYAK: DOG OF THE PEOPLE

c. 10,000 BCE — somewhere in Beringia
[Beringia was the subcontinent that extended from modern-day Alaska to Siberia during the last Ice Age. At one time, it was almost 1,000 miles wide (north-to-south).]

DYAK WAS HUNGRY. The smell of the sheep smeared the big rock where he lay. It covered the grass around him. It clung to the bark of the stumpy dark trees that grew in the middle of this place where he lived with the sheep. There would be no food until master came, and maybe none then, either. The smell of sheep was everywhere and, as Dyak had just nipped the heel of a fat ewe who strayed too far, the taste of them was on his tongue. Dyak thought again of taking one. The sheep were so foolish and so slow. But master was clear the sheep were not Dyak's prey. Bogh, who even master was afraid of, had used hard blows to teach this to Dyak.

Dyak liked the wet air. It held different smells from dry air. His heavy gray and white coat shed the water, the earth, and the cold well.

"Dyak?" A boy's high, cracking voice called out. Dyak couldn't see him, but the dog smelled the faint and comforting scent of master, called Attu by the other humans. Dyak fanned his bushy tail from side to side across the smooth stone.

Catching the eye of the biggest ram, Dyak curled back his lips, uncovering long white teeth. Warning his charges, his sheep, not to move. The ram and the ewes near him looked back at his teeth. Some made sounds that—as far as Dyak could tell—were the same for pain, hunger, happiness, rut, or death. Not like the sounds Attu and Bogh and the other humans made. Humans made many different sounds. Maybe that was why humans could not smell. They walked into places Dyak would not walk, places that smelled strong of longtooths or bears or biting insects. His tongue fell to the side of his mouth and he panted, remembering when Bogh walked into a nest of biting fliers. Those fliers bit Dyak, too—his nose stayed sore long—but Bogh was stung many times. Humans were blind in their noses like sheep were stupid.

Dyak trotted toward the voice that made him feel strong and happy as a pup.

"There you are, Dyak."

The boy ran to meet Dyak. His hands were hidden. Dyak smelled strong, good scents. Panting softly, he sat on his hindquarters and looked expectantly at Attu.

"That's right. I've got something. The Bent One made it and said I should give it to you." He knelt down before Dyak and then pulled some bones from behind his back.

Dyak loved no thing more. He had often seen humans eat bones, but only when they sat in front of their fires. For Dyak, a cold bone was as precious as a warm one. Both meant food, blood food in the marrow, tooth food from the rest. Bones were a great happiness.

He swished his tail faster across the ground.

Attu handed the bones to Dyak, who took them in his mouth and respectfully moved away from master before eating.

What was this? The bones—there were several—the bones were bare of meat on the outside, but there was meat *inside* them. Not fresh; no blood, but good meat, the dry meat humans ate when they walked.

Dyak had tasted stolen bits of this meat a few times as humans guarded it well. It was not as satisfying as fresh kill, but it was good. And it did not make his stomach hurt like some old meat did.

But this meat was behind the bones. There was no skin. Just bones and meat. Was this a skinless, bloodless animal that Attu captured and shared now with Dyak? Dyak crunched on the bones. They were big, hard ones. He bore down until his jaw hurt, but the bones did not crack or move out of the way so he could get to the meat in the middle of them.

Attu made the song Dyak knew meant he was happy.

"It's a game-trick, Dyak. The Bent One made this for you. Get the meat from inside it." Attu made the happy sound again.

Dyak lay down fully on the ground, the bone box game between his paws. He stuck his tongue as far as he could between the bones and licked the meat. Yes, it was good meat. It made him so hungry to taste this meat and not be able to bite into it. He *had* to get to this meat. What kind of animal could this be? He held down the animal with one forepaw and pulled at one of the bones on the edge with his shorter front teeth, trying to open it like he sometimes opened the hard, closed food that lived in the soft dirt next to the Big Water.

"What are you doing here, boy?"

Dyak dropped the bone animal on his outstretched paws, pricked up his ears, and looked back-and-forth between Attu and the human walking toward them. It was Bogh. Dyak became still and watchful as if bears were walking close.

"I came to check on the sheep, Bogh." Attu was very brave to make noises at Bogh. Dyak looked at Bogh's hands. The man did not hold a stick.

"I think you came to check on this worthless dog." Bogh was almost to them now. He was very big, big as the small bear. Not as strong or fast as the small bear, but strong enough. Bogh's teeth were small and he always smelled of human waste.

Before Attu could make human noises again, Bogh held one hand up and pulled a bag off the fur around his chest. He tossed the bag down at Attu's hands.

"Quiet. I don't want to know what girl games you play with this beast. Here, you do work for me. I need new spears. You know how to nap stone, boy?"

The hair on Dyak's back rose as he watched Attu's face and smelled his anger.

"Do I know how to pee, Bogh? I am of the People. I am not at my mother's breast. How could I not know how to nap stone?"

Dyak's rear legs tensed. If Attu was attacked, Dyak would lunge. Bogh's little eyes narrowed, his face was the color of meat without skin. Even if Bogh has a stick somewhere, I will help my master, Dyak thought.

"If you were not my mother's brother's son, you would learn manners today, boy." Bogh's hands twitched. Did he have a stick somewhere in his fine smelly furs? But Bogh's anger stench faded quickly, his face smoothed and, with that, so did Dyak's legs.

"I have feasted with the Dooma—on bear meat—and I am full. You are lucky, boy." Bogh patted his large stomach and paused, as if trying to remember, then said, "Two spear heads. By next light." He started to turn, then noticed Dyak.

"What does the dog have there, boy? Did you waste good meat on him?" Bogh reached down to take the bone animal from Dyak.

BOGH WAS NOT AS stupid as the sheep. And he knew Dyak. He knew Dyak well. It had been many lights now since Dyak was hurt in the hunt, hurt enough he could no longer chase the tall deer, but not hurt so bad that the hunters left him, or worse, brought him home for the pot. Dyak feared that when they put him on the dragging wood to bring him back. They gave him to Bogh and Bogh did not eat him; he taught him how to guard the sheep. Teaching meant that Bogh made loud human noises at Dyak, tied his throat tight with strips of watered hide, and beat him with sticks and kicked him. Dyak could not get away because of the hide strips. He chewed the hide when Bogh was not looking, but then Bogh put on new strips and beat him harder. He tried to fight, but Dyak learned quickly that he could not fight and win when Bogh held a stick.

BUT DYAK DID LEARN. He learned the sheep moved where he wanted when he bit their ankles. Stupid sheep. He learned they stopped when he showed them his teeth. And he learned to stay as far from Bogh as he could.

On a wet day, Bogh slept under a tree. Dyak smelled longtooth in the wind and ran to check where the longtooth scent came from. One longtooth could kill Dyak and all the sheep. So Dyak ran back to warn Bogh and the flock, barking his charges out of the way, and a sheep—a frightened stupid sheep—stepped on the sleeping Bogh. Bogh made sounds as if a longtooth was already eating him. Bogh was very angry. He kicked Dyak so hard that Dyak fell hard against the tree under which Bogh stood. Bogh kept making loud noises and kicked Dyak again and again.

When he woke up from the kicking, Dyak could barely breathe. Dyak knew he would die. He wondered what animal would eat him. Dyak hoped they would eat him soon as he was in much pain.

Instead, the boy Attu came to him. Dyak was too hurt to snarl or move or try to get away. He had seen some of the small humans poke sticks and throw rocks and pull and kick at animals that were dying. He did not want that.

But the People did not eat him. The boy brought him water in a stone. Dyak looked into Attu's eyes then, and he could see He was not like Bogh. He could not look long into the boy's eyes, though; Dyak was afraid He might change and become like Bogh.

For the second time in his life, they put Dyak onto the dragging wood the hunters used and Attu pulled him into a den of rocks. Twice every light, Attu brought water and meat to Dyak. After the Great Light rose and fell many times, Dyak stood and stumbled like a pup eating bulb weed so that he could watch Attu coming toward him, bringing water and food. When he saw the boy coming, Dyak's belly felt as if he needed to make water and like he was growling, but he had not had any drink and he was not angry. Each time Attu visited him, Dyak's tail moved back and forth, faster and faster. Dyak made sounds he had not made since he was a pup, and when Attu leaned down to give Dyak water and food, Dyak raised his head and licked Attu under the boy's jaw. Attu made Dyak feel like he did when the Little Light was round in the black sky. Dyak sang a song to the sky and Attu made the human sounds that meant happy.

Not long after that, Attu took Dyak back to *his* sheep, which were the same as Bogh's sheep. They were just as stupid as when Dyak last saw them. They smelled the same. But for Dyak they were different now. They were Attu's sheep—master's sheep— and Dyak kept them safe for Attu.

One day Bogh came with a stick. Dyak ran from the big man, but he would not go far from Attu's sheep, so Bogh kept running at Dyak—waving his stick. Dyak kept running away, then coming back. Soon, Attu came with another human. There were many loud human sounds, but Attu bared his teeth at Bogh and so Dyak was not afraid. Bogh threw down his stick and went away. Bogh did not come to the sheep field again. Until now.

NOW BOGH WAS TRYING to take food from Dyak. Special food that Attu had brought Dyak. And this time Dyak was untied and Bogh did not have a stick.

The big man squatted before Dyak, showing his teeth. Bogh's hand, which smelled of fish and human water, moved down to pick up Dyak's bone trick box.

Fast as fear into a sheep's heart, Dyak opened his jaws and grabbed Bogh's arm above his hand. He bore down, tasting Bogh's scent and then his blood.

Bogh made loud noises as he had the day when the sheep stepped on him. His hand struck Dyak's head. Dyak expected this, but since Bogh did not have a stick, he was not afraid. He bit down on Bogh's arm, not bone-crunching hard, but not like play. Bogh struck him again, but not as hard this time. The big man fell to the ground. He made whining sounds.

Dyak's fur felt longer and straighter; his eyes felt brighter;

the air was cleaner—despite or because of the strong smells of Bogh's arm and blood.

Other hands were on him now. Did Bogh have more hands than he knew? Dyak still held Bogh's bloody arm in his jaws and his nose was full of Bogh's smell, but the tugs and beatings from these others confused him. Attu called his name again and again, and made human noises that meant master was worried and afraid. Dyak ignored Bogh's weakening blows to his head, which were accompanied by the large man trying to bring his knees around to push Dyak away. But he could not ignore Attu's voice or the boy's fear. Dyak rolled his eyes upward to Attu and saw master's eyes were very wide and white. Were they being attacked? No. Attu was looking at Dyak—not for enemies; he called Dyak's name over and over.

Then Attu put his hands on Dyak's jaws and pulled at them.

Dyak knew Attu did not like Bogh and that master, too, was afraid of Bogh. Surely Attu did not want Dyak to release their tormentor? The taste of Bogh was so good. Each blow to Dyak's head made the taste sweeter. But master's hands pulled against Dyak's jaws and this confused Dyak's heart. How could he release Bogh and how could he not do what master wanted? How could these things be different? Dyak would have whined, if his jaws were not filled with Bogh's arm.

The taste of the victory over Bogh was strong. But Dyak's spirit moved with Attu's wishes. He slackened his jaw. A breath before, he could taste and smell and see only Bogh and his blood, now his nose and ears worked again and he knew there were other humans here. What did they want? Did they also threaten Attu? Would Dyak have to fight all of them? Something hard struck his head; he made the sound of pain, and then there was only blackness.

DYAK AND THE BODY EATERS

DYAK AWOKE in one of the pens where the humans kept sheep before they put them in the pots. His head felt as if he fell against a stone. Dyak cast around for sound or smell of master, but could not sense the boy anywhere. Maybe his head pain kept him from seeing or smelling or hearing.

He could smell Bogh, though. And he still tasted Bogh. Dyak yawned wide and his dry tongue lolled from his mouth. The other humans must have hit him with Bogh's stick. Would the other humans keep Bogh from hurting Attu? Dyak had never seen Bogh hit Attu, but he knew this could happen.

A human with long white fur on his head walked toward Dyak and stopped in front of his pen. He walked differently from the other humans and the noises he made were different, too. He smelled like dry plants pressed together.

"You made a bad hunt today, dog," said the old man with the stooped back. "Bogh may be the meanest of our tribe, but he's the Dooma's kin and a strong spear." The man stood and backed away a pace. "I'm sure he deserved your lesson, but he forgives no man any slight and you," the human pointed a finger at Dyak, "you are a dog."

The human squatted. Dyak turned his head, keeping one

eye on the old human. Humans liked to look straight on, but he could see them as well from the side. Humans did not know he could see them when he didn't look at them, and then they did not think he was trying to take their food. The old man looked straight at Dyak. The skin around his eyes moved so that his eyes looked small. "But not just any dog, I think."

"Kill the dog, Dooma. Kill him and eat him. Save a day's hunt."

Dyak's back rose as he heard Bogh's noises.

"The people do not eat dog. You know that, Bogh. You are angry this one bit you. It is fierce. That is as it should be."

Dyak knew the other human with Bogh. He was not as large as Bogh nor as old as the one with white fur, but he had been the leader in Dyak's last hunt. Even if Dyak did not know him from before, he smelled his sweat and knew he was not like Bogh.

"Fahh. You talk like Attu. The dog is not a woman to be played with. It is worthless meat. Worse, it is dangerous. Kill it, Dooma. I ask you as your father's sister's son."

Dyak's growl stayed low and soft in his belly at Bogh's noises.

The leader human blew air through his little nose. It was like Attu's happy noise, but also like the noise the hairy ox made before it pawed the earth and charged.

"Quiet, Bogh. Enough." He raised his hand and Bogh was silent. Dyak watched Bogh's back, leg, and face muscles soften. Bogh was frightened of this man. He must be a good human. "I will speak to Attu. It is his animal."

"I trained the dog..."

Quick as a snake bites, the leader human pulled a stick from his fur and hit Bogh on the head. *Hit Bogh! With a stick!*

Now Dyak *knew* this was a good human. His dry nose moistened with the scent of Bogh's anger and fear.

"Enough, Bogh. More words and I will put you in the pen with the dog and the People will watch." The Dooma turned his back on Bogh and walked toward the hide-covered sleeping places below.

Bogh rubbed his head with his hand and turned to Dyak. He spit into the dog's cage. Dyak heard himself making angry noises, and he quieted himself. The leader had hit Bogh. Did this mean the others would not kill Attu and Dyak? The leader had turned away from Bogh. So Dyak turned away too and lay down in the far end of the pen.

"Sleep now, cur. I'll be back for you...for your *meat*!"

Bogh turned to leave and only then saw the white-furred, stooped old man. "What are you looking at, old woman?" Bogh spit again. Dyak wondered if he had eaten something too long dead. Bogh always smelled like that, though.

"Nothing, warrior, nothing of importance to you." The old man spoke softly at Bogh's back.

DYAK DID NOT WAKE until Attu opened the pen and waved his hand to come out. It was in the dark time. Dyak trotted toward the sheep, but Attu ran after him, put his hand on Dyak and made the sign to stop. Then the boy put a sheep's-hide rope on Dyak and led him away from the People—in the other direction, toward the Big Water. Dyak was happy to walk with Attu, even on the rope.

But Attu was not happy with this hunt. The boy's smell was sour. His shoulders high and close. His breath hard. Maybe master thought Dyak could not help run down the game. Even Attu did not know Dyak was strong again and could run and hunt as he could before. Dyak's tongue dropped from his mouth as he thought how he would surprise Attu when they ran for the game.

Master made human noises as they walked. Sometimes he sounded Dyak's name, but although Dyak liked hearing the boy make this noise, Dyak did not feel good. Dyak shivered as if he had just smelled the giant bear ahead, too close to run away from. Dyak's ears and tail stayed down, even though he was with master and on the hunt again.

Dyak could hear the Big Water now. It was very loud and this made Dyak more wary than ever. There was much food by the Big Water. He liked the small food that lived in the soft wet dirt and that had hard skin. Many other animals liked this food and the fish that lived in the Big Water, too. Dyak did not like the fish. When he was a pup, a fish bit him after he ate it. He swallowed it, then it bit him inside his throat with a tiny sharp tooth and he did not trust fish again.

The noise of the Big Water was more dangerous than the fish whose bone bit after it was dead. And the smell was a great danger, too. The Big Water made so much noise and so much smell that it was hard to know when a bear or the longtooth or wolves ran nearby. All of these liked the food from the Big Water and all of these could kill Dyak and Attu.

Knowing these things, Dyak tried hard to smell and listen. Then Attu stopped and took the rope off Dyak.

Were they going to run for game by the Big Water? It was hard running in the soft flowing ground that was by the Big Water. Maybe Attu knew of some game they could catch here. Whatever master wanted, Dyak was ready. He sat, ears up, blue eyes focused on the boy for a sign.

Attu stooped. Strong smells sprang from the boy, cold and hot pouring off his sweating body. Master was unhappy. Dyak stopped swishing his tail and whined. Attu made the sign "run far," so Dyak ran as quickly as he could on the soft dirt. He ran until he could barely see master. He stopped and looked back. Attu again made the sign to run far. Dyak did not understand this, but he ran again. He ran and ran, until he past one of the great round animals that lived in the Big Water. He had seen these animals on the ground, too. Usually many of them stayed together as they lay on the rocks and called in loud voices. This one was not long dead. Its meat was still good. Some of the little hard-body animals that lived in the Big Water were eating part of it, nipping bites off with their sharp, pointed paws. This must be why Attu had wanted Dyak to run so far, to find this meat.

Dyak turned and ran back to where Attu was. But master was not there.

It was easy to find him. Attu was walking back to the human's den. Dyak knew Attu would be happy and surprised that Dyak had found this Big Water animal meat so quickly.

Dyak danced up to Attu and around the boy, his tail pointed in the air, tongue hanging happily over the side of his mouth. He yipped and stretched his front legs down and out, his rear stuck high in the air.

Attu did not stop walking. He only called "Dyak" very loud and made the "run far" sign many times. He did not even look at Dyak. Attu smelled angry and sad. The smell of the water from master's eyes made Dyak's legs weak.

Dyak wanted to do what Attu wanted Dyak to do. If Dyak did not run when master said to, then Attu was angry. If Dyak ran and came back, master was sad. Dyak stood in front of Attu and whined. Dyak knew master would help Dyak understand.

Attu stared hard at Dyak. Water no longer came from Attu's eyes. He went down on his half-leg and held Dyak's head between his hands, rubbing beneath Dyak's teeth where the boy knew Dyak best liked to be rubbed. Dyak licked under Attu's chin, to let master know that Dyak would always do what master wanted.

Then Attu stood and walked to a thorn tree. Dyak turned his head when Attu picked up a thorn stick and brought it back to Dyak. Maybe Attu would make fire here and they would sleep. Dyak did not like to sleep so far away from the other humans, from the hunters who could kill the longtooth when they were all together or even drive away the giant bear with their fire, but he would stay with Attu if that was what master wanted. He trotted over to the boy and looked up for direction.

Dyak did not expect what happened next. Attu hit Dyak in the side with the thorn stick and made Dyak's name noise very loud. Dyak whined and flinched in pain. The thorn stick hurt much. Even Bogh had not used such a stick. Dyak looked at Attu and whined again. Then Attu ran at Dyak, waving the thorn stick and making Dyak's name noise very loud. With Attu's other hand, the boy made the "run far" sign again and again.

Dyak jumped back from the stick. Attu tripped and fell on the ground. Dyak ran to his master to see if master was hurt. When Dyak sniffed the boy, Attu rose quickly on his half legs and hit Dyak on the nose with the thorn stick. The blow hurt Dyak so much that he almost couldn't feel Attu's anger and sadness.

Dyak ran a little way and rubbed his nose with his leg to make the hurt stop. When he looked up, Attu was running at him with the thorn stick, making loud noises again.

This time Dyak ran. He ran and ran. He ran from Attu. He did not know he *could* run from Attu. As easily run from the breath in his body or the food that gave him strength. Dyak ran from Attu not because master had hurt Dyak's nose but because Dyak was afraid. Afraid as he had never been when he smelled the longtooth near or even when Bogh had kicked him until he slept. Dyak ran because he did not know what else to do. When Dyak ran, the smell of the air and the story of the ground beneath his feet filled his life. When Dyak ran, he did not smell Attu; there was no room in him for that smell. If Dyak did not smell Attu, he would not feel Attu. Dyak's legs and lungs did not know his confusion; they knew only how to run.

When the Great Light rose above the trees, Dyak was still running. He splashed into the running water that was too wide for him to jump across. Dyak stopped, turned back up the bank, and fell to the grass. He slept, too tired to think of Attu and the hurt that went deeper than the pains in his nose, bloody paws, and aching heart.

❄

THE GREAT LIGHT and the darkness passed many times as Dyak walked and ran. Beside the running water there was much small game. Dyak tried not to think of Attu or of how Dyak did not know what master wanted Dyak to do. Attu's smell filled Dyak's nostrils whenever his side or his nose hurt from the thorn stick. Sometimes the air brought a smell of the stupid sheep or of Bogh, or of the human leader, or the old human with long white fur. Dyak missed the warmth of his place in Attu's den. But this longing for the den was not the same as how Dyak felt about Attu, about losing his master. When Dyak smelled Attu on the wind or in a bush or on the ground, it was as strange as finding a longtooth that smelled like a grass mouse. It was, but it could not be. It was a pain that did not heal. A hurt that blotted out all smell and taste.

And so Dyak drank and ate. He hunted and slept. And never did he forget his place by Attu's fire or the hurt he felt not knowing what he had done, not knowing what had made Attu strike him and send him away.

WHEN ATTU RETURNED WITHOUT DYAK, the white-haired old man, the Bent One, was waiting. Sitting under a sourberry bush, he picked at a bowl of sourberries and mixed them with wood grubs. He motioned Attu to sit with him.

"The Dooma is unhappy you took the dog before the judgment was made, Attu. Now he must either ignore, punish, or appease Bogh. None of those are good options—for you." The Bent One, who had a name none of the People could say, kept eating as he talked.

Before Attu could ask why this was, the Bent One raised his hand for silence and continued, "There are many things I must tell you, Attu. I hoped to teach you more and I hoped you would be older before these things had to be told, but it is important now that you hear them." He set down the bowl of berries and grubs, wiped his lips and hands with his long white beard, and then fixed Attu with clear gray eyes.

"The Dooma is a good man, Attu, and a good leader. But he is no longer young. He *will* be challenged, if not this season, then before enough seasons pass to fill a hand." He held his fist out and slowly opened one finger after another until all fingers and thumb stuck out. The old man continued, "Bogh will challenge him. Bogh is stupid, cruel, and not a good hunter. But he is strong and he can use his spear well in a fight. He will make a very bad leader for the People. You'll need the help of the spirits and the wind to survive if he becomes Dooma."

"I won't let Bogh become Dooma!" Attu said with great passion.

"Good boy. That's what I want to hear. But think, Attu, can you beat Bogh? With hands, with clubs, with spears?"

Attu's head fell and he spoke softly, "No. I do not think so."

"This is good, too, boy. It is good you know this. *That* is why it is important *you* become Dooma, and not Bogh—or even Grar. The Dooma needs to see things as they *are*, no matter how painful that is, no matter how difficult it is for him."

"But I *cannot* beat Bogh, I have said so and it is true."

"Yes. This is a point." The Bent One stroked his beard, then surprised Attu with a smile, "That's why I've been working with you for so long. You *will* beat Bogh, and Bogh will not even know you have won." Still smiling, he picked up his bowl again, eating and watching the boy.

Attu was used to the strange way the Bent One spoke. He used many words together and his speech was like the tricks he made for Dyak, with traps and treats that he could reach only if he worked at them. No one spoke like this, not even the Dooma or the other old ones. Most of the People stayed away from the Bent One. They said—behind his back—that he brought ill luck. He brought bad spirits. He was not of the People. They did not say this in front of the Dooma, though. Attu did not know where the Bent One came from, the old man did not like to speak about it, but he did know he had come from somewhere else, that his mother was not of the People. He had brought the first sheep with him, it was said, and other things good for the People. And Attu knew the Dooma listened to the Bent One, more than he listened to anyone else. Attu was the only one besides the Dooma who sought out the Bent One. Since Attu's father had fallen in the last hunt for the shaggy Grey Giant, the boy had grown very close to the old man.

"But this dog, Attu..."

"Dyak, his name is Dyak," Attu insisted.

"Oh! It is, is it?" Browning teeth showed slightly in the wrinkled face. "Dyak is gone now, isn't he, Attu? You took him out and killed him? Is this correct?"

Attu lowered his eyes.

"As I thought. You have broken the Dooma's promise to Bogh..."

"...but..." Attu began.

The Bent One stretched a spotted, gnarly finger and pressed it over Attu's lips. "...No, boy...listen." He took his finger from Attu and continued, "We must keep Bogh from using this broken oath to challenge the Dooma. We must make time for you to grow. We must do everything we can to help the Dooma."

Attu nodded and looked expectantly at the old man.

"Good boy. What you must do is go to Bogh and tell him you have killed the dog. That you are ashamed that he bit Bogh. And then you must make Bogh his new spears. And then make them again the next time he needs them."

Attu stood up, looming over the thin, white-haired man, fists clenched. "I will *never* say these things to Bogh. I will *never* kill Dyak. I will *never* help Bogh. He is as cruel as the longtooth. He says things that are not true and he does not do the things he says he will do. I will *not* be like Bogh."

The Bent One motioned for Attu to be quiet and sit again. On his third such motion, Attu sat, but he continued to glare. The old man shrugged his shoulders and let out a large breath between thin pursed lips. "That is as I was afraid it would be. It is true if you acted in this way, you will not speak all the truth in your heart and so will be like Bogh. But following this path for a time will help bring the People to a good place one day. You understand, don't you, Attu? If you speak all the truth to Bogh and to the Dooma, then that will be like a hot coal under a sleeping mat. It may not become fire right away, but the mat will burn. And it is as likely to burn the Dooma first as it is to burn you."

Attu stopped glaring, confusion growing behind his eyes.

"Here is the hard part, Attu." The old man set down his bowl. His brows drew together as he looked at Attu.

"Bogh *is* a good spear, maybe the best spear of the People. The People need good spears." The Bent One sighed again and placed his fingertips on either side of his own head. "That is why I am with the People now. My people did not have good spears. We lived far away in a warmer place where the running waters met the Big Water. Our village was larger than the People's, and we had many good things we do not have here. Life there was...it was much easier than here, Attu. Very good. With easy food, easy heat in the cold season, everything easy. It is from my people that the People learned to raise sheep. My people were... well, we did not have many like Bogh. We danced, we sang, we carved, we laughed. My female, Plana-alghaf-Lamana, was like the Dooma, she was a leader of my people."

Attu looked at the Bent One as if he had said their Dooma was a longtooth, "You had a woman Dooma?" He had heard many things about the Bent One, but none could match the strangeness of this tale from his own lips.

The old man smiled, "Yes, Attu, a woman Dooma. Some seasons, we had a man Dooma, too, but my Plana was a good and strong leader." His smile darkened into an old pain, "but then the Body Eaters came upon us." He looked at the ground, at the remains of his berry-grub mush, and picked at it with a long fingernail.

"But the Body Eaters are just spirits, aren't they, Bent One? What did they do with your people?" Attu's eyes were very wide, as they had been when he first came to the Bent One and listened to the old man's stories.

"That tale does not need to be told now. The Body Eaters were away far and a long time before you were born. I have not heard of them since I joined the People." The Bent One stood, walked to the edges of the sourberry bush and looked back toward the center of the People's place, then he squatted before Attu and continued, "What you do need to know, Attu, is that the Dooma saved me. I fell into a hunting pit and struck my head. The Body Eaters came upon my people as I lay without thought or light, and when I awoke I climbed out and stumbled to our living place. My people were gone or dead or worse. It is a long story, but Tabah found me and brought me back to the People. He was just a hunter then. His mother's brother was Dooma, but Tabah did not let the People leave me in the cold. He brought me meat and water until I became stronger."

"What of your woman? Did you have children? What..."

"Enough!" Attu had never heard the Bent One speak so rough. "I will not talk more of it." Then he squatted and put a long, thin hand on the boy's shoulder. "Return to your sheep. I will speak to the Dooma. Do *not* fight with Bogh. You *can* do that, can't you?"

Attu nodded, and went back to the People.

DYAK LAY on a soft bed of dead grass, eating a small white-furred Jumper, when he smelled humans coming toward the running water. He rose to find them. Attu might be with these humans.

He trotted toward them, head erect, nostrils quivering. He did not know these smells. He ran under a short tree and smelled and listened and watched. Humans could not smell him, no matter how close they came, and he crouched low under the tree.

He waited.

There were many humans. Human waste and water scents were stronger than Bogh's. Some stank like dead human meat. Dyak almost sneezed when he smelled this. He liked strong smells but this scent made his belly tight. He would not have rolled in it or brought it back to Attu. It was a bad smell.

These humans carried big sticks like Bogh. They walked on two legs like humans, but their backs bent over like the giant long-arm ones that moved slowly and hung down from trees.

Dyak did not like these humans.

Dyak followed their smell as they moved past him. He stayed far enough away the humans could not see him. When they stopped to sleep, Dyak found a place where he could watch. They did not make human noises like master's humans. They did not sleep together like dogs. They did not eat like Attu's humans. When they fed, they killed one of the small humans that they dragged behind them and then fought each other for its meat. After he saw this eating, Dyak moved away and found water. Then he sat. His pointed ears folded back against his skull. He filled his nostrils with air, air that did not smell of these new, bad humans. The fur of the small human they ate was like the fur on Attu's head.

When the Great Light came in the sky again, Dyak had not slept or eaten. He ran ahead of the bad-smelling humans. He ran while the Great Light shone and then in the darkness. He ran without eating and only stopped for water.

DAYS PASSED. Attu helped the Bent One with his colored dirts and grasses, his bones and needles. The boy slept near the sheep, now in their pens with no dog to watch them. Bogh did not come to find him when he was with the sheep, so he did not fight with Bogh.

His small hide shelter—he had moved from his mother's tent only two seasons past and had no need for a large one—was colder in the nights now. Attu wondered if he should find a mate to warm him and cook his food. He still ate from his mother's pots when the Dooma did not feed the people together. Attu smiled as he dozed: would a mate put up with Dyak's night noises? Then he remembered that Dyak was gone and would not be back. He covered himself in his sheepskin, closed his eyes, and tried not to think of his dog and the thorny stick he'd hit him with.

As the Great Light fell toward the edge of the land the next day, Tabah the Dooma returned from a long hunt. Attu watched as Bogh greeted the Dooma at the edge of the People's settlement. Holding his spear and shouting, Bogh moved his arms in big circles. He pointed at Attu and waved his spear.

The Bent One came out from his tent, close to where Bogh and the People's leader stood. The old man walked toward the Dooma, but when he neared them, Bogh raised his arm and struck the Bent One to the ground.

All movement around Attu slowed. He yelled something even he could not understand and started running toward the three men. The expressions on the Dooma's and Bogh's faces were large and bright, as if they were in front of him and not far away. The Dooma dropped the handful of birds he held and reached for the spear strapped to his back. The game fell to the ground too slowly. Attu's feet moved too slowly. As he ran, Attu wondered how he could so clearly see Bogh's smile, his small teeth yellow with bits of red and black between them.

Then the Dooma had his spear out and he and Bogh were trading blows, not with the deadly tips, but swinging the spears as clubs. The Dooma's mother's son, Grar, ran up between the two fighters. Attu was close enough to hear them now.

"This is a Dooma challenge." Grar shouted, his arms pushing out to hold the Dooma and Bogh apart. "It will be held before the old ones and the spirits of the People. Bogh! Tabah!

Be ready. I will gather the old ones. When the cooking pot is turned, the challenge will begin. Bogh! You are the challenger. What is the challenge?"

"Death!" Bogh spat. "Challenge to Death."

Attu stood by the side of the Dooma now. Tabah's expression did not change, but the muscles in his wrists tightened on the spears he held. They could be no tighter than the muscles in Attu's stomach.

Attu remembered the Bent One and ran to him. A gnarled hand grasped Attu's shoulder and the old man rose, a ragged knot and swelling bruise showing on his pale forehead.

"I breathe and I see, Attu. Do not be concerned for me." He propped his weight on the boy, and Attu could tell the old man was far from well. "Go to the Dooma and tell him to ask of Bogh's woman when they fight. Tell him to ask Bogh where she goes when she cleans his furs. Now help me to the fire, boy."

Attu helped the Bent One to his sleeping place and made sure his fire was warm. Twigs and dirt layered the long white beard and he looked much older than he had just days before when Attu talked to him under the sourberry bush. Leaving the old man, Attu heard Grar shouting. He hurried away, running between the People's sleeping places. He needed to deliver the Bent One's message to the Dooma.

As he ran up, Grar turned over the huge stone pot that was set in the middle of the Dooma's meeting place. This is where the Dooma made important decisions, where great hunts began, and where the People held communal meals and other ceremonies. Grar growled something at Attu as he passed him. But the boy ignored him and ran up to the Dooma, breathlessly telling him what the Bent One had said. The leader's eyes flashed as he listened, but he did not look at Attu. His attention fixed on his mate, Orena, and his twin sons.

Grar shouted for all to move back from the People's sacred place.

"This is a challenge for the right of Dooma of the People."

Grar looked around for anyone to say no to him and the challenge.

"It is a challenge to the death from Bogh against Tabah. None shall help either. The People are Strong. The challenge begins now." Grar moved back quickly out of the meeting place.

Attu expected Bogh to roar or shout like the big bear he looked and acted like, and then to run at Tabah. The boy was surprised that Bogh made no sounds at all. Both men circled around, well outside spear thrust from each other. They both danced the same dance.

Bogh was clearly bigger and stronger. None of the People were as large as Bogh. But the Dooma's muscles were hard as stone. He did not still play the arm-bending game, but Attu had heard that he only stopped because the Dooma did not want to hurt the arms of other hunters. It was said Tabah had never lost this game. And of Bogh and the Dooma, there was no question who was smarter. But Attu was no fighter and did not know if this would make any difference.

Tabah struck first with the spear he held in his wrong hand. Bogh knocked it down easily, but then the Dooma followed this attack with a strike so fast that Attu hissed in reaction. It caught Bogh on *his* wrong arm, above his wrist. Again, Bogh surprised Attu. He remembered how the big man cried like a child when Dyak bit Bogh on that same arm. Now Bogh made no such sound, but came down with an overhand strike, using his right-hand spearhead like a club and hitting Tabah squarely on his wrong side collarbone.

Tabah staggered. His grip on the wrong-hand spear was looser. Tabah stepped back a pace and yelled to Bogh, "And how is your mate today, Bogh? Do you make her happy under the furs?"

The People, who watched quietly, became even more silent.

Bogh stood very still. His lips pressed hard together and his face looked like he had run a long ways up a hill. The two men began circling again.

The men stepped in close. Their spears flashed one way then another. Brack-Crack! Crack-POPP-Crack! They traded fast blows for many heartbeats. The harsh sounds and the silences rang through the stillness of the watching People. So loud, then nothing.

Attu could see they slowed. Then, for no reason he could tell, both the fighters stepped back at the same time. Bogh's enormous chest heaved. His head and neck dripped with sweat. With a loud grunt he crammed his two spears a hand's breadth into the ground, tore off his upper fur, and grabbed the spears again, all the time breathing as fast as Attu could run.

The Dooma also panted, but not like Bogh's storm gusts. His collarbone where Bogh had hit him looked wrong, too big and strangely angled. He still held spears in both hands, though.

Just as Bogh's breathing started to slow, the Dooma called out to him, "I see now why your wife is so long gone when she washes your furs, Bogh."

At this, Bogh snorted like a goaded ox, then charged, holding both his spears like horns above his head.

Tabah waited calmly. He knew where this tree would fall. He knew when. He had only to step out of the way. Bogh thundered toward him. The Dooma stepped lightly to one side and drove a spear into Bogh's upper leg, spear-head deep, and with his right arm brought the haft of his other spear down on the back of Bogh's tangled head of hair. He struck this blow with such force that the spear-shaft cracked as Bogh fell, unmoving and face down, at the edge of the Dooma's circle.

Grar squatted, lifted Bogh's head and looked in his face. Still holding Bogh's head up from the dirt, he announced, "He is not dead."

Tabah stood tall with his spears, and cried out, "I am Dooma. The challenge is over. Bogh called it to the death. I did not. The challenge is over. The People are Strong!" He nodded at the healing women. Attu noticed they did not rush to Bogh.

The Dooma turned to Attu. The small smile that began on

Tabah's lips turned to a frown as his eyes tracked down to the boy's side.

THE SMELL of Attu filled Dyak's nose as he crossed the field of the stupid sheep. Master stood with the other humans by the human eating place. Dyak ran to Attu to pull him away—away from the bad-smelling humans who were coming behind Dyak. Before he reached master, the crack of the fighting sticks and the proud odor of the battle distracted Dyak. He stopped and stared as the familiar smell of Bogh's blood tracked into his nostrils. *The human leader had hit Bogh with a stick again! This was a good human leader.* Dyak wanted to lick him under the chin and bow for play, but Attu still smelled sad and angry; the bad humans were outside and coming, and so Dyak only shook his tail slowly when Bogh dropped to the ground.

ATTU FELT HIMSELF PULLED BACKWARDS. Someone tugged at his furs. He wheeled to deal with this indignity. Dyak—thinner but still sturdy, more gray-and-dirt now than gray-and-white—held firmly to Attu's lower fur and pulled him hard toward the sheep field.

The boy fell to his knees and hugged the dog, who did not release his hold on Attu's furs and who smelled of old mud. Attu had no thought for this, and fiercely embraced his friend. "Dyak! Dyak!" he cried.

A hard hand pulled him by the shoulder and he stood to face an angry Tabah.

"Malala-mananda-lal told me you had killed this dog."

"Malalal..." Attu stumbled, confused.

"...the Bent One," Tabah explained.

"I...I...did...not..." Attu began, eyes down.

"I see you did not. Did you lie to the Bent One or did he lie to me?" Tabah looked angrier than he had when he fought Bogh.

"Hold, Dooma." The Bent One's voice called, reedier and higher than Attu remembered. Tabah looked away from Attu, face washed of expression.

"The boy did as I told him." The old one stepped close between the Dooma and Attu, "I feared what would happen this day and did not wish to hasten it."

"Did you see this thing in the fires?" The Dooma's voice asked in a different tone.

"No, Tabah, I did not *see* it. But I *thought* it would come." The Bent One's voice was very low. He looked at Attu and Dyak and continued. "The dog has come back for a reason, Dooma. Do not judge the boy badly or quickly."

The Dooma turned from Dyak to Attu. He did not smile. But he did not frown, either.

"Why does the dog pull you, Attu? Does he want food?"

Attu looked down at Dyak. He made the sign of "run far." Dyak barked at him and did not move, then he seized Attu's fur in his mouth and tugged. Attu pushed him away, made the sign of "lie down and watch." Dyak barked again, but finally dropped down at Attu's feet. His blue eyes fixed hard on the boy.

"I do not know, Dooma. He does not act like this. He does what I ask. He knows better than this."

The old man turned and spoke softly to the Dooma. Attu could not hear what was said.

The Bent One spoke to him again, "Let the dog go, Attu. Follow where he pulls you."

Attu made signs at Dyak to rise and to run far, and then the boy grabbed and held to Dyak's thick neck fur.

Dyak moved swiftly toward the sheep field. Attu held on and ran beside him. Dyak ran across the whole field, Attu in tow. Still at speed, they made it to the edge of the grass and the Dooma shouted for them to stop. Attu dug in his heels and held fast to Dyak.

Dyak put a front paw on Attu's right foot, shoved his nose against the boy's leg, and whined. The boy stroked the furry pointed ears and looked down. He stared hard when his eyes met the dog's, and then he pushed Dyak's paw off his foot. In a moment, Dyak looked away, and when Attu made the "follow" sign and turned to run back, Dyak whined again. But the dog trotted at his master's heels as they ran across the sheep field. All the way back, Attu noticed the Bent One and the Dooma stood close together in deep talk.

"...like the longtooth has his smell. He must return, unseen, when he has found the end of the dog's trail." The Bent One finished as Attu ran up.

The Dooma turned and shouted for Grar, the People's fastest runner and best tracker. He had not gone far after the challenge. Tabah again spoke too quietly for Attu to hear, and then Grar ran off in the opposite direction from the sheep field, following some trail only he could see.

"You have not turned into an old woman, like some say, have you, Malala-mananda-lal?" the Dooma asked solemnly, but he smiled as he spoke.

"We should know before the first light, Dooma. It will not hurt to do this."

"Except your hands that will make Grar new foot pads."

Attu thought the Dooma was joking now. But he did not understand.

"We should prepare the rest." The Bent One was not smiling.

"As you say, old one, as you say." The Dooma walked away, leaving Attu and the Bent One standing in the People's sacred place.

"What is happening, Malal...Malala..." Attu began.

Malala-mananda-lal laughed now. "Bent One is fine, boy. Your tongue is not used to such sounds." He encircled Attu's shoulder with a thin arm. "Or call me BraDa, if you wish."

Attu looked at the old man who had been his teacher and friend for as long as he could remember. He would call him BraDa.

"Come, Attu. You can help me and the People. There is much to do before the dark ends."

DYAK'S TAIL fell when Attu did not run away with him, but he stopped trying to pull the boy because Attu made it clear they must stay. Dyak did not know what would happen when the bad-smelling humans found Attu, but it made his belly tight and his haunches weak with fear. He came back to master to get the boy away from the bad-smelling humans who ate other humans. Even though Dyak still felt the sting of the sharp-point stick, still felt the pain in his heart that Attu had struck him. But there were no sharp-point stick trees here. And when master turned and saw Dyak pulling on him, Attu's eyes and His breath filled Dyak's heart more than any pain.

Dyak smelled deep anger and confusion on Attu—even when they ran together. But now Dyak would find the scent of what master wanted.

ATTU DID NOT GO to his hides to sleep. The sky was clear and the Little Light was bright, so he was able to do the things that the Bent—that BraDa—asked him to do. They were strange and smelly things.

Dyak was no help. He followed Attu closely at all times. He whined. He nipped at Attu's legs. But whenever Attu became angry enough to strike the dog, the boy remembered the thorny stick he'd hit Dyak with and he reached down and stroked the rough furry head instead.

"I do not know what is wrong with Dyak. I think the Little Light took his sense when he was gone," Attu said as he struggled moving the stones that held back the worthless black ooze that pooled on one edge of the People's living place. He was already covered in its stink. At least the clinging drops on his legs had stopped Dyak from nipping him. Now the dog just stood close, wrinkled his nose, and whimpered.

"What I am afraid of most is that Dyak has *not* lost his sense, Attu," BraDa answered from the gloom. "Now tumble those stones and then come and help with this ditch. I am too old for such work."

When the Little Light had passed over most of the sky, Grar returned exhausted, collapsing in front of the Dooma's shelter, calling Tabah's name. Not only the Dooma, but most of the People woke at his calls.

The Dooma helped his brother up from the ground and under his resting hides. The Bent One, Malala-mananda-lal, stepped inside after them.

A few heartbeats later, the Dooma pushed aside his door flap. He strode quickly to his sacred place, Malala-mananda-lal at his heels. Grar was already there and the Dooma signed at him. Grar beat on the great pot, still overturned, and shouted for all to come. The Dooma stood and waited as the People came to the pit from their sleeping places. He banged his spears together for silence, but there was no need. The People knew some great thing was wrong.

"People! Spears of the People! Awake and Defend! Awake and Defend!" The Dooma called, then looked around at the People. None spoke. All eyes were clear.

"An attack comes at the People. We will be ready for this attack. The People are Strong!" Tabah shouted this last and beat his spears together. The People all shouted back at him. Those who carried spears beat them together, too.

When the responses faded, the Dooma continued, "Do not fear. I am your Dooma and I must tell you this. But DO NOT FEAR! Those who attack us are the Body Eaters. We..."

Many in the assembly began wailing and screaming, some ran back toward their sleeping places, two men ran for the sheep field.

The Dooma jumped up onto the great stone pot, raised his

spears to the sky and shouted his loudest, "STOP! IF YOU RUN YOU DIE! IF YOU HIDE YOU DIE!"

All this time he beat his spears together above his head. The Little Light shone on the Dooma's proud face and a storm seemed to gather around his shoulders as he spoke to the People. He made motions at Grar to catch the men running toward the sheep field and at his other brothers to bring back those who had gone to their tents.

When most of the People had returned and were calmer, the Dooma spoke again, still standing on the stone pot, "Yes, the Body Eaters are coming. But the People *are* Strong. We are strong in our Spears." He nodded at his hunters and spears and they beat their weapons together. "*And* the People are strong in wisdom." All voices hushed. They did not know what Tabah meant by this. He nodded at Malala-mananda-lal, who walked up to stand at Tabah's side. "This is a time for Wisdom *and* a time for Spears. You all know the Bent One." He nodded again at the old man. "He has saved many of you from sickness. He has helped the Dooma and the People many times. He has Wisdom that will help us turn away the Body Eaters. We *must* listen to him."

There were murmurs among the People. The Dooma nodded at Grar, who stepped toward those who spoke loudest. They quieted.

"Now. All who do not hold spears. You must do as the Bent One says. We have until first light to prepare for the Body Eaters. We Will Live! We Will Drive Back the Body Eaters! The People Are Strong!" He raised his spears to the sky and near all the People responded again.

Finally, still standing on the stone pot, Tabah called, "All Spears to Me," and he jumped down.

ATTU DID NOT RUN to his own hide tent when the Dooma told the People the Body Eaters were coming, but he felt the empty feeling he had felt when his father had not returned from the hunt. It was beyond fear. The Body Eaters were spoken of around the fires of the young to frighten them to stay in their sleep furs. When BraDa said their name under the sourberry bush, Attu had not heard it since he was very small. For Attu and for the rest of the People, the Body Eaters were like the spirits of the dead. They might be somewhere, but they would never be *here*. And none of the People knew any who had seen the Body Eaters and lived. At least, that was what Attu thought until BraDa had told him his story.

At least Dyak had stopped whining and biting at him. Could he have known of this? Why *had* he come back now? Attu reached down with both his hands and scratched under Dyak's chin, as he knew the dog liked.

"Did you come to tell me of this, Dyak?" The dog's bright eyes looked straight into his and did not blink.

THE PEOPLE SPENT the rest of the dark time preparing. Many grumbled under the orders of the Bent One, but Grar and another Spear stood close and all did as they were bid.

The Great Light rose above the edge of the world and the People stood, exhausted, looking at the work they had done during the dark time. Most were too tired to worry much now about the Body Eaters. Two of the Dooma's brothers and their women led the night workers to the great stone pot and the meal it held. All sat in silence and ate their stew.

The Dooma, the Bent One, and Grar stood on the small cliff that rose at one end of the living place of the People, just above the pool of black ooze—a pool that was much smaller now. They looked away from the meeting place, away from the sheep field. They lit a fire there. Attu knew it was cold on that barren rise.

Grar sprinted down the backside of the escarpment, through the sheep field and toward the meeting place. Tabah followed quickly but at a slower pace, and BraDa—The Bent One—walked down, leaning on a stick.

THEIR SMELLS TOLD him Attu's humans were afraid. Even the human leader. They ran from one human place to another. They scratched in the dirt. They did not sleep in the dark time. Dyak stayed close to Attu, hoping to see or smell or hear what He wanted Dyak to do.

The Great Light above moved toward the edge of the world. Dyak's nose twitched. The bad-smelling humans were not far. Dyak whined as he ran by Attu's side. *They were running* toward *the bad smell.* Dyak stopped and barked. Attu stopped. Master's lips curled and his smell was angry; he made Dyak's name noise many times. Dyak did not stop barking; he would not stop even if master hit him again. *The bad-smelling humans were almost here. Attu must understand. They must run. If Attu's humans could smell the eaters of small humans, they would run, too.*

The old human with white fur walked up and made sounds at Attu. He pointed at Dyak. At least Attu wasn't running toward the bad-smelling humans now. Dyak panted fast, but was quiet and waited. Then Attu ran again—Dyak by his side—back to the high place where all master's humans were in sight. Dyak looked the other way; his nose told him the bad-smelling humans were coming. The bad humans would have to go through the dead sticky water *and* climb up the hill. Dyak would not try to stop Attu from going there.

Attu made a noise on top of the rise. Dyak raised his ears and looked for the bad humans. He could smell them again now—even with the black water smell that was everywhere. Something moved far away where the sky and the ground met.

Attu and Dyak stood and waited together. Now Dyak could see the bad humans. There were many more than Attu's humans. They moved fast for humans. Dyak whined and Attu put his hand on Dyak's ears. Dyak looked up at master. Attu did not smell of fear; he smelled like play. Dyak did not want to play. He wanted to run. But he would stay with Attu until they ran together.

Below, the bad humans ran over the ground that Attu's humans had worked in the dark. Dyak had watched them scrape the ground with sticks. He stuck his nose in the scrape as it filled with the smelly black water. Even now, Dyak shook his head hard to rid his nostrils of that smell. If the bad-smelling humans drank that water they would be sick and run away. Dyak would never drink that water.

Attu held a stick with fire on it. Since it was not cold and it was not dark, Dyak was confused and turned his head to the side as he looked at Attu. *Attu would not hit Dyak with the fire stick, would he?* Dyak backed away a step. Dyak would not be hit by a fire stick, even by master.

But Attu did not hit Dyak. He dropped the fire stick off the high place into the pool of sticky black water below them. Dyak hoped Attu did not want Dyak to bring this fire stick back. *This was something else he would not do.* Knowing he would not do this made Dyak sad because he wanted to do what Attu wanted. But Attu did not make the sign to get the stick. The fur on Dyak's back eased flat. Heat waved up from below. Fire covered all the black water. Fire spread all the way from the rise where he and Attu stood, past the human's sleeping place to the big rock on the other side. Fire was everywhere the humans had scraped the ground.

Bad-smelling humans rushed through the fire toward Attu's humans. Many bad humans were on both sides of the black water fire now. There was fire on some of the bad humans and they made loud noises. Dyak wrinkled his nose and sneezed.

Dyak couldn't see any of Attu's humans. *Were they eating and sleeping?*

"Run!" Dyak barked at them, "Run, Run, Run!"

The human leader and a few others holding stone-pointed sticks appeared below out of the black air that rose from the fire water. The leader made loud noises, and the rest of Attu's humans ran out of their sleeping places and hit the bad-smelling humans with their sticks.

Dyak heard the tearing of flesh. Bodies smashed; the bad humans struck with rocks and sticks, their fists and their feet. And they bit. They bit the shoulders and the necks, the faces and the fingers and arms of Attu's humans. Sharp fresh blood smell was everywhere, adding to the black water stink, and the human scents of ripped flesh and, now, death.

The bad-smelling humans ran in all directions. Attu's humans stayed together in groups. A group hit one of the bad humans until that human did not move, then they ran together at another bad human.

Dyak stopped barking and watched.

"Dyak," Attu called and then made another sound. Then master ran down to the human sleeping places, *toward* the fighting and the bad humans. Dyak whined, jumped forward, and pulled at Attu's furs, but Attu did not stop and did not seem to notice Dyak at all. So Dyak stopped pulling and ran behind the boy, watching as Attu ran toward pointed sticks, fire water, and bad-smelling humans.

When they got to the fighting humans, Attu picked up a long stone-pointed stick like Bogh carried and ran toward a group hitting bad humans. Before Attu got to them, a bad human was on the ground with blood on him in many places. Dyak smelled him carefully; *the bad human would not get up again.*

Attu and the humans in that group made loud fast human noises together. Dyak held his ears back, his tail straight out behind him. These were Attu's humans, but they had sticks and Dyak was ready if they hit Attu next. But they did not smell angry at Attu. They smelled like the boy. They smelled as if they were hunting and playing. Smelling his master and his master's humans, water dripped from Dyak's mouth. He jumped around Attu, ready to bite any bad humans who came near. Dyak's legs and fur stretched out stiff to the air. His lips curled and a growl filled his belly.

Dyak looked around and sniffed for bad humans. As overpowering as their scent was, the smell of the black fire water was so strong he couldn't tell where the bad humans were. Dyak's tail swung slowly from side to side. His shoulders bristled in worry as they did when he was near the Big Water.

The bad human scent was everywhere, but he did not see any of them except the ones that did not move. Dyak's tail lowered further toward the ground. His nose told him Attu and his humans only wanted sleep now. They moved slowly, even for humans.

Dyak's ears pointed. Loud human noises rolled from far across the human sleeping place. A group of humans there were hitting and jumping. Attu made an angry sound by Dyak's ear and ran toward them.

Dyak ran swiftly and left Attu behind. Attu called Dyak's name noise. Dyak heard this, but he also did not hear it. Not heeding master was wrong, but Dyak felt its rightness, too.

Just ahead of him now, the human leader was hitting and being hit by some of the bad-smelling humans. They stood close to the scrape filled by the black water, very close to the fires.

Before he could leap at the bad humans, Dyak heard a terrible sound. It was a sound he knew, a sound he did not want to hear.

It was Bogh.

Face red, eyes bulging in hatred, Bogh ran up behind Dyak, carrying his big stone-pointed sticks. Dyak jumped to the side and started to run back to Attu. He knew he could move faster than Bogh.

But Bogh did not seem to see Dyak. The leg the leader had stabbed was dark with blood, but Bogh still ran. He ran at the human leader and made booming human noises only Bogh could make.

Dyak stopped again. Should he run and bite Bogh before he

hit the human leader? Dyak whined. Attu was still too far away to tell Dyak what to do. Dyak stood and watched.

Bad humans hit the human leader's head and he fell to the ground just as Bogh reached him. Before they struck the fallen leader again, Bogh jumped into the air and came down with each of his sticks hitting through the bad humans who were hitting the leader. The bad humans fell beside the leader and did not move.

Bogh bent to pull his sticks out, and Dyak watched as another stick flew through the fire—Bogh stood close to the black fire water—and this stick went through Bogh. Bogh looked at the stick that stuck through him. His dark eyes were round as he grabbed the point that stuck through his belly. Then he fell, slowly, face-down on the ground. His furs, his body, and his head lay near the People's leader, clear of the fires. His legs stretched out into the black water. Fire quickly covered Bogh's legs.

Attu ran past Dyak and knelt by the human leader. He made noises at him. He did not look at Bogh. Dyak went to stand beside Attu.

Bogh had fallen. Dyak walked sideways by the huge man. This was *Bogh* on the ground next to them. Bogh who had kicked him and struck him and strangled him so many times. Bogh who frightened Attu. Bogh who had penned him. Bogh who had tried to take the bone animal from him. Bogh. Dyak's ears were pinned to his head. His underfur bristled all over his body.

Bogh's body moved. Was Bogh rising again? No. Through the hot light of the fire, Dyak saw a bad human pulling Bogh across the black fire water, pulling Bogh to the other side.

Attu was on his half leg by the human leader. Dyak looked around. He could not see any bad-smelling humans on this side of the fire. Dyak looked back at Bogh's body as it moved into the heat of the scrape.

Dyak jumped forward and grabbed the fur that covered

Bogh's shoulder and pulled. He pulled to keep Bogh on his side of the burning as hard as if Bogh were Attu. The bad-smelling human on the other side was strong. Bogh's legs charred and shrank as the dog and the human pulled against each other.

An angry human cry spit from the other side of the scrape as Dyak dragged Bogh's smoking, blackened legs and feet through the fire. He pulled the big human two steps away from the scrape and then collapsed next to the smoking body, panting and exhausted.

He did not wait long before Attu and the human leader, who leaned on Attu, approached Dyak. They looked down at Bogh, and then back at Dyak. They made no human noises, but Dyak smelled that they were not angry.

There were still many bad humans on the other side of the fire water, though, and Dyak heard and smelled and saw they were angry. He could smell their fear, too, even through the black water stink. The human leader walked away from the fires, making loud human noises and waving his arms.

Attu gripped the thick fur on the back of Dyak's neck and turned to walk away. Dyak's back was still tight when he saw figures dancing on the other side of the hot light. Some were close to the scrape.

Human arms thrust through the fire from the other side. Dyak barked "DANGER! DANGER!" in short, sharp barks. Did the fire not eat bad humans? Dyak had seen many of them covered by it.

But no other bad human came through. There was a sound of great pain, and then a human on the other side dropped a small, lumpy fur next to Dyak. Scorched arms and human wails slid back to the other side.

The furry mound moved, rolling a half turn. Dyak walked to it. It had a strong smell, but not like the bad humans. It smelled lightly of plain human water and waste. And it made the sounds the smallest human pups made. Dyak stuck his nose into the thin fur around the lumpy pile. It *was* a human pup. Dyak licked its head and tasted bits of the black clinging water. He sneezed. The human pup sneezed.

When Dyak looked up, the figures on the other side of the fire scrape were moving away. They moved in different directions. He lifted his nose from the human pup and tried to sense what the bad humans were doing, but strong smells had made his nose blind, so he could not be sure.

But he could smell Attu, who loosed his grip on Dyak's fur. Master was on his half leg next to the human pup. And Dyak could smell the human leader, who stood behind them with many other of Attu's humans. Dyak smelled hunger. He smelled exhaustion. And he smelled happiness.

Dyak lay on his belly by the squirming, crying human pup. The gray dog's tail brushed slowly across the blackened earth. He had done what he should.

BARDO OF DYAK

FAR DOWN AND AWAY, Dyak saw the old dog lying next to the fire outside the lean-to. A young human woman—Mala, the human pup Dyak had smelled when she was dropped over the fiery scrape, now grown—squatted by the quiet gray dog and stroked its white muzzle. Dyak shook himself. The other dog did not move. Why did Mala stroke this dog that lay by Dyak's fire? Was this master's fire? Yes, there was Attu, sleeping behind Mala under their hides, on the leader's thick furs. But Dyak did not smell the fire. He did not smell Mala or Attu.

Dyak shook himself again. He felt strong, stronger than he could remember. Attu and Mala and the old dog and Dyak's fire and their sleeping place moved farther away from his sight as if he was running from it. He had not run since the last Long Cold when the ground stayed hard.

Dyak ran.

The ground gave beneath his paws, but it was not too soft like the wet dirt by the Big Water. As he ran, the smell and sight of Attu and Mala faded and there was only the running in his heart.

The ground moved below him, but this did not bother Dyak. The ground moved up, then it moved down. It was dark, then it was light. There was water beside him, then there was not. Dyak did not mind. He ran.

Ahead, he saw lights on a rise. And dogs and humans. Something was strange about them, but Dyak did not stop running until he was very close.

The ground rolled up around him as if he was inside one of the bone animals Attu brought him. Dyak was afraid and his back fur was tight.

A bright yellow dog, larger than any dog Dyak knew, appeared in front of him. It looked at him and did not move. Dyak's tail curled underneath his haunches. His ears pasted themselves to the sides of his head. He feared this dog, yet this dog did not smell or look to attack him. He did not turn his back and run from this dog, though. He walked toward the bright yellow dog, and he did not lower his head.

As he got closer, the dog turned away from Dyak and stepped to the side. When Dyak saw what was behind this other dog, he almost ran away.

The ground was gone. The sky spread before and below Dyak. It was filled with dogs and humans and strange things that should only be on the ground. Dyak did not understand. A dog sat in a box that moved faster than the fastest longtooth could move. Many humans pointed sticks at each other and then fell and did not get up. Many dogs stood together in one place—each with a human by their sides—and all the dogs looked different from any dogs Dyak had seen: tiny dogs as small as tree runners, dogs as big as the tall gray wolves who hunted the tusked Gray Giants, furless dogs short and wide as the flat-tailed tree biters. The dogs somehow seemed like they were him. They were not him, but they were. They had many different shapes. There were no other Attus or Malas, but the other dogs-like-Dyak had other humans with them.

Dyak glanced at the bright yellow dog standing next to him. The dog stayed silent, but his great brown eyes never moved from Dyak.

When Dyak looked away, back at the ground that was in the sky full of so much he did not understand; there were more new sights.

A broad land of grass floated in front of him. Bushy-tailed little tree runners scurried up and down low trees, deer stared at him and stood ready to be chased. And here also was the old human with the long white fur, the one Attu and Mala called BraDa, making the sign that meant Come to Me. BraDa's spirit had walked away from his body long ago, when Dyak could still hunt. Dyak and Attu and Mala all sang over the ground where they put him.

Dyak knew now his own body had fallen, too, and would not rise. He *was* the old dog Mala stroked by their fire. He raised his voice and sang his song of death.

When he stopped singing, BraDa was smiling at him, no longer making the sign to come. Then the old man walked away on the soft ground, walking as straight as Mala or Attu.

Dyak whined.

The land of soft grass, low trees, good hunting, and the kind old man lay before him. He had only to walk to it. Dyak's eyes stole a glimpse of the great yellow dog at his side. When he looked back from the shining dog, he still saw the soft ground and the old man walking away, but now he noticed that down the hill on the side away from the great dog was another land that looked more like where he and Attu and Mala lived. Far off, a group of humans moved together, dragging their den furs and their little ones, their stones that held fire, and all the things humans kept that Dyak did not understand. They walked on toward higher lands far ahead of them, the Big Water to one side of their trek. Though they were walking away, they seemed to be getting closer.

There—a young human. Was it Attu? Dyak's tale swished behind him, then stopped. No. But it smelled like master had smelled when Dyak and Attu had watched the sheep together. And there were the stupid sheep, and two black dogs running after them, biting the heels of the sheep when they did not walk where they should. That dog, the one closest to the Big Water: Dyak could see he sometimes bit the sheep when he didn't need to. Dyak's tongue fell from the side of his open mouth. He remembered this. Stupid sheep.

The other black dog was old, maybe as old and tired as Dyak had been before he last lay by Attu's fire. The human who was not Attu, but who looked and smelled like master, ran back and put his hand—a hand of kindness, on this dog. Dyak knew this hand. He knew the heart of this old dog.

Dyak's eyes and nose followed close behind the humans and the sheep. Their smells filled his nostrils. They were Dyak's smells. The sounds were *his* sounds. Where did these humans go? Dyak did not know. The hunt with humans: Dyak felt how *that* run, *that* hunt, *that* kill felt. The kills Dyak made on his own never quickened his heart like those; no meat tasted like that shared meat. Dyak felt Attu's hands, and BraDa's hands, and Mala's hands when they touched his fur. He heard their voices and his heart swelled when they made Dyak's name noise.

He lay on the strange ground by the great yellow dog, paws stretched out, head on his legs, and whimpered as his heart knew the sadness and pain and confusion they—these humans of his—felt. Dyak knew what *he* brought to their eyes and their hearts. Dyak knew that *he* filled their bellies with meat. Dyak knew their lives and his life were together.

DYAK'S PAWS hit the flowing wet dirt by the Big Water. This near the water, the smells were strong and complex. The loud sounds of the Big Water as it walked toward the ground made it hard to hear anything else. He remembered when he was young and Attu had hurt him here, but his heart left that behind and he ran on the soft ground, drinking in all the sounds and smells the Big Water offered him.

He stopped when a tree rose up in the Big Water just ahead

of him. His name noise came from the tree. The great yellow dog of light stood high in the tree. Dyak stayed solid still. His ears pointed. His bushy tail curled over his back. His sides panted softly. This dog *should* be in this tree, even though Dyak knew dogs were not in trees. The dog opened his mouth and a strong light came from it, and powerful smells—some Dyak knew and some he didn't. And the dog made human noises to him. When humans made their noises, Dyak knew his name noise and some other sounds, but he understood all the noises the great dog made.

As he listened, another path opened above the water next to the tree of light the great dog stood in. This path made soft ground over the water and led to the shining land where Dyak had seen BraDa. He could smell the smells of this place—almost as wonderful as the smells from the great yellow dog himself.

"Which?" The great dog asked Dyak. "The choice is yours, Dyak. Now and always."

Dyak understood. He smelled the clear smells of the green land. He knew the hunt would always be good in this place of perfect smells. He knew his paws would never be pierced by thorns; he would never be beaten; he would never hear pups or little humans cry or die if he went down this path.

Dyak raised his eyes to meet those of the great yellow dog of light. He saw there what he saw in Attu's eyes the first time, as he lay in slow death with his broken body after Bogh's beating. As Attu held Dyak's head in his hands and gave him water and soft food. As master handed Dyak the bone animal that BraDa made. And as Dyak saw in Mala's eyes when she last bent over her old dog, covering him with her sleeping fur.

Dyak raised his voice to the great yellow dog of light and sang his own song. It was a song that held Attu and Mala, BraDa, Tabah, and—yes—even Bogh ran in it. It was not a long song, but when it was over, the bright dog of light made no more noises. His yellow eyes, eyes that made Dyak smell and hear and feel all these things that Dyak knew and also things that yet had never happened, these eyes grew ever larger and warmer, and the fur on the great head shimmered in waves.

The yellow dog, the tree of light, and the path over the Big Water to the land of pure and perfect smells passed like the rain in the hot season and Dyak looked now only on the Big Water, it's great loud walking sounds beating against him again and again.

HE RAN for as long as the Great Light stayed overhead. Just before it moved into the water, Dyak smelled humans. They were the same humans he had smelled before, when he stood next to the bright yellow dog and looked down from the high place. He smelled the same sheep and the same dogs, the same humans and the same furs. Should he run to meet them? He did not know these humans. He did not know these dogs. And, he was dead. What would the humans or the dogs do when a dead dog came to them?

Dyak slowed his pace, but did not stop running.

After many breaths, a shift in the wind brought him their odors. Dyak glanced over the Big Water and saw the Great Light had moved to the edge of the world.

He must run. He did not mind running with only the Little Light above, but Dyak knew humans and their ways. When the Great Light fell into the Big Water, the humans would stop and make their sleeping places. They would make small mounds of fire and they would be more afraid until the Great Light rose again from the darkness. They would pen their stupid sheep and watch them carefully. It would be best if he came to the humans before the dark time was strongest. Dyak knew humans and their ways.

Dyak was coming back.

END OF *STONE DOG*: Volume 1 of *Tales of the Eternal Dog*

1

TEKHE: DAUGHTER OF ANUBIS

IN THE FOURTH year of the reign of Tut-Ankh-Amun, in Thebes upon the eastern bank of the Nile, in the house of Pharaoh's highest embalmer of household companions [c. 1327 BCE]

I AM ABU-WITI-YUW, *son of the sons of Anubis, servant of the Living Image of Amun, who makes the Earth shake, who makes the Nile swell with abundant life, brother of the storm and the moonlight, God on Earth, and father to his People. To serve the living God on Earth, I am all that I can be; I am the white death upon all prey that I turn my eyes upon. I do not fear the jackal or the leopard or the lion. I do not fear men's arrows or spears. I bow only before my living God, and before my progenitor, Anubis.*

This, my story, is the story of the sublimity of my Pharaoh, Tut-Ankh-Amun, who through his greatness knew that I, Abu-witi-yuw, would be the swiftest of all hounds, the surest at the kill, the greatest tracker of prey. My loins have filled the Pharaoh's traces with the hounds of my seed and so I and my line will serve all the gods on Earth as long as the waters flow in our mother, the Nile, and as long as wind blows in the reeds.

The Great Pharaoh, Supernal Image of the Self-Created, whose praises can never be fully told, brought me from his palace to hunt the gazelle that runs faster than the swiftest chariot and bounds higher than a man's head. In his own war chariot did Tut-Ankh-Amun, Son of Ra and Isis, take me. No other but he could command my proud head to lie down or my warrior's body to flatten before him. And so I waited in his chariot of onyx and gold, that shimmered like the stars in the blackness.

And lo, we did come upon a lion in the wilderness and before his generals could overtake him in their chariots and fulfill their duty to protect my master, He Whose Step Fells Mountains, the god on Earth, Tut-Ankh-Amun, had drawn back his great arm of bronze and cast six javelins into the heart of this lion—the like of which had not been seen since Horus overthrew the minions of Set. All of this time, I, Abu-witi-yuw, lay at the feet of my master, the great Pharaoh Tut-Ankh-Amun, fearing not and knowing that he needed the help of none against such a challenge.

Leaving behind even Hor-em-Heb, Fan-bearer on the Right Side of the King, who spoke now only of his fear of Pharaoh's prowess, great Tut-Ankh-Amun cried out to his chariot steeds, sons of the sons of Re-Sheph, who leapt forward to carry him to the silver gazelle of which the Pharaoh had been told.

"NOW THAT'S A STORY, if I do say so myself."

My master rose from his writing and his bench. The smell of the fresh papyrus wrinkled my nose, stronger even than the many interesting odors our usual work produced.

He stretched, leaning his hands down toward the backs of his legs. I heard small pops and cracks coming from his spine, and I whined softly in sympathy. My master was old. He had seemed old even in my earliest memories. Now I was old, too, and my master was not much changed. Maybe if my nose was as good as Abu-witi-yuw's then I could read the changes in him, but my sense of smell had abandoned me, as had much of my hearing, my sight, and my taste. Probably a blessing given where we lived.

"Don't think it's a little, well, a little much, eh Tekhe, girl?" My master looked down at me. I thumped my thin tail in support.

"No, I don't think so, either. Confidentially, you may look like cousins, but that little dog was no match to you in your prime." Having limbered up now, he picked up a stone canopic jar in each hand (they were empty, I hoped), spread the scroll out in front of him as wide as his hands could stretch, and weighted down the ends with the reliquaries.

"That should do it. I can just fit in the bit about the hunt now in this space." He sat back down at the bench. He pulled a knife from his broad belt, picked a fresh reed from the bronze stand on the edge of the table and idly began cutting it into the proper shape for writing.

"Let's see. 'Abu-witi-yuw, graceful as the Pharaoh's wife'... ummm...better not compare Ankh-ese-Amun to a dog... umm...'graceful as the water serpent'...no, that's not quite it...'graceful as the'...What in Set's name is graceful, Tekhe?"

Understanding that this was an important juncture, I thumped my tail on the dusty floor again.

"Right, I think you're right. 'Graceful as the clouds in the night sky.' Think I should add one of the gods in there, too? No, right, right."

The reed must've been to my master's liking now, as he turned his hands to watering the red and black ink cakes. By previous exploration, I'd found the red one wasn't too bad, but the black one tasted of ash.

"Where were we? 'I, Abu-witi-yuw, graceful as the clouds in the night sky, leapt from my master's chariot to chase the silver gazelle...King of the Earth,' and so on and so on." My master put down his reed and wheeled his legs around the bench to look at me. He did this so quickly that it startled me. I raised my head— it had been resting on my forepaws—and gave a little yip.

"This could make us, Tekhe. Fresh eel and fish stew for you, no more of this for me." He picked up one of the canopic jars with one hand and held his nose with the other. I understood what my master meant; he hated his work as an embalmer.

"My father and his father, far back as old Thoth-Mes, have been scribes, back to when Kilu-Hepa's great-grandfather came to us; when that Mittani princess married Pharaoh." He glanced at Saba, our Mittani servant, as he said this. Then he set down the jar on the bench next to him. I eyed it closely. Not because it was edible. I was afraid my master might knock it over and break it. Inside those jars were things I didn't like to see or smell.

"How I ever came to this?" My master held up his hands. "Embalming dogs." He sighed heavily.

I knew my cues. I sighed, too.

NEXT DAY WAS A FESTIVAL. I always knew the festival days because Saba, my master's *netcht*—his servant, made special Mittani cakes in the ashes of the fire. She always left a cake at the edge of the ashes. My master once found the cake there and waved an uncut reed at Saba for wasting food (he had no proper whip), but then I took the cake—as I always did—and went with it to my corner.

My master's face changed to a shape I did not understand, then he lowered his hand and told Saba to leave the cakes with him. He sat down on his working bench, picked up one of the cakes and started nibbling at it, looking at me the whole time. I didn't know whether to eat the cake or not, so I just stood there in my corner, the uneaten cake held in my mouth.

It was very hard to do this. I was not afraid of my master, though he had spoken loudly to me sometimes when I was younger and he had struck me once—I do not know why. He didn't look like he was going to beat me. He just sat there, eating that cake and looking at me. After a while, I dropped the cake from my mouth because I was confused. The smell of the sweet bread and the taste of it in my mouth was so strong. After a while I bent my head and ate it anyway.

When I looked up from this day's cake, my master was dressed in his finest cloth, with the bright yellow collar he wore when he delivered full canopic jars to the high priests. He also wore wide yellow collars on his wrists. The flashing of these didn't bother me, but I barked when I saw his eyes. They didn't look like my master's eyes. The shape around them had changed; it was darker. I barked and barked. Was this my master? He came over to me and when his hand was near (I was ready to bite this strange person in our house who wore my master's cloth and collar, and who looked so much like him) I knew that it was, indeed, my master. He even had the smelly new scroll in his hand that had the story of Abu-witi-yuw on it.

So instead of biting, I licked my master's hand, glad that it was him. His hand moved to my ears and stroked them gently.

"When I return, Tekhe, you and I and Saba will move out of this pit of stinks and back to the Scribe's District. Saba will have her own servant—she's getting too old for all this work, anyway." And then he walked out our open door.

MY MASTER DID NOT RETURN that night, so Saba built only a small flame and I lay down close to it. The winds from the desert blew faintly and even I could smell that the jackals were down from the hills. I slept, though, and dreamt of warm eels jumping from the water into my mouth.

"IS this the place of Dre-khe-mosul, the Embalmer?" A tall man ducked inside our door. It was morning. I could smell the cooking fires of our neighbors, the tanners.

Saba bowed her head low and said, "Yes, dread lord, this is his house."

The tall man snorted, "Rise, *baka*, I am no lord. I work for a living—like you. Where are his ceremonial things."

Saba looked up, but she did not stand. "Sire, my master would beat me if he knew I gave his things to a thief. May I ask who I should tell him took his pots and scrolls?"

The man laughed, "You're a cheeky one, *netcht*. If I didn't have a full house, I'd buy you for amusement." He stopped laughing. "I am Ay-ne-tul. I have the honor of acting on order from the High Scribe. As humorous as you are, I have no time and you have no say in this. So be still. Where are his ceremonial items?"

This man was from the High Scribe! Had my master succeeded and melted the Pharaoh's heart with his tale about Abu-witi-yuw? My tongue tasted my dream-eels!

Saba rose now and spread her hands over the table in the middle of our room, "These are his scribe's tools, master."

The man stepped forward and examined the reeds, the ink cakes, and the papyrus ends carefully, "Well prepared." He set them down, "I'm looking for his work tools, *netcht*, not these. Where are his embalmer's tools. They are sacred and must be removed forthwith."

"In the other room, master. If the master will follow me." And she took the newcomer down the stairs behind the fire to my master's smelly work room, where I was forbidden to go.

I stood by the fire pit and shivered. The hearth was cold now and so was I. Where was my master? Were we moving? The new man came out of my master's work room carrying large boxes of wood. He stepped slowly and carefully.

"Others will be here to take the rest. Do not interfere with them, *netcht*. They will not have my sense of humor." He walked out.

Saba squatted next to me and set her hand on my head. She said nothing, but I could smell her fear and worry. It was the same as mine. Where was our master?

NO "OTHERS" came that day, or the next. Neither did our master. Saba made small fires and we both ate the plain food from our pot. It tasted like sand without my master's talking and laughter. At night, the desert winds blew strongly and Saba moved a screen in front of the door.

THEN THE "OTHERS" did come. Large Nubians from the Royal Court by their belts, young and male, and another older one who told them what to do. They went into the master's work room and came out balancing huge bundles, things I had no notion of, though some of them smelled very interesting. I stayed out of their way, under the table.

The one who told the others what to do told Saba that she was not to leave. "I'll be back for you." When he left, Saba smelled very afraid. After a little time, she slipped out the door.

This was very strange. Saba never went out of our house unless the master took her with him. Did she know where he was and would she bring him back?

I sat by the cold fire and waited. The screen was gone from the door. The desert winds blew fine sand into our home.

While I slept, I dreamed I was young. I was again, like Abu-witi-yuw, swift as the gazelle, without the ache in my legs that had caused the master to have Saba weave me my own mat of thick gauze. I could smell and—best of all—I could see again. Not the near dim sight that I had now, but as when I hunted on the plain, before my master found me, when I ran down the marsh deer with my littermates. I could see from one edge of the world to the next. When the prey twitched its ear to be rid of a fly, I could see it. When the crocodile scuttled through the reeds far away on the banks of the Nile, I could hear it. There, there— a fat young buck deer bounded through the marsh grass and I was after it. I was ahead of my three brothers. I would have first strike. Ears flat, eyes steady on my prey, my body was an arrow through the still air.

TWO DAYS PASSED before the tall man in temple robes came for the second time to Dre-khe-Mosul's house. He did not see the frightened eyes, lids stained in Mitanni green, that watched him from across the way as he hurried inside.

Cursing into the murky interior after stumbling through the thin screen that stood by the door, he glanced around the small room.

"Everything's covered in dust." He rubbed his broad chin, freshly shaven by the temple barber. "I wonder if the neighbors took in that *netcht*." Still stroking his face and looking around, he continued to himself, "Poor fool embalmer, smart enough to scribe, he should've known the fate of blasphemers and those who rise above their sacred duties."

Ay-ne-Tul stepped across and fingered a black stone figure of Anubis that rested in a wall sconce. "Still, if he'd just not have mentioned Hor-em-Heb, he might've got away with it. Hard fate." He set down the little jackal-headed god.

"Ummm...I'm the fool. Walked across this foul district in the summer's heat and all that's here is a stinking dead dog."

With that, Ay-ne-Tul turned away from the small white dog curled before the cold hearth. He left the dusty house and its last guardian, Tekhe, the white death of all prey that she surveyed, daughter of Anubis, whose path was as swift and sure as the winds that blew through the reeds or across the threshold of Dre-khe-Mosul, formerly Third Embalmer for Tut-Ankh-Amun, Living Image of the Self-Created One.

THE KA OF TEKHE

SANDS FLEW ALL AROUND HER. She'd never been in the deep desert before and Tekhe shivered with fear in her dream. *This is a dream.* She was sure of that as she looked down at her sleek, white legs.

My paws haven't been this small since I first sat by the master's fire.

At the memory of her master, Tekhe whined. She sat on the blowing sand. She could not move because of the nothing she felt, the emptiness in her Ba, her heart.

The wind and the sand swirled around her for a long time.

The light dimmed and she realized the sand no longer moved. But she was moving, along with where she sat. Downwards.

The sand is swallowing me!

She jumped up and ran to escape. She had seen animals swallowed by the sand. Tekhe ran and ran, but she stayed in the same place. The sky above her and around her was gray. Sand still flowed below her paws.

Is this what death in the sand is like?

Tekhe stopped running. *No, I am dreaming.*

A shape rose out of the dimness. It was a great gate, like she had seen when her master took her to Karnak. Higher than many men, but only as wide as one. A tall woman stood in front of it. She was bare-breasted, but wore many ribbons, and carried a whip. Over her head hovered a shining blue-pointed star.

"Welcome, child of He Who is on His Mountain. Do you pass here?" The woman spoke to Tekhe.

This is a very strange dream, Tekhe thought; *I like the eel dreams better.*

"Do you pass here, Tekhe of the white sides, or do I cast you into the flame?" The woman repeated.

As she said this, the tall woman gestured with her whip and a great pit opened to the side of the gate. Tekhe felt the heat from where she stood. She smelled the sharp scent of burning stone. It blazed as if the whole world was fire and rock.

Tekhe whined. *No*, she thought, *I do not like this dream.*

"You are not here to like or not like, daughter of He Who is In the Place of Embalming. Now answer. What am I?"

Tekhe squinted and shook her head until her ears slapped her cheeks. *The woman can hear me. It would have been convenient if the master could...Oh...is the master "He Who is In the Place of Embalming"? Didn't he talk about these gates? There was the Goddess Who Repels the Serpent, and...*

"You have named me, Tekhe, swift death who walks the sands. You may pass through."

Tekhe's head rocked back in surprise. But she trotted quickly through the gate as the Goddess Who Repels the Serpent stepped aside.

She passed through and the sand and the greyness around her changed. Now she stood on a green plain, waving grass and river reeds growing as far as she could see in every direction.

In front of her rose another gate. This one was as wide as the other had been tall, and barely high enough for the tall woman who stood in the middle of it to walk through without bowing.

They are littermates, Tekhe thought. For this woman did not just stand proudly like the other or wear kohl in the same way as the other, she smelled the same as the first one.

Smelled! Ah, this is a good dream, Tekhe thought; *I can smell again, as well as run. This one, though, is not bare-breasted, because she wears so many necklaces they cover her chest. She does not carry a whip, but above that long knife Over her head hangs that same blue five-pointed star.*

"Speak, dog, or suffer."

I liked the first woman better, Tekhe thought.

"Name me, dog, or move in endless pain."

Like the woman before, she waved her hand—the one with the rod in it—and a chasm of fire opened all around them.

Tekhe thought back to the scrolls her master read when he prepared the remains of dead humans. *I've already seen the one who repels the serpent—I wonder where the serpent was? This woman's wearing a lot of jewelry...*

"Speak now, dog." The woman lifted the hand that held the knife. The heat from the fiery chasm flared. Tekhe whined despite trying not to show her fear.

She looks like she's going to cut me in half with that thing, Tekhe cringed and looked around, knowing there was nowhere to run.

Tekhe blinked her eyes and thought: *she must be The One Who Cuts through Ba.*

Responding again to the little dog's merest thought, the tall guardian grimaced.

"Pass on, cursed whelp of Anubis." The tall gatekeeper snarled then vanished, as did the burning chasm. Tekhe pushed off hard with her hindquarters and ran swiftly through the portal.

This time as she passed under the gate, the sky became bright blue. The sandscape returned, but splitting it in front of her was a river that stretched from one side of the world that she could see to the other. A river wider and far brighter than the great Nile itself. In the middle of the river a woman stood on a thick sheet of papyrus. On the other side of the river was a round-arched gate.

Must have been a large litter, Tekhe thought. For the woman did look and smell exactly like the last two women, except this one wore a short, torso-covering robe of deepest blue and gold. On her head was a helmet of gold, and above that hung the now familiar shining, blue five-pointed star. She carried an ankh of lapis lazuli in her hand.

Even in her magnificence, that wet papyrus still stinks like old beans.

"Greetings, Tekhe. Do you know and name me?"

At least she is polite, Tekhe thought.

"Alas, child, you have little time. Name me or you shall dwell forever in the river of souls and be eternally consumed by He Who Devours Himself."

Maybe not so pleasant after all.

Tekhe closed her eyes hard. She remembered the many nights when the master had read aloud to her. Her belly full of the meals he'd shared with her. His fire guarding against the cool dark. His voice warming her even more than the fire. *What are the names of those goddesses? Splitter of the Heads of the Enemies of Ra?—No, don't see any enemies lurking about. Lady of the Night? —The sky's blue and bright. The One Who Beheads Rebels?—The last woman had the knife; she looked like she would have been happy to behead anyone. Not this one, though. The Witness to Ra's Magnificence?—We all like the sun, but there's no sun to be seen here.*

"Name me now, daughter of the dog-headed One, or I must cast you into the watery abyss."

Tekhe trembled in terror. She had always been most frightened of drowning, never venturing close to the death-hiding water of the Nile. She closed her eyes and thought of her master smiling and beckoning to her from the boat, she too timid to walk on...*Ohhh*...his reading had taken her on trips as surely as any...

You are She Who is On Her Boat, lady, Tekhe thought at the woman with the ankh.

The goddess smiled. She floated toward Tekhe and, as she did so, the papyrus on which she stood grew wider, growing a broad prow and deck.

"Come, little chaser of life, I will bear thee to thy true Master and the one you seek."

Still quailing inside at the thought of the river beneath them, Tekhe daintily pranced onto the papyrus barge with the goddess.

THEY FLOATED TOGETHER SLOWLY over the river. More slowly than Tekhe would have liked. She wondered what would happen to her next.

I'm dead, Tekhe thought. *Not dreaming, dead.* Her legs and sides trembled, but she stood and did not fall.

The goddess looked down at the thin white dog, raised her ankh, and smiled. "You must find your Ba. Without your Ba, you will become only a shadow, little one."

The papyrus boat reached the other side of the river and Tekhe willingly hopped out and ran underneath the arching blue stone.

On the far side of this gate was a place so beyond her imagination that for a long while she could do nothing but stand, breathe, smell, and stare.

Tekhe had not gone with her master when he visited the Pharaoh's palaces. She had never traveled with him to the temples, where her presence would have been a defilement. But even had she seen these places, she was sure she would not have been prepared for the enclosure in which she now stood, shivering and alone.

It is not open to the sky. It is a space of stone over stone. It is not outside, like the desert or the river. Though it seems large enough to hold a desert or a river.

Even with her keen new eyes—sharp as they'd been in her youth—she could not see the ceiling when she looked up. The span was so vast she could only make out the color and the way that color changed in the creamy distance. It was deepest blue toward the middle and became greyer and mistier as her eyes searched for the edges of this place.

Tekhe's heart beat swiftly in her chest, as if she had been chasing sand deer all day or as if she heard her master return after a long absence. And it wasn't the size of the room that caused this quickening. Her heart pounded because of what filled this impossible room.

There were as many inhabitants as there were palms along the Nile, as many as there were stones in the hills. Tekhe's thoughts swirled as she raised her head and her hunting sight revealed the whole panoply of beings in front and to the sides of her.

Many, perhaps most, were like the woman goddesses that she had met at the gates.

They look and smell and move like humans. Almost like humans. Those by the throne are too tall. Those in the pool are too short. Those down near the wall are too wide. None smell altogether human.

But many of the room's occupants were like the statues that the master kept in nooks and mantels in his house. Their bodies were the bodies of men and women, but their heads—and their smells—were those of birds and animals. Owl, jackal, lion, ibis heads on human bodies. Most of these animal-headed people sat on huge stone chairs. Some walked up and down the giant hall and many of the humans followed each of them.

"Welcome, daughter." A proud voice filled her ears.

Tekhe turned slowly and, though she knew they had not been there a moment before, standing a pace behind her were several of the animal-headed humans.

The one that had spoken was the tallest. He was far bigger than a human. He had the head of a gigantic, beautifully elegant jackal. Looking upon him, Tekhe felt a deep calm, and when he looked at her, an enormous excitement welled up inside her. She tried hard not to yip. Yipping did not seem right in this place.

A figure, ochre-robed and human-headed but as tall as any of the animal heads, stepped forward. This goddess—for surely this is what she was—plucked the bright ostrich feather from the ribbon in her hair and held it over an ivory box that a more human follower raised before her.

A different animal-human spoke; this one had the head of a catfish: "I see you have no Akh. You are a dog. You have only Ba and Ka. Meskhenet—She Who Carries the Cow's Uterus On Her Head—disagrees."

The jackal-headed god, Anubis, curled his lip at this comment, then looked down at Tekhe and spoke, "Your Ka resides here, daughter. It is no longer with the body you left in the Small World. But your Ba cannot be reunited with it until Ma'at has measured your heart."

The gods and their followers towered above her. They loomed all around her now. Tekhe felt that the entire enormous space held its breath as a solemn ceremony began—a ceremony about her. Her smooth white sides shook. Her tail fell lank. She was more afraid than she had ever been when she was alive.

This is not as it should be, Tekhe thought. *I grieve for my master. He is dead. I am dead. I will find my master. What these gods do is not what I choose.*

The thin white dog turned away from Anubis and Ma'at and Meskhenet and all the gods and trotted in the other direction, down the great, endless hall of Duat. She did not see the expressions of anger, amazement, and—on one face—amusement that she left behind her.

"You cannot run from the gods, dog!" cried one.

"You cannot run from your fate, Tekhe of the white sides!" cried another.

"You cannot run from your own Ba, my daughter," said a deeper, gentler voice.

Tekhe did not look behind. Her heart beat so quickly now that it felt as if it would burst from her chest, but she ran on, in the only direction that she could—to find that part of her that she would never lose. Somewhere, somehow, she would find her master again.

2

IN THE SLEEVE OF FU HAO

THE 27TH YEAR of the glorious reign of Wu Ding, born Zi Zhao, son of the Provident Xiao Yi, grandson of Xiao Xin, 22nd in the line of kings after and descendent of Ching Tang of Shang, in the palace of his capital at Shangyi [c. 1277 BCE]

"GIVE HER TO ME, you silly girl. You could not properly hold a stone." Lady Fu Hao accepted the small dog from her second handmaiden.

"And my fingers are cold," the High Lady added unnecessarily.

She is very strong, Quan Qi thought. *Cool, like all humans, but not cold. I will smell-taste-clean her.*

Quan Qi's small grey body squirmed in Fu Hao's grip. But after puffing out two tiny snorts, she subsided and twisted so that she could press her short black muzzle against her captor's hands, her tiny black tongue darting in and out between fingers.

THE LADY FU, eighth wife of Wu Ding, Emperor of Shangyi and descendant of the Most Illustrious King Tang, chose not to notice this mild indignity of Quan Qi, her new sleeve dog. Instead, she stretched her other hand out to Ma Tze, her eldest slave and she to whom Fu Hao had given access to the Repository of Soul-Speaking Tools.

Ma Tze, from long practice and knowing her Lady was not slow with the bamboo rod, bowed, bent low, and swiveled on her knees to retrieve the bronze ting stored behind her in the Lady's pavilion. She rose to her feet, careful to maintain a bent back so that her eyes never rose above the Lady's, then turned and placed the heavily decorated urn in front of her mistress.

"Well, are you going to open it, Ma?" Fu Hao set Quan Qi in her lap and reached toward the ting in anticipation of Ma's removal of the top.

Liberated from Fu Hao's hold, Quan Qi rejoiced in this opportunity to scamper around the chamber.

Her fingers taste of fowl and honey. They are wonderful fingers. She is a wonderful mistress. I am happy. I will make her fingers happy. What else could this human have on her? She will be happy and I will taste it.

Quan Qi danced and cavorted near the High Lady, dodging back and forth around her flowing skirts.

Lady Fu glared at her second handmaiden, "What are you feeding this dog? She is having fits. Ma! Take Quan Qi to my chambers and massage her belly until she calms!"

Ma Tze, used to Fu Hao's quick turns of interest, rapidly set the ting's top beside the now open receptacle and shuffled to pick up the small dog with the black, mashed-in face so like the face of Dai, the god of rice and rain.

As the slave headed for the rear of the chamber, Lady Fu called out, "Do not put rose petals in her water, Ma; that is probably how this crack-brain Qim Su has ruined the dog's constitution." Fu Hao then took up the heavy bronze pick from inside the ceremonial ting and turned her attention fully to the formal observance of the tortoise-shell inscription, preparing for the evening's divination rite where she would supply the High Priest with the questions the Emperor, her husband, had instructed her to scribe.

In Lady Fu's rear chambers, Ma released Quan Qi and

watched as the young dog sniffed each corner of the room. The Lady's two older dogs, Kagi and Dou Fun, slept in one corner. Unnoticed for now, the aging Ma sighed gratefully. This little one was trouble for her old bones. She could no longer bend and scrape as swiftly as she once could and Quan Qi was no respecter of age, position, or anything else. Despite herself, she smiled as the puppy stalked a jade courtier the size of Ma's hand, ready to battle this ancient warrior of Xia. When she began to yip and bark her challenges, Ma scuttled over to hush the dog, lest the wrath of a disturbed Fu Hao come down on *Ma's* head. The great lady would tolerate much from the dog, but her temper was slim with her human retainers.

AFTER THE CEREMONY of Soul-Reading and after the Oblations to the Ancestors had been discharged by the Emperor and the High Priests, Wu Ding held an informal dinner for his Dukes and chiefest ministers and generals. Also at the banquet were the High Priestess of the Ancestors' Closets, General Hu Gao's first wife, and Wu Ding's second and eighth wives, both priestesses and diviners. None of these worthies were accompanied by more than three of their closest attendants.

Wu Ding was in a contemplative mood. The bones cracked into good omens in the ceremonies and General Hu Gao had this day arrived from the south with news that the Gong were well repressed and an emissary would soon be arriving in Shangyi with tribute and, probably, a new treaty wife for the Emperor. Wu Ding did not shrink from battle and knew violence would always be necessary to maintain order in his expanding realm, but it was a good day when a new war did not have to begin.

So, he addressed a question to the table that might otherwise have remained interior to his consideration, for it held within its answer the seeds of civil discontent. A dangerous question, one that the answerer need consider well before opening doors in the Emperor's mind that could not be easily shut.

"Twice every celestial aeon, Di, the King of Heaven, opens the draperies that surround his Jade Throne and beckons the least among his Court to sit in judgment upon his actions. And so I ask, O Friends, what is the best path for the country? What would you tell your Emperor? Where should his eyes travel? What injustices should he address?"

Wu Ding paused to glance at each of his dinner guests. He took a slow drink of wine from his tripod dragon cup of bronze.

"What" he added, "are the shortcomings of your ruler?"

The hush that fell on the table could not have been more profound if the Emperor had asked the company to listen for the waving wings of the moths in the walls outside the eating pavilion.

As this silence built upon itself, the cast of the Emperor's face grew graver and graver. Finally, he spoke again, "Am I so dread a Lord? Do I not honor my ancestors with oil, ash, and blood? Do I vouchsafe my honor when my word is promised? Have I so timid a Court?" Further silence ensued, and the Emperor asked again, "What words have you for me, Members of my Family and Trusted Advisers? Is my path truer than the King of Heaven's? For surely that is Blasphemy and the Ancestors have decreed the penalty for Blasphemers is to join their blood with the mortar of sacred temples. Is this your answer, *Friends*? Should I call the sacred architects to begin new shrines?"

General Hu Gao cleared his throat and began to speak, but his first wife—who sat unfashionably next to him at table, as she was a barbarian from Ba province—reached her hand under his robe and sank her thumbnail into his thigh and he quieted.

"Oh my husband," Lady Fu spoke in her clear, ringing voice. The eyes of all at the table stayed on the Emperor, as was the way of the Court (except for General Hu Gao's first wife, who openly stared at Lady Fu—she was, as mentioned, a barbarian who did not know the ways of the Ancestors). The silence became more intense as the Emperor's gaze turned toward his eighth wife. His eyes were hard as the jade dragons that watched from the arms of his carved chair.

"Oh my husband," Fu Hao began again, "I speak to you not as your wife, nor as a Lady of your Court, but as Bonz of the Divination of Soul Speakers."

The depth of the creases in Wu Ding's brow became shallower.

"And what, Priestess, does the shell of the Celestial Tortoise of the Ever-Flowering Heaven tell you of the reign of Wu Ding?" The Emperor asked in a calm, steady, and terrifying tone.

"O Son of Heaven, your knowledge of the Oracles is surpassed by none in this land. And you know well what the Priests have said of this day's bones. What they have revealed is great and good, and only to be expected from the rule of Zi Zhou."

Fu Hao paused briefly, but long enough for the Emperor's eyes to widen in displeasure.

"Can it not be said the Gods know what men do not?" Fu Hao did not pause long, but continued after the briefest of nods from her husband. "Conversely, though men are above them in most things, the beasts of the field and the air and the water know things which men do not. The fox knows where to find the pheasant's eggs that are hidden from the wisest human eyes. The crane knows where to fish, though the water and air he searches are trackless to us." Again, her husband inclined his head slightly.

"So it is, great Emperor of the people and land of Shangyi, that women know some things hidden from men." There was a slight stir by the high priests and ministers, but as the Emperor nodded again, they were quickly silent.

"The oracle shells have long been favorable for the kingdom of Shangyi. This is good. This is without doubt a judgment from Heaven accorded to the reign of Wu Ding." The table had regained its stone silence. All of the attendants knew the Lady Fu Hao's head lay in the noose of the next words she would utter. As if in response, her shoulders seemed straighter, her posture more erect, even though none could tell she had moved. She now looked directly at her husband, the Emperor, in such a way that some thought he would take offense.

"However, great Emperor, what women know, what is writ in our bones as surely as the will of Heaven is writ on these shells, is that the favor of Heaven passes—even for the greatest of kings and kingdoms. What women know is that time passes and time *means* cycles of ebb and flow. And that even the power and will, the victories and plans of the great Wu Ding are subject to these cycles of fortune and of *Heaven's* will. This is what women know and this is what is best for you, great King, also to understand."

After these words, Lady Fu rose from her dinner seat to kneel in the temple fashion before her husband, hands together on her thighs, head bowed.

The silence that had covered the King's dinner before was as a tempest of noise compared to the quiet that now held the hall. None looked at the Emperor directly, though all eyes tried, averted, straining to assess his reaction to Fu Hao's words, that they might immediately fall to the side of the Emperor's reactive mood.

Wu Ding himself was still, his face impassive.

Moments passed, then more moments.

The members of the dinner party dared not watch their ruler as closely as they wished, but it did not escape their notice that the Emperor's expression was slowly changing. The outside tips of his long eyebrows were tilting downward, to match the slant of the corners of his wide, thin lips. Was he about to speak?

This unnatural and overpowering silence was broken by a peculiar noise, like sea crabs clattering over stone or tree branches brushing bronze statues in a high wind. Another strange sound was added, as the clicking and scratching drew nearer, a high, piercing piping noise as of someone violently stomping again and again on small bladders of air.

Even the Emperor now looked up to find what spirit, what denizen, what foolish human might so interrupt this grave moment of Court decision.

A bundle of grey and black energy, the length of Wu Ding's forearm and less than two handspans wide and tall, hurtled into the midst of the sovereign's dining chamber. It scurried under a low table, between General Hu Gao and his first wife, eliciting a small gasp from her as it passed beneath her gown, then it continued to the middle of the dais, where Fu Hao still knelt before the Emperor.

When it reached Lady Fu, its linear movement slowed, but it made a quick circuit around her, searching for the correct launch trajectory, then—upon finding her lap—it leapt, executing a half twist, and landing on its back, legs writhing, tongue out in determined attempts to lave her mistress' chin and neck.

General Hu Gao's first wife's breathy expostulation of surprise was caused by the entrance of Quan Qi. Restive at Fu Hao's long absence preparing for the oracle, the puppy's impatience led to disconsolate moping as the Lady Bonz conducted the oracle ceremony, and then as the state dinner progressed and Fu Hao remained missing, sad passivity became desperation. Ma Tze, who was guardian of the small nuisance, had underestimated the dog's wiles and her determination to be with her Lady Mistress.

Fu Hou's back straightened as she knelt and, for a heartbeat, held the quivering dog and appeared to ignore this intrusion. Quan Qi rolled in her lap, licking any exposed skin, then barked, then yipped, then yowled, softly and in quaint imitation of human noises. Fu Hao succumbed to the attentions of her little charge, petting her enough to let her know she was welcome and loved. The Lady even took her eyes off of the Emperor, who

—the rest of the dinner attendants saw—continued to watch Fu Hao closely.

After a few moments, the Emperor cleared his throat. This was not a gesture to which he was accustomed, as it was more blatant than was usually necessary for him to regain the focus of a meeting.

Fu Hao's eyes and attention snapped from the dog to the Emperor. She continued, though, to hold the wriggling Quan Qi affectionately—if *very firmly*—between her two hands.

"It is apparent, wife, that there are some things not only Emperors and men cannot know, events even wise priestesses and Queens cannot predict. Some things that are brought to us by very handsome little dogs."

At this, the Emperor of Shangyi rose from his chair of state, the Bench of the Jade Dragons, and stepped down toward his eighth wife, the High Lady Fu Hao, who rose and bowed as he held out his hand to her.

"Come, wife." Against the rules of the Ancestors, the Emperor held the hand of his eighth wife after she stood.

He turned and spoke to those who had shared the dinner. "General and Ministers, Priests and Priestesses, observe the lesson Heaven has sent us this day: The wisest of us make our plans; Heaven favors the prudent. But what we see and hear is not all nor ever is. And so, no matter how far-sighted our plans, no matter how fortunate our lives, there will always come a time when a small thing we cannot control overtakes us and our wisdom, our power, and our plans collapse and fade like the shadows of Heaven's will that they are."

The Emperor gently pulled the Lady Fu, who still tightly gripped Quan Qi in her other strong hand, out of the Imperial Pavilion toward his private chambers.

As he stepped under the entry arch, he turned and spoke once more to his attendants. "Think on these things, my Court. Tomorrow we will talk of cycles and turns. And, General, we will speak of your plans for the kingdoms of Tu-Fang and Yi. My

Lady Fu Hao has some stratagems of interest that we will discuss. I believe Heaven is bringing *their* cycles into interesting positions."

Wu Ding released Fu Hao's hand and the two stopped, turning toward each other. The Emperor reached forth and stroked the little dog's upturned belly and scratched her wrinkled black ears.

"A small thing, wife, a small thing indeed."

3

THE CASTOFF: A DOG OF ROME

ROME: The year of the XIVth Consulship of Imperator Caesar Titus Flavius Domitianus Augustus, Dominus et Deus, and the co-consulship of Lucius Minicius Rufus, 841 years after the founding of the city [c. 87 CE]

I

"Hoi, Lucius. Get yer weight on it, boy." The bulkiest of three men grumbled from behind a massive two-wheeled cart. In it were stacked bodies of dead animals, parts of dead people: a leg, a hand, a dog, some unrecognizably mangled flesh. Hardly noticed by the sweating crew, the dark iron smell of old blood clung to the living and the dead.

Thump...Plop...Thump...Scrape...Thud...Squeak... Thump

The cart was the unfinished dream of an evil child: leaning crazily to one side, parts missing all over. The men moved slowly around it, sorting, picking up, casting in. After clearing a small area, the big man in the back kicked out the rear bracing board while the other two heaved on the pole that protruded at an odd angle from the front. They pushed, pulled, and shoved the cart to the next pile of broken body parts. The wagon teetered on uneven wheels and mismatched hubs, threatening to dump all their work back onto the stained sand of the Flavian Amphitheater.

"Push up yourself, cowbreath. We're holding our end." A reply grunted from in front of the cart.

The vehicle tilted far enough that the last body tossed in slid out over the top of the blood-greased pile. It was a dog. An enormous war mastiff with most of a wicked-looking, iron-studded collar still on its tawny neck. The body hit the sand with a soft thud, shifting the balance so the cart righted itself. The dog lay unnoticed as the three men wrestled the wain along fifty feet to the middle of another pile of bodies. The day's fading rosy light lit the empty marble tiers that surrounded them.

PAIN. DOG GROUND. MAN? NO FIGHT. PAIN.

After a few minutes of stacking, the biggest man, Baractes, threw in a dark severed arm, wiped the sweat from his small, black eyes with a forearm better suited to a bear, and regarded his crew.

"Drop the grue and get over here," he began, "Time for a dump, boys."

The other two men continued tossing dead human fragments into the wagon.

"There's just this bit to do, horsemouth. Leave off and we'll finish." A balding, thickset blonde worker replied over his shoulder.

"Leave off yourself, poxnose. It's already too heavy. If your wits were as large as your stomach, Titus, you'd..." Baractes began.

"...I'd not be in this line of work—sure not with a surly Illyrian like you." Titus finished.

"You're lucky to have the wage and you know it. Your mother..."

Tempers escalated as Baractes and Titus argued about

whether to pull the load down to the *Spoliarium* and dump the remnants into the abattoir that led to the *Cloaca Maxima*, the largest sewer in Rome.

Lucius, youngest and smallest of the three, looked forward to these arguments as opportunities for breaks from the filthy, hard labor. The noises of the other men were like gnats in his ears when they went off like this. If he did give their jarring exchanges a thought, he tacked up their animosity to familial feeling. Baractes—who was, indeed, from somewhere in Illyricum—won Titus' sister after winning freedom in this same arena. Lucius had seen that sister and suffered the barbs delivered by her well-honed tongue, so his sympathies tended to fall on Baractes' side. On the other hand, the looming Illyrian had persuaded his brother-in-law into this despicable job. Further, Baractes was an evil bastard.

Lucius took these interludes as moments to dream of a return to his grandfather's land in Picenum, to raising cattle and grapes. Generations ago his family owned their land, but the famously greedy Gnaeus Pompeius Strabo took title with some trumped up charge of *tributus familiaris* and they'd been tenants now for a hundred and fifty years. Their landlord, Marcellus Pompeius—also known as Strabo because he'd inherited his ancestor's crossed-eyes—was a current favorite of the Emperor's.

"How's our poet? Thinking about the right color for a maiden's flowers?" Baractes brayed at Lucius. "Can we bother Prince Homer to help us dump THIS THRICE-CURSED CART?" Though not joining in with Baractes, Titus grinned, too. Lucius merely nodded and gripped the lever-handle. He considered again whether escaping to Rome to live his poetry might not have been his best decision.

Ready to pull and strain the unwieldy vehicle back into the noisome *Spoliarium* where they'd dump this stinking mound of flesh and then return for another load, Lucius wondered again how he'd gotten into this miserable position. As he began to heave and grumble to himself, he noticed movement behind Titus, in the area from where they'd just pulled the cart. "Hold!" He cried.

"What is it, princess? Should we call for a scribe to cut your pens?"

"I'm letting down the cart."

"Rat spit in your eye—we're not!" Baractes shouted from the back.

"Brace it, numb-wit; I'm letting it down at three: ...*unum*...*duo*..."

"All right, all right—this best be for more than a pee-break..."

Lucius felt Baractes place the block-brace. He glanced at Titus, and they lowered the cart. As soon as it was as steady as they could make it, he trotted around the pole handle.

Baractes walked up next to his brother-in-law. "Where's the fool going?"

Titus shrugged.

"HE BREATHES." Lucius called out to Titus and Baractes as he crouched down by a large beast.

MEAT. MAN. DOG DARK. BLOOD SMELL. DOG HURT.

"We dropped the cart for *this*." Baractes snorted and squatted where he stood, watching Lucius. Titus leaned against the cart.

Lucius stood up from the recumbent dog and trotted toward one of the gaping holes at the edge of the field. He vanished in one of the dark entrances into the netherworld that lay below the arena and the stands.

Baractes shouted, but before he could work up a proper fit at Lucius' desertion, the young man ran out, carrying a fish-emblazoned *myrmillo's* helmet before him in both hands.

"See, he *is* alive." Lucius balanced the helmet precariously on the ground, stood, and faced his coworkers with a broad smile. The massive dog tilted his head and neck as his broad tongue dipped in and out of the water in the helmet.

DRINK. DRINK. DOG MOUTH WET. DRINK. DOG DRINK.

Baractes glanced at Titus with a clear, unvoiced, "so what?" Scratching at the leather mitt that covered his mangled left hand, he walked toward Lucius.

"I'm not picking up that creature while it can still bite. It must weigh two-hundred *librae*." Baractes looked around for a weapon, but the arms crew always cleaned up first. The mastiff was the only detritus left on the blood-soaked sand. "And it's too damn big for me to strangle. Fetch me something from the wagon, brother."

Although senior in the crew, Baractes seldom ordered the others directly. He knew there were limits to what they'd take in this dirty, grueling job. He'd worked arena cleanup long enough to see dozens of men walk off in disgust, often without collecting their last coin from the surly paymaster. But this was too much. Stopping work for a dead dog—or a dog that *ought* to be dead.

Titus hesitated, then walked to the cart.

"I'm keeping him." Lucius said, looking down at the panting behemoth.

"Jove's Testicles!" Baractes snorted.

"His name is Iace. I'm taking him with me. I can use a good dog."

"ee-yAII-kay?" Baractes repeated, incredulous. "*Castoff*? A dog name that suits a red-headed green-eyed bumpkin, I s'pose."

Shrugging back to anger, the Ilyrian added, "I don't care whether you name him Flower Bird or Worthless. He's meat for the sewer." Turning toward the cart, he added, "Where's that damn sword?" Titus ambled toward them, carrying the shredded reins of a charioteer who would not drive again.

"I'd rather have a blade, but I can strangle him with these, I suppose." Baractes held out his hand to Titus, who passed over the leather strands to Lucius instead.

"Jupiter's beard—that's a good one, brother. The boy should kill the cur himself for holding us up." Baractes chuckled.

Ignoring the larger man, Titus stared at Lucius, who held the strips of leather harness limply in his hands. The older man smiled and nodded in the direction of the arena exits.

Lucius' eyebrows rose, then he returned Titus' smile and knelt down by the dog. He ran his hands over the network of pale scars that stretched across the expansive yellow-brown side and back. Bones were visible under the skin, but none protruded, and the blood smears that covered the dog's hide appeared to come from other bodies.

Baractes shifted his weight and stepped nearer. Remaining prone, the dog emitted an ominous, subterranean noise from somewhere in the vicinity of his belly.

"See, he's a fine judge of character." Lucius grinned.

Baractes snarled.

"On your neck be it, poet." The large man called out as he walked toward the cart. "We've got to clear everything by dark or pay's docked. Do what you will with that bag of bones, but get back over here and finish what we're paid for."

"Yes, Centurion." Lucius tossed the leather straps into the van, winked at the unruffled Titus, then bent his head down to the now-silent dog.

"Here's the rest of your water, Iace. Tonight we go home. You'll have food and a warm place to sleep. You're a good dog. I can tell."

DOG. MAN. WATER. WATER. DOG FEAR? MAN PAW COOL. SMELL MAN. MAN NO FEAR. MAN NOISE. DOG NO FEAR.

Iace dipped his tongue into the dead *myrmillo's* helmet, sighed, and flopped his head down on the hard sand. Twice more before the bloody sun set over the white edge of the amphitheater, he raised his head and watched the one who brought him water.

. . .

FOR THE TWENTIETH time that day, the three men dragged the empty wagon behind them as they trudged up the ramp from the *Spoliarium*. Reemerging into the arena, they turned before reentering the Gate of Death and traveled down a long colonnade under the outer ring. They parked their cart in a small alcove beneath the statue of a nameless demigod.

"All right, all right. That was the last load. Next time, no more dog breaks, Country Boy." Baractes smiled savagely, grabbing Lucius' *tunica* sleeve in a scarred fist, "If I have to move that scabby cur in the morning, I'll take my trouble out of your hide."

Lucius' hand looked like a child's as he grabbed Baractes broad wrist and brought his blue eyes up to meet the big man's taunting gaze. Baractes' grin widened in anticipation of the beating he hoped to administer, but Titus stepped between, tugging on the Illyrian's burly arm.

"Ehe, what's that? Trouble with the hides?" A toothless face arose out of the murky shadows and held out a hand encrusted with relic filth.

"You boys selling to the tanner on the side? I'll need my taste or the curule aedile will be unhappy."

"No, Sporinus, you old scob, pull in your talons, there's no taste for you here. We've nothing but blood on our hands. And there's no money in that." Titus replied to the hoary paymaster.

All four men chuckled at this professional witticism. The paymaster, Quintus Sporinus, blinked constantly as he reluctantly handed each man a silver *denarius* and two *sestertii*. As soon as this was done, he silently disappeared into the umbral darkness from which he had materialized.

"That old coot is second cousin to Pluto, I'd swear," Titus breathed.

"It would explain his fondness for *our* coin and *this* place," Lucius replied.

Titus grunted an acknowledgment of this wisdom, then headed out the nearest arch toward the closest wineseller.

"Tomorrow, poet." Baractes added, then followed his brother-in-law.

II

Lucius stumped down the outermost ring of the maze that was the underbelly of the arena, the grand structure begun by Vespasian and finished by his youngest son, the current God-Emperor Domitian. When he'd made a quarter way around, he turned and ran out Gate XXXI, facing east and the *Oppius Mons*.

In this shadow of the great arena was a gathering place for the carters that couldn't afford donkeys or horses, who pulled their wagons themselves in Rome's active night transport system, in a city that outlawed wheels on city streets by day.

"Hoi, Lad! Two *sestertii* for an easy load to the Subura."

A bandy-legged boy Lucius would've sworn knew no more than six winters looked him over with eyes that could've seen a hundred. "Ten. Five there and five back." He piped in a high register and a pure Roman street accent.

"I only need the trip there."

"And what am I supposed to do with me cart when I get to the Subura? Offer it in trade for the jewels that grow on the trees there?" Two urchins who sat nearby laughed.

"Three *sestertii*, a crust of bread when you deliver my load safely, and I'll not report you to the Censor for violating luxury prices." Boys in the shadows snickered, but not as heartily.

"Tell you what, *Senator* (another snicker from the other boys), I'll break bread with you—*all* Glaubus' loads are delivered safely—six *sestertii*, and *I'll* not tell the Urban Praetor you're trying to take advantage of a *poor child*." At this last, he moaned, squatted, and broke wind, triggering great mirth in his audience.

"All right, you Tyrian whelp, I know when I'm overmatched."

Lucius smiled and handed coin to the tiny boy, who grimaced at his palm, "Three now and three when we get there. Follow me."

Lucius turned back toward the amphitheater. The light was almost gone. He looked behind him. The boy hadn't moved.

"Ain't goin' in *there*!" The boy stood behind his cart and crossed his arms.

"What? That's where the load is. What's wrong?"

The young carter hesitated, then said, "Ghosts," and looked back at his mates for support. All the heads still visible in the falling dusk nodded solemnly.

"Oh, Hercules and Diana!" Lucius stomped over to the boy and held his hand out for the leading pole.

The boy looked at the outstretched fingers as if they were snakes, "Ain't handin' over me cart, neither."

"Well, then," said Lucius, "you can toss back the coppers."

Face contorted with doubt, Glaubus passed him the pole.

Lucius turned toward the Gate of Life.

MAN. WATER-MAN. COOLHANDS. DOG BITE?
TOO MUCH HURT. SOFT MAN. DOG NOT BITE.
FLOOR MOVE? DOG MOVE. DARK.
FLOOR MOVE. DOG REST.
WATER-MAN WALK.

BY THE TIME Lucius pulled his load into the open space where the carters were now playing a game of bones, it was dark enough that he feared he would hit one of the many potholes and flip his injured dog onto the cobbles.

Glaubus, with night vision surer than Lucius', ran up and grabbed the cart handle as soon as Lucius was well clear of the boundary of the arena.

"What's this, then? You stealin' the consul's pets? I'll need a silver *den* to keep me mouth shut 'bout that." The now-expected laughter floated up from the darkness beyond them. "And another for each of me mates, too." Laughs were replaced by cheers.

"Just pull the cart, boy. The dog's injured—left for dead." Lucius growled, no longer in the mood for this small miscreant's banter.

"Dog, is it? More the size of a bear. Don't know I *can* pull no bear, Senator. I'm just a tiny bit of a boy."

"That's enough, Glaubus. He's a large dog, true, but there's no more than bones and skin on him. It's the same as if you were pulling me."

Glaubus eyed the quiescent Iace from a pace away, unable to make out much detail in the shadowy gloom. He sidled up, sticking his face close to the dog, as if sniffing for hidden treasures.

SAUSAGE AIR! SAUSAGE AIR!

SAUSAGE LITTLE-MAN FACE! LITTLE-MAN SAUSAGE FACE!

With no warning, Iace lifted a gigantic paw onto the boy's shoulder, bringing him to his knees. In the same motion—before Lucius could round the cart to save the lad from what might be a fatal mauling—a tongue that would've done justice to Cerberus himself snaked out and laved the urchin from chin to forehead.

NO SAUSAGE. LITTLE-MAN FACE. SWEET SAUSAGE.

There was just enough light for the cart boys to see the whole scene. They exploded with laughter and catcalls, "You finally got a kiss, Glaubus!" "Too bad her tongue's longer than your sword!" This turned into a sing-song chant of "*Cave Canem*, Glaubus, *Cave Canem*, Glaubus."

Ignoring the unwanted bath and the attention of his mates, Glaubus grabbed the handle of the cart and pulled hard northwest, toward the Subura, the stewpot of Rome, where only the brave or the desperate ventured, and where *no one* with a choice *wished* to domicile.

THE CASTOFF: A DOG OF ROME

DOG move. DOG hurt. dark.
water-man walk. little-man sausage-face walk.
DOG move. floor move.

III

Shortly after the sun rose, Iace woke to gentle stroking of his neck and shoulders. His eyes stayed blissfully shut as knuckles kneaded around his ears, lightly rubbing the shreds of the right one, then moved underneath his massive jaw. Involuntarily, his chest rumbled approval and ecstasy as faint memories of an immense, rough, cooling tongue washed over him. He'd never known such touches before, not known such existed. The pot-sized muscles of his haunches and back unknotted. His belly grumbled, not in hunger, but in a repositioning of organs that until now had been held in tense, unnatural order.

"...sweet puppy...*canis dulcis*...*canis bonum*...good dog...you like that don't you...*puerum bonum*...good boy..."

Never had Iace heard humans make noises like this, except the night before when the cool water-man found him.

FEMALE MAN SMELL. SOFT PAW...HAND? TOUCH DOG. GOOD GOOD GOOD.

NOT FOOD, LIKE FOOD. NO-FEAR, NO-PAIN.

GOOD...DOG?

"Come on, boy. Out of the cart. You can't be comfortable there."

FEMALE MAN HAND? DOG TAKE FLOOR-ROLLER. FOLLOW SOFT-HAND GIRL.

After sliding off the back of the cart, Iace took the pole handle in his mouth and pulled it as he followed the girl who had wakened him.

"Stop! You don't need...no, no, *Canelillo*. You don't need to bring that old thing."

Confused, as one human command and emotion he understood well was "stop"—Iace let go the cart, dropped to the stable floor on his belly, and whined softly. It was never good to show you hurt. Men whipped you longer then.

"No, no...*puerum bonum*. Leave the cart. Eheu! You don't understand what I'm saying. Oh, poor boy. Here..."

Iace's wrinkled forehead winced as the girl knelt by him, sure hard blows would soon follow. She put her hands on either side of his out-sized, dirt- and blood-stained jaw, and kissed his brow. Iace stopped whining.

"Here. Is this what you want?" Still kneeling, she reached over and grabbed the handle of the little cart and pulled it close to the drooling black edge of Iace's muzzle.

The giant dog tilted his round black eyes up at the girl.

FEMALE MAN NOT-FEAR. FLOOR-MOVE SAVE DOG.

DOG TAKE FLOOR-MOVE. DOG FOLLOW GIRL.

FEMALE MAN WATER-MAN LITTLE-MAN-SAUSAGE-FACE SAVE DOG. DOG GOOD. DOG WARM.

Cart pole gripped between thumb-sized teeth, Iace followed the girl.

LUCIUS WOKE TO FIND GLAUBUS, whom he could see in the daylight was dirtier than he'd thought last evening, sleeping in a fresh pile of hay. Lucius picked bits of straw out of his own back. They both reclined in Lucius' home, a corner of Sappho's Stables he rented for two *denarii* a week from the owner, a Greek named Menaeus. Despite his sensible professions as stable owner and farrier, the common view was that Menaeus was insane. He was a poet. Everyone knew all poets were crazy.

Lucius brushed himself off, nodded at Admetus and Bucephalus, the mules who shared the next stall, and looked around. A small stab of panic hit him when he didn't see Iace. They were so tired when they arrived at the stables last night, they hadn't even unloaded the dog. He *should've* still been in the cart. The cart! The cart was gone, too. Someone had stolen the dog *and* the cart.

Why would anyone steal an almost worthless urchin's cart and an almost dead dog? Lucius ran through the stables, looking under horses, mules, and various pieces of Menaeus' farrier gear.

"Iace! Iace!" Lucius called, pelting back and forth in the close confines of the stable.

"Upon the necks of men, no doubt. Morrow, good poet. Have you my rent?" A dark, lean head and shoulders peaked around the rump of the jenny, Aurelia. A tiny, well-knit adult body followed. "Whereon do you cast your nets, friend Lucius? The sea's breezes cool our brows, but a man can lose his sense in their scents." Menaeus smiled broadly, then held out his palm, "Do you have my coin?"

Lucius waved the little Greek off and continued calling Iace, as if the dog could know the name he'd been given the night before.

"I expect this must have something to do with a creature the size of a trireme that accompanied you here last night?" Menaeus asked. "I don't suppose he's worth the eight *denarii* you owe me?" He added, pensively glancing up at the rafters of his workplace.

"Yes. Of course. No, of course not. Where *is* he? Do you have him?" Lucius grabbed a handful of coarse wool at the neckline of the traditional Greek chiton the blacksmith poet sported.

"How could *I* have *him*? He's half as big as Bucephalus—and much more intimidating." Menaeus' black eyebrows tilted into the peculiar "V" that expressed both puzzlement and approval. "He's around the back with Livilla. They've been together all morning." The Greek placidly returned his attention to the jenny's hooves he'd been cleaning.

"Juno's Breasts! You might as well have given him over to the Furies themselves! What are they doing?" Lucius shouted as he ran to the front of the stable, so as to circle to the back—there was no rear exit. Outside the pens, he yelled at the side of the building, "And my rent's only two *den* per week, you Greek fraud."

Reaching for his favorite hoof-pick, Menaeus muttered, "But you owe me for four weeks, gentle Lucius."

. . .

LUCIUS WHIRLED around the rear of the stalls, ready to lambast Livilla for taking the dog. Turning the corner, he stopped. Iace—canine exterminator, veteran killer of dogs, lions, and bears, terror of the Flavian Amphitheater—wore bits of ragged scarlet cloth around his neck and over part of his head. Livilla, a slender girl in a juvenile's threadbare *toga praetexta* wrapped tightly enough to show she'd not much longer wear this garment, rested a hand on the dog's head, which in turn grasped the pole of Glaubus' cart between powerful jaws. Together, they ceremoniously promenaded around a collection of clay forms that stood propped up in the dirt.

"By Anchises' scraggly whiskers, what—" Lucius began.

"Hush! We're almost through." The flash in Livilla's green eyes brooked no argument.

The dog, the cart, and the girl made a final slow circuit around the clay and cloth figures. Livilla stopped, patted the top of Iace's stone-solid head crown, and faced Lucius, who was struggling hard to maintain his angry expression.

"We're circling Thebes, asking Creon for my brother's body. It's a very serious business."

The furrows in Lucius' brow smoothed as his mouth widened. "You're spending altogether too much time with my Muse-besotted Greek landlord."

"I heard that, friend Lucius—the girl could do worse than to re-enact the classics," the trained voice of Menaeus projected from out of the stable.

"Go shoe a horse, you corrupter of youth." Lucius yelled back. Turning to Livilla, he added, "Fine. I see you've met Iace." He picked a final haystraw from behind his ear and added, "You gave me a start though, little wench. Does your mother know you are here again? Playing with dogs, dolls, and grown-up men?"

"eee-OCH-ay? That's a stupid name." Her mouth twisted in mild distaste, then she looked away from Lucius. Her palms gently kneaded the broad sides of the dog, "Livia has little care with where I am, as you well know."

The sudden sadness in the girl's defiant face shocked Lucius into reverie. A blurry gauze covered his mind; he sat on the back of a lurching market wagon on its way to Spoletium and thence to mighty Rome. He memorized the deeply lined face of a beloved old man who pretended not to watch him leave the only home he'd ever known because of...he could not now remember why. Lucius paused a moment, walked over and squatted by the girl and the dog. Near the same size, the man's and the dog's heads were on a level.

"Let's see what you taught this great beast of ours."

For the second time in less than a day, and the second time in his life, Iace's gigantic tongue whipped out and slathered a human.

WATER-MAN. DOG DRINK TASTE WATER-MAN. COOLWATER-MAN.

Lucius, despite witnessing the premonitory bath Glaubus received the night before, was surprised enough by this slobbery service that he lost his balance and fell backwards.

"Eheu!" he cried, extracting a now shapeless mass from under his backside, "I think I may have angered the gods."

Livilla's eyes opened wide as she gasped between giggles.

"I seem to have crushed Creon and the entire Theban court."

IV

Glaubus liked his new berth and the Subura's business, so he stayed on at Sappho's Stables, sharing the straw with Lucius. During the day, he snored, but his cart was idle. What use was a wheeled cart in Rome when the sun shone?

And so the next day and the next found Livilla and Lucius behind the stable with Iace, Glaubus' pole cart, and two very frayed cloth ropes.

"Pull, Iace! *TRAHO! TRAHO!*" Lucius' tone rose in frustration.

The great tawny dog sat in front of his young Picentine

master, one end of a rope tied around his neck, the other around the front of Glaubus' street cart.

"I don't think yelling is going to work." Livilla commented.

"Oh! What do you suppose will work? Reciting verses, perhaps? Do you think he prefers Catullus or Horace?" Lucius violently expelled breath through his nose, which remained flared with frustration. "Look at him! He's *laughing* at me!"

Iace's mouth was, indeed, gaping wide and his gigantic black-splotched tongue lolled several inches down from the side of his copiously drooling jowls.

WATER-MAN NOISES. WATER-MAN PAWS WAVE. WATER-MAN LOUD.

"Well, I didn't have any trouble taking him 'round Thebes, you know—and that was the first day he was here."

"My luck to save a dog who only responds to Sophocles— and me without a touch of Greek."

"He is a wise animal." Menaeus' deep voice rumbled from behind the stable wall.

At that moment, a loud commotion began with a clank—as of a kicked and overturned pail—then a shout of "Minerva's Whiskers! I've got a ten *sestertii* commission at sundown! Where's my cart!" Curses and blasphemies a ten-year-old boy should not have known, much less uttered, soared over the wall. These were followed by the sounds of sandals slapping hard on the ground as Glaubus—bleary eyed, dark hair poking sideways from his sleep—hurtled around the back corner of the stables, eyes searching for his cart.

Quick as the young urchin was, Iace was quicker.

MEAT! MEAT RUNS! MEAT NEAR! CATCH MEAT!

QUIET! GRAB MEAT!

Glaubus made three steps around the corner of the stable and Iace pounced. Lunging forward, he snapped the fabric rope around his neck as if it were a child's play-string, overturning the cart behind him—noticing neither cart nor rope. He loomed on his back legs, seemingly twice the height of the little Roman boy who fell on his face in terror.

"*Mater Mea! Mater Mea! Adiuto!* Help!" the boy cried.

Lunge complete, Iace descended onto all four feet, pinning Glaubus underneath him.

MEAT? SAUSAGE-FACE LITTLE-MAN? WHERE MEAT?

Iace peered down into Glaubus' grimy, moist, twisted face as Lucius and Menaeus (who'd followed hard behind when the little carter skimmed out of the stable bier) each tossed ropes over Iace's head and tried, with no effect, to pull the dog backwards off the boy.

"Off, Iace! *RETRO!* Back! Back!" Lucius shouted—as he'd been shouting since Iace first surged forward.

The dog stood still as a brick; Glaubus quivered and quieted beneath him.

Livilla knelt by the big canine's scarred side and stroked his spine. Muscles involuntarily rippled in relaxation. "Pull softly now." She told the men quietly. "And stop shouting at him, Lucius."

The two men eased the gentled Iace back and Glaubus lost no time in scrambling up.

"Gods! That's twice this Cerberus of yours has got me! I'm used to havin' to crawl out o' trouble, but not from under no dog." Glaubus puffed, as out of breath as if he'd run laps around the Circus Maximus.

Iace sat next to Livilla, Menaeus, and Lucius now, his tail swishing rhythmically in the dust, his great tongue falling from the side of his mouth as he watched Glaubus stand up and edge widdershins around him.

"I don't know what you three are playing at here—*you* should certainly know better, Master Greek. No wheels inside the *pomerium* during daylight, with or without a dog. And nighttime's too dangerous for a girl. Even if you *did* have a cart." Glaubus said as he stood up.

Before he completed a step toward his cart, Livilla spoke up, "Do it again, Glaubus."

The boy and the two men swiveled their heads toward her and responded as one, "What!?"

"Go around the corner and run back here again." Livilla expanded.

"You're wolf-crazy, little girl." Glaubus reached for his cart pole.

"I am *not* a little girl!" Recovering her aplomb, she added, "And I'm not crazy. Go on—go back and run up here again."

"Why should I? I'm already late for a *very profitable* fare. And I don't need no dog Colossus to scare my *tunica* up me legs."

"Oh, are you bringing toadstools to the old poisoner, Mirella? You know they *execute* poisoners—*and* poisoner's apprentices."

"She ain't no poisoner; she's an apothemclary. It's honest work."

"Oh, I guess the Praetor wouldn't mind then..." Livilla trailed off.

"You...you...fish-faced daughter of Pluto...you skirted robber of..."

"Yes, yes—I've got the idea, *little boy*. Now. Quicker we get this done, the quicker you're off for your fare. It shouldn't take long."

"The dog wants to *et* me!" Glaubus whined—defeated, but still defiant.

Livilla lowered a shockingly white arm around his sun-baked shoulder, "No he doesn't, Glaubus. He's just startled—thinking you're a coney or a stag or such. He stopped on his own, didn't he?" She patted his arm.

"Well..." Glaubus leveled a gimlet eye on Iace, who paid him not the least attention.

"Good. Now get back out of sight around the corner and wait until I call you."

Casting glances back at the dog—and Livilla—every few

feet, Glaubus walked just out of sight behind the stable's perimeter fence.

Livilla moved around to kneel in front of Iace. She put a hand on either side of his drooling, crenelated black muzzle and rubbed with short, soft strokes. The dog's dark eyes closed in bliss.

"Now, *puerum bonum*...my good good Iace" she said in almost a whisper, "Glaubus will run around the side here and I will keep rubbing you as long as you are a good boy."

"Pardon, Mistress Diana—or is it Athena today, for surely this is a wisdom that escapes the senses of such a poor mind as mine." Unable to restrain himself any longer, Menaeus began.

"Now you two," Livilla continued, not deigning to respond to the Greek. "*If*—and I do mean *if*—Iace lunges for Glaubus, then you'll want to restrain him with the ropes."

"Oh!" Lucius blurted. "Oh! *If*? And 'we'll *want to restrain him*'? Oh, well...that's just *fine*, then."

Livilla fixed Lucius with a stabbing, quieting stare.

"This *will* work! But we must *all* play our parts." She said with perfect assurance.

"As long as Cerberus here doesn't sprout any new heads, I suppose we'll follow our goddess' commands. Play on, spirit of Olympus—play on." Menaeus added.

"All right," Livilla called out, "Run to us, Glaubus."

Glaubus was several steps around the corner and very visible before Iace made any move, before he even seemed to notice the runner. When he did see the boy, though, Iace leapt forward—and Livilla just as quickly stepped to the side to allow him room. It took all the effort of even the forewarned Lucius-Menaeus team to restrain the mastiff from repeating the previous scene.

Breathless, but not quite as frightened as he'd been in the first encounter, Glaubus quipped, "*That* went well. Now—can I have me cart?"

Iace was already seated again—relaxed, seemingly unaware any activity was in process or planned for him. Livilla took the slack restraining rope from Lucius and nodded to Menaeus—a grin of dawning knowledge grew on the horse-trader's face.

"Yes," she replied as she gently pulled Iace back a few feet to his original position, "I agree—that went well." She tossed a phrase over her shoulder at Glaubus, "Again."

"What! You..." the boy released his cart and began to splutter...

"Mushrooms." Livilla smiled, then added, "Wave your arms this time as you run around the corner."

Mumbling as he passed her, Glaubus scurried past Iace and his keepers.

Livilla released the rope and silently handed it to Lucius, indicating he and Menaeus should leave full slack. Then she knelt before the dog again and rubbed his jowls until the drool covered her knuckles and Iace's eyes shut tight in sweet pleasure.

"It's only Glaubus, Iace. Good boy, *Puerum Bonum*. He's our friend...*Amicus*...our friend." She continued her massage for a few seconds and called out, "Come around again, Glaubus."

The little carter hurtled around the corner of the fence, whirling his arms about his skinny frame. He slowed and veered slightly as he neared Iace and Livilla. Glaubus whisked by them and the dog never acknowledged the boy's presence.

"GOOD BOY, Iace! *PUERUM BONUM!*" Livilla redoubled her jowl kneading.

"The dog's claws curl in ambrosial ecstasy," Menaeus observed. He and Lucius still held the loose ropes in their hands.

"*Now* can I take my cart, *domina*?"

"That was good." Livilla left off rubbing Iace and wiped her hands on the edges of her juvenile *toga*. "Let's try without the massage."

V

A few mornings later, Menaeus—who'd often spied on Iace's training through cracks in the stable walls, offering disembodied advice in Greek hexameter—joined the group working in the stable yard.

"No. No. You will strangle the poor beast. Let me show you."

The little man removed the cloth straps from around Iace's neck and nimbly tied several clever and complicated loops.

"Well?" he glanced up at Lucius. "Raise his foot, this side first." Menaeus slid one harness loop up the dog's sturdy left front leg, "Now the other one." Then he pulled a loop up the other leg, adjusted the top over Iace's patiently upturned head. "Don't look at me like dinner, you yellow monster!" He tried to reach under Iace's chest to pull the straps around to tie up behind the dog's neck, but his arms were too short.

"All right, all right. Girl, hand me that end!"

"*Girl*! Girl, indeed. I'm fourteen, you...you...*old* man!" Livilla blustered, but grabbed the end of the makeshift harness and passed it to the Greek farrier.

"Your pardon, Artemis. The air is so thin in your presence, goddess, that my unbidden tongue spoke in a haste of its own. Strike me not down in your raven anger. Fourteen is a magnificent age. My own mother was hardly older when she brought me into this world of pain and wonder."

Appeased, Livilla grimaced as her nimble fingers checked the strange and complex knots Menaeus had tied to create Iace's makeshift harness.

FEMALE MAN DOG GOOD. IACE GOOD.

"There. Now the animal can pull many times his weight and the tension will be carried on that wall of rock that is his chest." Menaeus stepped back and rubbed his palms together in satisfaction. "So, let's see what you have taught him."

Lucius sat on a cleft column pediment, nodded to Livilla,

and flamboyantly waved his hand for her to proceed. "It's your show, my lady."

Livilla's eyes stayed on Lucius for a moment, then flashed back to Menaeus. "Iace has learned ten commands."

"Ten! Did you master dog language to teach him these or does he speak the Latin of little goddesses?" Menaeus smirked.

Livilla knelt by Iace and held his head between her hands. She kissed his scarred forehead, and then stood.

"Iace! *TRAHO*! Pull Iace!"

FEMALE MAN NOISE. IACE GOOD. IACE GO.

The formidable dog stepped forward and effortlessly pulled Glaubus' small cart behind him.

"*SISTE* Iace! Stop!"

The dog halted.

"Just a moment." Menaeus stepped to the cart. He bent over and tugged on first the front axle then the back. Then he sat daintily on the edge and swung his legs over. The cart creaked.

"Let's see him go again."

Lucius and Livilla exchanged glances. Lucius nodded.

"Iace! *TRAHO*!"

With no more noticeable effort than when the cart was unladen, Iace stepped forward. Metal-clad wheels dug into the hard-packed clay, but rolled on as Iace walked toward Livilla.

"*VERTE*, Iace! Turn, Iace!" Livilla called every few moments. Menaeus struggled to find balance as the little wagon rolled and chugged, describing a slow arc around the yard.

Menaeus succeeded in sitting. "Ve-ry im-press-ive." His voice shook with the vibration of the cart.

Livilla flashed a look at Lucius, then called out, "CURRE, Iace! Run, boy! *VELOX! CURRE!*"

Menaeus' hand-tied harness strained around the dog's gigantic chest as he dug his paws into the hard soil. "*VERTE*, Iace! *CURRE! VERTE! CURRE! VERTE!*" Livilla called. The dog's pace picked up speed to a brisk trot. The cart wobbled and careened behind him. The wheels wiggled and turned, sometimes acting more as sleds when the dog and cart turned abruptly in response to Livilla's commands.

IACE RUN. RUN. TURN. PULL. AIR COOL. RUN.

Menaeus' movements were less predictable than the cart's erratic swings. He fell from his sitting posture to a prone position as he desperately clung to the wagon's sides. After three quick turns—with Iace accelerating—the rear wheels locked over a hard piece of sod and the back end of the wagon bucked up half a foot. Arms flapping, Menaeus flew over the side, landing face down in an well-aged pile of stable hay at the back of the yard.

Lucius and Livilla bent over almost double in laughter. His load abruptly lightened, Iace stopped in the middle of the yard. Then he turned, too, and—still pulling the cart behind him—walked over to the still form of Menaeus.

"Gods, Livilla, I think you've killed the man." Lucius breathed.

"I never…" Livilla's eyes widened and the two ran together to the fallen Greek.

Iace reached him first. He sniffed interestedly first at Menaeus' hands, which lay at his sides, then moved up to smell his neck. Livilla and Lucius reached the body of the stable-keeper just as Iace bent to smell the back of the farrier's head.

MULE-MAN SLEEP. MULE SMELL GOOD. MULE-MAN! SOFT-HAND… LIVLA…NOISE. MULE-MAN!

"Menaeus?" Lucius whispered. "Menaeus? Do you live?" He gently rolled the small man's body over onto his back. Menaeus' eyes were closed; he did not move.

Livilla and Lucius knelt on either side of him. "He's still warm and breathing." Lucius whispered.

As Lucius stared down at the little Greek, Menaeus' eyes popped open. He swiftly raised both his hands—his left to Lucius' face and his right to Livilla's; each hand clutched a nice mush of stable waste that he smeared over each recipient's nose. As the stable owner accomplished this, Iace leaned down and swiped Menaeus from chin-to-forehead with his broad wet tongue.

"Aaaaghhhh," all three humans spat and jumped to their feet, flailing their hands at their faces.

Menaeus, the first to recover, brushed himself off, wiping his face on his leather apron. He raised a finger, pointing to the sky, and declaimed, "Whom the Gods would honor, first they cover in dung and dog spittle."

VI

On the *nones* of *Julii*, the month the divine Gaius Julius Caesar claimed for himself when he reset the calendar, Lucius woke to Greek-tinted imprecations, hammerings, and much stranger sounds.

"Blast my soft knuckles to Hades!" *Bang! Squeak!* "A dryad's curse on the tree that begot this board!"

Shuuunng! A saw ripped through wood. "Where is the pity of Haephestus for his poorest nephew?" Screeching noises of various sorts followed.

MULE-MAN NOISE. MULE-MAN ANGRY NOISE. HARD NOISE. MULES SMELL GOOD.

Lucius rose and picked the straw from his clothing, dipped his head in the fresh-water bucket, and then touched his toes three times. Iace sat like an Egyptian statue: front paws forward, head erect. Every time Menaeus cursed, the dog tilted his head to one side.

Lucius knelt, resting his hand on Iace's shoulder. Together, they peered into the gloom at the back of the stable. "What's he doing, boy?" Lucius inquired seriously, "Forging Achilles shield?" He called the last bit out more for the farrier's benefit.

LUUKYUS NOISE.

"Hoi? Much more like work for great Hyperion, friend Lucius. There. There." There was a final bang, then several dull squawks. Menaeus' dark-bearded face popped out of the shade. "Where's Livilla?" He asked.

"Livilla? How and where in the Seven Hills would I know?" Lucius stroked Iace's spine as he answered. "She's usually here by now, isn't she?" he added, looking around.

"Thought you didn't notice the comings and goings of 'that little wench'?"

"I..."

A pile of rags topped by thick brown hair cast itself down on the other side of the dog from Lucius. Pale, thin arms thrust outward around Iace's tree-trunk neck.

Lucius's hand moved unconsciously from the dog's back to the girl's heaving head and shoulders. "There, there, Livilla. What's wrong, *caria*?"

LIVLA SAD. IACE SAD.

The massive dog pressed his moist black muzzle into the crying girl's side.

"Money." A tiny voice emerged, hardly recognizable as Livilla's. "I must have money."

Face blackened by soot and shiny with grease, Menaeus stepped out of the back of his stable. "Then, how about *this*, my little goddess?"

As he emerged, he pulled behind him a wooden cart, half-again the size of Glaubus', with much higher rails. Festooned over the wagon were two harnesses of red leather.

Livilla's red-rimmed eyes cleared and began to shine, "For me?"

"Hoi-phoi—for that great beast that's eating more than my two mules!" The corners of Menaeus' mouth turned down and for an instant he looked true kin to the limping God-smith of Olympus he so often invoked. Then the shine of his teeth burst from between his lips and he was once more Menaeus. "And for *you*," he pressed a sooty finger to Livilla's forehead, "And *you*, friend Lucius. He's *your* charge, after all," and pressing the same finger on his own brow, leaving a clear greasy spot, "and for *me* as well—at least till the harness is paid for."

"Menaeus! Have you lost what wit the gods left you? This girl can't cart in the night. She'll be murdered or..." Lucius paled, blanched, reddened, and stuttered in succession as he realized he could not bear to describe what he thought would happen to a lone teenage girl on the streets of Rome at night, much less one carting around other people's valuables.

"Ah, give me some credit, friend Lucius." Menaeus grasped Lucius' upper arm, leaving three faint greyish stripes behind as he released him. "She will *not* be alone. Few single thieves would care to tackle our mighty Iace. They've seen what dogs such as he can do in the arena."

Involuntary shivers ran down Lucius spine. "But if there is more than one attacker?"

"Then she will be guarded by as good a heart as any I know." The white teeth in the blackened face flashed.

Lucius tilted his head in query.

"*You*, good Lucius. *You* will be guard and companion—and profit share—in this little company of ours. Now. As to the cost of the harnesses. It required..."

Lucius did not hear what else the farrier said. He looked at the strange dark visage of the animated Greek as he explained to Livilla how to hitch the carting harness. He watched Livilla's pretty young face move from despair to hope, and he watched the gladiator dog endure all the indignities and ministrations of the pair as they hooked him up, released him, and hooked him up again. The die was cast. He just wasn't quite sure *when* he'd crossed this Rubicon.

"...and here's the other piece. This is my own invention. I've not seen its like before." Menaeus took another complicated piece of leather and straps out of the back of the cart. "Let me show you how this attaches."

Iace, well-used to such procedures by this time, allowed the sure hands of the little man to affix the contraption that covered most of his back and sides.

MULE-MAN. IACE CLOTHES. IACE HARD CLOTHES. IACE MAN?

"...and thus." The Greek stood back and opened his arms in proud display.

"And thus—What?" Lucius asked. "What in Pluto's name is it? Are we going to hire him out for local gang battles?"

"It's not for warfare, friend Lucius." Menaeus grabbed Livilla by a sleeve and Lucius by his *tunica* front and pulled them close to him. "There are *many* factors who do not like to wait for nightfall and dawn before they have their goods delivered."

"Yes, yes certainly that's true, but—" Lucius began.

"—we can leave the cart behind and bring them their stuffs in these satchels." Livia hopped up and down in excitement. "Parchments and papers to copyists and booksellers and libraries, herbs and drugs and sands to apothecaries! In the day! And we can go more quickly and cheaply than mules! And, as long as we stay on the best roads, there is little danger! Oh, Menaeus! You're Archimedes! Daedalus reborn! Oh! Oh! Diana be praised!" She wrestled Menaeus to her in a tight embrace and blackened her heart-shaped lips with the soot from his cheeks.

"I told you she had a relationship with that goddess." Menaeus winked at Lucius.

VII

The street smelled of fish guts and vinegar.

"I hate garum." Livilla muttered to herself. "Why does it always smell like *garum* here?" "*SISTE*, Iace. Stop."

The girl and the dog were clothed in belted pale pink cloth. Livilla's wool *palla* was gathered like a modest Greek chlamys. On Iace, the pale fabric covered most of the sturdy leather harness on his shoulders and the metal-studded paniers that were strapped over his back and muscled flanks.

The colored fresco wash on the wall of the corner building

had once been a sportive scene of Baetian dancers, frolicking with what might have been satyrs or small and remarkably nimble bulls. Now the tints were faded, the lines broken, and the stucco cracked. Most of the dancers and satyrs were missing limbs or heads or bodies.

Livilla knelt by the giant dog. "Stay here, Iace. *MANTE.*" She sighed and patted the iron-hard top of her companion's wrinkled head.

Inside, several crude tables furnished the windowless room. Two aging, rough-hewn men were seated on a splintered bench. Rustic shelves held amphora of varying sizes. Old wine and ancient human fluid smells almost overcame the *garum* stench that permeated the neighborhood atmosphere. A stuffed, moth-eaten wolf's head hung on the wall. Livilla ignored the odors and the clientele and walked through the archway at the back of the room.

"Here's my little *regina barbarorum!*" A large-breasted woman in a tight *tunica* rose from a sleeping alcove and staggered toward Livilla. "Did you decide your Mumsy's company is as good as that Greek boy-lover and his stinky donkeys?" Words slurred from a darkly rouged mouth.

"I brought you my rent—Mother." Livilla opened her palm, showing several silver coins.

Livia—Livilla's mother—quickly straightened her stance, running well-practiced hands down her *tunica* sides to ensure modesty. Her gaze focused and her sloppy speech resolved as she counted the coins with her eyes.

"That's four silver *den*. I think we'd decided on five, hadn't we, my chick? *My* landlord's not as forgiving as *yours.*"

Before Livilla could reply, a booming voice called out behind her.

"Not forgiving, am I? I'd say I was about the most generous 'landlord' in the Subura—sweetling." A great bear of a man filled the archway. He strode in, picked up the older woman in one arm and sat down with her in the alcove.

"Now-now, my bold *Centurion*. Don't scare my little daughter. She's not used to real men and their ways." Livia spoke now in high and lisping tones.

"Well, then, we'll have to teach her men's ways, won't we, *pretiosa*?" A muscular, encircling arm, terminating in an oddly shaped leather glovelet, squeezed Livia till she gasped. His eyes never left Livilla.

"Now, *carus* Baractes, dear. What will she think of such goings on? She's only a child?" Livia breathed out, catching her breath.

He released Livia and leaned back against the wall.

"So, what's this about rent?"

"I pay my Mother rent, Centurion."

"I ain't no centurion, girl."

"What's her name?" Baractes' other hand clenched Livia's thigh.

Livia threw a leg over the big man's lap and breathed into his ear. "Forget about her. Aren't you still my brave conqueror? Let's play Walls of Troy again—"

"Shut it, whore." Baractes idly picked up Livia's leg and tossed it and her toward the back of the large niche. "Later." He added, striking the woman's cheek with a casual backhand.

He stood, looming.

The air and sound in the room stilled, disturbed only by Livia's light gasps and the heavy breaths Baractes took as he stared down at the young girl. Livilla's fists were clenched and her eyes were dark with rage.

"Hoi." He sneezed a laugh. "A tough one, eh?" He grabbed Livilla's wrist in his good hand, fingers encircling her arm.

"Baractes." Livia weakly objected from the wall.

"Hush, woman—I won't warn you again." Baractes grunted.

"I'll take that." He pried the money from the girl with his gloved half-hand, and then released his bruising grip. Gaze still locked on Livilla, the Ilyrian stepped back, flopped down on the couch, and absently cupped Livia's knee in his broad palm.

"Your rent's paid, little woman." Speckled teeth flashed a broad grin. "For now."

Livilla felt a warmth by her side. Baractes' mouth melted from smile to slack gape. His small, black eyes stretched open as a subterranean growl rolled across the room.

LIVLA SMELL. BAD SMELL. NOT FEAR SMELL.

BIG SOUR-MEAT MAN SMELL. KILLER FEAR SMELL.

IACE GO LIVLA. STAND.

KILLER SOUR-MEAT MAN FEAR.

IACE STRONG. IACE STRONG NOISE.

"What's that cursed cur doing here!" The leather finger slots of Baractes's mauled sword-hand swept reflexively toward his empty belt. "Get it out of here! Get it out of here or I'll have its ears—and yours!" The large man made no move to rise.

"*STA*, Iace." Livilla spoke quietly, resting her hand on the dog's head.

"Back, *CEDITE*." Holding Iace's collar close, Livilla backed out of the room.

The cold fear and hatred in Baractes' small black eyes followed hard by as she raced down the cluttered street.

VIII

"Lucius Viterbus? Is there a Lucius Viterbus here?" The young man panted as he leaned against the entry post to the stable. Although about Lucius' height, he was so thin that he seemed much taller.

"I knew a Lucius once," the unseen voice of Menaeus projected from behind Bucephalus' bier.

"Lucius Viterbus? Do you know Lucius Viterbus? I'm told he lives near here." The young man caught his breath, but not entirely his wits.

"Ahh...why-Der-booz...no...not sure about that. Do know a Lucius, though." Menaeus rolled in a heavy Greek accent.

"Oh." The runner slid down to the ground in one movement. "Oh," he repeated.

The small dusky farrier strolled out from the rear of the stable, holding a large pair of tongs that the runner eyed with anxiety.

"I could ask around. I know most of the good folk in this quarter. What did you say his name was? And why were you searching for him?" Menaeus asked, eyes wide.

"Loo-key-us Why-Tur-Bus," the young man corrected with no irony whatsoever. "I have news from his family in Picenum. A letter." He spoke ever more slowly as he watched Menaeus and the pincers, visibly upset by the demands of conversation with a non-native speaker.

"A letter." Menaeus scratched his beard. "From Picenum." He rubbed his head. "I'll ask around for you..."

"...Marcus Dramius..." the youth supplied.

"...mar-Kooz Draw-me-ooz. I see. And where should a message be brought if your elusive Lucius is found?"

This question stunned the young fellow, who had begun to brighten. Having stood back up, he now looked in danger of collapsing to the street again.

Menaeus smiled at him beatifically. "You're familiar with Heraclitus, no doubt? 'The Stones of Heraclitus'?"

Marcus Dramius shook his head and stared in painful confusion at the grey pavers under his sandals.

"A strange man. Cast off a brilliant legal career to splash around in various rivers."

"That...doesn't seem like a..." the runner began to reply.

"...very smart? Ahhh, you Romans. He discovered—among other things—that water *flows*. It always flows. It coalesces. It pools. And at the same time it continues to move on. It *appears* to have no integrity at all. The water that washes across your feet in a stream," Menaeus undulated his hands, miming the movement of a stream over the Picentine's dusty feet, "is never *exactly* the same water again. But—on the other hand—it's *always* the same water. It just includes some other water and it, itself, is—in it's entirety—somewhere else."

"I don't understand what—"

"*Of course* you don't understand." Menaeus looked offended, crossed his arms tightly over his chest, and backed off a step. "You are not Greek!"

At that moment, Lucius emerged from a small crowd gathering in front of the bathhouse in the middle of the block on the other side of the street. He jogged up to the stable in the darkening light and clapped the unsuspecting messenger on the shoulder.

"Spotty! Spotty Dramikins! Does *Pater* Ferrelas know you've hopped the fence? I'll not tell, but your Mum will take the lashes if you don't, knowing Grandfather."

The thin young man's face contorted in an impossible mixture of grief, relief, and some set of unrecognizable emotions. He began to weep.

"What's wrong, Marcus?" Lucius squatted beside him in the dust and hay of the stable entrance. "I know Grandfather can be hard, but we can square it, I'm sure. Don't take on."

Marcus Dramius shoved a hand deep into his scruffy, ill-fitting *tunica* and retrieved a small, sealed scroll that he handed to Lucius. "Master Lucius. This is for you, sir."

Without taking his eyes off Marcus Dramius, Lucius accepted the scroll and stood. He broke the seal, stepped into the street, out of the shadow cast by the stable, and scanned the parchment.

IX

"Where's Lucius, Menaeus? Don't tell me he's out drinking. We've got two boxes of glass eyes to deliver to statue makers on the *Via Sacra* tonight and it's ten *denarii*—unless we're late."

"Please sit, little goddess." Menaeus motioned toward a nearby stack of hay.

"I don't have time to sit." Livilla smiled at the farrier, "We can talk theater when I return. I was hoping you'd recite more of the Bacchae to me." She patted Menaeus on his balding pate. "So, where's Lucius?" Her tone bit down again into business mien.

"Sit, Livilla. I'm afraid the glass eyes will have to wait till tomorrow." Menaeus began.

"They *can't* wait. I told you there's a penalty—"

"Lucius is gone, *caria*. He went home."

Livilla sat. Abruptly.

"He's *gone*? *Home*?" Her voice was young and small. "*This* is his home." She added. Then her hand covered her mouth, "Oh! You mean…he went back to *Picenum*?"

"Yes. His grandfather sent a slave to fetch him. There's something very dire going on." Menaeus sat down next to the girl and put his arm around her shoulder. "He left us…you…a letter."

Livilla stood up as quickly as she'd sat down. "A letter? Where is it?"

"Ummm. I set it here somewhere. Oh yes—I left our good Cerberus to guard it."

Iace watched the exchange between the man and the girl with some interest as he cleaned his paws and then his undersides with his long, loose tongue.

SMELL SAD. MENYUS FEAR. LUKYUS GONE. LIGHT GONE.

PULL CART SOON. NO SMELL LUKYUS.

LIVLA SAD. MENYUS SAD. LUKYUS?

WHERE LUKYUS?

Iace nosed a small scroll off the edge of the hoofing bench.

LUKYUS SMELL HERE.

EAT LUKYUS SMELL. TASTE LUKYUS SMELL. LUKYUS NOT-FEAR SMELL TASTE.

"It should be right…Iace! Stop! Give that over!" Menaeus pulled at the protruding bits of paper that hung in the mastiff's drooling maw.

Livilla unceremoniously pried open jaws in a head larger than hers and Menaeus retrieved the remnants of the note.

"Zeus Phradoxes!" Menaeus looked over the girl's shoulder at the shredded, dribbling, blurred scraps. "Zeus!" He repeated.

Livilla pressed the ravaged pieces down on a paving stone. "Can you make anything out?"

"Let's see. '...friends...Let...kind *Felix*...Keep me away for more seasons...Menaeus...send coin...for Iace...Livilla...take...your own cares...and...I say to you...return...the dog and to pay all debts...Lucius'" Menaeus raised his head and looked into moisture-dimmed eyes. "What do you make of that?"

"We're on our own." Livilla lay down by the broad side of the reclining mastiff.

LIVLA SAD. LUKYUS SMELL GONE. IACE SAD. IACE MAKE LUKYUS SMELL COME BACK. IACE FIND LUKYUS. LIVLA SAD. IACE HURT.

A great tawny leg terminated by a clawed paw the size of her palm gently flopped on to Livilla's knee.

X

Livilla had little trouble persuading Glaubus that two carts, a colossal fighting dog, a tough girl dressed as a boy, and a street-savvy 10-year-old were a harder mark for footpads and night-thieves than a single boy and cart. And from *Martius* through *November* the team was busy enough and collected sufficient coin to leave the loss of Lucius locked in the understory of Livilla's mind (almost 18 months now since "the *betrayal* of Lucius" as she thought of it, when she let herself think of it at all—"leaving Iace to that madman! As if *I* wasn't the one who trained him and *I* wasn't the one that let the wispy-haired librarians and stinking copyists and smarmy perfumers stare at me like I was for sale just so we could get their business!")

And the coins were rolling in. Glaubus had even purchased a new red linen *tunica* and sandals he swore were elephant leather. Livilla smiled as she and Iace waited while Glaubus dealt with their latest client. Those sandals were certainly as ugly as an elephant. But her smile persisted when she thought of the *armarium* Menaeus kept under his mules, a strongbox that would soon hold enough for her future and Iace's, a future away from her mother and that evil-smelling, one-handed man who frightened and oppressed them both.

"Where is that dirty mite of a pest?" Her smile turned to a scowl. "I'd better not find him dicing. We still have two deliveries before dawn."

She ducked her head under the canopy outside the shop of the musical instrument factor to whom they were delivering an array of Egyptian reeds and stage whispered, "Glaubus? The rosy fingers of dawn crawl up the night." Their instructions from this new client emphasized that he would *not* deal with a female. She waited another moment then cried out more forcefully, "Glaubus? Other deliveries—remember?"

Snorting impatiently, Livilla patted the stoic dog on the flat, but wrinkled, plane between his ears. "*Mante*, Iace. I must find our *partner*." She curled around the front of the building and entered the alley on the side where Glaubus had gone to find the rear entrance and the proprietor.

A few moments later, an indignant Livilla—with Glaubus and his empty cart in tow behind—trotted back up the alley.

"What do I care whether he has Cretan wine? We're not on a bacchanal! This is not a festival! We have *business*! You have *responsibilities*! And you're too young for fortified spirits, anyway!" She sputtered, looking backwards every few feet as she chided.

"I *was* doing business! You have to develop client relationships! And nothing does that better than sharing a bowl of wine. Of course, *you* wouldn't know anything about that, being a *girl*— Hey! Where's the beast?" Glaubus stopped at the corner of the alley.

Livilla's head whipped around. Their cart sat where she'd left it, a small sack of indigo in one corner and a stack of blank parchment in the middle. The tooled red leather harness hung empty, sliced away in three places.

Iace was gone.

XI

COLD DARK. PULL CART TIME. LIVLA ANGRY. ANGRY IACE? NO. LIVLA ANGRY. LIVLA TELL IACE STAY. SMELL MAN-WATER AND MAN-DIRT. EVERYWHERE. IACE THIRSTY. LIVLA GONE. LIVLA TELL IACE STAY.

MAN SMELL. SOUR-MEAT MAN SMELL. SOUR-MEAT KILLER MAN CLOSE. BIG KILLER MAN SMELL. IACE MAKE BIG NOISE. IACE TELL LIVLA. IACE STOP SOUR-MEAT KILLER MAN NOT HURT LIVLA. BITE SOUR-MEAT MAN. BITE...

. . .

"I'M GOING to enjoy this, you ugly brute." Baractes swung the leather-covered cudgel down hard on the back of the neck of the huge dog. It was a blow that might have cracked a man's head, but sufficed only to stop Iace's deep growl of warning and to propel him into unconsciousness.

A second man, who could've been Baractes' smaller twin, held the dog's head, then his front legs, then his rear as Baractes bound Iace with several turns of cord. The two together heaved the limp animal like a sack over the back of an otherwise unladen pack mule that stood behind them, staring at the paving stones.

"Here's your pay, Quintus." Baractes tossed a thin pouch to the smaller man. "This never happened or..."

"I know, I know. I'm leaving Rome anyway, Centurion." The other man replied.

"*Don't* call me that—*ever*." Baractes countered quietly, quickly, and savagely, "Now...*git*." With a final glare and triumphant grin at the unconscious dog, the Illyrian turned into the night.

Quintus and the mule, hooves heavily muffled with cloth, bore Iace into the darkness and an unknown future.

XII

"Hoi! What's this?" A small, half-naked manikin shouted down at Quintus and his dog-laden mule. "We don't need no carrion. Turn around and get back to the mudball you reckon from, *culus*." Nasty as they were, the insults were delivered as casually as morning *Aves*.

"You be Caspius, weren't you?" Ignoring the imprecations, Quintus legged down from the grateful mule, using his falling momentum to pull at the cords around Iace's muzzle, dropping him hard to the gravel road. The dog made no response. "Here be yours, now, it is." And he made to climb back on the placid mule.

The tiny man who'd accosted Quintus from above nimbly jumped down from the broken Doric pillar on which he'd perched and ran to Quintus speedily enough to interrupt him before he succeeded mounting again.

"What're you doing, Fish Nose? This ain't no dumpin' ground. This is official property of the Roman *Populi* and I'm *Praefectus* herein. Pick up the dead cur and be on your way." To punctuate his tirade, he brandished a rusty gladius and spat a thin stream that splashed lightly on Iace's nearest paw.

Quintus stopped his ascent onto the mule and turned. "That's what I were saying. You be Kepseus?" And he pointed at the gladius-wielder.

"Cleptius, yes..."

"Clepseus...ah, now, you don't look like no Greek, do you?" Warming to his interrogation, Quintus paused only a moment before resuming, "*Praefectus* of this here Tiburininni rock quarry?" Accompanied with another jab of his finger.

"Yes, but..."

"You be in business with a large Illyricainian fella with...err...a...errr...big glove?"

Cleptius the *Praefectus* of the Tibur marble quarry lowered his sword and rubbed his stubbled chin. "You're from *him*, then." He glanced at Iace, still motionless on the ground. "Why's he sending me a dead dog?"

"Ain't dead. Just clipped in the head a time or six. Watch 'im; he came from the *Ludi*." Quintus yelled the last warning over his shoulder, as he'd already remounted the mule placidly retracing his steps to the Via Nomentana.

XIII

"I know she treated that great brute like it was her babe, but we've got contracts." Glaubus sat on the hay at Sappho's Stables in the late afternoon, chewing on a bread and fish breakfast.

"She's the one's always mewling about 'business' and 'responsibility'."

"Her heart's strong as Artemis and her head's harder than Hera's, but she's still a wisp of a girl, Glaubus. She can't pull that cart like Iace could. And she's smart enough to know it." Menaeus called back from the gloom. His shadow moved around the depths of the rear stable: the ring of a small hammer, the jingle of harness metal-on-metal, and the occasional *huffle* from one of the mules punctuated his replies to the young carter's complaints.

"Well..." Glaubus pressed a finger against the tip of his nose and expelled air and detritus; he was unused to the emotions he was feeling, "well...she could come along with me and...errr...scout...and...errr...tell me when the footpads were likely near...and..."

"And call down the fury of the elements on the heads of malefactors. No, young Glaubus. I'm happily surprised by this turn of sentiment from you, but it's to no good. Livilla's out of the transport business unless we can get that great dog back." Menaeus strode out and sat opposite the boy, "And that, my young friend, is only the beginning of her troubles." He flicked a mote of soot from the back of his hand and added. "How will she now pay her Mother's dues?"

Squinting his brows and eyes into a lugubrious face, Glaubus was again silent. Finally, he ventured, "*You* could hire her. All your animals think she's the queen of the feedbag."

Menaeus smiled with downcast eyes, "That would delay her fate a while. But she would see the falsity of the offer and the girl's too proud for that. And I'm too poor to keep such a position paid for long. In a season, maybe two, she's back where she is now."

"A season's a long time!" Glaubus chirped.

"Ah, youth!" Menaeus' smile grew even sadder. "No, Livilla will soon face a new life. And that hard head and strong spirit of hers will do her no favors in the world she'll be moving into."

That evening after dark, the wistful half-smile still pasted on his face, Menaeus dropped the canopy over the rear of the stable and knelt between his two mules.

"Now don't pee on an old Greek, 'Metus, I'll only be a moment."

He pried up two dusty boards with forge tongs and a hoof pick and pulled out a small, very flat boiled leather box, cinched with a thong and a complex knot. He jiggled the box, shifting it from one hand to the next. The hollow sounds indicated scant contents, perhaps eight or ten coins.

"Ah, youth." Menaeus repeated and sighed. "This was full a fortnight ago, dear Livilla."

He carefully replaced the box and the boards, then kicked stable dirt and straw over the spot.

Stroking its sides, the short stable owner confided to the quiescent mule under which he'd been delving, "Nothing an old Greek fakir can think of for it, my little goddess, nothing for it. Welcome to the world of man."

XIV

HEAD HURT.

Iace rose to a sitting position. He was in a strange place, lying on hard dirt. There were dogs on each side of him. He turned his head. The world was small, dirt walls rose to the sky all around, narrow roads led down to deep holes where many men were striking the dirt walls. And there were carts, many carts.

DOGS CHAINED. DOG NECK CLOTHES. LIKE LITTLE MULE-MAN DOG CLOTHES.

He stepped forward and felt the tension go taut on the chain.

IACE CHAINED. BREAK CHAIN. FIND LIVLA.

Heedless of the whines from the dogs on either side of him, or the building pressure on his chest as he lunged forward, Iace strained. More dogs yelped and growled. Iace didn't stop, dragging the dogs forward with him a pace at a time.

IACE BREAK CHAIN. FIND LIVLA.

The yelps become yowls of confusion. Iace continued to strain and lunge.

Several men appeared from over the rise just beyond the dogs. The smallest man was at the fore; he was tinier than Menaeus and indescribably filthy. He wore only a few leather strips that so poorly covered him, he would have been thrown out of the poorest *caupona* in the Subura. But he carried a heavy stick a bit longer than his forearm, and a many-tongued flail tipped with wooden balls. He stopped ten *pedes* from Iace, regarded the straining, plunging dog, and motioned overhead without looking behind.

"Next three: unfix the *torquem magnam* on that one. One of you on tail, head, and short chain." He squatted and spoke directly to the dog. "So you woke after all, *preciosa*? You were in the lime-pit tomorrow if you hadn't." The toadish man stood and grinned. Still without looking away from the splayed-out dog, he ordered "Quantus! Take the short chain and put him on the *mille* load cart! You other two, if he bites Quantus bad enough to lose a day, you'll both lose fingers."

MEN FEAR SMELL. IACE WALK. LITTLE MAN...LITTLE MAN SMELL DEAD. NOT DEAD.

"You a fighting dog? What arena did you disappoint, cur? Let's see what those muscles can do. Hurry, Quantus, or you'll feel it."

"Sorry, Feotor." The tall blonde holding Iace's lead chain stopped, his face full of terror, "Sorry, *Magister*, sorry!" As he bowed, the imp deftly and casually cracked the blonde on his shin with the club he carried in his left hand.

"Humph...harness him, you Gallic *culus* or you'll get far worse than that."

The crew of men walked Iace over the small hill. There were several carts strewn in a wide place in the path, some loaded with piles of raw stone. Quantus led Iace to the cart with the smallest pile.

"*Stultus*! Look at this brute, this *muta*. He's like you: all stupid muscle. I said to put him on the *mille* cart." Feotor's hand motioned with his truncheon. Quantus quickly led Iace to the largest cart with the heaviest load and attached the chain that ran through his rough collar harness.

Iace stood. He looked at Quantus, standing a pace away, a deep frown of concern creasing the man's dirty forehead.

"Hoi! MUTA! Here! Bring that load here! Now!" Feotor shouted.

Iace stood. The crease in Quantus' forehead became deeper.

"Now, *MUTA*! Here! Now!" Feotor's voice rose in pitch.

Iace stood.

BIG MAN, PIG SMELL. LICK BIG MAN.

Iace moved forward toward Quantus, but when the chain went taught, he stopped, sat and his tail brushed the chalky soil as it waved back and forth.

"Well, isn't that sweet. The dirty Gaul and the dirty Cur: two bulls who are lambs." The tiny man hurried to the side of the dog and looked down at him again, this time with contempt.

"We *work* here, *MUTA*! Work or die! I knew I was too kind with you. Should've softened you first before hitching you up."

With no pause before his action, Feotor raised the many-tailed whip and began beating the giant dog at his feet. Each wooden ball sounded an obscene "Pop!" when it struck bone on Iace's back or head.

LITTLE DEAD MAN HURT IACE. LIVLA SOFT-HAND GONE. SAUSAGE FACE LITTLE-MAN GONE. LUKYUS WATER-MAN GONE. GIRL SWEET-SMELL GONE. IACE HURT. IACE STOP LITTLE DEAD MAN.

Even knowing the ways of the giant dogs, many *bestiarii* in the *Ludi Romani* were taken to their doom by the surprising quickness with which the great fighting beasts could lunge from a fully reclining position. And though he was *rector canibus*, Master of Dogs, Feotor had never faced Iace's type, so the lightning lunge that ended with the 200 *librae* dog on top of him was entirely unexpected.

"Quantus! Toss this *Muta* off me! Now—Or lose a hand!" the somewhat muffled voice came from underneath the quietly standing dog.

The big Gaul led Iace off the little man, who jumped to his feet, sputtering and slavering.

"You two! Yes, you. Hold his tail. Quantus: hold the cursed chain for this worthless beast. He will learn his lesson now. Before he goes into the lime pit!"

IACE HURT. LIVLA SOFT-HAND GONE. SAUSAGE FACE GONE. LUKYUS GONE.

HURT. DEAD MAN HURT DOG. HURT. HURT.

A blonde curl brushed Iace's muzzle and pale lips whispered to him: "You must pull, dog, or Feotor will kill you sure as Cairnunnos has horns. Pull! Traho!"

In the dim haze of concussion and near death, Iace heard the word "Pull."

TRAHO, IACE. *TRAHO*.

Somehow he crawled forward. There was a giant pulling behind him. He must move a building, a temple.

Cool hands caressed his dry muzzle--too dry for the relief of slobber. A sweet voice filled his ears.

TRAHO, Canis Bonum

TRAHO, Canelillo.

As he collapsed insensible, the great dog felt the mountain behind him move forward.

XV

The *kalends*, *nones*, and *ides* of twenty months passed; it was now the 843rd year since the founding of the City of Rome. Many men and animals died in the great Flavian Amphitheater in the 842nd year. Crowds cheered. Many more died in wars fought on various borders of the empire. For his fifteenth consulship, the Emperor Domitianus Caesar Augustus chose as his co-consul the distinguished Senator Marcus Cocceius Nerva, surely without the foreknowledge that in a few short years, his co-consul would replace him on the throne. The small folk continued as the small folk do. In the marble quarry outside Tibur, a great many dogs died. Sometimes a mule stepped wrong or a dog was run over by a cart. Sometimes hearts failed as dogs pulled carts up hills. All the animals brought into the vast pit-works in the previous year were now dissolving in the deep lime-filled trench kept for disposal of no longer useful beasts. All dogs but one.

Summer heat in the pit was unremitting and inescapable, but the hills were dry and footing was sure.

Summer ended.

With the fall came rain.

MURMURS PRECEDED the tall legionary who picked his way around the refuse in the center of the Subura's *Vicus Lorarius*, the Street of Harness Makers. His leathers were worn, but that only validated him as a real soldier and not a Campus Martius practicing want-to-be. His scabbard was empty, as dictated by the laws of the *pomerium*, the ancient inner border of the city. His dark green eyes were haunted and hungry.

There was something familiar about this veteran, the regulars at Grimio's wineshop whispered as he marched by them.

A considerable disorder was stirring in front of Sappho's Stables, which stood in the middle of the block the young legionary so purposefully strode down. Two large wagons piled with bundles and casks and hung with tools blocked most of the narrow street.

Adipus Culicus, the Syrian owner of the *insula* across the way, was shouting at the backside of his neighbor, the Greek Menaeus.

"My girls can't get to the baths. Customers don't want *dirty* girls. Even a Greek should understand that!"

Menaeus was hitching up Bucephalus to one of the wagons.

The small, dark man called back to Culicus, "As I told you, we'll be gone by sundown." Then he turned and flashed his grin at the portly businessman, "And don't overestimate the fastidiousness of your clientele."

"Why you—" the young legionary thrust an interceding metal-braced arm between the Syrian's belly and Menaeus' face.

Nostrils flaring, Culicus shot a gaze at this impudent intruder and just as quickly doused his anger, "Your pardon, Centurion. This citizen is blocking commerce. I was—"

"I could see and hear what you were doing, *Culus*." The young soldier commented, relishing the punning insult.

Jowls quivering, he stared again at the legionary, eyes heating up and bulging, "Luc...Luc..."

"Yes, that's right. Luc...Luc...Lucius. Lucius the stable bum. Lucius the poet." A smile followed. "I'd like to talk to my friend now. In private."

"Yes, of course, Centuri—Lucius." And with greater alacrity than his bulk would have suggested possible, Culicus retreated into his darkened doorway.

Lucius and Menaeus stood face-to-face. The soldier's mouth split into a wide smile—unlike the grimace he'd directed at Adipus Culicus. He opened his arms and embraced the smaller man.

Menaeus' face flashed through many phases: anger, fear, hope, sadness, but settled on mild panic.

"I don't know why I did it! I don't know why! Don't turn me in to the Praetor, Lucius! Please? I'm all me Mum's got." He blubbered in his deep voice.

"You haven't seen your Mother since she left you as a babe on the steps of Diana's Temple." Lucius folded his arms and his forehead wrinkled, "What's this game you're playing, Menaeus?"

"Artemis, my boy, Artemis." Menaeus slapped himself on his cheek and continued, "You see, you see—even the gods were none too good for her Moochikins." Menaeus ducked several times as he spoke, anticipating a forthcoming-but-unpredictable blow.

When it became clear that Lucius wouldn't immediately resort to violence, he sighed like his working bellows and sat down hard on the stone bench that ran along the front of the stables.

"Good Lucius, you know I was fond of that dog of yours. And I haven't spent *all* the money you sent, despite serious needs on my part—look at these sandals!" Menaeus ducked again, watching Lucius for signs of incipient mayhem.

Eyes hard and green as agates, Lucius stared down at Menaeus. After a moment, his shoulders fell into a slope that mimicked his friend's and he sat down next to his former landlord.

"What are you talking about? What happened?" He asked. "What money?"

"Four months ago. The astrologer warned me, but I was possessed. I'd just lost 50 *sestertii* on the Blue. Then I went drinking anyway because this fellow Baractes was buying—he'd bet the White."

"Baractes? Great slab of an Illyrian?" Lucius' face slackened in surprise.

"Yes, lots of meat on large bones. Illyrian? Hmmm. Don't think religion came up and I'm not one to gainsay a barbarian anyway. But yes, Baractes bought that day and then for the rest of the week. I had a fine head by the time the *Lupercalia* rolled around, I must tell you. Painted myself like an Etruscan and told fortunes all day. Women *love* fortunetellers. Did I ever tell you about the time…"

"Menaeus. You'd just lost on the Blue and—" Lucius prompted.

"Sorry, yes. Oh, the money—don't play coy spirit with me, Lucius, the 40 *denarii* you sent—with that godawful dithyramb. I thought we'd covered that meter problem of yours, my boy. And watch those internal rhymes. They're as attractive as a Gorgon's body, but deadly as her head."

"I have *no* idea *what* you're ranting about, Menaeus. Even less than usual."

"*Well*, Livilla and Iace and Glaubus. You know how attached those three have always been."

"Yes."

"They took him, Lucius. Some thieves stole him."

"Glaubus?"

"No. The dog—Iace. Gone. Livilla's not been the same since."

Lucius did not speak or move.

Menaeus fidgeted, but waited.

"Tell me more about Baractes." Lucius said in a low, flat voice. "What did you talk about with Baractes?"

"Oh, you know, the usual stuff—women, gambling, gambling debts, the easiest bookies to dupe, the easiest women to confute."

"Nothing else?" Lucius' voice was so quiet, Menaeus leaned in to hear him.

"I don't know. It was a long time ago—thousands of conversations over wine since. You've been gone most of two years."

Lucius raised his eyes and stared at the Greek.

Menaeus slapped his thigh and smiled back at Lucius, "Oh, yes. Baractes had some sort of new investment, something about marvelous cards, cards of Mars, yards of marvels. He was getting it from the river. You know Baractes, always some scheme."

"Yes, I know Baractes." Lucius frowned, then asked, "The river, you say?"

"Yes, yes, Father Tiber. He was getting his marvels from the Tiber."

"What do you suppose he meant by that?"

"He was drunk, friend Lucius. He's always drunk—his wife drowned, you know. Zeus' beard! I could almost feel sorry for the scoundrel." Menaeus' eyes squinted in remembrance. "In any case, that's about it."

"What? What do you mean?"

"Well, I got home somehow, woke up the next morning—oh, it *might* have been early evening—like I told you, the week before the *Lupercalia* was one to remember, or not to remember if you know what I mean."

"Yes, yes, you woke up *and*..."

"And he was gone. Slick as spittle from a Phoenician trader."

"What about Livilla and Glaubus? Where were they? Where are they?"

"Oh, I don't know. Glaubus is running more clients across the river now and I don't see him every day. Livilla. Well, Lucius, our little goddess Livilla has grown. And, once Iace was gone and her livelihood lost, it's just been a matter of time till...well... you know her mother..."

Lucius stood. He reached down and squeezed Menaeus' shoulder. The Greek looked up at him and nodded.

"I'll get you the coin back, Lucius, I promise. Times have been hard."

"Menaeus." Lucius spoke very slowly as the little man looked up at him. "I did not send any money."

"You didn't?"

"As Jove is my witness. I did not."

It was Menaeus' turn to pause. "That little vixen. I *knew* you'd never have rhymed Agamemnon with hepastaikeon!" Eyes glittering, Menaeus slapped his thigh and leapt up from the bench.

"But these are mysteries for young hearts, Roman hearts, friend—*legionary* Lucius. I have still to harness strong Admetus and make my way from this stew of excess. I must be outside the Servian Wall before dawn."

"What—another banishment?"

"Yes, our master and god, Domitian, has once again decided that philosophers are corrupting Rome." Menaeus ran his palm in front of his bearded face, wiping all expression from it. "Life is an illusion. All government is evil. Live for the day. Seek wisdom, not pleasure." His smile crept in at the edges of his eyes, "Seek pleasure, not wisdom. Forget today, plan for tomorrow. Order is good, social order doubly so. This world is the only world." Bending his knees and grasping them, he laughed. "Oh, Lucius! I have one unbroken amphora of good Sicilian red. And one lost friend refound. Let us drink!"

"I must seek my dog and my friends, Menaeus." Lucius hesitated.

"We will plan and think best together—you and I and the great god Bacchus!"

Lucius slapped the farrier on his broad back, "Dionysius, friend philosopher, Dionysius!"

AN HOUR and a pot of wine later, with Admetus harnessed, Lucius and Menaeus prepared their farewells. But neither they nor the gods had advanced a plan to find either Iace or Livilla. Menaeus, demonstrating "the dances of my forebears," was hopping around so boisterously that his dung-stained grey chiton fell off one shoulder.

Lucius laughed. "You old drunkard. I've missed you." He clapped the other man on the shoulder again. "This *is* all you know, is it not?"

Menaeus stopped his capering and looked back into his friend's eyes, "As Athena is my witness, Lucius, I'd give my right thumb to have that dog back for you, and I'd go dry for two days just to have more or better news." He continued, "But what of you, *legionary*? For certain there's a tale there. You left a boy and now...well...you saw how our good Culicus responded? You are most intimidating, soldier Lucius—and it is not the uniform or the broader shoulders, it is *there*." Menaeus pointed the fork of two fingers at Lucius' green eyes. "They have seen things that boys do not see. Where dwells thy spirit now, Lucius the legionary?"

Lucius emptied the dregs of his bowl on the stable floor and leaned against a vertical beam. "Here it is from start to finish, Menaeus, unglossed as the 'poet' Lucius could never have made it. My grandfather called on me because our cursed patron, the fifth cross-eyed Pompeius, had wind the Emperor needed support in Germania Superior to put down revolt there."

"Some word of this reached here. Saturninus and this revolt were duly squelched, no?"

"Yes, they were. And, as a new *vexillatio* attached to *Legio XXII*—under Pompeius' command—I played my small part in it."

"You fought the Germans?" Menaeus' eyebrows rose an inch. "Were they seven *pedes* tall?"

"We fought ourselves." Lucius scowled. "We fought other Romans. Auxiliaries. From Gaul, from Macedonica…I know not where." He paused. "I fought. I killed, Menaeus." Lucius' face was immobile, then a smile flashed across it—on and off as quick as a strike of lightning. "Mostly I dug latrines and walked picket and drilled and coughed from the cold." He spat. "The short of it is that the Emperor was greatly pleased. He conferred enormous wealth on Pompeius for his assistance and—for once and for reasons only the gods understand—Pompeius did not keep all for himself. He offered to let my family repurchase our estate at Pausulae. I have the coin, but I need an almost equal amount to fix the damage it's suffered, replace the livestock, and feed us all until next harvest. I thought to hire out in Rome to raise the funds."

Lucius poured the last of the wine into his bowl as the two men stood in silence. After a swallow, he wiped his mouth with his wrist and continued, "But what is this of Livilla?"

Menaeus' mobile face registered considerable surprise, every part of it appearing ready to crawl off its own far edges, "You are concerned?"

"Concerned?" Lucius' head jogged upward, startled, "Of *course* I'm concerned. Livilla is, well…a good friend. I have been worried about her and presumed the use of Iace would alleviate her...errr...difficulties."

"The note you left gave no such indication, friend Lucius. In fact, it rather dashed the girl to the stones."

"What! What? What was wrong with the note?"

"As memory serves, it read 'fates keep me away for many seasons' and 'Menaeus send coin for Iace'—I remember that one well, and 'I say to you return the dog and pay all debts', and —the one that faired to crush the child's spirit, 'Livilla take your own cares.'"

"I never wrote such!" Lucius protested, slapping the boiled leather cuirass that covered his chest.

"Ummm, suggests Clotho and her sister Lachesis have played us rough, friend soldier. I believe you, but Livilla will take more convincing. She's a fair woman now, you know, and her will's no weaker than it was."

Both men sighed in tandem and raised their bowls in mute tribute—to Livilla, to the lost Iace, to themselves.

Then they stood and embraced: the middle-aged Greek farrier-madman, bearded and balding, dark of eye and hair, and the Roman with russet hair and eyes the color and shape of fresh olives, once a carrier of the dead, a poet, a want-to-be philosopher: now, a soldier.

"Well, flee the Emperor's wrath, you impious corrupter. You're always welcome in Picenum, if they kick you out of Tarentum for making bad rhymes. And send your wisdom in a letter. You know where to send it, do you not?"

Menaeus jumped up from their bench, solemnly poured the dregs of his wine on the ground, and began a slow rhythmic shuffle as he declaimed, "Do I *know* where to send it? I'll drop it into Boreas' cheeks and bid him blow it home. I'll toss it into the sea and ask Poseidon to ferry it to you on dolphins' backs. I'll tell Helios to turn copper into the spun gold of the sun and let it fall down on you like Zeus' engendering rain."

XVI

Lucius left Menaeus declaiming to the street his own rude Latin translations of the poet of Lesbos as he, his mules, and his apparatus made their way south toward the *Porta Latina* and Magna Graecia. He heard slops pouring down from the offended—or amused—or amused-and-offended locals. The old reprobate would never change. What had he been thinking leaving *anything* in the hands of that flighty, good-hearted, lunatic? He had had little choice, though. His grandfather's summons had been less a plea and more a desperate last request.

But now he had to find Iace. And turn up Livilla somewhere along the way. That little wastrel needed a piece of his mind. Although Menaeus was the culpable party, Lucius wouldn't have hesitated leaving Iace with her. Those two were soulmates. Or so he had thought.

Still musing, with only enough of his street-mind engaged to prevent treading in puddles best avoided, Lucius rounded a corner he'd walked by every day when he worked at the great arena in the shadow of the Colossus. In a narrow alleyway just past the bend in the main road, an indeterminate number of street urchins crouched over a game of bones. A scene passed a hundred times, Lucius scarcely nodded as he hurried on.

"Lucius! *Amicus*! Wait up!"

The smallest and filthiest of the urchins hopped up from the street dice game and ran toward him.

"Glaubus! You're the fellow I most wanted to see in all of Rome!" Lucius held out both his hands as his smile shone on the dirty young urbanite.

"Ho, Lucius." Glaubus stuck his thumbs in his rope belt and chuckled, giving his old friend a slow once-over. "Hoo-oo, Lucius! A soldier boy, now! Good pickings for poets in Picenum, eh?"

"I was seconded to a little action following the Emperor into Germania Superior. It turned out well for Domitian, and—to everyone's surprise—the *viri boni* didn't keep everything themselves."

"Saved a taste for your old chum? For 'the fellow I most wanted to see in all of Rome'?" Glaubus stuck out an open palm.

"Tell me about Iace and Livilla."

The corners of Glaubus' mouth turned down, as did his shoulders. "Ah, Lucius. The dog...the dog is gone." The boy looked down at his remarkably ugly sandals and kicked a clod of filth in the gutter.

Lucius reached out and settled a hand on Glaubus' arm, "I know." He waited till Glaubus raised his eyes to meet his. "What happened? And where's Livilla?"

"Some'un took him, Lucius. Some'un took him. We were makin' a deliv'ry to a new client all straight and proper and then he was gone." The boy blinked and swallowed. "There's thieves in Rome takes anything." He confided in a whisper.

"And Livilla?"

"She don't have no money, Lucius. The Greek helped her out some, but she pays her Mum regular and..."

Lucius had turned and was running deeper into the Subura before Glaubus could finish.

"Ruined me contacts in the *Vicus Sutorius* it did," Glaubus yelled at Lucius' back.

XVII

PULL *TRAHO* PULL. DOG STRONG. PULL.

LITTLE DEAD MAN BEAT DOG.

The rains of *November* struck the quarry like liquid pebbles flung down from an angry Olympus.

Overseers were in their shed, drinking wine laid back for days like this. High-value quarry slaves were under drenched skin roofs, or sheltered as they could out of the downpour. Only Feotor, the senescent half-mad dog master—the *rector canibus*—

still braved the elements and steadfastly beat his charges up and down the slick, man-made hills, cliffs, and valleys.

In full harness, Iace was near the top of the first level. Behind him on the steepest downslope was a young dog new to the quarry. The *rector* stood beside the hapless beast and screamed at him and at the rain, with every curse slicing down his rod onto the dog's straining harnessed back.

DEAD MAN BEAT DOG

DOG NOT PULL CART DOWN HILL

DOG PUSH CART?

CART NOT ROLL DOWN?

With a final blow delivered to the head of the confused animal, Feotor hobbled around to look below the cart, to find what had stopped its progress. As the man stooped to remove a wedged stone, the exhausted young dog leaned against his side of the over-laden wagon. The cart jerked forward, picking up speed. Now in front of the moving vehicle, the *rector* stumbled and vainly pushed at it, trying both to slow it and to get out of the way. When the slack stiffened, the young dog pulled as hard as he could, but finding no purchase didn't slow the plummeting acceleration of the cart.

In a sliding rush, the wagon made the bottom of the pit, scudding across a small landing space, crushing the flailing *rector canibus* against the wall of the quarry. Falling and rolling behind it, the young dog in its harness piled against the front of the wagon with enough force to elicit an additional groan from the still-conscious man pinned against the rough wall of stone. The dog stood up, wet and dirty but more-or-less unhurt. The man crumpled forward, red spittle rolling out onto the marble slabs in the cart where his head drooped.

When the hated *rector*'s head dropped forward in mortal finality, Iace closed his eyes, raised his head as high as his harness allowed, and listened.

He listened for Lucius. He listened for Livilla. He listened, through the sheeting rain, for the agitated whinnies of Admetus and Bucephalus.

He stood, effortlessly holding five-hundred weight of Tibur *lapis* on the wagon that stretched at the end of his harness, and an image, a smell, a light, and a sound came to him in the misty downpour.

Somewhere in memory, the mule-smelling Menaeus settled *his* harness—the harness Iace pulled for Livilla—over his neck and shoulders. He smelled *her* smell and felt the harness slip over and off his head at the end of a night's work. He smelled *its* smell and felt *its* soft feel on his scarred shoulders as the rain stretched and softened the badly cured pit leathers around his neck.

TRAHO, dog, Pull
SISTE, dog, Stop
LAXO, dog, slack
Iace's feet moved.

He was pulling a triple load—Feotor had bet another overseer on "how long that arena brute can last" and so Iace's wagon was always heavier than any other dog's.

He was almost to the top of the hill. There was a downward incline beyond that—always tricky for the dogs to negotiate.

Iace pulled on. The feel and smell of Livilla's hands and breath were on his face. With even his own name forgotten, the taste of the rain was like the water Lucius brought him in the arena, the water that led him to the wonderful life only his heart and nose could remember.

TRAHO DOG *TRAHO*
HILL TOP *SISTE*
WATER COLD
COOL-HAND WATER-MAN
DOG LICK WATER, LICK WATER-MAN.
WHERE SWEET GIRL? WHERE WATER-MAN?

He stood past the top of the hill now, on the downward slope. The wagon was far enough behind on the other side of the peaked rise that it still tugged against him. A paw's breadth at a time, Iace strained forward until the cart balanced at the top of the rise. Now there was no pressure on his harness, only slack.

He backed up until his rump touched the balancing cart. Twisting his corded neck, he shook his head. One eye was almost out of the stretched, wet, and now loosened harness, the rest of the strapping settled on his jawline and, no matter how hard he shook, the last leather loop refused to slip over his head.

There was just enough give so that he was able to bend his nose to the ground and step on the edge of the harness with one wide paw.

TRAHO. SISTE. LAXO. SISTE.

DOG MAKE CLOTHES GO.

TRAHO. LAXO.

DOG SLACK. DOG PULL.

Now he was able to pry the soaked, deformed harness over one ear. The other side caught under his enormous jaw.

DOG *TRAHO*. DOG *LAXO*.

DOG STRONG.

His gyrations dislodged the balanced cart. Pointed at the bottom of the hill where the dead *rector canibus* and the confused young pit dog lay, the wagon sped downwards. Iace's partial success getting the harness off meant he could no longer use all the pulling power of legs, shoulders, and back to slow it. He pulled against the full weight of the rolling marble-laden cart with only the muscles of his neck.

Iace strained. He pulled. For longer than he'd ever fought in the arena. Harder than he'd ever pulled Livilla's cart up the Esquilline or Caelian Hills. The great cords of his neck muscles knotted. Exhausted, against his will, they relaxed, smooth and limp and powerless, and then spasmed to rock-hard immobility. The cart pitched downhill, Iace skidding helplessly behind.

TRAHO. *TRAHO. TRAHO* DOG.

DOG HURT. DOG PAIN. PAIN.

DOG FEAR. DOG DIE?

Iace had always bested his opponents with his raw strength. He would *not* lose to a *cart* and to the *rain*. He would attack!

RUN. *CURRE.*

DOG RUN FAST. *CURRE VELOX.*

DOG STRONG. DOG FAST.

DOG BITE CART. DOG BITE DEAD MAN.

DOG STRONG. DOG NOT DIE.

Iace stopped pulling and ran *at* the cart as it now careened down the hill.

The dog at the bottom of the hill yelped and jumped aside as Iace's cart smashed into his.

CART BREAK.

SMALL DOG JUMP.

LITTLE DEAD MAN DIE.

Only half-a-pace behind his own cart, Iace leapt at the last instant and stood—for a moment—atop the now-sideways overturned wagon.

Drawing the last of his strength, he flailed his head from side to side and the worn pit harness, hated by him and countless dogs before him, slid from his broad black muzzle and over the top of his head.

He fell off the cart, fully spent, just as it toppled again and slipped into the murky water of the deep pit—the final pit—that lay beside the wreck.

HURT.

CART GO DEATH WATER.

CLOTHES GONE.

Under the pummeling rain and with only the energy of will, Iace limped up the endless maze of ramps and turns and flats of the vast quarry. Past drenched, uncaring, half-dead slaves, past drunken or sleeping overseers.

As he reached the top, climbing out of the hole that had been his life for six seasons, the rain ended.

Behind him, the red sun set above the darkling pit.

City bred and raised, Iace paused, confused by the enormity of the horizon. Nothing hard defined his world now. No walls of rock or clay, no paving stones, no circumscribed paths. He remembered trees. They grew in pots and next to buildings and walls. He had seen grass, or glimpsed it through openings to peristyle gardens when Livilla's deliveries took them to Palatine or Esquiline villas. But here—as far as he could see—there were no buildings. There were no humans. There were more trees than he could understand, scattered around an immensity that stretched on forever to the sky.

GOOD SMELL. NOT-FOOD, GOOD SMELL.

WHERE WALL?

HARD PATH.

LIGHT STRONG. SMELL STRONG.

DOG HURT.

TRAHO DOG *TRAHO*.

NO CART *TRAHO*.

DOG FEAR.

DOG GO HARD PATH.

There was a road, even if there were no sides to it, only trees and dirt. Iace understood roads.

DOG GO GIRL. DOG GO COOL-HAND WATER-MAN.

WHERE SOFT-HAND GIRL?

He turned to his stronger side. Limping north on the *Via Tiburtina*, each painful step carried him farther from Rome.

XVIII

Lucius ran into the dankest part of the old Subura. He'd passed near Livilla's mother's "wineshop" once or twice when they were on deliveries, but Livilla always arranged the route so they never went directly by Livia's *insula*.

Lucius understood. The truth of the little lies Livilla told about her home life was clear enough in her tough, young face. But he was certain her mother Livia would have some idea of where the girl would be. And Livilla, in turn, should bring more news of Iace.

Sidewalks played out. He hadn't passed a fountain in the bleak squares of the area for a mile or more. Refuse, plain and unmentionable, was strewn here and there in the streets. Some debris looked and smelled mature enough to walk away on its own. Lucius slowed his pace to avoid an accidental slip in the oozes that flowed from the nearest pile.

A satyr-and-cattle fresco emblazoned walls of a corner three-story *insula*, images Livilla had referred to—with considerable distaste—a number of times.

There was no door on the corner archway.

"*Put your heart in your pocket, Lucius.*" The young man reflected before stepping inside.

The smell of old wine—both before and after it processed through a human body—overwhelmed him. A bearded denizen, passed out on one of the rickety tables, snored freely. Another customer, sans beard, but with an interesting collection of scars and tattoos on his sunburned face, sat at the same table, ignoring his sleeping companion and nursing a bowl of (no doubt sour) wine.

At almost the same moment that Lucius entered, a woman came through the open arch at the other side of the room. She had—not too many years before—been beautiful, Lucius noted. Her beauty might even have inspired him in his recent past. Perhaps an ode to the inevitable transience of human splendor? Now, Lucius had seen too many faces and bodies like hers. Molded by fear, greed, desperation, and driving self-interest. Her beauty hung on her like flesh on a corpse. It simply did not belong there at all, and something about its clinging vestiges was more disturbing than outright ugliness would have been.

"A tribune from our Emperor's legions!" She trilled in an impossibly high voice, sliding over to put her arm around Lucius' waist.

"Oh, great conqueror—what can I possibly provide for you

here? Have you come for our wine—only the best Falernian—or something else?" Her free hand stroked her own still-smooth and creamy cheek.

"I've come to ask you where your daughter is, Livia?" Not ungently, Lucius pulled her fingers from his side.

"My...*daughter*? My *daughter*?" Her voice retained its strained high register. "Surely, tribune, you can't think *I* am old enough to have a *daughter* that might interest such as you?" Her fingers, freed from his side, went to her lips. She moistened the tips with small kisses and fluttered a wave.

"No games, Livia. I know Livilla. I worked with her for a year. Where is she?"

The remnants of glamor evaporated and Livia's color turned from cream to splotched pinks. Her stance moved from coquette to something befitting an Ostian dock worker. Hands drove to her hips, feet squared apart. Her brown eyes shafted Lucius with an anger made hotter by the fear that backed it.

"You! You're that *poet*! You and that black Greek boy-lover filled her head with...with...*thoughts* and ideas! You *ruined* her! If Baractes were here, he'd rip that smug expression off your pansy face. He was a *real* centurion. Where'd you buy that outfit, *poet*!"

Lucius stepped forward and grabbed one of her wrists firmly enough to startle and stop her ranting.

"Where...Is...Livilla?" He asked as she flailed her other hand around, beating him ineffectually on his shoulder and side.

Realizing he would not let go, Livia stopped striking him. Her skin tone returned close to its original pallor. She looked at him again, this time more like a frightened animal. Her knees collapsed.

Lucius caught her as she fell to the floor and carried her through the archway into the back room, where he laid her on the sleeping alcove.

There was a half-finished bowl of wine on the side table. She gulped the wine he handed her. She sat up, back hunched over, and sobbed.

"Tell me about Baractes." Lucius asked.

Her head darted up and she looked frantically about the room. Satisfied after a moment, she whispered, "Baractes is my...my...landlord."

"Really?" Lucius replied, all tone washed from his voice.

"Yes," she said, her head turned down toward the floor again. "He purchased this *insula* over a year ago. He has options on many of the *insulae* near here. Those he doesn't own pay him to assist them and keep them safe from the *collegia* gangs. He's a very respected landlord."

"Is he?" Lucius said. "So he is a wealthy man? Is he a senator? An *equites*?"

Livia's head turned up again and her glances darted around the room. "No, he is...he is...a man of business. He made his money in construction. He told me..." Her eyes opened so wide that her speech stopped.

"Yes? He told you?" Lucius urged. As if caressing a wilting flower, he stroked Livia's nearest wrist for a moment, then removed his hand.

"I think...I think he said something about repairs for the Emperor's Amphitheater. He owns the quarry in Tibur. He's a very important man. He's a very good..." Livia's sobs began again. Lucius waited for them to subside.

She grabbed Lucius' hands with surprising, harpy-like strength.

"He wanted *her*! He wanted *her*! 'She's too young', I told him. I did *everything* he ever asked. *Everything*. *I'm* not old. Why did he want *her*? I'm *beautiful*, aren't I?" Her pleading eyes stared into Lucius'. "I *am* beautiful?"

Pulling her hands away from his, ignoring the small scrapes left by her nails, Lucius held her gaze and asked once again, "Where is Livilla?"

Livia's mobile face flashed through disappointment, fear, and anger. Then she hung her head. "I don't know." She said quietly, then repeated in a hoarse whisper, "I haven't seen her in five days. I don't know where she is."

XIX

THE SKY WAS DARK.

Blood seeped from the pads of his paws, leaving pink prints in his wake.

Still, Iace saw no humans, no buildings.

NO WALLS. DOG GO HARD PATH.
TIRED. SMELL DOG BLOOD. HURT. TIRED.
WHERE SOFT-HAND GIRL? WHERE WATER-MAN?
HARD PATH LONG. DOG FALL SOON.
DOG SMELL WARM OLD SMELL. NO, NOT OLD, REMEMBER.
MULE SMELL? SWEET MULE SMELL. MULE-MAN?
NO. NOT MULE SMELL.

It was not mule; it was the other animal like a mule. The animal like a mule that humans sat on.

It stood next to a building! Iace did not stop in the road, because he was afraid he would not be able to move again if he stopped, so he trudged forward toward the horse and the building.

The horse stood next to a wagon! Not like the rude carts Iace had left smashed behind, but a great, high wain with tall, thin wheels. It smelled strongly of human.

DOG NOT DIE.
DOG FALL.

Eyes half-closed, his knees buckled and he collapsed underneath the horse-cart. By the time his heavy head hit the grass and the tiny fragrant violets that grew there, he had fallen into the unconsciousness of complete exhaustion.

DOG PULL GREAT CART. DOG FALLS UNDER CART.
MAN AND GIRL RIDE CART.
SMALL MAN AND MULES AND BIG DARK MAN WITH STICK LEG.
DOG PULLS WAGON EASY. *DOG ALONE.*

ROAD LEADS TO BIG SUN DOG. DOG BIGGER THAN DOG. SUN DOG SMILES.

MAN AND GIRL AND MULES AND OTHER MAN LAUGH.

DOG SMELL MAN. DOG KNOWS MAN. MAN SMELL CLOSE AND STRONG.

DOG PULLS AND PULLS.

XX

With the help of the brown vinegarish wine she generously provided, Livia's tongue had wagged for hours. To Lucius' frustration, she was silent as the *Styx* when asked about her daughter, but she'd rattled on about Baractes until Lucius left her nodding, sodden and sour as her wine.

"So, Baractes the Senator! Landlord and Protector of Livia and Livilla! Owns the state quarry at Tibur! My, that Illyrian freedman has come up in the world." Lucius mused half out loud as his pony trotted up the *Via Tiburtina* toward the ancient city of Tibur.

In the dark forests of Germania Superior, he'd saved the life of and become close with the son of a well-off baker who lived at the base of the Palatine. Originally slaves, the Corelli became wealthy selling honey-cakes and wedding pastries to the *viri boni*, Rome's "best" men. Manlius sent letters home from Germania naming Lucius and so he'd been recognized and able to borrow a stable horse for this trip. "Our home is your home," the elder Manlius Corelius said and had warmly embraced Lucius. But somehow there was no empty room in their commodious house, and it seemed none of the family would be eating-in that day—would he like an apple? A cold sausage? And the horse they gave him was a sad little pony so small that Lucius' feet near touched the road on either side.

"Still better than walking, eh Pegasus?" So the Picentine had named his mount, who was placid if nothing else.

"What could that blackguard be playing at?" Lucius

continued speaking to himself as he and Pegasus sauntered down the road. The pony couldn't maintain a faster pace for long.

"I'm sure there must be some answer at the quarry—I wonder if I should present myself as an inspector? That would put a Gaul at their doorstep." A brief smile flew across his face.

But he was too worried for levity to last. He passed five mileposts, then ten.

The landscape became more bucolic: copses of olive trees, perfectly round oaks, waterfalls, and brightly colored wash-outs lined the road. "No wonder Tiberius retired here," he mumbled to the patient Pegasus.

He pulled the pony's reins to the right at milepost XXVII, leaving the setting sun behind him, ambling toward the ancient quarry from which stone had been pulled for so many of the finest Roman buildings of the past two hundred years. Broken chunks and slabs of the white, variegated *lapis Tiburtina* lay strewn everywhere.

The path that led off the *Via Tiburtina* was almost twice as wide as the great northern road itself. Untidy collections of broken, unfinished columns—some with fluting and pediments, some merely rough cylinders—clustered casually every few hundred feet. On a few of these dwelt half-done statues and busts: an ear and part of a senator's face, the tall curling hair of a matron piled up on a blank square, the lower legs of Hercules and part of a snake's tail.

Before long, Lucius and his mount were on a broad declining path. Ahead of them spread the cyclopean expanse of pits and ramps cut into the beautiful hillside, scarring it with man's ambitions.

A half-naked gnome sat on a large pediment at the side of the road. He was toying with a long wooden pole, a broken *gladius* stuck through his thong belt.

Lucius pulled up his horse, swung his leg over and dismounted with what he was sure was some degree of elegance.

"*Ave!*" He even went so far as saluting the man by lightly thumping his left breast with his right fist.

With great economy of motion, the small wiry man of indeterminate age raised watery eyes and hairless brows and inspected Lucius. "No orders today, soldier. We're closed." He lowered his gaze and continued twirling his wooden pole.

Resisting all impulses to react to the man's dismissal, Lucius turned as if about to mount his pony. "That's unfortunate. Baractes said there's a great deal of coin involved. I suppose he'll have to decline the contract."

The demeanor of the man with the pole altered instantly. He jumped up and ran forward, placing himself between Lucius and Pegasus.

"Ho, there, Centurion! I didn't know who'd sent ya! Hold now. There's no need to return empty handed." The man hopped up and down in excitement.

Lucius rubbed his stubbly jaw, "Ummm...Baractes said we could count on immediate delivery. It *would* be a shame to disappoint the Urban Praetor..."

"No need to disappoint no one...no need..." The fellow started to grab Lucius' arm in a "friendly" gesture, but— glancing at the soldier's eyes—pulled his clay-encrusted fingers back, turning the gesture into a bow of welcome. "I am Cleptius —but you knew that, I am sure, Centurion. Come, come to the side of the road. I...I have a *congium* of good Campanian to wash away the dust. Come...come."

Holding his head stiff and high, Lucius followed Cleptius, who pulled a large leather flask from behind the marble stanchion he'd been sitting on and, barring a gap-toothed smile, handed it proudly to the ex-poet/ex-legionnaire.

"Thanks, good Cleptius." Lucius poured several ounces of an unexpectedly mature wine into his mouth and swallowed, then handed the jug back to the grinning quarryman. "Thanks, indeed. However, my business is with stone, not with grape."

"Hoi!" Cleptius clapped his hands and beamed, revealing the

three teeth in his upper jaw. "Ho," he repeated, "This is well said! Errr...*Vir*?...?" He cocked up one side of the long pale line of his hairless brow in question.

"Vindicius. Callidus Vindicius, of the Legion of the Bronze Ox." Raising his nose and chin, Lucius struck a pose and glanced off in the distance, "most recently from Brittania."

"Ahh...Centurion Vindicius, it is an honor. I am Cleptius, *Praefectus* of the Emperor's quarry here at Tibur. But you know that, do you not? You know that?" Cleptius clapped his hands as he spoke. "What does our friend Baractes have prepared? Where are your carts, your sleds?"

Nose pointed high, Lucius rolled his eyes downwards at the overseer, "I am here to place the order, not to cart stone."

"Of course, of course...Centurion." Cleptius' hands jigged and jerked, clapping or rubbing together, or grasping then dropping his wooden pole. "We can begin filling *any* order from Baractes in the morning."

"The morning!" Lucius raised his voice almost to a shout, "The morning! There's an hour of light left, *Praefectus*! I understood you were not soft with your slaves here! This order must be filled by tomorrow at midday, when the carts arrive from Rome!"

"No! No! We can fill *any* order...any order." The hands flew together and apart, "It's...well...we've had a bit of an accident today and it..."

"An accident?" Lucius asked, filling his face with disdain as his belly shrank in fear, "It's a *quarry*, man. Of *course* you have accidents. Why does that stop the work?" Lucius' hands moved to his hips.

"It's the dogs, Centurion. And the poxed *rector canibus*. Mud slide, path blocked, cart broken. Chopped old Feotor almost in half. Lost a dog or two—don't know 'xactly."

"How can you let the loss of a dog and an old slave stop you, man? What are workers for?" Lucius fueled a snarl with his growing horror. "Dispose of the trash and let us get to our business!" Lucius hardened his stare and added, "You *have* disposed of the bodies?"

"Yes, Centurion Vindicius...yes...Feotor...the...err...*rector canibus*." Cleptius licked his lips. "The new *rector* beat the dog what caused the mess right proper, then tossed him in the dead pit—big fighter dog, it was."

Lucius' eyes swam. Intuition struck him like a stone in his gut. Swallowing hard, he asked, as casually as his pounding heart allowed, "Baractes told me he brought you dogs sometimes. From the arena, if I recall?"

"Yes, Centurion. He has done that. Just one dog, though. Humongous brute he was. Seasons ago. Never saw one last that long." Cleptius ended in a mutter, not noticing Lucius' stance had become unsteady or that his eyes had closed tight for a moment.

Rubbing his forearm across his face in camouflage, Lucius responded, "I will take more of your wine, good Cleptius, before we discuss our weights and shapes."

AFTER ENDLESS CONVERSATION with the stinking *praefectus* about slab sizes, types of cuts, and timetables, Lucius assured Cleptius the carts would soon arrive with full specifications and cash payment. He, Lucius, would leave now to intercept them and explain the quarry's plight and then head back to Rome to clear things with Baractes. Rubbing his hands in furious gratitude, the little man insisted that "the Centurion" take the wineskin as small recompense.

With soldierly dignity, Lucius mounted his sad little pony in the growing dark. It was the first hour of night, *prima hora nocte*. Rain moistened his bare head and his pony's patchy coat. "There's a *caupona* just west along the main road, Pegasus. There might even be decent stabling for you." Lucius's face felt stiff as his heart. Iace was dead. Gone. Lost in a pit of lime, tossed there by such as the vile creature he'd spent the past hour with. And Baractes was behind it all. *Baractes*.

And that broad sack of excrement had Livilla. His heart's eye recalled the battle-marked dog—festooned with Livilla's clothes—marching in ceremony around her clay gods and heroes. Their endless arguments about the merits of lyric and tragic poetry—shouted at each other over Iace's tawny wide back and fine red harness, as they made their deliveries in the dark Roman streets. He'd celebrated those nights—every night he'd been on the frozen picket lines of Germania Superior. When his ice-crusted *caligae* were so hard and cold he couldn't take them off until he'd held his feet by the barracks brazier for an hour. In those rare moments after an actual attack, after he'd thrust steel into a stranger's face or guts or leg. Even as he sat and patched his cloak or armor or weapons. It had always been the three of them—the dog he saved —the formidable canine of the bloody amphitheater, the quick-witted, harsh-tongued wisp of a girl that the dog worshipped, and himself—Lucius Viterbus of Pausulae, the young Picentine poet. Not Lucius the legionary, not Lucius the soldier, the killer.

A black, unnatural shape loomed on his left. Sauntering up the *Via Tiburtina*, he'd ignored Pegasus, letting him have his head. Tibur was well behind them now, but the way station, the *caupona*, must be near. Yes, that was it. That was the looming shape—the inn at the *stationem*.

Even in the gloom, Lucius noticed the draught horse tethered to a large two-wheeled *cursus publicus* cart that huddled under an overhang on the near side of the *caupona* building. There was no further room under this eave. "Sorry...no stable," he muttered to the tired pony. When he rode to the far side, a withered old man sat there on a board on the wet straw. Lucius dismounted and tossed the reins and a few coppers to the old slave. "Dry him," the young man ordered simply as he turned to enter the inn.

It took several moments for his eyes to adjust to the mix of deep darkness and oil-lamp glare that filled the stopover's interior. Standing just inside the leather drape that functioned as a door, he inspected the tall room with a mild suspicion borne of his experience and training on the northern marches. High benches clustered near one wall functioned as drinking tables. Two men—one very short, one very large—stood there with crude calix cups and wooden bowls in front of them. A third figure, a slender rat of a man, leaned against another wall, drowsing.

All conversation—if there had been any—ceased. But Lucius did not mind the silence and continued with his observations. There were ladders affixed to three walls, leading up to tiny, railed sleeping ledges. Large troughs and amphorae lined the fourth dirty wall, no doubt the inn's stores.

"Xth or XXIInd?" The larger man at the standup tables boomed out into the quiet and boldly stepped forward.

Lucius blinked. Now that he heard him and saw him move, the man had an unmistakable air—a military air. Ugh—a *Centurion's* air. He was surprised by the strange and complex feelings that arose in him and almost strangled the breath in his throat. "Strabo's XXIInd—reconstituted from the Xth."

"Eheu...I heard about that decimation. Rough stuff." The dark face of the big man squinted at Lucius, "But you weren't part of that, were you?"

Lucius allowed his sigh to be visible this time, "No, thank the gods. I was just there as food for the cold and the lice—and a nice slow target for barbarian archers."

A vast, toothy grin softened strong features: "That would be the life, boy, wouldn't it?" He extended a pale-palmed melon-sized hand and grasped Lucius' forearm. Lucius completed the gesture with his grip on the corded muscles of the other man's arm. "Talo, lad. The name's Talo. *Ave!*" A thick eyebrow of coarse black and silver hair flicked up in question.

"Lucius." Trying to match the fellow's iron grip, Lucius added, "*Ave*, Talo."

"Lucius. A fine soldier's name." Talo swung a dusky arm around the younger man's shoulder, an arm so strong Lucius knew he couldn't evade it if he'd wanted to, and pulled him back toward the benches. "Come drink this swill with me, Lucius. The rodent in the corner there claims it's Cretan, but I think they drain the swamps and privies for it. Well—it warms, though, it warms."

Eyes now adjusted to the dim and varied light, Lucius noticed the thumping limp of his new friend and looked down. Talo's right leg ended just below the knee, where a shallow metal cup held the terminating flesh. Below that was a dark pike or post, ending in another inverted cup.

"It's me old *gladius*. The boys of the XXth—that would be Agricola's XXth—they were a sentimental lot. Had the *ferreus* there refashion it into this fancy cup and leg pole. Even a stone in here from our camp at Inchtuthill. Swear I can still feel the cold from that dreary place" Talo winked a black eye. "Can't complain 'bout the sturdiness." He stomped and laughed. "And it's fireproof!"

The older soldier's meaty palm slapped Lucius' back, "Now let's trade, good Lucius: you give me your stories of the North, the borders, and those Germans of yours, and I'll curdle your guts with tales of blue tattoos and wild swordwomen in chariots."

Lucius felt his face, his shoulders, and all the muscles of his body relax in the open-heartedness and cheer of this new comrade. Thoughts of the dead Iace and of Livilla in danger did not disappear, but they receded—powerful shades to be re-engaged on the morrow. The simple warmth of this bluff ex-legionary soothed his battered spirit. Perhaps—after enough bowls of wine and improbable exaggerations. Perhaps he could rest tonight.

Iace was lost. But he would find Livilla. And Baractes. Oh, most definitely Baractes.

XXI

"Ho, there! What's this?"

A broad dark face split by a massive nose and punctuated with glinting black eyes peered under the wagon at Iace.

"I've seen your like before, fellow, but not beyond the cold mists of Brittania. One of your cousins took off the wrist of our *primus pilus*."

"Hmmm...What would be your name, *pugnaces*?" The man rubbed his squared chin, "Herakles? Those shoulders could bear the world on them. No? Brutus, perhaps?"

"No. Your eyes are too filled with the sadness of life, *canis mi amice*."

"Ah, I have it!" He slapped his own substantial thigh, "Fido—the faithful one—Yes, fits you well! A trueheart if I ever saw one beat."

"*Ave*, Fido." Talo bowed and cross-fisted his chest in salute, "I am Talo."

Iace rolled up from his side. He staggered out from under the cart where he'd slept the night, thick tail swaying back and forth.

"Rough night, Fido?" With no further word, the post-legged man bent over, wrapped his arms under the enormous dog and effortlessly lifted him into the small wooden bed of his *cisium* wagon, behind the strongbox attached to the frame of the cart.

"There now, *canis bonum*. You'll ride up here with the mails. Old Rufus won't mind."

At the sound of his name, the red draught horse whinnied.

Canis Bonum, GOOD DOG. GOOD SMELL MAN. STRONG MAN. DOG TIRED.

As Talo turned toward the horse, Iace's head tracked the old soldier's movements and lashed out his tongue, successfully swiping the big man's cheek.

"Right you are, dog. No baths here. But now only the one side is clean." Talo stooped and bent over the dog, exposing his other cheek to Iace's ministrations and simultaneously scratching the canine's ears, which were even darker than his own.

Iace did not disappoint as his prodigious tongue washed across the mailman's face.

"Clean and ready for the day we are!" After a final pat, the old soldier stepped away and began to unhobble his horse.

Curses and the sound of breaking crockery wafted from inside the *caupona*. This was followed by a high-pitched chittering noise Iace had not heard before. Thin brown furry arms and legs clambered up Talo's side.

"Oh! Pluto and Dis! I almost forgot our expedition leader!" The mailman turned his head and looked with a solemn eye at the monkey now perched on the broad ledge of his left shoulder.

Rufus waited in full repose as Talo informed Iace, "This, good Fido, is my partner Artemidorus. He is in charge of eating our maps, fouling himself, and frightening sleepy tavern keepers —all of which are activities at which he excels!"

Artemidorus lept from Talo's shoulder to the back of the cart's bench seat. He seemed to notice Iace for the first time. Canting his head to one side, the monkey stretched out a long finger, a finger that proceeded to explore first the top, then the underside, then the interior of Iace's left ear.

MAN? HAIRY LITTLE MAN? NO.

DOG? NO?

COOL LIKE MAN. TOUCH LIKE MAN. MEAT SMELL.

BITE? NO—BIG GOOD MAN—FRIEND? NO FEAR. NO BITE.

EAR SCRATCH. GOOD LITTLE NO-MAN.

HAH! DOG PLAY LITTLE NO-MAN! HAH!

Iace lay still during this exploration, eyes half-closed, filling the wagon's shallow bed that he stretched across. But as the monkey began to reach down with his other hand, perhaps to explore both ears at once, Iace lunged up with such speed and force that the wagon rocked and even the placid Rufus started.

Artemidorus was taken thoroughly unawares; his concentration had been focused on his journey of discovery through the strange new world of Iace's ears. And so the mastiff engulfed the little simian's head in his cavernous mouth, closing his jaws just enough and for just long enough that the monkey's entire hairy cranium was trapped during its initial reflexive pull backwards.

As startled as his tiny companion, Talo reacted with a loud "Hunh!" By the time the big Numidian hoisted himself up into the cart, Iace had already released the spindly little imp, who immediately jumped onto the top of his master's shaven head, screaming and jabbering monkey imprecations.

Talo's long-fingered left hand cupped most of the monkey's side in comfort and support. He spoke in a soft croon, "Not many crawl from the mouth of Cerberus and tell the talk, friend ape. Best mind your manners. Come down now, lad." The man's dark eyes filled with mirth as they slanted over to share the jest with the great dog panting nonchalantly behind him.

It took a few moments of pulling, then stroking accompanied by verbal blandishments, for Talo to move the terrified Artemidorus back to his shoulder. And the small monkey was none too pleased after Rufus was hitched and Talo foolishly climbed up on the cart alongside the monster that had swallowed him.

Loose reins held in one hand, Artemidorus hanging from his left shoulder—as far away from the monkey-eating devil as he could get and stay on the cart—Talo glanced back at the relaxed dog reclining behind him. His eyes crinkled and shone and he briefly rested a broad hand on Iace's softly panting side.

"Well, friends...Back to Rome we go." He shook the reins and Rufus moved off at a slow trot, "Till we reach the *Porta Collina*... then it's straight up to Reate on the *Via Salaria*. Our letters may not be urgent, *amici*, but they buy the bread and the wine."

Artemidorus glared at his latest nemesis around the safety of his master's neck and chattered insults. In idle response, Iace lowered his muzzle onto his outstretched forepaws as the cart rocked up the

Via Tiburtina and the morning sun beat down in soft massage. His muscles and bones—tested and strained so long in the stone pits of Tibur—uncorded as he rode beside this honest man on this pleasant day. But to Iace, the hay by the roadside was the scent of a musty stable in Rome, the bright flowers along the ditch were the smell in a girl's hair, and the clanking shushs of the wheels turning below them were a Picentine accent reciting bad poetry.

XXII

Lucius woke with a head the size of the amphora he'd shared with Talo the night before. Except the amphora resting on his neck kept swelling and shrinking, each expansion and contraction providing exquisite pain.

"If he hadn't told me he was a centurion, I'd have known it by the way the man drank. *Juno Acieiorum!*" The young man stumbled outside, registering from the corner of his eye that his borrowed horse was still *in situ*, then thrust his head into the cool water of the animal trough.

Dripping and shaking water from his ears, he staggered back inside, to be greeted by the grinning publican and a bowl of browned specks. He frowned at the "beans," but accepted them, and called for wine, which he watered thoroughly.

By the third hour, he was back on the road to Rome. Half his attention was bent toward hurrying the stable-spoiled pony and half to musing about his next moves.

Baractes. Baractes? How did that oaf get the wherewithal to buy an *insula*? To bribe imperial quarrymen? Slaves, yes, but imperial slaves. Where did he come by the idea for such a scheme?

In Lucius' experience, Baractes notion of deep thought was remembering which *popinas* still served him wine on credit. The Illyrian hulk's actions came most often from the needs of his gut or the desires of his loins—no forethought apparent past where the next amphora of wine or the next leggy woman might be located.

His mind refocused on the girl.

Little Livilla. Could that brute see her as a woman?

Why hadn't that trollop mother of hers told me more?

I could try to find Titus. He'd landed those fabulous jobs cleaning gore from the sand for me and sister's husband, Baractes. He'd surely know where his sister is, if not his brother-in-law. But I've no better notion where he is than an Etruscan madman. And, if found, he might not be forthcoming about family whereabouts.

The Amphitheater. That's the place to start. Sporinus will know something. His skinny fingers are in everyone's stew. He'll talk for silver.

And if not for silver, then for steel.

Lucius tossed down three coins on the greasy counter and stepped outside. The old slave was absent, so he unhobbled his pony himself and mounted.

"Come, Pegasus, let's fly now. You'll have your home oats by the first watch of the night. Then I'll find our little girl and perhaps, too, that ill-favored panderer."

XXIII

Angled shafts of dim light filtered through sand and boards onto Baractes tangled hair and the dark forbidding path he walked, revealing glimpses of Erebus—Hades on Earth.

A glint of deep yellow reflected from behind rough bars of forged iron—the rarest of killer cats from the east lurked there. The size of a lion, but striped in deep oranges and blacks, and flashes of white. No common killing creature, this animal was saved for the Emperor's most delicate whims. A smile faced with toothy daggers, a growling roar that froze bones with its stealthy anger, not like the lion's simple challenge, this sound roiled with raw hunger and pride. This was the sound of darkest death, of a stolen soul consumed by fear and lust for the kill.

Baractes raked his short blade, his *sica*, against the bars of the tiger's cage. "Nahhh!" he slurred, "You filthy dog eater. Bite your own mother! No food from me."

He pressed the stiff leather that covered his half-hand flat against the cage, then stumped down the narrow aisle.

The gloom deepened, but he knew this path well and was near his destination.

He stepped unafraid past cages of bears, hyenas, and lions, but the big Illyrian moved to the middle of the aisle as he whispered by the leopard cages.

On his right side, huddled at the backs of the smallest enclosures, were human smells of anguish, terror, and resignation. Flashes of a bone-white leg, a heavily scarred brown arm, and a shattered hairless face gaping in silent horror were all ignored equally by Baractes.

"Water. Please, water."

"My child is dead. Help me. He's dead. He's dead."

"...there was no reason for it, no reason...I told them everything...I told them...there was no reason...no reason...no reason..."

He'd seen and smelled and heard such and the like too many times. From both sides of the bars.

His first time in the *Hypogeum* was in one of these cages. He'd shared it with two of his brothers and several cousins. The arena was fresh built and it was Titus' playground then, the last *Ludi Romani* held for Vespasian's golden successor. Yes, Baractes knew the feel of these walls. The taste of the brown water that trickled from the serving pipe, a taste that never lost its flavor of excrement. A flavor even the deadliest thirst did not overmatch.

He pulled the flat leather *congium* from under his belt and wet his throat with cheap wine.

He'd been the only survivor of his clan that day. After three rounds against beasts—he'd lost a sister to a great bull, one cousin was mauled to death, and two others were dispatched by the Nubian cleanup crew—the finale was a match of his barbarian family members against each other.

Baractes gutted two of his cousins with a *sica* such as the one he held now. Grestac, his mother's brother's son, cursed and spit blood in Baractes' face as he died. They'd had their first women together.

Then he'd strangled his youngest brother with a *retarius'* net.

The crowd was ecstatic. He'd been manumitted on the spot by the Emperor himself. Then enlisted in the XIVth Twin Legion as a free man.

He reached the center of this underground world. The strands of creeping light from the dusk above were almost gone. Taking a final pull from the *congium*, he smashed it to the dusty, chalky floor, then snatched a torch from a wall sconce and lit it from a nearby brazier.

The smoky flickers from the torchlight conjured a constantly changing madness of shadows on the arches, cages, and walls.

All around him, eyes reflected back the light in liquid whites and yellows.

Baractes saw none of this.

With an incongruous delicacy, he picked his way through

the machinery and controls of the central *Hypogeum*, until he faced the last cage.

"Honey buns, Daddy's home." He whistled softly through the bars.

XXIV

BRANG. THUNK. Snop. Thud. Thud. Thud. Brang.

The bent bronze shafts springing Talo's seat groaned and sang. Iace reclined on the payload bench that lay directly over the axles, and so he was constantly jostled, sometimes airborne, as the little *cisium* cart of the *cursus publicus* bounced up the cobblestones on the ancient path.

The sun hung a thumb's width above the great umbrella pine rising to their right, back beyond Tibur—the way they'd come.

The burly, dark-skinned cart driver would have looked more natural sporting a plumed soldier's helm than wearing the leather tricorn *petanus* of an imperial mailman. Talo's spindly man-mocking monkey clung to his bulging shoulder, well out of reach of the giant lemon-brown dog. The travelers were on their way through the *ager Servii Tullii*, the field of Servius Tullius, which extended outside the great wall that legendary king had erected around the outer edge of his city.

Shoddy tenements filled in the space on their right. Well outside the *pomerium*, the sacred border of Rome within which no citizen could bear arms, these hasty, ill-built structures sported narrow porticoes under dangerously extended awnings of colored linen. Stuffed under this shade, vendors spread an immense array of foodstuffs: bundles of dormice hung braided by their tails; mounds of clams, snails, ducks, fig-peckers, apples, quinces, lemons, and doves crowded makeshift tables. Cranes, geese, chicken, and hares were displayed strung up by their necks.

Iace's head lifted. Drops of ropey drool fell onto Talo's bare thigh.

"My stomach rumbles too, *amicus*. Not the place to stop for a feast, though," Strong hands shook the reins and the old soldier clicked at Rufus.

Beckoning temptations did not end with the food. In every third arch, a brightly clad and even more brightly painted woman lounged and smiled—or gestured in some more obvious way. On each corner, open doorways revealed benches and tables and patrons with jugs or bowls of wine.

Talo informed his companions as the cart clopped along. "Best to keep with the ridge, lest the sands cover our heads, amici. Praetorians are always spoiling for a fight."

"Another mile and we'll have passed their *castrum*," he added, eyes rigidly forward.

The ladies at the corners continued their attempts to attract the notice of the large, dark, mailman, but no soldiers emerged from the *cauponae* or *stabula* or marched down the *Via Principalis* from the *castrum* of the Emperor's Praetorian Guard.

The four companions rolled on unaccosted.

The wall to their left ended in a wide, looming structure. The road they were on, though in good repair, was narrow. It doubled its width as it passed the northeastern corner of the Servian Wall, Rome's primary defense line. Another major track, larger than their current course but not as broad as the one extending northward, forked to the northeast.

"That's ours, friends," Talo informed the company, pointing to the smaller course on the right, "the *Via Nomentana*. By Hercules, it goes bloody nowhere." The big man sighed and slapped the top of the worn *armarium* strongbox,"But delivering letters to out-of-favor senators exiled to their *latifundia* beats stabbing blue-painted men in the cold north—or sleeping with their women either, for that matter." A bright smile popped from his mouth.

The cart neared the egress through the defensive wall, the

Porta Collina, and the northeastern gate rose to their left. Across from the gate, on the right of their current path, stood an impressive temple of veined pink-and-white marble. No pitted rock from the Tibur quarry here. Polished alabaster facings magnified rosy tints on the skin of outdoor devotees, and the reflection of the sun's rays on the gold-threaded marble walls cast a rich glow. Male and female attendants smiled and raised their hands to Talo as the cart jostled past.

The ex-legionary nodded and grimaced, but did not stop, "Temple of Venus Erycina," he rumbled and adjusted his seat and *tunica* on the cart bench, "No time and no more talk of that."

STRONG MAN SMELL. MOUNT DOG SMELL? NO DOG HERE.

STRONG MAN ANGRY? STRONG MAN FEAR?

Iace sensed a change in his new friend and sat upright on the hard boards.

Another building faced the shiny temple of Venus, huddling under the great wall on the near side of the *Porta Collina*. Or perhaps it had been a building. Not much more than a few pillars, what might have been an altar stone and the cross pieces of a portico. Iace's nose and ears twitched at the two black cats reclining symmetrically on either side of the largest recumbent stone.

Talo pulled up the reins and halted the cart.

The big man thrust a long index finger into his mouth, then removed the moistened digit and rubbed the spittle behind his ear.

He twisted toward Iace, who sat up in the back of the cart, "By Mercury, I don't believe this, dog, but I've been told it works whether you believe it or not." He gestured with the same finger toward the ruined temple and the cats below, "That's the Official Good Luck Temple of the Roman People, friend Fido—*Fortuna Publica Populi Romani*. Same old king built it what built this wall. And *he* was one lucky fellow."

The two cats stood up together as if in a dance, stretched, and darted off in opposite directions.

SHARP PAW SMELL. LITTLE SHARP PAWS?

STRONG MAN NOT RUN. STRONG MAN NOT FEAR SHARP PAW? LITTLE SHARP PAWS RUN.

DOG STAY. REST.

Talo shook the reins and navigated the cart through the intersection and up the *Via Nomentana*, away from Rome and into the Italian hinterlands.

XXV

The same unease he felt before a battle stirred his belly and prickled the hairs of his neck as Lucius approached the hulking enormity of the great Amphitheater. He passed the Emperor's palace on his left, up the Palatine. The last sunshine lit the crown of the Colossus, the enormous golden statue of Helios, or Nero or whoever they were calling it this week, stood sentinel up there. Looming beyond, and barely recognizable in the swiftly descending darkness of early winter, the overwhelming size of the shadowy structure humbled and oppressed him. Cold-eyed and steady-handed, he'd faced swords and screaming murderers in Germania, but Lucius shook his shoulders and head to free himself of the little defeats signified by this bundle-of-the-past. There was no room for sadness, only anger for fuel, and urgency for purpose. Livilla. poor Iace. And—not to be forgotten—Baractes.

He was on foot, having dropped off the old pony at the *domus* of the *gens* Corelli. To Lucius' disgruntled amusement, their house master was surprised at the return.

Now it was time to come back here, the last place he'd ever wanted to see again.

First: to find Quintus Sporinus, his former employer and chief factor of the Emperor's arena. Sporinus would know something of Baractes. That old spider's webs stuck to most of those who'd worked in this house of pain.

Unconsciously holding his breath as he entered through Gate LXV, Lucius turned east, searching for the semi-hidden panel covering the small vestibule in the inner wall where Sporinus counted his coin before it was removed to the temple of Jupiter each evening. Past Minerva Locres, two statues of Castor and Pollux, a startling cast of Hercules pierced by one of the Stymphalian Bird's iron feathers, three nameless heroes—Heruli by their garb. There. Between a Romulus and a Scipio

Africanus Minor, the latter's foot upon a dying Carthaginian bowman.

Even in the dimming light, it was clear the panel was ajar.

Lucius slowed and edged around the opening.

There was a good deal of blood on the floor. Near the door, a pool of red with a dead slave lying face-down in it, arms outstretched, a wooden cudgel not far from his right hand.

Lucius bent, retrieved the club, and slid it into his empty scabbard.

In front of him, at the back of the vestibule, Quintus Sporinus' bald head slumped on the proscenium desk. His face lay flat on an open scroll; he appeared to be standing, leaning against the desk. In the quiet of the enclosed space, Lucius could hear a dull drip-drip sound; brief inspection identified thick blood falling from the edge of the table to the mosaic floor and matched his vivid memory of fresh bloodsmell.

Sporinus' muffled voice drifted across to him, as if from another world. The man had not lifted his head.

"Marcus could read Greek, did you know?" The voice creaked. "Not very useful here, but he was a gentle lad." It added.

"No more Greek for him." Sporinus coughed blood from his thin lips, "Nor none for me, neither." A dry hack followed that might have been a laugh.

Lucius curled around the edge of the desk and supported Sporinus' emaciated body to a seated position on the floor, back to the wall. A steady drool of blood dribbled from the corner of his mouth and down his chin.

"Ho...the Picentine lad...Mucius? No...Lucius. Ha."

"Who..." Lucius began to ask.

"Who else? Baractes, that Prince of Toads. You know him, don't you, country lad? Smelly...sheep-lover." Sporinus' bloody gurgle turned into a racking cough. Lucius held his thin body upright until the fit subsided. There was little life left in him.

Lucius pulled the small man's ratty toga apart at the breast, revealing a ragged wound.

Sporinus shook his head, as if to dissuade Lucius from further examination, "Neat bit of blade work there with poor Marcus. Course he is an Illyrian, so I'd expect him to know his way around a *sica*. I think he caught my spleen."

"Why?" Lucius began again.

"Hoi...why, indeed." Sporinus raised faded, rheumy eyes of blue and yellow to look into Lucius' face for the first time. "You're a poet, I understand."

Lucius inclined his head.

Sporinus' filming eyes roamed over Lucius' boiled leather cuirass, the rest of his legionary dress. He expelled a deeper breath, forming small sudsy bubbles of blood around his lips.

"A soldier." The croak of a laugh came again, then a little light crept into those wasted, weary eyes. "Perhaps," he said, "perhaps." Another breath: each one weaker than the one before.

The dying man shrugged his shoulders, "It's the woman, isn't it?"

Lucius stiffened, "A woman? A girl?"

"Yes, a girl." Sporinus sighed. "I told the lout 'no.' Then he went mad with that little blade of his. We'd had...well, he'd been a good factor...good business. Fool...for a girl..."

"Where?" With less care than urgency, Lucius shook the old man.

"Center pit...beasts...fool...for a girl..."

A final spasm squeezed the life and a few last drops of pink foam from the well-used body of Quintus Sporinus, chief factor of the Flavian Amphitheater.

Dropping the old man's corpse to the floor more gently than his past deserved, Lucius sprinted out of the vestibule, heading for the depths of the *Hypogeum*, the dark, hidden world beneath the arena.

XXVI

Talo was in no hurry. The *cursus publicus*, his cart, and his animal confederates rolled and bounced up the emptiness of the *Via Nomentana*.

"Something to be said for 'nowhere,' eh, *amici*?" Talo swiveled his bald pate around, flared his nostrils full of pine and rosemary scented air. He reached blindly behind and stroked Iace's wide forehead. The dog closed his dark eyes and exhaled.

Evening was settling in around them. Tree shadows, some fat, some spindly, lengthened across their path; they rolled and creaked through the soft pattern of shadow bars.

"If I had my cithara, I'd sing." Talo offered.

Instead, he started humming—with no words but with considerable vigor—in his deep voice. Iace settled down on the board behind the *cisium*'s strongbox. The cobbles of the *Via Nomentana* were smoother and more closely laid than the old stones paving the path up the *ager Servii Tulii*, so he did not bounce with every turn of the wheels. He was still tired deep as his bones, though; all his muscles still ached. He was tired from the endless toil of months at the quarry. Tired from his search after his escape. Though his name and theirs were lost to him, he was tired most of all from the long heartache of losing Livilla and Lucius. The sounds this new friend made soothed him, in many ways as Livilla's voice soothed. But the balm of the human noises also triggered memories of the voices that directed and gave meaning to his earlier life.

Iace's head raised and he woke as Talo's humming stopped in mid-breath.

"Jupiter's Beard!"

Big hands shook the reins and Rufus picked up his pace to a slow trot.

Moments later, Talo looped the lead leathers over the beak of the *armarium*, planted his left hand on the riding bench, and vaulted down to the side of the road.

The metal cup at the end of his left leg rang dully as it struck the pavers and scraped forward, but Talo ignored the pain and hobbled briskly into the ditch where another mail cart—identical to his own—lay on its side, the breeze turning the wheels a notch one way then the other.

"*Ave? Ave!*" Talo boomed out, hands fanned on either side of his mouth.

A short, thin, red-tunicked man emerged from the far side of the wrecked cart. The crown of his head reached to Talo's chin, and where Artemidorus' master was colored in ebons and ambers, this man was palest creams topped with orange.

"*Ave* yourself!" The other man responded, with no great warmth. He stepped squarely up in front of Talo, looked up at the far larger man, and appraised him as he might have his only daughter's first male caller.

"Umm...s'pose you're *some* luck. Mailman, I see. Well, help me get the *armarium* down." With no further words, he turned his back and started to climb onto the fallen cart.

But the man came close enough for Talo to take matters into his own capable hands. Before the other mailman ascended one rung of the cart ladder, Talo's right hand grasped him by the shoulder and turned him around again.

"*Ave, amicus!*" The bright grin returned to light the dusky face, "Talo's the name. And yours would be?"

For several moments, the stranger's features shifted colors. Just as the high pink color of rage drained and a more-normal fish-belly white was returning, Artemidorus—who had hopped off Talo's shoulder even faster than Talo had jumped down to the road and who had remained since on the *cisium*'s bench—leapt through the air and landed on another of his favorite perches, the top of Talo's smooth head.

"Gahh!" The stick-figure man cringed backwards, thrusting his hands in front of him. Artemidorus capered up and down on the smooth round skin of Talo's baldness, chittering and waving his arms. "Pluto and the Penates! What demon rides you?" The pale stranger gasped.

Talo pulled the monkey down and held its paw as he dropped it to the ground, "My travelling companion." Talo bowed to the tiny simian clinging to two of his fingers: "Artemidorus: meet..." Talo swept his hand to encompass the scowling stumbler before them.

"errr...Metellus...Quintus Sextus Metellus Tertullius."

"Ah, Artemidorus, we've royalty here—a *Metellus*, eh? Complete with cognomen." Talo winked broadly at the monkey and bowed to the man in front of him.

"It's a large family." Metellus sniffed.

"So I've heard."

After a brief silence, Metellus sniffed again and continued, "I have vital papers in the *cisium* box. As a member of the *cursus publicus*, I charge you, in the name of the Emperor, to bring these forthwith to the Magistrate of the Treasury. They are timely and of great import." As he spoke, Quintus Sextus Metellus Tertullius drew himself up straight and his eyes seemed to focus just beyond the end of his long nose.

"'Great import,' 'Magistrate of the Treasury,' is it?" Talo repeated with earnest solemnity.

Then he slapped his thigh and laughed. "Tell you what, friend Metellus. I'll help you right your wagon here, then I'll give you a pull at my wineskin, and *then*. I'll be on my way. *I've* got 'papers of great import' to be delivered, too—to the pig-keepers up the hill. Hah!"

Talo started to move toward the overturned cart, to make good on his pledge. Before he'd gotten halfway, Metellus scurried around the draught pole (and his mule, which was placidly munching dry grass in the ditch), clapped his hand on Talo's shoulder, and hoarsely admonished in a throaty whisper, "No, no—these papers *are* of great importance." He crawled up to the top of the overturned cart, pulled a large iron key off his belt hook, opened the *armarium*, and handed down a scroll to the big Numidian.

Talo glanced at the parchment roll in his hand and whistled. "The Emperor's seal."

Metellus nodded so vigorously that the cart on which he still perched creaked in warning.

"All right, all right. I'll take the lot. The Praefectus of Nomentum can wait for his hog count, I suppose." Talo stepped over and accepted the small leather bucket of documents Metellus handed down to him. His smile became a sigh. "Magistrate of the Treasury, you say? I suppose that'll be at the Temple of Jupiter Optimus Maximus?"

Metellus bobbed his head, "Marcellus Crispus Ammianus or his clerk Pertinax."

"Right. Some purple-striped senatorial ponce or his pet Greek *pedisecus*." Talo nodded and ignored the returning scowl on Metellus' delicate features. "You want help turning this rig right-side up?"

Metellus raised a pale eyebrow. "I'll send boys from the nearest *mutatio* to handle that. Those papers are, as I said, *timely*, Mailman Talo. And they are now in *your* charge."

With no further comment, Talo climbed back up into his cart, patting Iace's brow as he settled into his seat, and pulled the reins on Rufus, executing a neat turn back toward Rome.

Not far down the road, his right hand resting on Iace's wide flank, the skin around Talo's eyes crinkled as he murmured, "Don't suppose our friend Sextus Metellus has often been up this way. Don't expect he knows our ever-frugal Emperor has closed down all the *mutationes* and *mansiones* between the *Porta Collina* and Reate? Ah, but it's a pleasant evening and he's got a mule to ride. No matter how sleepy and hungry he might get." He riffled the reins and grinned, "Step a leg, Rufus, we've *important* papers today."

XXVII

Lucius had never ventured much into this area of the underworld of the Emperor's Amphitheater, even though he'd worked above it for over a year. Even though he'd pulled the meat wagon back and forth to the *Spoliarium* more times than he could count—the *Spoliarium*, which should have been a more dreadful place than this. But there it was only the bodies of the dead. Sometimes the near dead, but they never remained in that state for long. It had been much like working for a butcher. Though a poet, Lucius was country bred and not easily made squeamish by the dismemberment of non-living bodies.

But the *Hypogeum* was a different matter. It was full of life. Life of a sort that made death a comfort. Baractes, and even Titus, made fun of him for not taking advantage of his position to assess the competition in the pits below and then bet "intelligently" on the *Ludi*.

Thinking of the wretches that waited here, he could not even watch the games. How could he stroll through this obscene pit of hate and fear and desperation and *make odds*.

Lucius the Picentine lad ran down these dark corridors, shrinking from these walls and bars that trembled from shared nightmares; he tried to stop his nostrils from breathing, his eyes from seeing, and his ears from hearing. Then thoughts of Livilla and Baractes brought another Lucius into the same running body, the soldier created on the picket lines of Germania Superior, the one who could thrust a Roman *gladius* under an enemy's sternum and touch a human heart with steel death.

Both these men ran through the darkness, green-hazel eyes lit with fear as great as any who stared out from the cages they ran past. Both these souls knew the sort of man Baractes was. That Baractes had become. This new Baractes was driven by grand desires and hard perversions. Caution no longer moderated his path.

This brute had Livilla. Somewhere in this worst place in all the Roman world, he had Livilla.

The two Luciuses reunited as they ran, fear and anger pounding through their heart.

XXVIII

The sand around her was smooth and clean. The marble seats above her, the Emperor's box that loomed behind, were empty. The sun was down beyond the stands on her right and, since she now wore only a thin *tunica* and no *palla*, her arms felt the chill of the evening. Her beautiful blue woolen *palla*. It was the last thing she saw before Baractes and his men dragged her, screaming and biting and kicking, into the street and stuffed her into a thick sack chained to their cart bed. Her *palla* fell in the muck of the gutter and Livilla stopped her screaming for a moment at the shock of seeing Baractes' studded caliga slide down on it, ripping holes that instantly filled with brown goo.

The time that passed until the wagon stopped was a blur of curses, threats, and rough hands gripping her through the sackcloth. Then her bag was unshackled and she was carried blind as she shouted "*Adiute*, Help!" When she was pulled out, she was in a dungeon. The smell and sounds of the place were unbearable, even for someone born and bred in the lower end of the Subura. In the constant gloom, she slept little, for unknown lengths of time. Baractes seemed to always be there when she woke. Ever drunk, he made lewd proposals to her, suggested things she did not even understand but that made her belly tighten in disgust and her mind reel in fear.

He'd never opened the cage. He'd never touched her after the first day.

Until tonight. He'd threatened her as was his habit, telling her in one breath of the love that burned in him and then of all the vile things he would do to her. Then he'd opened the cage, pulled her onto a strange platform that rose through the air into this empty place of horror and death. The wooden cross waited for her. He'd shackled her here, and then returned below, laughing and mumbling to himself.

Reverie over, these recent episodes did not concern Livilla. Nor did she have any interest in the place she was in—a place she'd never visited as a spectator; she'd been too young, a female, and had no liking for blood sports—except in how she could escape from it.

She considered her partners, Aristopolus and Maenax, of the tiny shop on the *Vicus Librarius* that her *armarium* silver had funded. Aristopolus had just bought his contract out and was a *liberto*, a freed man. She'd seen him only days before and the light in his face was a wonder. He'd tried to kiss the hem of her *palla*—the one that lay torn and besmirched now in the gutter. She'd laughed. Maenax laughed. He'd been freed by a grateful master years before, but had fallen on hard times until Aristopolus—a distant cousin—pulled him, drunken and filthy, out of Livia's vile *popina*. Now the three of them had one of the smallest copy shops in Rome, but one with a growing reputation and a solid client list. Livilla's investment had done well.

She laughed out loud, hard enough to rattle the chains that secured her wrist manacles to the small wooden crosspiece. Ari and Maenax would wonder what had become of their benefactor, but one must ride the tide the Fates stirred. They would be fine, even better off. Perhaps they'd dedicate a *Lares* or a Greek shrine to her.

Of course, the shop, the money, the freedom she thought she'd bought herself—all of it was because of the great yellow-brown dog. Her Iace. Pins of heat gathered around her eyes, up her spine, even warming her chilled arms. Where had he gone? Who took him? Her poor *canelillo* Iace.

Anger rose and took the place of sadness. It was all Lucius' fault! How dare he leave them so, she thought for the thousandth time. That worthless, rhyme-spewing wretch. *He'd* always maintained Iace was *his*! How could he leave the dog like that? How could he...how could he...how could he leave *them*?

For an instant, Juno-brown eyes wavered as she looked over the empty arena floor where multitudes of others—weak and strong—had fallen. Long black hair curled in and down as her head bowed. Then fire crackled deep in the brown, her head bobbed up, her jaw set. Her mind turned over catalogs of heroic escapes. She *would* be free. Tears of bitterness and resolution fell on the sands that covered countless other victims.

XXIX

The sun set beyond the Caelian Hill off to their right, as the horse Rufus, the wagon, and the three companions rumbled in the cart down the broad back of the Esquiline.

They rolled through yet another sculpture garden. Massive clay elephants (Iace growled at these—he had seen their like crush two dogs in the pit at Tibur), godlings, nymphs, goddesses, flying horses, sea serpents, Gorgons, Chimerae were frozen in stately dignity as the mail crew clomped past.

Talo was unimpressed. Occasionally, he'd spit green juice at one of the statues if they rode close enough to give him an opportunity for a direct hit.

"Dead gods, dead people, creatures what never lived except in some dreamer's drunken fears." He expectorated at a seven-headed hydra the size of a small trireme. "Men want heroes and monsters. Artists have to eat." He spat again, catching the hydra on its center brow.

More statues and more followed. Iace dozed. His travels with Livilla, Glaubus, and Lucius never brought him this far past the city center.

With no preamble, Talo halted Rufus, dropped the reins, and climbed off the *cisium*.

Iace jumped down behind him as the Numidian examined an almost nude marble man. The statue was semi-reclining, a

Celtic or Germanic torc around his neck. He leaned on one hand, which rested on the ground near a large sword.

Talo's dark hand merged with the twilight shadows as he placed it on the shoulder of this fallen, bright marble warrior.

"Eheu! That sculptor knew his business, friend dog. See how the wound angles so." Talo motioned with his hands, "That shows this fellow here has both his spleen and his lung punctured. No wonder he dropped his sword!" Talo leaned over for a closer look, "One of those damn ox-butchering blades. Great for show when you jump screaming out of a bush, but I'll take our trusty little *gladius* any day."

SMELL.

SMELL...WATER-MAN?   COOL-HAND   WATER-MAN?   WHERE WATER-MAN?

DOG FIND.

FIND SOFT-HAND SWEET-SMELL GIRL.

DOG RUN.

Talo let out a heavy breath, patted the white shoulder of the statue, and climbed back in the wagon.

"They'll be no excuses taken from such as we're to deliver to tonight, *canis amicus*. These types are born with a *pilum* up their bum." He shook Rufus' reins and looked down at Iace, who'd remained on the ground, "Need to stretch after the ride, do you? Keeping your fighting weight—very smart, Fido."

The Numidian clicked his tongue and Iace ran alongside as the cart moved apace down the *Via Tiburtina* into the eastern edge of the Subura.

XXX

The torches ahead were bright. Closing his ears to the moans and entreaties, Lucius plunged forward, into the darkest heart, the central command point from where the living were served up to die for the pleasure of the cruel.

Unlike the holding cells of the *Hypogeum*, this chamber's

walls rose high. So high, the barrel-vaulted ceiling was lost in shadows the torches could not illumine. Cage doors lined the walls. In the vast middle span of the floor were enormous cogs, giant wooden levers, and huge coils of rope. These workings reminded Lucius of the siege engines he'd watched the engineers construct outside Mogontiacum.

But that idle memory vanished when he saw the large man at the far end of the chamber whose long stringy hair waved across his back as he worked some machinery attached to the far wall.

"Baractes!" Lucius did not shout, but his anger forced the word from him when stealth would have served better.

Baractes' head whipped around. Even from this distance, Lucius could see the changes in the man. His eyes were wide, bloodshot. But his forehead was smooth with the lack of care felt only by the innocent and the mad.

A dull streaked line split his lips as Baractes smiled. "Where'd you get that costume, poet? Rob a dead soldier?" The big man walked forward confidently.

Hands by his sides, holding the cudgel he'd recovered in Sporinus' office, Lucius was silent and still.

"Hoi! And I thought you'd be glad to see your old *amicus*." Baractes continued closing the space between them. "Your little girlfriend was glad enough to make up for lost time." Baractes shimmied his head and shoulders, "She's a wild one, she is. No wonder you took up with her." The smile stabbed across the distance, "Of course, now things are different and she's got a real man."

"Where is Livilla?" Lucius' entire body vibrated with anger.

"Oh. Yes. Well, she's waiting for me upstairs." Baractes stopped ten paces from Lucius. He put his hands on his sides and laughed. "I've got a surprise for her. A BIG surprise." He made a rude gesture and laughed again. "If you're a good little legionary, I'll let you watch."

Wordless and planless, Lucius launched himself at Baractes.

Quicker than his bulk would have suggested possible, the experienced gladiator side-stepped the young man's charge, slid behind Lucius and hugged him, pinning Lucius' chest and arms with his own arms, thick with corded muscle.

"Always wondered if there was anything but watered Picentine cabbage in your veins, boy." Baractes hissed in Lucius' ear. "Hunhh…you've gained some meat since I last trounced you." Baractes huffed as Lucius struggled.

"You're too much a handful now, guess I'll have to truss you up while I take my pleasure with the little slut."

The senseless fury of Lucius-the-poet transformed into the cold, calculating anger of Lucius the veteran warrior. The close red tinge of terror widened into stark greys and blacks. He smelled his own sweat of fear and, now, that same acid scent from his opponent.

His booted right foot drove down on Baractes' sandal. The big man bellowed; Lucius followed by smashing elbows back into the Illyrians' ribs. Baractes' arms loosened and Lucius sidled out from under them. He darted forward and spun to face his foe.

Baractes was no more than six boot-lengths away, but his breaths were coming fast and deep; his shoulders slumped, his gloved and ruined left hand rubbed the lower ribs of his right side. His eyes stayed fast on Lucius, eyes as full of wordless hate as any of the primeval killers behind the bars of the cages around them.

Lucius watched for an opening, grip firm on his small cudgel. He'd learned how to kill, but Baractes was a killer too. And the Illyrian was far stronger—even than the newly forged Lucius. His mind raced through options: Groin? Solar plexus? Neck? He dismissed each of these points of attack as quickly as they occurred to him. The temple? Yes, it must be a blow to the head.

He crouched, ready to feint first with a kick and then follow with his left fist before making the finishing move with his club.

When Lucius raised his hands, Baractes seemed to notice the cudgel for the first time. Wild brows rose and plump lips puckered. His blood-rimmed eyes narrowed into focus. He reached across his torso with his gloved hand and pulled up the hem of his filthy *tunica*, baring a thick, dirt-encrusted thigh. He slid a long, curved knife from a leather sheath concealed there. Lucius could make out irregular-shaped rusty stains along its wicked edge.

"I slaughtered many sheep with this when I was no bigger than you, poet." Baractes let his hem fall, then crouched crab-like, moving both his hands in slow small circles. "This should be much the same." He sprang forward, the scythe-like *sica* rising then falling in a blow meant to cleave Lucius' where his neck met his shoulder.

Lucius leapt sideways and drove his weaponed hand down on the nearest target of opportunity, Baractes' left shoulder.

The big man howled in pain. His left arm fell limp. Yet he never broke gaze with Lucius, and his bloodstained weapon was still held high in his other hand.

"I'll make it a slow death now, you Roman dog." Baractes cursed through clenched teeth.

The two men circled in a timeless dance.

Baractes spoke again in a violent whisper, "That reminds me, *Lucius*. Your dog..."

Lucius' attention wavered for the briefest instant and Baractes feinted forward with his knife, then retreated and laughed, "...yes. The cur you stole from the arena. He's dead. Worse than dead..." Baractes slashed the air with his *sica*, eyes on Lucius' eyes, "...I stole him from your slut. And took him to the marble pits to be crushed."

As Baractes finished his goading, Lucius noticed a pattern to his speech and movement and rushed forward, wrong footing the big man.

Off balance, Baractes sliced down. Lucius thrust his club half-way through the blow, catching the edge of the blade in the grooves carved in his cudgel. Using the downward momentum of Baractes' powerful but awkward swing, he pressed and slid his club sideways and down with the caught blade, twisting and then yanking forward at the bottom of the curve. Baractes' own strength caused him to lean forward, his grip loosened on his weapon by this unnatural angle. Lucius pulled and struck Baractes' wrist a hard, rapid knock.

The knife fell to the floor. Lucius' foot slid forward and kicked the *sica* well out of either man's reach.

Baractes' stumbled toward the knife, but Lucius struck a quick blow to the other man's knee as he passed him.

"Lucky *nugator*...fahh..." Baractes panted, crouching low and trying to circle round Lucius to get closer to his lost knife.

Likewise crouching, Lucius sized up his now-weaponless opponent.

Baractes ran.

But he didn't run back up the long, evil-smelling, pitch-dark hallways, he just started running—crisscrossing the great open middle space where the two men had met. He ran around a gigantic supporting pillar that stretched to the arena floor above. Then he glanced out from the edge of it, glaring at Lucius with insane eyes. Then he ran in front of Lucius, perhaps ten paces away, and stopped by a wide cistern, crouched down, sprang up again, scowling and grimacing at his young foe.

Lucius did not chase him. Both the poet and soldier were puzzled by this behavior. Obviously, the Gods had stolen the few wits left to Baractes, but Lucius' grim mission was still clear. Barking mad or cruel and sober, Baractes heart must be stopped. His life must be ended or Livilla would never be safe.

So, he watched the big man randomly sprint from one place to another. He stalked toward him, closing the distance between them, and making sure any retreat Baractes might try would have to be past Lucius.

The dirty gleam of Baractes' smile flashed. The Illyrian stood again by the central pillar, his mauled left hand behind it.

His empty right hand rested on a tall wooden crate. He hadn't moved from this spot now for several moments. This would be the closing place.

Lucius strode resolutely forward, watching Baractes for any further sporadic rushes. He didn't hear the groaning, creaking sounds of wood scraping on stone or of tautening ropes until the grate he stood on gapped downward and he was falling.

Frantically, fingernails ripping, he tried to find purchase on the board edges.

With a dull thud, he struck sand and stone and a softer, unknown refuse.

XXXI

SOUR-MEAT MAN? TAKE DOG FROM SWEET-SMELL GIRL. SOUR-MEAT MAN?

"...then there was a time in Eboracum, with three *taberna* girls, two rabbits, and an amphora of Falernian that would've filled a lake. In fact, we were near a lake and one of the girls—Brandellia, that was her name—one of the girls decided...Here now, Fido *amicus*, catch up. Can't keep those pee-soaked empty togas waiting at the Temple."

Talo pulled up, dismounted, and stumped toward Iace, who stood in the dark moonshadow of the Flavian Amphitheater. They'd just emerged from the narrow ways of the Subura and had broken into the northwest edge of the wide piazza skirting the great structure on its eastern side.

Iace was walking slowly in erratic movements, nose to the ground, emitting whining sounds interspersed with soft growls.

Talo caught up with the mastiff, knelt beside him on his good leg. He took the dog's giant head between his own oversized hands, and looked hard into his eyes. Proud experience and understanding met deep brown confusion and hope. Iace's whine came again, asking an all-important question of the big soldier.

STRONG MAN WARM. GOOD STRONG MAN. FIND WATER-MAN.

"I don't know, dog. I don't know."

Iace's head twisted in query as Talo stood straight. A big black hand stroked the back of the dog's head, "Nothing for old soldiers like us to worry about anymore, though, is it, Fido? The sand blows and the wind knows."

Iace sneezed twice, glanced up at Talo, and returned to snuffling the pavement.

FIND GIRL, *DOMINA*. FIND *DOMINUS*.

Talo sighed in a soft chuckle, "Not so faithful after all, are you, *canis, mi amice*?" Then he turned and climbed back onto his *cisium*. With one more glance at the searching, preoccupied dog, he added, "Then again, perhaps that is exactly what you are. *Vale*, soldier! *Ave atque Vale*, Fido!"

"And the pity of Mithras on the *culus* who crosses you." Talo clucked and shook his reins, head filling with visions of soon-to-be appreciated *popina* and *caupona* girls.

XXXII

There was a muffled thump and Livilla lifted her head. Baractes walked toward her, having appeared out of nowhere. He limped and there was a trickle of blood at the left corner of his mouth. He also had an evil-looking curved knife in his hand. She couldn't take her eyes off the line of blood splitting his unshaven chin.

"Enjoying the moonlight, my dove?"

Livilla pulled her head back as far as she could, trying to escape his sour, wine-soaked breath. But the big Ilyrian grabbed a full handful of her hair and held her face in front of his. He kissed her hard and off-center, teeth grinding against her upper lip. This ordeal was brief; he released her hair, wrinkled his lips into a sneer, and stepped back a pace.

"Ho. Still pining for your Picentine? Funny thing that..." Baractes held his hand above his brow and pivoted side-to-side, as if looking for spectators. "Guess who've I've got downstairs, waiting to play with the Emperor's kitty cats?"

Livilla, stunned from days of ordeal in the unreality and horror of the *Hypogeum*, said nothing, but her stare was as intense as the shine of the moon.

"Yes...that worthless bumpkin has returned."

Anger and disgust forgotten, Livilla's heart raced. She felt it pounding. She could hear it. Lucius was here? Why? What could he do if this savage villain had him caged below? What could she do? She must win him time. Why had he come back?

"...Lucius?..." She murmured. It had been most of a day since Baractes had brought her water and almost that long since she'd spoken.

"*Lucius*?" Baractes mocked, crouched into a cringe, arms pulled in to his chest, hands dangling in front of him like a rabbit. "*Lucius! Come save me, Lucius!*" Baractes pranced and sang in a falsetto. "Like you saved that cur dog I sold to the quarry." His voice shifted, but remained in a high, crazy register, "Like you saved your girlfriend..." He stopped his dancing and stood; his stare at Livilla was even and dark as the oil of Africa Nova, "Like you saved her slut mother when I torched that fleatrap she worked." A toothy smile mirrored the horror spreading across Livilla's face.

"My mother? You burned my mother?" For a Roman of the Subura, fire was the greatest, most frightening of horrors. It stole livelihoods and lives in the night. It destroyed families with no warning or reason. Arson was one of the few crimes besides treason that guaranteed a death sentence. Livilla thought she was beyond shock, but this shook her as a lion shakes its prey.

"*You burned my mother?*" Baractes returned to his mincing falsetto and dance.

Livilla cried tears she did not know she had, for a mother who had been a mother only in name. Weak as the bond had been between them, the woman had not deserved this.

Baractes mouth gaped in rictus grin as he watched Livilla

process the murder of the woman who'd given birth to her. After her shock diminished, he approached. He wore the blank face of a madman, a face that was brother to the full moon hanging above the stands.

"I've entertainment for you, girl." He began. "And you won't have to sit way up there," he waved at the matrons seats in the third tier. "In fact," he delicately lifted the back of his hand to cover his mouth, "You won't have to do anything." He wheeled and ran three steps back to Livilla, grabbed her hair again and whispered into her face, "Except *die*."

Still struggling with the unexpected feelings Baractes stirred with his revelations about Lucius and her mother, Livilla watched her tormentor as he walked away.

"Baractes?" She called after him. Lucius was still somewhere, she *had* to give Lucius time to do *something*, to get away. *Why* was he here?

The ex-gladiator slowed, but did not stop.

"Baractes? Did you love my mother?" She tried again.

The big man stopped now, and turned.

"*Love*? What dolly child's game is that? Your mother was made for love. She was Venus Erycina herself. Eheu! *Love*? I *loved* your mother, girl." He laughed. His look coarsened, the moon-face of madness gone and the old sadistic bully returned. "Is that of interest to you? We can make that game last a while." He didn't move toward her, but his body leaned, and his eyes filled with lust.

"I...I...haven't known any men. You could teach me. You could show me, Baractes." Bile filled her throat as she spoke. She did not allow herself to contemplate anything beyond giving time to Lucius, time for him to escape from below.

Baractes rubbed his chin with his good hand. He tapped his foot on the sand. He looked up at the moon, then back at Livilla. Turning again, he walked slowly away.

"No, I think not, girl. I've got better sport for us." He called back over his shoulder.

Livilla watched in fascination as he began vanishing downward, the sand swallowing him where he stood.

She squinted in the moonlight, trying to understand what was happening. Not having been to the *Ludi*, the games at the Amphitheater, she had no idea of the stageworks that were commonplace and well understood even to such as little Glaubus.

After Baractes' head disappeared, Livilla could make out a square hole of blackness where he had been. She'd never seen a trap door or even a stage door, such as they had in Pompey's Theater, nevertheless she did not think Baractes had the wit for witchcraft.

Had he gone below to kill Lucius? Could she have been more seductive? Could she have persuaded him to stay longer? And Iace? Brave Iace. Her dog had been stolen and *murdered* by this evil filth. *She* would not cry again, but she saw no options for herself and, very probably none for Lucius. They had all been abandoned by the gods.

XXXIII

Iace did not notice Talo's farewell as he'd encountered something even more compelling than Baractes' scent.

WATER-MAN. BELOW.

His thick, ropey tail fell and curved toward his belly, remembering.

DOG BELOW. DOG FEAR BELOW.

Iace curled his back, shrinking, and moaned.

WATER-MAN FEAR SMELL. IACE SMELL WATER-MAN.

His head rose. His ears lifted.

IACE?

DOG IACE.

His back stiffened straight and he sniffed the air for memories.

LUKYUS? LUKYUS FEAR.

Stepping forward one paw before another, his momentum accelerated. At speed, Iace plunged into the arena's underground.

IACE *CURRE*. IACE RUN.

IACE *ITE* LUKYUS.

XXXIV

Waking and sitting up, Lucius could see his trap was no more than nine or ten *pedes* deep. And he'd fallen less than that, as he'd slid part-way, so he was uninjured, even though he'd been knocked out. For how long?

He stood unsteadily and made a circuit of his enclosure. A few scraps of leather, what appeared to be two shin bones and a large animal jaw, nothing on the walls of the pit—nothing he could make out in the near absence of light.

Though the floor's edge was less than the height of two men above him, it might as well have been the deepest cavern in the blackest part of Hades. The trap door hung down flat against the wall, but the closely-set boards offered no chance of purchase.

Baractes' pale, strangely empty face hung above him like a diseased moon.

"Picked up some spirit in the legions, didn't you, poet? Well, I'll be back for you after I make arrangements with our little queen. She's upstairs now, waiting for me." He spit into the open pit, "As I remember, you were always partial to the cats. I'll find one to tickle you when I return. Then we'll see what kind of guts you brought back from the picket lines."

The muscles in Lucius' neck and shoulder tightened. There was nothing to say, no taunt that could damage or hinder the crazed Illyrian. There *must* be a way up, a way to save Livilla.

He reexamined every inch of his enclosure. Maybe he could make a rope from the leathers? A grappling hook with the jawbone?

But the leathers were too short and too thick and he had no blade to strip or split them.

What light there was angled in through the dangling trap-door. When he was only a hand's-breadth away, he saw that the frame was not completely featureless. Seven *pedes* above him was a hole, drilled for some unknown reason, and, as he pored over its surface, he discovered a similar hole two handspans away at the same height. But the holes were hardly large enough for him to fit two fingers in. Lucius had become strong under the tutelage of the harsh centurions of the XXIInd Primigenia, but he could not pull himself up by two fingers.

Further squinting showed holes of the same sort drilled every foot or so above the first ones he'd found, reaching all the way to the top edge of the hanging door.

"If I were a man of sticks, I could climb such a ladder," he whispered into the dark silence.

Disconsolate, Lucius flopped into a practiced hard squat. Filled with anxiety that threatened to become hopelessness, he picked up the cudgel that had also rolled into the pit with him and idly struck the stone flooring.

tap...tap...tap

He looked down at the club and tapped the floor again with it. Then he leapt to his feet and ran to the wall. Holding the slim club tip over his head, he slapped an end of it into the first hole he'd found in the suspended door. It fit as if milled for the purpose, leaving plenty of wood sticking out for a good grip.

Lucius pulled himself up till his eyes were level with the cudgel. He pulled and pushed and rose inch-by-inch over that point. The edge of the floor was only a few *pedes* above him now, perhaps two arm lengths.

He took one hand off the cudgel, raised an arm, and fell.

It was no good. Almost worse than never having found the holes at all. Maddeningly close, there was no way to reach the edge with only the single purchase.

Scrambling into one of the darker corners of his cell, Lucius looked for the bright glint of metal he'd seen underneath one of the crumbling leather harnesses. He jabbed his hands into the dark piled detritus, flinching as he cut himself on a sharp edge. Digging with greater care, he soon unearthed a well-worn sword. Rusty at the hilt, shorter and wider than he'd practiced with in Germania, he was surprised at how the steel lifted his spirits. Finding a broken cog on the floor, he wedged the blade between tines, so that one sharp side faced up, then straddling the ancient *gladius* and holding his club tightly, one hand clenching hard on each end of the wood, he raised the club over his head and drove down with all his strength, aiming the center of the cudgel directly on the upturned edge of the sword.

A satisfying crack resounded as the cudgel malformed. It was beginning to split. Lucius rotated the wood and repeated the exercise. It took a dozen blows, then another brief time to bash down the sharpest ends of the resulting two staubs of wood.

He shoved the venerable sword through his belt. Holding a piece of his climbing gear in each hand, Lucius reached up and inserted an end in each of the two first "rungs" in his doorladder. The muscles in his neck and shoulders extruded with each "step," but he managed to rise almost level with the holes. Then he realized a single step approach would be more efficient. He pulled the broken cudgel from his left-hand hold and shoved it into the hole a foot above the right-hand hold he still clung to. Pushing with his right hand on the lower piece of wood and pulling with his left above, he rose another foot and repeated this hand-over-hand process until he clawed three fingers of his right hand over the edge of the pit. Moments later he stood, panting hard, on the floor of the central chamber in the *Hypogeum*.

Now he had to get to the arena.

Sounds penetrated the thick flooring above him: a thud as if a titan had fallen, then a bellow that could well have come from such a behemoth.

Lucius' eyes raked the deep shadows around the chamber, searching for a ladder or some means to the surface.

Baractes knew these levers and cogs and platforms, but Lucius was baffled. Within a few breaths, he found a long, braided leather rope with a step-harness at one end. It was threaded over a pulley that Lucius could just make out in the darkness of the ceiling above. The other, plain, loose end fell to the floor by the step-harness.

"If only that giant were down here, he could haul me up in a trice." Lucius whispered a prayer to the dank *Lares* of the *Hypogeum*.

He turned to make the long run back through the underground, hoping he could find entry to the arena in time to foil Baractes' plan. He did not allow himself to reflect on the unreasonableness of that hope.

The torches were guttering at the far end of the chamber, and Lucius could not see to run at full speed. Then, just as he passed into a pocket of blackness, two blows struck him on his chest and he was thrown to the ground.

Breath driven from his lungs, he forgot the sword at his waist as he panicked and flailed at this new unknown antagonist, who was warm and covered in short hair.

"Furies and Ghosts!" His mind fogged with fear for Livilla. He was stunned by this attack, which was followed not by claws or daggers, but by a slopping wet toga bathing his face.

"Iace?" Lucius clasped his arms around the neck of the shivering, excited dog. "Iace," he repeated, pressing his check in the blind dark against the slobbery muzzle of the big canine.

Lucius did not linger in this reunion. Arm braced on the steady canine's spine, he hoisted himself up and trotted back toward the far wall of the chamber he'd just left in frustration.

Iace kept pace, tongue lolling and dribbling from the side of his black maw.

At the wall, Lucius put both his feet into the step-harness attached to the long leather rope.

He leaned over and put the other end of the rope in Iace's mouth, then knelt down and pressed his lips just above the dog's nostrils.

As he stood upright again, he called out in command, "*TRAHO*, Iace! Pull!"

Iace stood with the rope fixed in his closed jaws. Lucius called again, "*RETRO*, Iace! Back! *RETRO...TRAHO!*"

Four wide paws struggled backwards, then dug in as the

rope had already become taut and Iace now had to pull and bear all of Lucius' weight between his teeth.

One *digitus* at a time, Iace backed up. His massive head stayed level and straight. His rear legs described a sharp angle as he found purchase with the front, then leaned back, pulling through his teeth with his mighty back and neck and rear thigh muscles.

Lucius rose in the air, more swiftly than he could have climbed a ladder.

"*TRAHO*, Iace, *TRAHO!*" Lucius cried out, more in awe of the dog's power than as instruction. He'd given this scheme a meager chance, thinking he'd climb the rope himself as Iace kept it taut. But now he was half-way to the arena floor. His concentration shifted to the next problem, finding handholds at the ceiling and making it over to the opening in the arena floor that was now only a few *pedes* distant.

Somewhere on the other side of that hole, on the bloody sand of the Flavian Amphitheater's arena, Baractes held Livilla.

XXXV

Baractes' head was clearing from the wine he'd imbibed steadily since rising. And the departure of those spirits was followed by the onset of a cold hatred, a determination to set things right with these Romans. Two of them were at his mercy now, the stupid hayseed poet he'd wet-nursed in their job together, always mewling about virtue and truth and other seaside southern Greek twaddle. And Livilla, who's eyes betrayed her disgust every time she looked at him. Looked at him as if *he* were the filth that *her* mother was.

He stepped onto the small platform on which he'd ridden up to the arena and lowered himself to the *Hypogeum*.

All was prepared for Livilla's surprise. He'd have plenty of time to ponder what to do with the poet after he savored watching Gigans work on that little whore.

He ignored the noises coming from below where he'd so cleverly trapped the boy, except for a quick shout of ironic encouragement to the arrogant lad in the pit—and began working the engines he'd set up over the past day for just this moment.

There. He pulled a wooden lever. Another. And another, each the size of his leg. Rope-on-wood creakings emanated from just before him, behind the biggest cage of the chamber as the lift, cage, and contents rose slowly into the arena. Baractes had lashed three slaves to pull down the counterweights that allowed one person to operate this, the largest of the lifts.

He ran back to his platform and pried off the safety to the spring that gave him one last assisted rise to the world above. If he was quick, he could see the girl's eyes when she first caught sight of the instrument of her fate.

He came level with the sand, swung his head around and—yes—he was aboveground ahead of the ponderous lift that was raising Gigans.

Excited drool dribbling into his beard, he jumped off his platform and ran to the girl, whose head was down as if she were dead or asleep.

Baractes reached out and ripped a wide swath of cloth from the hem of Livilla's soiled *tunica*. He took a flat ceramic vial from his belt and spilled its contents on the cloth.

Livilla lifted her head. She said nothing, but stared. Well, this would be the last time he bore her insolence.

Smiling in triumph at the girl, he darted forward and smeared the moistened cloth over her chest, shoulders, and tethered arms. He made attempts to wipe down her legs, but she kicked too violently.

"What? " She sputtered—as if he'd stuck the rag in her mouth and not across her breast.

"Oh, just a little something to attract your new suitor, my little duck." Baractes bowed back a pace, mincing like a deferential courtier.

"Or should I say, my little white *heifer*."

He had placed himself strategically between Livilla and the platform upon which Gigans was raised. Now he stepped aside to let the girl see the creature.

The bull's body was black as the tar in Dacia, but its horns—extending four *pedes* on each side of its huge skull, filed to points sharper than a *pilum*—were a light creamy brown that reflected prettily in the moonlight.

As if on command, the enormous bull from Hispania bellowed and struck his feet against the platform to which his restraints were attached.

"May I introduce you to Gigans, *Lady* Livilla. He's a most *experienced* suitor, my white-breasted little *columba*. He's enjoyed the favors of four maids in this very arena. And, as I know how you girls hate to be ignored, I've taken the liberty of helping your courtship along. The sweat of his greatest rival in the pens and blood from a cow in heat now perfume you for your *amasio*."

"The gods curse you for your impiety, Baractes. Hera of the Cow Eyes, and Zeus who loved Europa, and Heracles to whom the blood of the innocent is sacred—they all curse you, Illyrian. They are your gods and they know your twisted heart."

Baractes' smile cleared. "You can speak their names, little wench, but no Olympians will listen to the smug daughter of a Roman harlot." He turned, limping back to release the shackles of the furious bull.

XXXVI

WATER-MAN! WATER-MAN! LUKYUS! LUKYUS! LUKYUS!
TRAHO LUKYUS. *TRAHO* IACE. *RETRO* IACE.
BACK. PULL. HURT. TOOTH HURT. TOOTH GONE.
TRAHO. TRAHO. RETRO. IACE BLOOD.
LUKYUS GONE.

Iace sat in the shadows cast by the failing torches. He could no longer see or smell Lucius. One long canine and a bloody molar lay on the ground next to him as he panted in pain and exhaustion.

WHERE LUKYUS?

He looked up and could just see a lighter grayness above and sense more smell and air coming from the opening where Lucius vanished. His nose and ears quivered, straining for some sign from his master and friend.

Then he heard it. Drifting down from the hole above him was the sound, the sound of Her voice.

LIVLA.

He opened his nostrils as widely as he could. Yes, there was her smell, too.

SWEET-SMELL SOFT-HAND SMELL ABOVE. IACE...LIVLA. LIVLA!

The muscles around his mouth and neck relaxed as they had not since he was stolen in the night.

Her scent was not right.

LIVLA HURT.

Iace had never smelled fear from Livilla.

FIND LIVLA. STOP HURT. STOP FEAR.

Another scent pearled into Iace.

SOUR-MEAT MAN SMELL. ERRRRRRR...IACE BITE SOUR-MEAT MAN. BITE HARD.

The growl began in his belly. It filled his chest. It covered the aches in his muscles, aches from months of impossible strain and little rest. His torn mouth and gums were forgotten.

FIND LIVLA. SAVE LIVLA.

He ran. Through the mad darkness of the *Hypogeum*. Past the cages of desperate animals and more desperate humans. Overturning rakes, benches, and buckets unseen and unnoticed as he galloped through the noisome alleys. He was *not* DOG, the mindless killer, he was Iace, and he would find Livilla.

IACE LUKYUS IACE. IACE LIVLA IACE.

IACE NOT DOG.

IACE IACE.

XXXVII

Sand drifted down and into Lucius' eyes. He negotiated his way across the *Hypogeum* ceiling by grasping ropes with unknown fastenings and half-hidden wooden knobs and squeezed through a gap between the platform and the edge of the arena floor.

He rolled into a crouch and stood.

The moon shone as haughtily as the sun after the Stygian shade of the arena's underworld. Its pale light revealed Livilla tied to a wooden cross thirty paces to his right, under the Emperor's podium. At the same distance to his left, Baractes knelt before a chained, gigantic black bull, horn tips sharpened for the arena.

Lucius ran to the bound girl. The sand was thick enough on the boards of the amphitheater floor to muffle the sounds of his sandals.

Livilla called out no sign of recognition, but her eyes cleared in recognition. Lucius realized he was blushing.

His rusty *gladius* was out and he'd cut the rope from her closest hand before Baractes shouted curses at this discovery.

"Now you'll die, foul Roman!" The huge Illyrian rushed toward them, his dagger raised in the practiced move of a *sicarius*, blade down, curve out, ready to stab a glancing blow down the side of Lucius' head, ready for the successive upward yank that would tear out the carotid artery.

Lucius pulled away from Livilla. Her free hand clutched his shoulder.

Baractes struck the classic downblow, but feinted at its finish, attempting a disarming sideswipe. Steel rang on steel. Lucius used the curve of the *sica* blade and his opponent's force to sling Baractes off guard and off balance.

Momentarily shocked by this skillful riposte, Baractes stood fixed, calculating in madness.

Equally unexpected, Lucius mind was occupied by the remembered snarl of a hated centurion.

"STRIKE, *boys, strike! Strike until your hands bleed, then strike again! That's blood you made, so use it!*"

Hour upon hour, the primus pilus of Legio XXII drilled his legionaries. In the snow, in the rain, in winds that lifted a man from the ground. Every day they did not fight a battle, including the days spent morning 'til dusk digging, every day they drilled until their hands were hard as the leather of their loricae.

Such a sword hand bore down on Baractes' *sica* now.

CLANG! *slither-ring...Clang! Clang!*

Though he had a hundred *librae* of meat and muscle on his opponent, Baractes fell back at this onslaught. Then he just fell.

The big man held his *sica* above him like a slim shield; Lucius beat down on it again and again, anger and fear for Livilla powering every blow.

When it seemed the steel of one of the weapons must give way, Baractes cried out, flung his dagger away from his numb fingers and held his hands and his feet up in the air in an ageless gesture of surrender.

Breathing like a bellows, Lucius picked up the *sica* and thrust both blades into his belt. Beaten, weaponless, Baractes crawled to his feet and reeled away from Lucius. Certain he could catch the big man at any time, Lucius turned back to Livilla.

"Took you long enough, poet."

"I had some errands to run."

Her smile brought a strange disquiet to his gut as he chopped at the bonds that held Livilla's right hand.

"Luci...The bull! Lucius! Behind you!" Free from restraint, Livilla shouted. Baractes drug the opened chains behind the monster; Gigans was unfettered. "Give me the *sica*—we can stand him off between us!" She held her hand out.

"You may be Diana's chosen, but you couldn't hold a flower until the blood's back in your hands." He tenderly pushed her behind him.

"Across the field," he nodded, "under the Vestal's box, there's a hidden gate. It should be unlatched for the cleanup crew. Get there. Move like an Etruscan soothsayer: with *dignatus*." He stepped sideways, edging toward the opposite side of the arena from the Emperor's box, under which they now stood.

The bull, though pointed generally in their direction, stood still. Baractes shrank several *pedes* behind it, otherwise unmoving.

"It's not far. Slowly...slowly." Lucius warned.

They made several paces of sideways progress.

The bull was a statue.

Then it was not.

Gigans accelerated at an impossible rate, horns bearing down on them. Lucius realized there was no possibility they'd make the far gate before they were intercepted—trampled under that dreadful weight or skewered by those living spikes, long and deadly as the legion's spears.

He pushed the girl hard toward the gate, then jumped in front of her and ran toward the oncoming bull, screaming like the Germans that attacked out of the trees in the frozen North.

"Hai! Hai! Bull! Here!" Waving and flailing his arms. Gigans altered his path and swerved toward Lucius. Lucius stole a glance and saw Livilla more than halfway across the arena. If he could stay alive for this first pass, she should make it.

Now the bull was slowing, almost as if he were ignoring Lucius. It halted. It raised its head into the air and rotated its glossy black nose in a small circle.

Then its head turned down and dark, lustrous eyes fixed on Livilla.

Like trumpet cries from Olympus or Hades, a proud and

horrible noise rolled from it. It scratched the arena floor so deeply that the boards boomed hollow sounds that echoed across the sand.

XXXVIII

Gigans charged a second time with a quickening speed as preternatural as its first onslaught. But now there was no chance that Lucius could intercede before the bull struck Livilla.

When the bull charged this time, Livilla abandoned stealth and ran as fast as a city-bred girl in light sandals could. She was two paces from the wall when she realized she did not know the mechanism by which the gate opened.

She glanced behind her. Gigans was coming at terrible speed, head and deadly rack lowered. It would reach her in heartbeats. Lucius was shouting something, but she couldn't hear him for the blood pounding in her ears.

She turned to face the hurtling death.

"Athena, Diana, and Hera—save Lucius," she whispered.

Unable to take her eyes off the monstrous beast, time slowed and she noticed the softness of the night air, the small streak of white that played down the center of Gigans forehead. Her *tunica* was shamelessly short—what would Lucius think?

The angry ruttish smell of the bull's breath filled her senses.

She raised her fists in final defiance against the enraged horror. Between her outstretched hands, a flash of yellow-brown covered and hid the front of the bull, altering the course of its head and her death.

EMERGING FROM THE *HYPOGEUM*, Iace slid to a halt. He lifted his nose. He listened.

LUKYUS LOUD NOISE.

IACE RUN LUKYUS.

LIVLA! LIVLA SMELL. BIG MEAT SMELL.

LIVLA FEAR SMELL.
IACE JUMP.

SPRINTING TOWARD HER, Lucius was thirty paces out when the bull reached Livilla. He stopped in awe as the mastiff appeared, flying over the elephant-tusk inner fence of the *euripi*, landing jaws first—grappling onto the muzzle of Gigans.

IACE BITE BIG MEAT. DOG BITE.

GIGANS WOULD HAVE BELLOWED if he'd been able, but the powerful jaws holding him by the nose also clamped his mouth closed.

Gigans had never suffered indignity or pain like this. The thing holding him was so insignificant in size. How could it keep him from trampling the smell of his rival?

The bull flexed his great muscles and shook his head and neck and spine with all the strength of unprecedented frustration.

The "thing" on his nose stuck. In fact, it seemed to hold harder; the pain in Gigans' muzzle increased.

"IACE!" Livilla cried. Fearing her call would distract the heroic canine, she fell silent. What could she do? She hesitated, then began to move toward the violent tangle of dog and bull.

A muscular hand grasped her arm, pulling her from her daze of concern.

"This way. Now!"

She followed Lucius the few steps to the wall. He reached behind a column and the heavy wooden facing—painted with triumphant *myrmillones* bowing before a ridiculously huge Emperor—swung out a handspan.

Lucius tried to lead her through, but she stood hard and looked up at him, "What of Iace?" Unshed tears welled in her brown eyes. "We cannot leave him. *You* cannot leave him—again."

"I will not." Lucius' jaw set, firm as Livilla's feet. "You cannot help us. Go." He looked down at her and whispered, "Please, Livilla. I will not leave him."

Livilla swallowed. Her eyes narrowed in acquiescence. She stepped through the gate.

IACE HELD to the great bull's hairy nostrils. He had never battled such power, such strength.

Again and again, the frenzied bull tried to sling away the hated load cutting and crushing its sensitive muzzle.

Iace held. He dangled from its head, his back feet brushed the sand.

Then the creature began to vibrate. A paroxysm shook it, growing from its tail up its back until it reached its stupendous neck and head. The violence of the movement ripped the tired dog from his mooring and he was flung far and high through the air.

STANDING HALF-COVERED by the gate opening, Lucius watched the struggle between the giant dog and the even more gigantic bull. Before the power and determination of the combatants he was as helpless as he'd made Livilla feel.

Then Gigans shook with a mighty shudder, the effort that dislodged Iace.

Gouts of blood streamed from the bull's shredded nostrils, but Lucius saw only the long trajectory of Iace's flight.

XXXIX

Baractes throat was dry and scratchy. It yearned for wine. Enough wine and he could forget this little Roman slut that had ensnared him with her wiles, had led him to spoil the beautiful arrangement he had laundering funds for that old spider Sporinus. And that damned milksop whining poet. How'd he learned to swing a blade like that?

"I must've slipped in the sand," Baractes mouthed to himself, watching with hatred as Lucius unfastened the little whore from her bonds.

Then he remembered the bull. Yes, the bull would bring things right. The little legionary might best a half-drunk Baractes, particularly one that slipped in the sand, but he'd have no chance against Gigans.

So he'd unleashed the animal, stalking at a safe distance behind it, ready to dash for the same gate Livilla was making for.

"Stupid girl, doesn't know how to open the gate. Hoi! That's it, then." He smiled as the bull made its final charge.

Then the unthinkable happened.

The fact that the mewling Picentine had escaped had been bad enough, but now this *dog*!

And the cursed animal was fighting off Gigans! That could not be. It had taken three *bestiarii* and two special handlers from the *Forum Boviarium* to corral the horned titan.

Baractes' hand flashed for the empty *sica* scabbard on his thigh.

A cold sweat covered his forehead as he realized he was unarmed.

Standing there, immobilized by fear, his vision dimmed, his senses faded. He was barely aware of the tawny bundle of muscle and bone that rioted through the air at him.

. . .

LUCIUS GAPED as Iace flew in an arc of deadly height, then smashed in a jumble into Baractes, who was himself dashed hard against the arena floor.

Lucius ran toward the two fallen enemies.

Baractes wobbled, trying to creep away on hands and knees.

Iace's body lay contorted and unmoving on the arena sands.

Lucius knelt by the dog and tested for heart and breath. As he'd done once before, he lifted the dog in his arms. No cart to help this time, he staggered for the gate. Though bleeding and confused, Gigans bellowed his presence and his anger—very much still alive and still near.

BARACTES WANTED nothing to do with the Picentine or the dog—or Livilla. He needed to escape this rotten arena, this rotten Rome. He wiped his clammy forehead with the smelly rag that hung on his belt. He'd stashed some coin at a temple on the *Clivus Pullius*. He could strongarm Pecius and Durithon. A smile returned at the thought of Durithon's daughter. Maybe a brief diversion before he left this cursed city. He rose from his hands and knees and stumbled toward the platform that would let him back down into the *Hypogeum* and then out. Out. Out.

XL

Gigans stood dripping blood, smell-blinded and in pain. He had shadow memories of this place. There had been loud noise. It was bright. There were bleating things all around him. He had buried his points in soft runners and his anger was soothed when he trampled them.

No thing had ever injured him like this last thing. Little bites sometimes, but nothing like this.

A smell entered his mauled nostrils. *It is stronger now*; it was a smell he knew. *It is the smell of the white bull* that lived next to him below. He hated that bull. And *it is the smell of a heifer ready to be covered.*

His eyes filled with flame.

Finding the source, he pawed the ground to show his intent, to make his enemy fear him.

Then, for love and for war, he charged.

THOUGH MOST OF LUCIUS' attention was on holding Iace, not falling, and making it to the gate, the bull stood between him and the exit gate. So he chose a wide arc and not a direct path. All alert, he watched Gigans' erratic behavior. The bull was confused. It pawed the ground. Then it charged.

It did not run toward him.

Changing angles, he angled straight for the exit, tripping almost to a trot.

Livilla's gammon face peeked around the edge of the gaudily painted gate.

"What are you doing here? I told you to get out!" He panted, exhausted, arms aching.

Livilla flashed a well-known look at him. But before she could insult, her eyes filled with horror.

An evil sound reverberated across the sand and against the polished walls of the arena, as of a titanic butcher's knife cleaving through the body of an equally titanic sheep. A cry of final agony followed, then only distant stampings and thumps.

Lucius turned in response to Livilla. Gigans—at full gallop—skewered Baractes in the center of his back, raising the big Illyrian into the air like a child's cloth toy, and then tossing him to the arena floor.

Livilla looked away, her hands over her eyes, but Lucius was transfixed as the bull stamped down on Baractes body, nudged and gored him, until—even at this distance—it was clear the Illyrian would trouble no one again—this side of Hades.

Strength failing now as adrenaline drained, Lucius staggered.

Small, strong fingers grabbed him and supported Iace's drooping head, and the two young Romans slipped out of the Flavian Amphitheater, away from the graves dug for the Emperor who built it and the city that reveled in its brutalities.

XLI

Pausalae: The year of the XVIIIth Consulship of Imperator Caesar Domitianus Augustus, Dominus et Deus, and the consulship of Quintus Volusius Saturninus, 845 years after the founding of the city

"LUCIUS! Don't torment that poor dog! Lucius! Don't ignore your son!" Holding a large woven basket against her hip, Livilla scolded.

Her husband, Lucius, reclined on the grassy hillside, a bowl of olives and fresh goat's cheese on one side of him, a stylus and wax pad on the other. He wore a very broad and somewhat tattered straw hat. Just above her, on the hilltop under a spreading hazelnut tree, the other Lucius—their two-year-old son—was climbing on a huge yellow-brown mastiff, who seemed to be asleep.

Lucius—the elder Lucius—glanced up the hill at the dog and the toddler, then peered out from under his hat at his wife. He regarded her with appreciation. She was wearing the dark blue *palla* he'd traded his best ewe for. And she was wearing it over her short Doric-style *tunica*. The women of Pausulae, Firmum, and Ricina whispered about her scandalous attire. But only behind her back. Well after she'd passed them by. Lucius grinned. None crossed his redoubtable Livilla.

"The child loves the dog. The dog loves the child. What would you have me do, wife?"

Livilla set down the basket of apples and hard, dark bread,

then set herself down by her husband, staring into the shade around his eyes.

"Iace is old. Little Lucius might injure him. Iace might retaliate." She began with a tone of concern, but the conviction left her voice and she, too, smiled.

She took Lucius' hand between both of hers.

"You are my dear and worthless husband."

Lucius pulled her hands to him and kissed them.

Livilla began to pull away, starting to rise, but Lucius put his hand on her shoulder, "Eat. Breathe. Watch the river below, Livilla. I'll tend to the boys."

Little Lucius was mountaineering on his best friend, the fierce dog of the arena that had seen him into the world, had licked him clean almost from the womb, had watched over his crib, and slept by his cradle for the past two years.

Other than ancient scars, there was little purchase on Iace's sides, but Lucius was not daunted.

He'd reached his favorite spot, astride the dog's muscular neck. Small hands patted down hard on the crown of Iace's head.

The dog blinked at the pummeling.

Then the boy lost his balance and slid off the side of the dog, tumbling to the ground in a soft, laughing lump.

Quick as he was down, he was back up again.

Using Iace's rock-solid chin as a pull-up point, he stood in front of the dog and grabbed a floppy, scarred black ear in each of his tiny fists, twisting and grasping.

A glint appeared in Iace's glossy eyes.

LITTLE-MAN LUKYUS LIKE LITTLE HAIRY MAN.

IACE TASTE LITTLE HAIRY MAN HEAD.

The edges of his great black muzzle quirked upwards. There was a memory of a monkey's head in his mouth and the monkey's face and chittering after he'd released the monkey's head.

LITTLE-MAN LUKYUS.

IACE WARM.

IACE LITTLE-MAN LUKYUS.

Small human firmly attached, stubby fingers poking and manipulating his ears, Iace turned his head and watched the larger Lucius climbing toward them.

As he neared the top of the hill, Livilla stood and called ambiguously, "Lucius…"

But before she could continue to shout out the warnings, admonitions, imprecations, and advice that were on her practiced tongue, her bow-shaped lips pressed together, their edges flexing upwards until her smile was so full it crinkled the soft flesh around her eyes.

Under the hazelnut on her hilltop stage, she saw Lucius—the poet, the soldier, now the farmer and husband—holding the ankles of Lucius the two-year-old terror, whose trim little belly (bared now as his undertunic had fallen over his eyes) rippled with peals of convulsing laughter that rolled down the slope to his mother's ears.

At the bottom end of this tableaux, the hands of Lucius—the littlest Lucius—maintained a fervent grip on the tips of the ears of Iace: his dog, his brother, his servant, his protector, his confidant.

Below those hands, Iace—bullfighter, unmatched quarry dog, fighter and killer of the Flavian Amphitheater—stood on canine tiptoes. The wrinkles in his black (now trimmed in gray) muzzle joined with the deep whorls covering his yellowed, scarified head.

The curve of Livilla's smile straightened as she registered the dog's fraught expression.

"Lucius," she called again, "You're hurting Iace!"

Quick as boiled shellfish, the scene changed.

Lucius released his grip. The black skyward-pointing triangles of dog's ears fell, becoming dark pendulous squares.

Lucius shifted his arms and cradled his son.

Lucius the smaller began to cry.

Iace's weathered brow, which smoothed when his ears were released, became again lined and he tilted his head up toward his youngest charge.

"Yahkay...Yahkay...Lukyus love Yahkay." the child burbled in distress.

Lucius lowered his son to the ground beside his dog.

Short arms tried and failed again and again to encircle the giant neck; tiny fingers grasped and massaged the loose folds of skin around Iace's shoulders.

"Lukyus love Yahkay..." the boy's vocalizations ended as he pressed his moist nose and mouth against the dog's bony side.

The Picentine sky was a perfect blue. The briny fragrance of the Mare Adriaticus drifted in, filling the old dog's nostrils with strange and powerful smells. Beyond and below lay the sparkling green line of the river they splashed in where Iace sometimes caught fat and sour frogs.

Lucius, who had saved him from the arena, stood by him. Livilla, who had taught him to live, was below. And the littlest Lucius, who hung on him, clinging to his neck, sobbed into his ribs.

His chest expanded, drooling jowls ruffled out in a heart-deep sigh. Iace, the castoff, was home.

GLOSSARY FOR THE CASTOFF

Achilles, shield of – Legendary shield given to Achilles by his mother Thetis, forged by the Greek god Hephaestus
Adiuto! / Adiute! – Help!
Admetus – Ancient Greek king, friend of Apollo and Herakles, spouse of Alcestis
Africa Nova – The conquered lands of Carthage formed part of this Roman province, more-or-less equivalent to modern-day Libya
Agamemnon – He and his brother Menelaus were the chief kings on the Greek side of the Trojan War; murdered in his bath (when he got home after the war) by his wife Clytemnestra
ager Servii Tullii – Literally "the field of Servius Tullius"; this was a large field just outside the *pomerium* (the original sacred boundary of Rome)
amasia – Lover
amic-us, -i – Friend(s)
amphor-a, -ae – Popular tall, double-handled clay container of liquids, also a Roman unit of liquid measurement (*amphora quadrantal*) of approx. seven gallons
Anchises – Trojan father of Aeneas, who founded Rome (according to Virgil in the *Aeneid*)

Archimedes – A Syracusan Greek regarded as the greatest scientist of the ancient world
armarium – Strongbox (for money)
Artemis/Diana Greek/Roman goddess of the hunt
Athena/Minerva – Greek/Roman goddess of wisdom, daughter of Zeus/Jupiter, born directly from the god's head
AUC – *Ab urbe condita*: "from the founding of the City"; the traditional year of the founding of Rome is, in the modern Western calendar, 753 BC
Aurelia – Popular name for Roman women (Julius Caesar's mother was named Aurelia)
Ave! – Roman greeting, roughly equivalent to "Hail" or "Hi"
Bacchae, the (or **Bacchantes**) – The cultish female worshippers of the Greek god Dionysus (roughly equivalent to Roman Bacchus) known for their fierce abandon and orgiastic ways, also a famous play by the ancient Greek playwright, Euripides
Bacchus/Dionysius – Roman/Greek god of wine and pleasure; Dionysius is typically considered a more "serious" god than Bacchus
Baet-ia, -ian – Area on the coast of the southern part of Roman Hispania (Spain)
bestiar-ius, -ii – Gladiators fought other people; *bestiarii* fought animals in the Roman *ludi* (games): some were voluntary fighters, others unlucky victims; also referred to as the keepers of the beasts
Blue, the [chariot races of the Romans] – One of the four racing teams that competed in the Roman *ludi* (games), along with the White, the Green, and the Red; competition on and off the track was keen and often deadly—both among the competitors and the fans
Boreas – Greek god of the North Wind (sometimes borrowed by the Romans and sometimes meaning just "the wind")
Bucephalus – The famous horse of Alexander the Great
Caelian – One of the (eastern) Seven Hills of Rome: see Seven Hills of Rome

Cairnunnos or **Cernunnos** – Gallic/Celtic god of nature; sometimes called the Horned One as he wore the antlers of a stag
calig-a, -ae – Hobnailed sandal-boots worn by the Roman legionaries
Campan-ia, -ian [wine] – Fertile area of Roman Italy lying just south of Rome on the Tyrrhenian Sea; includes the important cities of Capua, Benevento, and Neapolis (Naples); part of Magna Graecia
Campus Martius – Literally "Field of Mars," large area just outside the *pomerium* (official and sacred border of Rome) where military practice, plays, voting, and other public events were held
canelillo – [Affectionate diminutive] "little doggie"
canis bonum – Good dog
canis dulcis – Sweet dog
canis mi amice – My dog friend
caria / carus – Dear or "dear one" (feminine / masculine forms)
Castor and Pollux – Demi-god sons of Leda the Swan and Zeus, twin brothers of Helen of Troy and Clytemnestra; also known as the Gemini, the Twins, the Dioscuri; they were martial (liked to box, for instance) and were very popular with the Romans
castrum – Camp; specifically, a Roman military camp, usually built for one or more legions (*legiones*), built to a very precise size and form; usually a square fort with high wooden palisades, a gate in the middle of each wall, and the administrative headquarters at the crossroads in the middle
Catullus – A famous patrician Roman lyric poet who scandalized many with his poems and behavior
caupona – Disreputable tavern, usually offering accommodation, often placed at or near important mileposts and near fancier sleeping arrangements like *tabernae*
Cave Canem – Beware the Dog!
CEDITO!/CEDITE! – Back! [command]
Censor – Senior Roman magistrate (typically an office held

post-consular) who oversaw the census and ruled on matters of public morality

Cerberus – The giant three-headed dog who guarded the gate to Hades

chiton A simple garment very like a tunic (*tunica*)

chlamys – An ancient Greek garment, something like a robe, usually attached by a brooch or pin at the shoulder; not generally worn by Romans

Circus Maximus – Literally "the biggest circus," the largest site for the Roman *ludi* (games); for most of its long history, it existed in the valley between the Aventine and Palatine hills; could accommodate over 150,000 spectators for the races held there

cisium – A small, highly sprung open carriage, similar to a gig; drawn by horses or mules

cithara – Ancient Greek instrument (the god Apollo played a cithara) with between two and 8 strings, U-shaped with a deep wooden sounding box

Cloaca Maxima – The largest (and most ancient) sewer in Rome

Clotho – One of the (Greek) Fates [see Fates, the]; Clotho spun the thread of human life

Clivus Pullius – Street running south from the Subura across the western end of the [*Mons*] *Oppius* to the Fagutal

cognomen – Having few given names (*praenomen*), Romans often attached a descriptive fourth name to differentiate, for instance, *Quintus Caecilius Metellus Numidicus* was the conqueror of Numidia (thus Numidicus) and his cousin *Quintus Caecilius Metellus Macedonicus* was the conqueror of Macedonica (there were always a lot of Metelli)

Coins of Rome – The most common Roman coins at the time of the Emperor Vespasian were, in order of least-to-greatest value:

as (bronze)=10 grams bronze

sesterce (copper/bronze)=4 *as*

denarius (silver)=4 *sestertii*

aureus (gold)=25 *denarii*

Colleg-ium, -ia [gangs of Rome] – There were several official

Collegia of Rome, including the College of Pontifices (Priests) and the College of Augures (Augurs/State Fortunetellers), but most Collegia were semi-criminal gangs that controlled territories in Rome based on important crossroads, usually meeting in a crossroads *taberna*

Colossus – 100 ft. bronze golden statue of the Emperor Nero as the Sun God Helios; it was moved several times in and around the Colosseum and the Forum until it was torn down

columba – Dove

congium Large, but portable Roman liquid holder, sometimes treated leather, but could be of any material, also a unit of liquid measurement, roughly 3.5 quarts

Consul Highest elected office in the Roman political system; two consuls were elected every year, alternating their rule (*imperium*) of the Senate from month-to-month; while in office, Consuls enjoyed complete legal immunity from civil prosecution

Creon An ancient king of the Greek city of Thebes; he is featured in many famous Greek tragedies, including those of Sophocles

culus – Anus

CURRE! – Run! [command]

cursus publicus – Literally "the public way": the state-mandated and run postal/delivery system paid for by the public purse (the *Fiscus*); most important documents were not carried directly by the military and were handled by the *cursus publicus*

curule aedile – Important, but junior, magistrates who looked to the care of the city, the provisions coming into the city, and managed the *ludi* (the games); at any given time, there were two curule aediles and two plebian aediles (roughly equivalent in duties and power)

Dacia – A war-like country of the Roman world corresponding to modern-day Rumania and Moldova, not colonized by Rome at the time of the Emperor Vespasian

Daedalus – The greatest mortal engineer-scientist of Greek mythology: built the labyrinth for King Minos (to contain the

Minotaur) and, tragically, the wax wings fitted to his son, Icarus, who flew too high and subsequently fell into the sea (along with his melted wings)

denar-ius, -ii – A common Roman silver coin: see Coins of Rome

Diana/Artemis – See Artemis/Diana

digitus – "Finger," Roman inch: see Roman units of measurement

Dionysius/Bacchus – See Bacchus/Dionysius

Dis – Short for Dis Pater or Dispater was a Roman god of the Underworld, which he shared with the other Roman gods of that place (Pluto and Orcus)

dithyramb – A passionate form of ancient Greek poetry that usually celebrated the god Dionysus

domina – Mistress, as in Lady or "Mistress of the House" (no connection to any sexual activities or preferences); with or without slaves, the Roman *domina* ruled her household

Domitian – Full name: Titus Flavius Caesar Domitianus Augustus, Roman emperor from 81-to-96 CE, younger brother of the previous (much loved) emperor Titus, son of the Flavian-dynasty establishing (general) Vespasian; he was no monster (as Roman emperors go), but not well liked by anyone, assassinated in 96 CE

domus – House/household

Doric – The plainest Greek style of architecture, also any style or object thought to originate from the western (Doric) part of Greece

Eboracum – Roman name for the city of York, UK

equites – Member of a high Roman social order; only the Senators were of higher social class than the *equites* (and the *equites* were often wealthier)

Erebus – Literally: Hell on Earth

Esquiline – The easternmost of the Seven Hills of (central) Rome: see Seven Hills of Rome

Etruscan – Most powerful and important civilization in Italy prior to Rome; the last three Roman kings (before the Republic)

were Etruscan; Rome continued to be influenced by Etruscan customs even after conquering all Etruscan strongholds: gladiatorial combats were originally Etruscan funeral games; Etruscans were always considered the wisest soothsayers, etc.
euripi – The ditch surrounding the floor of the Colosseum that prevented animals from leaping into the stands
Europa – Name of (at least) two of Zeus' lovers and mothers of some of his extra-marital children
Falern-ia, -ian [wine] – Reputedly the best wine available in ancient Rome
Fates, the – In Greek mythology, the three sisters—Clotho, Lachesis, Atropos—spin the destiny of all; Clotho spins the thread of life; Lachesis measures how much is allotted for each person; Atropos cuts the thread
Februarius [month] – Second month of the (Roman) year; 28 days long
felix – Luck, also Felix—the god of luck
ferreus – Blacksmith
Flavian Amphitheater – Better known today as the Colosseum; it was built during the rules of Vespasian and his son Titus, who founded the Flavian dynasty
Fortuna Publica Populi Romani – Good Luck Temple of the Roman People, a simple and ancient temple standing just outside the *Porta Collina* (the northern entrance to Rome), built by Servius Tullius
Forum Boarium – Site of the major cattle market of Rome; located where the original docks of the Tiber had been before Rome's shipping moved to Ostia
Furies, the – Mythological Greek flying demons who endlessly tormented the damned (or those the gods chose to torment)
garum – An extremely popular fermented fish sauce used as seasoning on almost all Roman food; the preparation of garum involved allowing raw fish to ferment in the sun and so its production was notoriously odiferous
Gate of Death, the [in the Colosseum] – Western entrance to the

Colosseum, between Gate LVII and LVIII; there was a direct connection to a tunnel leading to the Spoliarium

Gate of Life, the [in the Colosseum] – Eastern entrance to the Colosseum, located between Gates XIX and XX; this was where the gladiators entered the games

Gate LXV [in the Colosseum] – One of the 76 public entrances and exits to the Colosseum

Gate XXII [in the Colosseum] – One of the 76 public entrances and exits to the Colosseum

gens – Family or family name, as in the Julian *gens*, the Metellus *gens*

Germania Superior – "Upper Germany," a Roman province in the time of Domitian that mostly extended along the west bank of the middle Rhine; major (Roman) towns included the capital Mogontiacum (Mainz), Aquae Mattiacae (Wiesbaden), and Argentoratum (Strasbourg); it was an area in a more-or-less constant state of uprising

gladius – The Roman sword used by the legions: primarily a stabbing weapon shorter than a longsword

Haephestus/Vulcan – Greek/Roman god of invention, mechanics, the furnace and the smithy

Helios – Greek/Roman god of the sun

hepastaikeon – From Greek mythology: a fantastical spherical weapon with seven spokes

Hera – Queen of the Greek gods; the Roman goddess Juno is similar

Heraclitus [The Stones of Heraclitus] – Greek philosopher of the 7th Century BCE who spoke in obscure poetic riddles and believed in the constantly changing state of reality; "The Stones of Heraclitus" was one of the names given to his work

Hercules/Herakles – Roman/Greek hero of remarkable strength; most popular Greek hero among the Romans (who tended to think Greek heroes were not very trustworthy or honest)

Horace – *Quintus Horatius Flaccus*: Roman lyric poet and statesman, contemporary and friend of Octavian (later Augustus Caesar)

Hyperion – Technically a Titan and not a god in Greek mythology, always associated with the Sun; his own children were Helios (god of the Sun), Selene (goddess of the Moon), and Eos (goddess of the Dawn)

Hypogeum – The vast underground portion of the Flavian Amphitheater (the Colosseum) where prospective victims, human and animal, were incarcerated for the games, alongside enormous and complex mechanical devices that allowed for the raising and lowering of trapdoors, lifts, stairs, and scene changes that would enhance the drama of the slaughter occurring above

iace – Cast, cast-off, throw, throw away

Illyr-ia, -ian – Someone from the Roman province of Illyricum, which would include today's Croatia, Bosnia-Herzegovina, Montenegro, Albania, Kosovo, Slovenia, parts of Serbia

insul-a, -ae – Literally "island" in Latin: in the city, *insula* could refer to either a single apartment building or an entire city block; most people, including many of the wealthy, lived in *insulae* in ancient Rome

ITE! – Go, Go to [command]

Jove One of the Roman names for the chief of the gods, similar to, but not quite the same as Jupiter

Julius [month] – The "fifth" month in the Roman calendar (corresponding to modern-day July), renamed after Julius Caesar by Marcus Antonius

Juno – Roman version of the Greek goddess Hera, spouse of the king of the gods; in the case of Juno, this would be Jove/Jupiter

Juno Acieiorum – One of the many forms of the goddess Juno; literally "Juno of the Regiment"

Jupiter Optimus Maximus – Literally "The Biggest and the Best Jupiter": see Temple of Jupiter

Lachesis – One of the Greek Fates [see Fates, the]

lapis Tiburtinus – The marble quarried outside the city of Tibur, just north of Rome; many of the larger buildings of 1st and 2nd Century Rome were rebuilt using this marble

Lares, the – Along with the Penates, the Lares were the Romans much-favored household gods, usually kept in some small statuary form in all Roman households

latifundia – Large country estates owned by wealthy senators and equites that employed the majority of slaves in the Roman Empire

Leg-io, -iones – Legion(s)

Legio XX – AKA *Legio vigesima Valeria Victrix*, the Twentieth Legion of Victorious Valeria; one of the longest serving Roman legions in Brittania (modern UK), Talo's legion

Legio XXII – *Legio XXII Primigenia*, Fortune's Twenty-Second Legion began service in the Roman province of Germania Superior, guarding the border of the empire on the river Rhine; Lucius served in an auxiliary unit with this legion

Lesbos, poet of – The Greek lyric poet Sappho (fl. 600 BCE), often considered the greatest lyric poet of the ancient world

libert-us, -i / liberto – A freed person, a slave who has been freed either by purchasing their own freedom or by manumission by their owner; Roman *liberti* had many rights in Roman society that were denied to slaves; the children of *liberti* were born as full citizens of Rome

libr-a, -ae – Roman pound (weight): see Roman units of measurement

loric-a, -ae – Body armor: there were several types of armor worn by Roman legionaries, the most famous being the form-fitting boiled leather body piece normally worn only by tribunes or higher ranks; Lucius wore the *Lorica hamata*, a type of metal ring armor

Ludi Romani – The games of Rome: catch-all name for the large-scale games held in Rome, particularly at the Flavian Amphitheater (the Colosseum) and the Circus Maximus

Lupercalia – One of the oldest and strangest festivals in Rome, included the practice of anointed male youths running nude around the Palatine hill, striking anyone they met with ceremonial thongs (thought to bring fertility to women); associated with the sacred goat fig, the *Ficus Ruminalis*, thought to have nurtured the founders of Rome, Romulus and Remus

Magna Graecia – Settled by Greeks before Rome existed, the southern coastal areas of Italy were so called by the Romans; included many famous towns and cities–Tarentum, Metapontum, Heraclea, Cumae, Capua, Neapolis, Croton, and all of Sicily

mans-io, -iones – Official waystations on Roman roads, maintained by Rome for those on official state business

MANTE! – Stay! [command]

Martius [month] – The third month in the Roman calendar

Mater Mea – My Mother

Mercury – Roman version of the Greek god Hermes; god of speed, crossroads, and messengers

Metell-us, -i [gens/family] – A prolific, wealthy, influential, and long-standing clan of the highest-born plebian Roman stock; there were many famous Metelli; there were even more never-famous Metelli; almost all were wealthy

milepost – Marked every mile, every *mille passus*, on official Roman roads like the *Via Tiburtina* and *Via Nomentana*: see Roman units of measurement

Minerva/Athena – See Athena/Minerva

Minerva Locres – Like most Roman (and Greek) gods and goddesses, Minerva had many aspects; Minerva Locres was the "local" spirit of the goddess of wisdom

Mogontiacum – Capital of the Roman province of Germania Superior, modern day Mainz (French: Mayence)

muta – Brute, beast, monster

mutat-io, -iones – Part of the support system of way stations on Roman roads; *mutationes* offered veterinary services, cart and carriage repair, and some lodging

myrmill-o, -ones – A class of gladiator that fought with the standard Roman sword, the *gladius*, the large rectangular shield (the *scutum*), an armored sword arm (*manica*), shin guards, and an odd, ornate, grill-faced visored helmet (*cassis crista*)

Nomentum – City and terminal point of the *Via Nomentana*, approximately 23 km northeast of Rome, modern Mentana

nones – Fifth day of the month on the Roman calendar

November [month] – The eleventh month of the Roman calendar

Nub-ia, -ian – Not part of the Roman empire, but well known to Rome, the area (and inhabitants) south of southern Egypt; more-or-less modern-day Sudan

nugator – Mild expletive: liar, faker, trifler, lightweight

Numid-ia, -ian – Modern coastal Algeria and Tunisia, became the largest part of the Roman province of Africa Nova

Oppius Mons – Southern spur of the Esquiline Hill (one of the Seven Hills of Rome); the valley of the Subura lies below the Oppian to the north; the Colosseum is to the south: see Seven Hills of Rome

Ost-ia, -ian – Port (and town) of ancient Rome, lying to the west of the city on the Tyrrhenian Sea

Palatine – The most famous, most prestigious of the Seven Hills of Rome; most early emperors had their primary dwelling on the Palatine: see Seven Hills of Rome

palla – An overwrap garment worn by Roman women, a large rectangular piece (generally wool) worn with one or more clasping brooches

pater – Father

Pausulae – A large town in Picenum (modern region: Marche), northeast of Rome, on the river Flusor (modern river: Chienti) and the coast of the Adriatic Sea

pedisecus – Servant, familiar, lackey

Penates, the (*Di Penates*) – Along with the Lares (see Lares, the), the most important of the *di familiares* (household gods) in a Roman home; associated with the family ancestors, the gods protecting health, hearth, and threshold

pe-s, -des – Foot: see Roman units of measurement

petanus – Distinctive tall, leather hat worn by Imperial postmen

Picenum – Ancient Roman region between the Apennines and the Adriatic Sea, northeast of Rome, modern Marche (plus a little bit of Abruzzo); ancestral home of the *gens* Pompeius

pilum – The primary medium-range weapon of the Roman legions, basically a 2 meter-long spear with a pyramidal iron head and an iron shaft running half-way to the wooden butt-end shaft; designed to bend after striking, encumbering the target and becoming unusable to the enemy

Pluto/Hades – Roman/Greek god of death and ruler of Hades

pomerium – Religious boundary circumscribing the original environment of Rome, essentially consisting of the Seven Hills; legend held that it was originally drawn by Romulus' plough, then Servius Tullius built his wall on it; different laws and customs applied to citizens within and without the *pomerium*, for instance, no one (except the Praetorian Guard) could carry weapons inside the *pomerium*, a law often breached

popin-a, -ae – Cheap tavern/bar

Porta Collina – Supposedly built as the northern entrance to the city by the ancient Roman king Servius Tullius (see Servian Wall) sometime in the 6th Century BCE, the Colline Gate stood at the crossroads of the *Via Salaria* and the *Via Nomentana*; nearby were the important temples of Venus Erycina and Fortuna

Porta Esquilina – Ancient arched gate through the Servian Wall on the *Via Tiburtina*

Porta Latina – Marble, single-arched gate at the southeastern entrance to Rome on the *Via Latina*

Poseidon/Neptune – Roman/Greek god of the sea

praefectus – A managerial or oversight position, roughly equivalent to "prefect" or "manager," Ancient Rome had military prefects (like *Praefectus castrorum*–camp commander), civilian prefects (like *Praefectus urbanus*–city prefect), police prefects, and even provincial prefects

praetor – One of the most powerful magistracies in the Roman empire, their power was only less than the consuls (and, of

course, the Emperor); the *Praetor Urbanus* (city praetor), for instance, had more-or-less complete control over everything related to the functioning of the city of Rome
pretiosa – Pretty one
prima hora nocte – First hour of the night
primus pilus – "First spear," the senior centurion of an army, commander of the first cohort; for comparison to modern military ranks, the duties and privileges of a *primus pilus* were a mix of the those of a First Sergeant and a Sergeant Major, generally being more hands-on than either, as the *primus pilus* was also the top training officer
puerum bonum – Good boy
pugnaces – Fighter
Reate – Ancient Italian city, supposedly the source of the women who were stolen as wives for the first Romans (the Sabine Women) and who stopped the last Roman-Sabine war (the Battle of *Lacus Curtius*) by running between the two armies and (successfully) appealing to their relatives on one side and their husbands on the other side
rector canibus – Master of dogs
regina barbarorum – Queen of barbarians
retari-us, -i – Depending on speed, the *retarii* were a type of gladiator who fought with few clothes and little armor; each was equipped with a weighted net (*rete*), a trident (*tridens*), and a short dagger (*pugio*); a *retarius* wore no helmet and no armor other than a metal shoulder guard (*galerus*)
RETRO! – Back! [command]
Revolt of Saturninus – During the middle of the reign of the emperor Domitian, the Roman Senator Lucius Antonius Saturninus led a revolt of two legions in Germania Superior; two legions and a number of *vexallationes* were called up and successfully put down the revolt; Lucius Viterbus (Iace's master) fought in one of these auxiliary forces
Roman units of measurement – The Roman units of length,

weight, and size used (or implied) in the story of Iace and their rough Metric and U.S. equivalents:

Units of Length

Roman unit equal to Metric equivalent

```
digitus = 1/16th pes = 18.5 mm (.72 in)
pes = 1 pes = 29.6 cm (.97 ft)
cubitum = 1 1/2 pedes = 44.4 cm (1.5 ft)
mille passus = 1.48 km = .92 miles
```

Liquid measure

sextarius = 1/6 *congius* = .55 liters (1.2 quarts)
congius = 1 *congius* = 3.3 liters (3.5 quarts)
amphora = 8 *congii* = 26 liters (7 gallons)

Units of Weight

uncia = 1/12 *libra* = 27 grams (1 oz.)
libra = 1 *libra* = 329 grams (11 1/2 oz.)

Romulus – Founder and first king of Rome, brother of Remus; he and his brother were adopted by a she-wolf as babies

Rubicon – A small river in northern Italy that defined the extent of the Roman *imperium* at the time of Julius Caesar; when he crossed it along with his Legion, he said *"alea iacta est"* (the die has been cast), signaling that civil war was inevitable

Sappho – See Poet of Lesbos, the

Scipio Africanus Minor – Formally Publius Cornelius Scipio Aemilianus Africanus Numantinus, generally known as Scipio Aemilianus or Scipio the Younger, one of Rome's greatest generals, friend of the Greek historian Polybius, adopted grandson of Scipio Africanus; he destroyed Carthage in 146 BCE

Servian Wall – (*Murus Servii Tulii*) Built in the early days of Rome, supposedly by the sixth Roman King, Servius Tullius, it encompassed most of the Seven Hills of Rome and had 16 gates

Servius Tullius – Probably legendary sixth King of Rome (fl. 545 BCE); first elected king, second Etruscan, builder of the Servian Wall, very popular, but suffered an evil end, murdered by his daughter and his son-in-law Tarquinius Superbus, who succeeded him, becoming Rome's last king

sester-ce, -tii – A small copper Roman coin: see Coins of Rome
Seven Hills of Rome, the – The oldest (most sacred) and central part of Rome comprises these hills and the valleys between them: Quirinal and Viminal in the North, Esquiline and Caelian in the East, Aventine in the South, Capitoline in the West, and Palatine in the center; the Servian Wall surrounded all seven hills
sica – Short, curved sword or long knife with about a foot-long blade, used by the Thracian-type gladiators (the *sica* being similar to a Thracian sword)
sicarius – Assassin, someone who used the short, easily concealed (somewhat illegal) *sica* knife
SISTE! – Stop! [command]
Sophocles – One of the most famous ancient Greek playwrights; his best known work centered around the history of the royal court of the city of Thebes
Spoletium – Modern Spoleto, on the eastern branch of the ancient Roman road, the *Via Flaminia*
Spoliarium – Large, underground chamber with direct access to the Colosseum where dead gladiators and animals were taken (dragged or in a cart), armor and weapons removed and stashed for later use, and bodies disposed of; a vile and horrific place
STA! – Stand! [command]
stabul-a, -ae – Stables
Strabo – Cross-eyed; a name sometimes given to children who suffered from Strabismus
Styg-ia, -ian – Refers to the river Styx, which separates the world of the living from Hades, the world of the dead (in Greek and Roman mythology)
Stymphalian Birds – Mythical man-eating birds with bronze beaks, metal feathers that could be launched like arrows and poisonous feces; removal of these birds was the Sixth Labor of Heracles (Hercules for the Romans)
Styx, the – According to Greek myth and religion, after death

every person had to be ferried across the river Styx to begin their eternal stay in Hades

Subura, the – Notorious low-end part of ancient Rome lying between the Viminal and Esquiline hills; there were few individual homes in the Subura; most of it consisted of large apartment blocks (*insulae*), often with *cauponae* or some other commercial enterprise on the ground floor

stultus – Idiot, fool

tabern-a, -ae – Originally, hotels for wealthy and official travelers on the Roman road system, as *tabernae* proliferated, they became less exclusive, more like local pubs or small lodging houses

Tarentum – Modern Taranto, important (mostly Greek) city, unofficial capital of Magna Graecia

Temple of Jupiter/Jupiter Optimus Maximus – A temple of the great god Jupiter that also functioned as the primary bank of ancient Rome

Thebes – One of the major cities of ancient Greece where many of the early Greek tragedies (plays) were set

Tiber/Father Tiber – As pantheists, Romans believed in many gods and one of the most important was the god of the Tiber, the great river that snaked through the middle of the city and offered so much to the settlers there

Tibur – Modern Tivoli, known even anciently for two things: a watering hole for the wealthy and one of the finest quarries near Rome

Titus – Officially (as Emperor): *Titus Flavius Caesar Vespasianus Augustus*, renowned warrior (he captured Jerusalem, ending the First Jewish-Roman War), eldest son of the emperor Vespasian; he succeeded his father, but died after less than two years of wearing the crown; immensely popular, particularly for his generosity after the eruption of Mount Vesuvius in 79 CE and the great fire in Rome the following year; his brother Domitian was probably his least enthusiastic fan

toga – Official, but not ever really popular, garment of Rome, primarily for the Roman upper classes; the *toga* was a single piece of (usually white) wool, cut into an enormous semi-circle; difficult to put on, uncomfortable to wear, unsuited for any physical work, it became the ceremonial dress for the upper-class; complex rules governed which of the many types of *toga* a citizen could wear (only citizens were allowed to wear the *toga*); the bright whiteness of *togas* was achieved by a combination of laundering in urine (which breaks down into ammonia) and an application of chalk

torquem magnam – Literally "the long chain," a chain that threaded together many slaves

TRAHO! / TRAHE! – Pull! [command]

tributus familiaris – Literally "assigned family," a form of claim or taxation similar to feudal dues widely practiced in ancient Italy

tunica – Tunic, a popular item of clothing for both sexes; often worn as an undergarment

Tyr, -ian – An ancient city on the far west coast of the Mediterranean, known from ancient times as the original home of the Phoenicians and the source of an intense purple dye

Urban praetor [*Praetor Urbanus*] – Top-level magistrate of the City of Rome

Vale…[*Ave atque Vale*] – The "Farewell" portion of the most popular Roman greeting, "Hail and Farewell": often accompanied in the military with a clenched fist thumped once against the opposite side of the chest; *Ave* and *Vale* were both used separately as well

VELOX! – Faster! [command]

Venus Erycina – An aspect of the Goddess of Love; the popular Temple of Venus Erycina followed some of the more ancient and licentious rituals of this goddess

VERTE! – Turn! [command]

Vespasian – *Titus Flavius Vespasianus*, began life as an *equites* (that is, not from a Senatorial family), became a famous general (fought successfully in the Roman invasion of Britain and in

Judaea); Vespasian was the "winner" (that is the final survivor) of the civil war called the Year of the Four Emperors (69 CE); a great general, a good ruler, his difficulties arose from a scrupulous thriftiness; he ruled as emperor for ten years and was succeeded by one of his sons, Titus, and then the other, Domitian; he named his family's rule the Flavian dynasty

Vestal Virgins – At the time of the emperor Domitian, there were six Vestals (or Vestal Virgins), women who vowed complete chastity for 30 years in order to serve the Roman goddess Vesta, goddess of the hearth; their primary sacred duty was to make sure that the sacred fire of Vesta never went out; as Vestals, not only were their bodies sacred and untouchable (immediate death was the penalty for violating this proscription), they enjoyed many other privileges such as the right to free condemned persons simply by touching them

vexillat-io, iones – Specifically, a detachment from a regular Roman legion that was on a temporary or special assignment; these were regular troops and not auxilliaries (though auxilliaries could be assigned to a *vexillatio*); Lucius Viterbus soldiered in a *vexillatio*

Via Nomentana – Road leading northeast from Rome to the town of Nomentum (modern Mentana: 23 km)

Via Salaria – Roman road that led northeast to Castrum Truentinum (modern Porto d'Ascoli), passing through Reate (modern Rieti) and Asculum (modern Ascoli Piceno), and then on to Ancona (in Picenum) on the Adriatic coast.

Via Tiburtina – Ancient road that originally terminated in Tibur (modern Tivoli), a wealthy vacation spot and the location of the primary marble quarry near Rome

Vicus Librarius – Street of the Scribes: concentration in central Rome for copyists, bookbinders, scroll and parchment repair shops, and where Livilla had her copy shop

Vicus Lorarius – Street of the Harness Makers, and other leatherworkers

Vicus Sutorius – Street of the Cobblers

Vir? – Literally "Man?"; a Latin idiom used in spoken language (the question mark was implied) essentially requesting that someone tell you their name

viri boni – Literally "the good men"; the *viri boni* were the most important and prestigious men in Rome

White, the [chariot races] – One of the three racing teams that competed in the Roman *ludi* (games), along with the Blue, and the Red

XIVth Consulship of Caesar Domitian, 840 AUC – Fourteenth consulship of the emperor Domitian; his consulship ended on mid January of 88 CE (840 AUC) and was taken up by his co-consul, Lucius Minicius Rufus until April of that year

Zeus/Zeus Phradoxes – The Greek king of the gods; Zeus appeared in many different forms, often in the form of the husband of a human woman he wished to ravish; Zeus Phradoxes is an unknown attribute of Zeus, probably attributable to Menaeus' poetic imagination

END OF *IRON DOG*: Volume 2 of *Tales of the Eternal Dog*

GOLD DOG

Tales of the Eternal Dog, V. 3

ALEC ROWELL

1

INUJIKI-NO-KAMI

MUTSU PROVINCE, the Tsubaki Shrine of Sarutahiko-No-O-Kami and Ame-No-Uzume-No-Mikoto, in the 2nd year of the Ten'an era, in the reign of the Emperor Seiwa-tennō (c. 858 CE)

I SEE MORE colors than I did when I was alive. Humans make much of colors and I understand now.

Of course, that is only when my eyes are open. Squirrels and pigeons are still grays and dirty whites. As are all the small things that crawl and fly. Deer, too. There is some blue around their ears and heads. Lynx and bears reflect flashes of yellow and pink.

Crows, now. Crows and raccoon dogs are bright in their reds and greens and blues—colors melting around them like walking rainbows (which I can see now, also).

Inumiko, my mate on the other side of the path, tells me that these colors mean something.

Like me, she is a statue. She and I, Inujiki-No-Kami, are guardian kami of the Tsubaki Shrine—*Komainu*, temple dog statues. She is more fearsome than me. She is also usually correct.

Humans are the big show here. The young ones are clean, simple colors, usually of one or two hues. Most often girl children are yellow and boys red. As they get older, strange vertical stripes of darkest purple and green mark them. Sometimes these colors are frightening and bold.

There are flashes and explosions when humans touch. Pools of color expand around their clasped hands. Swirling masses of green and gold race across their heads and groins when they put their lips together, which they do not often do inside the Shrine.

That action is very confusing. Sometimes I close my eyes and wake when two humans do these things.

For it is only when I close my eyes that the true world begins for me. It is then much as it was before I died. The swirling intensities of color wash into comfortable tones. My feelings are closer to what they were before I became a god.

And—most importantly—I can move again.

THIS DAY, two humans—a man and a woman—stopped at the *Temizuya*, the cleansing spot just outside the *Jinja* pavilion. They followed the private cleansing ritual: pouring sacred water over left hands, water over right hands, rinsing their mouths, rinsing the handle of the *Hishaku*, the long-handled bamboo ladle. They moved together between us—the kami guardian lion-dogs—and proceeded to the pavilion. After a moment of silence, I heard their prayers. Prayers always sound clear in my stone ears, even though I sit well away from the *Jinja*.

MAN'S PRAYER: Oh, Sarutahiko-No-O-Kami. Dissolve this shame from me and my family. Cleanse my wife of her unclean connections.

WOMAN'S PRAYER: Oh, Ame-No-Uzume-No-Mikato. Please hear my humble petition. My family has disgraced my worthy husband. His family has ostracized him from their home. My disgrace should not be his disgrace. Help me, Lady.

Following at once upon this prayer, the Lady Ame-No-Uzume's light—the white of milk—shone on the small woman.

It reflected off of her and upon her male companion. He was tall, but stoop-shouldered, as if some heavy weight had once dropped on him, and his dark eyes darted about, ever watchful for that stone to fall on him again.

The small woman was dressed in plain, light-brown peasant garb, though her companion wore bright silk. She, too, was bent —perhaps from the same weight—diminishing her already slight stature. Her hair was pulled back hard into a farmer's planting bun. I decided to smell her. That was my most trying limitation as a god-statue, so I closed my eyes to enter the shadow kami world.

I leapt down from my stone perch. As always when I was in this mobile form, my sight now beheld only black and white and shades of shimmering silver. But my keenest sensor, my nose, was again my own and the world's secrets opened to me like a well-dug-out rabbit's den.

I was right. The young woman smelled of the faint fresh scent of river flowers, of newly planted earth, and a soft bitter aroma that brought me up short. I do not sneeze in the shadow kami world, but I felt as if I should. The light that shone upon her in my statue world was even brighter in the shadow world.

IT WAS time to follow my Lady Ame-No-Uzume's bidding.

It is not that I am ungrateful for the work that is mine and for the gifts that I have been given to accomplish this work. But I look forward to some chores and others I perform as a dutiful servant of my Lady Ame-No-Uzume and Lord Sarutahiko. Such it is with soul watching and heart leading. If I could speak to my Lady and my Lord, I would ask them if these are truly a dog's path. No doubt they would tell me that it is *Kami No Michi*, a kami's way. Two hundred years and I still do not understand.

Rising in the air (except to other kami, I am unnoticed in the shadow world if I do not choose to reveal myself), I gazed eye-to-eye with the small woman and so entered her heart.

AIOKI'S HEART

"We must leave Mutsu and never return, Aioki. We must leave today." Kuro's fierce brows glowered down at her, but Aioki knew the gentle heart her husband strove to hide with this scary show, so she lowered her eyes and spoke softly.

"Your family would be disgraced—more disgraced than they are already with a daughter like me. We cannot leave, husband."

Kuro grabbed a *bokken*, a wooden sword affixed to a bracket on the wall of their small receiving room and slashed the air, then bashed the floor, leaving marks Aioki would have to repair. He cast the sword down and fell to his knees, craned his head back and shouted at the ceiling: "The heavens have forsaken us! I will not bear this shame. I will not allow you to bear this shame! I must...I must..." Then he twice beat the floor with his palms.

Remaining in *seiza*—a good wife's supplicant position—Aoki raised her head and spoke, "We must endure, husband. I know that my family has caused this grief and I will do anything you ask--or anything that your family asks--in order to redress the shame as much as my poor efforts can. Please direct your anger at me."

Kuro rose from the floor, hands clenched into fists. Wordless, he stood over Aoki, disarmed between frustration and affection.

I SIFTED through her dark hair, like smoke I fell from her ears and lips.

My Lady—for whom time itself is but another illusion—spun the wheel backward and I entered the heart of her husband.

KURO'S HEART

"I will protect you, wife. My parents are unreasonable. We will survive. Do not worry." Kuro stood straight and tall.

Aioki knelt on the ground, crying quietly: "What are we to do? What are we to do? Oh, husband, I do not know where we should turn."

Kuro knelt by his wife. He firmly lifted her chin and looked deep into her beautiful dark eyes, the whites reddened now in sorrow and distress. "I tell you, Aioki, in Dewa we will put this all behind us. Never fear. My blood is noble and I can find refuge elsewhere. I have a kinsman in Dewa."

Aioki sniffed and stopped crying, looking up dutifully at Kuro. Her eyes were filled with concern. "But what of my shame? Of my family's shame?"

"This will be of no matter. We will not speak of it again." He gently held her upper arms, never losing her regard. "Go and make us ready for departure, wife."

Aioki bowed slightly, then rose and left the room.

AND SO MY shadow-self fell from the ears and mouth of Kuro and, as spirits do, I found myself again the stone kami in the shrine of my Lord Sarutahiko and my Lady Uzume.

EYES OF LADY AME-NO-UZUME-NO-MIKOTO

"Finding problems in human lives is not a difficult task, is it, Inujiki-No-Kami?" Soft gold notes emanated from the Lady Uzume as she radiated her thoughts to me.

"Are you hearing what I think, Lady? Or am I thinking to myself? It is confusing when I make no motion and do not even detect smells."

"Yes, little one, I understand all that passes through you."

"Yes, Lady Uzume, humans are full of troubles and little else. I do not know how they have survived." I would have lowered my head if I could, not just in deference, but at my defeat in the task the Lady Uzume had assigned me.

"Where there are problems, there are also answers, Inujiki."

"I told you the dog wasn't up to it." A new voice and new form filled the air. A giant dressed in crimson and black, with a red round face and enormous pointed nose floated aggressively up to the Lady Ame-No-Uzume. It was my Lord Sarutahiko-No-O-Kami, Lord of All Earthly kami. "He's a dog, Uzume."

In one smooth, sweeping motion, Lord Sarutahiko swished

his huge, blade-leafed *Hoko* spear through the air, then held it perpendicular to the ground. The blunt end touched the tip of his fantastic nostrils, and he spoke so firmly, his crimson and gray words would have been a snarl had he not been the kami of positivity and protection as well as of justice. "There's only one way to cut through this mess."

The small pink cloud upon which Lady Uzume rode slid between Lord Sarutahiko and the very still statue of Inujiki. Her immaculately perfect right arm extended and she stroked the puffing crimson cheek of her husband with her long white fingers. "My Lord, these matters are well in hand. You must allow new ascendants to exercise their abilities. Do not take so much on yourself, mighty Sarutahiko. It will trouble your divine sleep."

"...'must allow'...Hunhh...Well, the cursed dog *does* trouble my sleep. Why did the priests raise dog kami in the first place? Kamaitachi and Inari have fine service from their *kitsune*. Foxes are refined. We know their powers. Dogs...dogs are..." Though calming at the beginning of his words, the Lord Sarutahiko grew redder and redder and ever more solid as he spoke.

During his speech, Lady Uzume never removed her alabaster hand from his cheek. Now she lightly and slowly stroked it as she continued: "My cherished Lord, as always, it is your will that I have chosen to be in accord with. As you have so often pledged that it is my will that you follow as well. There is no discord here. Indeed, there is no reason for misapprehension. Inujiki-No-Kami was just relating to me how matters in this issue stand and what outcome he foresees."

At this, my Lady Uzume turned upon me and my stone heart melted.

Indeed, my heart did melt, as did all my body. I stood neither as a statue nor in that silver shadow world. I stood again as in life, a dog with a fine bushy tail, a nose that smelled life as it was, and eyes that saw the world in ways I understood. But I knew this was only to make me more presentable to my Lord Sarutahiko. What would I say to him? How should the prayers of Aioki and Kuro be answered?

I scratched my chin with a rear leg as I thought. It felt very fine.

Lord Sarutahiko stared at me in silence. His hard eyes flashed red like his nose. As his mouth began to open, I spoke.

"Great Lord and My Lady: I know a seemly way to address the prayers of your two supplicants. It is a simple matter."

"No foolery, dog!" Lord Sarutahiko thundered. "Speak your plan and I will judge its worth."

It seemed I still had some shadow-world abilities, for I rose in the air so that I hovered between my Lord and my Lady, and then carefully but quickly explained to them what I hoped to do and what I believed it would accomplish.

My Lord scowled when I finished. "It can do little harm. I will watch for further prayers and offerings. If this does not prove out, then this will not be an end, Lady Ame-No-Uzume-No-Mikoto." Then, as suddenly as he appeared, he was gone, leaving behind only the odor of seaweed and snow.

My Lady turned upon me. The slightest of smiles tipped the edges of her mouth. Pale light shone from her eyes and she nodded her head. "Do as you have spoken, Inujiki. You have my blessing."

THE PLOY OF INUJIKI-NO-KAMI

Kuro rolled from his sleeping mat at dawn. In the next room, Aioki was already boiling water.

"There is no time to eat or drink, wife. We must leave before my father's agents come here today. Then we at least will not have the shame of being thrown into the street added to our burdens."

"Yes, husband. I have prepared the bundles we will take with us. But we have no cart or horse."

"Fujimori the blacksmith owes me many favors. He has a

wagon and a pony that he has pledged to me. I will leave now and bring it back at once." With that, Kuro stalked from the house in his high patent sandals.

Still bending over the hearth fire, Aioki paused to consider her best actions.

After a moment, resolution straightened her face and her back. She tied her painted straw *kasa* on her head, wrapped a shawl around her shoulders, and hurried out of the house in the opposite direction from her husband.

THE TSUBAKI SHRINE stood near the house of Kuro and Aioki, so the trip there afforded Aioki little time to consider her future when strange noises suddenly arose in front of her—a loud flapping and sounds like a flute blown with no tune, all combined with very deep growls. Rounding a corner of the path obscured by cascading purple blooms of wisteria, she witnessed a horrible struggle. A large crane stood over a nest, pecking and waving its wings at the largest dog Aioki had ever seen. Its teeth and saliva glistened over midnight black gums as it feinted moves in and out toward the beleaguered bird.

Aioki's eyes surveyed the area for a stone or stick that she could use against the monstrous dog, which was nearly as big as herself. She found a small but sturdy branch and with no hesitation ran at the huge dog, shouting "Hai! Hai!" and waving her meager weapon at it.

Paying no attention to her, the dog continued to harry the protective crane.

Aioki drew closer, raising her arm to strike the dog and continuing to shout at it to leave off.

Finally noticing this new combatant, the dog turned its enormous head. Its red eyes stared viciously and it quit its attack on the bird. In an instant it enveloped Aioki's delicate wrist in its slavering jaws.

It was the luck of the gods that the creature's intelligence did not match its ferocity, for it grabbed Aioki's left wrist, leaving her other arm free to attack with her pitiful weapon. Which she now did, vigorously but with no apparent effect.

Aioki could not hear it amidst the tumult and strain of her fight, but a loud shout of her name came from close behind her. Her husband had forgotten his coin, returned home near the time she had left and had rightly guessed the destination of his devout wife, following hard on her heels to reprimand her for unexcused absence in their time of crisis.

Petty rebukes forgotten now, all Kuro could think of or see was that his beloved, kind, selfless, dear wife was struggling in the jaws of a hideous monster—a demon out of ancient tales. What she had given him, uncomplainingly! All he could give her in return was his protection and this was her fate? Kuro dashed in, grabbing the gigantic dog by its furry, pointed ears. He had heard that this would loosen the jaws of the wildest beasts.

Kuro's information proved correct. The dog-demon immediately released Aioki's wrist and--with unmatchable speed--twisted and turned, fastening its great mouth around Kuro's unprotected throat.

The man and the dog wrestled on the ground, Aioki frantically scurrying around them, trying to beat the dog away with her large twig.

Abe Masuko and his small band of retainers appeared from around the wooded corner that sheltered the Tsubaki Shrine, brushed aside the wisteria vines and beheld this terrifying scene. Masuko had come to try to speak reason to his wayward son, Kuro, and persuade him to leave his bride, whose clan name was now soiled by their connections to the reviled *emishi* barbarians. Although Masuko had seen his son leaving his home, he was too proud to call out and so following behind now found himself witnessing the awful fight before him.

"Save my son! Mayumi! You and Kaneko kill that beast!" Abe Masuko commanded.

Mayumi and Kaneko, though loyal to the head of the Abe

clan, were household men: scholars and men of business. Seeing the monster before them, they quailed.

"We have no weapons, Lord. How are we to help him?"

Levelling a gaze upon his men that might itself wound the beast attacking his son, Masuko snorted, "Cowards!" Pushing back the ceremonial dress he wore on such outings, he pulled his sharp *koto* sword and rushed into the fray to save his son.

Masuko was unable to strike immediately, as Aioki continued to swing wildly at the giant dog that was mauling her husband, heedless of any danger to herself. Her blows lacked precision and effect, but her boldness and passion were supreme.

After trying to get around the young woman for a few moments, Masuko finally held up a palm, blocking a slicing blow of Aioki's switch. He grunted, "Step aside, girl, I have a sword." Then, without further pause, he struck a strong blow that cut clean down the ribcage of the attacking creature.

There were instant and gratifying effects to the sword strike. The creature released Kuro. It howled. It dropped to all fours. And before Masuko could continue with his assault, it bolted away, into the woods and out of sight within a heartbeat.

Aioki and Masuko knelt by Kuro's side, expecting grievous wounds. Kuro sat up. Where they expected a slashed and mutilated throat, there was no evidence of the attack other than some already swelling bruises.

"How did you escape injury, Kuro?" The astonished father asked.

Kuro shook his head in equal disbelief.

Aioki wrapped her arms around his chest and sobbed, "Oh, my dear husband. My prayers are answered. You are whole."

"But what of you, wife? You fought the beast first." Kuro stroked Aioki's hair gently.

"It is nothing."

Still kneeling by the side of the couple, Masuko took Aioki's injured arm in his grip and examined the work of the dog's teeth. Blood covered her arm and half of her simple smock.

"A moment." Masuko spoke, then used his sword to slice three long strips from his embroidered ceremonial robe. Patiently and with great care, he bound his daughter-in-law's wound.

"This will hold until I bring my apothecary. He will clean your wounds and bandage them properly."

Masuko rose, motioned to his men, whose heads had remained down through the entire adventure. Stepping a pace away, he bowed deeply to Aioki and his son, both still seated on the ground, holding each other. When his head rose, his face was flushed and solemn.

"I ask you, son and daughter-in-law, to attend my house for the New Moon Ceremony in two days. We will celebrate together the great good fortune of having such bravery in our family." His eyes took in Aioki's simple dress, then turned down to the ground, and he added, "My tailor will bring a 12-layer *Juni-hitoe* before the visit, Lady Aioki."

Kuro's face furrowed, then he stood, helping Aioki to stand beside him. Her expression was soft yet serene. Together, son and daughter-in-law bowed.

"We would be honored, father." They said in unison.

Masuko returned their bow, bending as deeply as he had initially.

INUJIKI-NO-KAMI RETURNS

"Thank you, Crane, for your assistance." I bowed to my fellow kami. He and his mate resided as guardians in the nearby shrine to Fukurokuju.

"It was the will of our Lady Ame-No-Uzume-No-Mikoto. It was also an amusing diversion, Inujiki-No-Kami. Anytime you require such assistance, I will gladly comply." Crane kami bowed in that awkward-graceful way that only such legs could achieve.

And so I returned to my shrine.

I stood below my statue and blinked. And so the world of colors and motionlessness returned to me. I was once again a god and a statue.

SOMETIME—I do not know how to measure it as the colors of day and night do not impinge upon me as a statue—but sometime later, the small woman Aioki returned to the Tsubaki Shrine. I watched her cleanse herself at the Temizuya. I watched her make obeisance at the Jinja pavilion, clapping hands, bowing, and ringing the Suzu bell. She made her Senpai, her prayer, there:

AIOKI'S PRAYER

Lady Ame-No-Uzume-No-Mikato: I, Aioki, thank you for the gifts you have given me: music and song and a good husband. I ask that you bless our marriage and may we have children that will honor you.

THEN AIOKI PAID a high-crowned priest for a ribboned *Yakayoke Omamori*, which she hung carefully by it's woven chord to Lady Uzume's offering board.

She did not come to my shrine. I felt sadness at this.

Some other time—again, I do not know how much later—the pink cloud of my Lady Ame-No-Uzume appeared before me. Her eyes of indescribable color looked into mine and, once more, I felt my stone heart melting.

"You have sadness that the lady Aioki made *Senpai* to me, Inujiki, and ignored you." As always, her words were the deepest comfort, even if I was afraid there was some rebuke inside of them.

"No need to answer, friend dog. Your greatest power is the clearness and openness of your heart. There is not nor has there ever been a lie there," she continued.

Nevertheless, I raised my courage and my voice to her. "I thought she would *know*. That somehow she would *know*." I sounded very small.

My Lady smiled at me. Her light brightened and covered me. The colors that swirled everywhere flowed into and out of her light and then it shone through me, bringing joy and peace like I had never known.

After a time, her light dimmed. The joy I felt became bearable. Lady Uzume's cloud began to drift away. As her presence faded, her smile brightened and she whispered to me, "And did you not know, Inujiki-No-Kami, that this Aioki who made prayers to me—and that did not visit you—is the great-great granddaughter of the Aioki who was 'saved' from the dog monster? The story of 'Aioki and the Demon Dog' has grown great in the annals of the Abe clan." Then my Lady Ame-No-Uzume-No-Mikoto laughed. I had heard her laugh only once before when she cavorted with her husband, my Lord Sarutahiko. "It is a tale that will live as long as their children have children. You have done well, Inujiki-No-Kami."

As her cloud drifted away, my eyes remained open.

2

LIONHUNTERS OF BAM-I-YAN

VALLEY OF BAM-I-YAN, Bukhara region of Khurasan, during the rule of the Saffarid Amr ibn al-Layth, in the 259th year after the Hijra of the One True Prophet [880 CE]

THE BOY STUMBLED and fell on the dusty road. What was left of the knees of his tattered breeches shredded as they grazed the gravel. Old scabs opened and bled.

Mas'ud hardly noticed these small indignities. They were the aftermath of far worse cruelties he'd suffered over the past three seasons as his bruised body trudged southwestward. It had been almost a day since he'd had water. That was far more on his mind than the pink oozing from his knees and feet. He didn't remember when last he'd filled his belly with anything warm.

The final wisps of that strength that only accompanies youth were almost drained from his thin, torn body and spirit. For days beyond count, his mind had washed in memories of bloody flashing swords, harsh voices shouting words of lust and hate he couldn't understand, pain, and a blackness with no peace. "Where is Thy Mercy, Allah?" And then the ashen remembrance of waking in a charred ruin, surrounded by broken walls, broken skulls—the remains of his family, his village—everyone and everything he had known in his life of fourteen years. "*Where* is Thy Mercy, Allah?"

At least the road had been flat this day. Vast high mountains that he knew he could not cross lay to either side of him. An enormous outcropping of red stone jutted in front of the snow-topped range on his right. Even in his febrile state, Mas'ud wondered at the hundreds of small black openings that dotted the near surface of this cliff-hill. The road swept ever nearer the sandstone cliffs. It soon became clear that these specks were small caves.

Caves? So many caves? Perhaps I could shelter there?

"But then, what would I eat on such a mountain of stone?" He muttered to himself, "Better to stay on the road. There will be another village."

And there were buildings that seemed to have been carved into the sides of the mountain, too. And what were those stones of men? It must be his thirst. There could be no figures of that size anywhere. Surely they were as tall as ten men. No, a hundred men. Mas'ud shook his head and almost fell from dizziness.

Now he saw more apparitions, two beasts—one silver and one golden—highlighted like angels flying against the dark red stone of the cave-splattered mountain. They did *seem* to be flying. No, they were running. Faster than the deer of the plains. What were these wondrous creatures? For a moment, Mas'ud forgot all the pain in his body and all the horrors in his mind, breath held as he watched the cohesive motion of these animals in their course. His eyes focused well enough now that he could see undulations of gold and silver wave and flow in concert with the movements of their legs: a vertical fall of line as front feet scissored down, pushing through until they met the back feet that dug in to plunge forward, then horizontal as the front legs stretched ahead and the back stretched out behind in an impossible elongation. Mas'ud stood, transfixed at this perfect expression of will and muscle. He watched them grow smaller and less distinct, and so too did his vision of everything else around him. The browns of the road, the patches of green that had begun showing up around him, and the red of the nearby mountain all shifted toward a darker and darker grey and then, finally, to black.

"ALLAHU AKBAR, my son. God be praised in his infinite mercy and goodness."

Mas'ud's eyes opened to the unusual sight of a finished roof above his head. And not just *finished*; this ceiling was covered with thousands of fantastic, colorful insects or animals. Had he fallen into Sijjin? Would he be burned for eternity? Had he not suffered enough? But someone had spoken God's name. Surely that would not be done in the realm of Shaitan?

He lifted his head and found that he was reclining on carpets and soft sacks or pillows. An ancient with an enormous grey beard squatted beside him, holding two bronze bowls.

"Praised be the name of the Prophet and all his kin. Praise to Allah and his Mercy. Thou art well, boy." The greybeard did not smile, though it would have been difficult to find teeth in the mass of brush that covered his face, but he extended his hands to Mas'ud.

"Here, child. Eat and drink. But do so sparingly, else you will swoon."

Keeping a wary eye on the old man's face (or, rather, beard), Mas'ud accepted the offering. He drank—not too deeply—then looked at the food. Chunks of grilled meat—lamb, his nostrils told him—and white tubers. His stomach growled audibly in impatience.

"Allah speaks though no word is spoken." Was that a low chuckle rolling out from behind the beard?

Maintaining his vigilant view of the old one, Mas'ud ate. Whenever he sensed he was not being watched by the patriarch, his eyes searched this dwelling with the same hunger his empty belly had recently felt. He was in a great room. There had been no such place in his home of Taloqan, the home that had been destroyed by the ravaging infidel Turks. Mas'ud had some learning and he recognized parts of the Book written on the arches and walls in palest greys and softest blues. Now that his mind was not so fogged, he could see that the insects were not crawling across the ceiling; those figures were carved letters and shapes, too. His grandfather had instructed him and his two brothers (Oh! He saw the slashed bloody faces of his brothers, Ali and Umyad, as they fell at the feet of his dead parents) and had read the Prophet's words to them. He could even make some marks himself: his and his family's names, the benediction Allahu Akbar, and the phrase "the donkey knows his tail, do you know yours."

Something cold struck his foot, and Mas'ud looked down to see that his slack hand had spilled some of the water onto his own foot. A small shadow passed above him, and he canted his head up to see the old man's gnarled, long-fingered hands (missing the right thumb) held out before him.

He handed back the almost empty bowls.

"I am Abu Fadl," the old one said simply, then turned and walked out through the nearest arch.

Mas'ud returned to his examination of the room.

At head height, all walls ran long and wide and were decorated with the grey and blue letters, sometimes joined in fantastic ways with squares and other shapes. There was a deep indentation in the wall opposite the arched entry door—almost another small room. It had its own arch, inlaid with stone whiter than all the other stone. The lettering and shapes in this area were in deep blues, red the color of the cliffs he'd seen on his way into this valley, and yellows bright and vibrant as sun's rays. It was the most beautiful wall Mas'ud had ever seen.

"The *mihrab* points the way, boy. Rise and we will approach. It is almost time for the *adhan*." Abu Fadl had noiselessly returned and motioned once for Mas'ud to get up, then turned his back on the boy.

His head pounding as he did, Mas'ud rose and stepped carefully, barefoot, behind the old man. He heard a distant voice singing, a song he almost remembered. His vision and his hearing were still clouded, but then Abu Fadl knelt on the enormous rug that covered most of the broad room and bowed down in the direction of the magnificent wall inset. Following him, at first from the weakness that still pervaded his body and his mind, and then from memory, Mas'ud knelt and spoke the powerful words of his faith:

> *God is Great*
> *I bear witness that there is no god except the*
>   *One God*
> *I bear witness that Mohammed is the messenger*
>   *of God*
> *Rise up for prayer*
> *Rise up for salvation*
> *God is Great*
> *There is no god except the One God*

As he began this prayer a third time, the blues and reds of the *mihrab* seemed to pulse; the greys became a mist that spread over him and Mas'ud's mind slipped into the swirling, welcoming colors of the prayer carpet on which he knelt.

He awoke again with the now-familiar bearded face of Abu Fadl above him.

"My name is Mas'ud." He spoke softly and roughly, throat and tongue oddly dry.

"A good name, Mas'ud." The old one replied. "You have family in the valley?" He added.

"Which valley is this, grandfather?"

"Ah. You are a wanderer. And you are a believer found. Allah be praised." Abu Fadl's eyes rolled toward the ceiling.

"Did you carry me here, grandfather?" Mas'ud could not bring his eyes to meet Abu Fadl's watery brown ones.

"No, my son, an infidel found you on the road. A good man, but like many in this valley, he follows false gods and knows not the peace of the surrender to the One God's will."

Mas'ud did not know what to say to this. After a moment, though, he remembered what he had seen on the road before he collapsed, and asked, "Do you know of the dogs, grandfather, the great grey and yellow dogs that move like the wind on the water across the face of the hills?"

The portions of Abu Fadl's face that were not covered by his beard contracted at Mas'ud's question. When he replied, his voice had lost the soft kindness with which he had so far addressed the boy, "I know of these dogs, Mas'ud. What of them?"

"They are...uh...beautiful...grandfather."

Tensions and ripples traversed Abu Fadl's wrinkles: his brow relaxed, the edges of his mouth rose and his cheeks bunched, his large ears pinned themselves back against his balding skull. Finally, as Mas'ud was sure he was about to reply, some rattling and chuffing noises outside drew their attention. Abu Fadl looked down at Mas'ud, his proud straight eyebrows—stiff and black as an adder—told the young man to stay still, then the old man shuffled out of the room.

Abu Fadl had hardly been gone when he returned. His face was now smooth and unreadable. He motioned to Mas'ud to stand and follow him.

Unsteady on his feet, Mas'ud walked behind his benefactor into a long hall. In the open archway at the end of this space stood a small man. He was dressed in the dark blue-stained garb that Mas'ud had come to associate with the people of the mountains he'd sometimes met on the road.

Abu Fadl continued to beckon Mas'ud onward with hand gestures.

When the boy came within three paces of the entrance, Abu

Fadl spoke, "This is Perzo. He is the man who found you on the road. The one who brought you here."

Mas'ud stepped out of the building to more closely see his rescuer. There, in the sunlight, two large dogs stood near the outside wall. Drifting layers of their hair fell almost to the ground; one was grey, the grey of bright silver, and the other was furred in golds and yellows and browns. Their great plumed tails curled up behind them like fern banners. These were balanced by heads held high on proud necks. Most prominent in these extended heads were snouts full of teeth, some teeth so long that they stuck down over their lower gums, even when their mouths were closed. The dogs paid little attention to any of the men, not even glancing to Perzo, who stood by quietly. These were the visions he'd seen running, limned by the sandstone hillside. Mas'ud could not take his eyes off them.

"And these are his dogs."

MAS'UD WOKE to the challenging call of a distant rooster. The sun was not yet up. He was alone on a dusty straw mat in a tiny, dirt-floored hovel.

He stood and stepped outside the uncovered doorway. At the far end of a small animal pen stood Perzo and his dogs. The hillman carried a long pole and a bulging bag over one shoulder. He was walking away from the house toward the sandstone hills.

Mas'ud quickly sat back down and emptied the gravel from his heavily worn slippers, then hopped up and ran after.

HE HELD BACK a dozen yards as he followed Perzo and the dogs. The golden one swiveled its head in Mas'ud's direction a few times and even once might have waved its tail. Neither Perzo or the silver one acknowledged the boy's presence in any way.

After they passed the last tilled field and began to climb into the open scrub and small willows that sheltered in the southern lee of the great cliffs, Perzo and the dogs began trotting uphill. The boy was still weak—and had never been a great runner—but he kept up as best he could.

They came to a vast flat red rock. Mas'ud thought he could pace a hundred times before he'd reach the end of this one stone. At its northern end, it abutted the sheer front wall of the ruddy sandstone cliffs.

Perzo squatted down, swung the bag from his back, and pulled something from it, which he held out toward the dogs. The gold one stepped up, smelled what looked like an old rag—and sneezed. The grey moved closer to Perzo, but did not come as near as the gold. It shook its head side-to-side, a simple move that resulted in a brief sample of the rippling and flowing shimmers that Mas'ud had seen the first time he saw the dogs.

Perzo stood, rapped his staff against the rock twice and called out two words that Mas'ud did not understand. He held the rag high in his hands. Both the dogs took off, sprinting away parallel to the cliff face. Within a few moments they were out of sight.

During those few moments, Mas'ud held his breath at the wonder of their fluid beauty. He didn't notice that the small hillman had crossed the space to stand beside him.

"Those are my treasures—Barsala and Khwaga. They *are* the breath of Heaven, are they not?" Perzo spoke toward the now hidden dogs.

Afraid to speak the blasphemous answer in his heart, Mas'ud looked down into the dark, lined face, which after a moment smiled and added, "Let's eat."

OVER THE NEXT WEEKS, Mas'ud ran with Perzo, and sometimes with Barsala and Khwaga, though the pace they made when with the humans was more like a quick walk for them. He saw and learned many things: how the valley and hillsides were put together, where the dogs could run, where a man could walk and where he'd have to climb, water caches, blind spots—some hidden ankle-breaking drop-offs, the names of farmers and herders that employed Perzo, how to skin rabbit and weasel and—finally, one day—a pard.

"No spots. Your knife, Malquin." Perzo named Mas'ud after one of the local melons, which he claimed had the same color flesh. Mas'ud had yet to see one of these.

"Spots go to Balkh. Worth two farmer's pays. Learn to skin on the black." Mas'ud stared at Perzo, as much in surprise at the value of the hide as at the tough little man's volubility. There were many days when Perzo spoke no more than a sentence from dawn to dusk. But the reticence of Perzo's tongue did not extend to his small, hard hands. They guided Mas'ud's first cuts on the pard's belly and the tricky trims around the head. Just as they had shown him how to climb the ancient handholds into the caves where they'd often sheltered from sun and the night, how to milk goats in the valley, how to choose mountain berries that didn't curdle the stomach.

The sandstone cliffs, impressive and mysterious, were filled with ghosts. Ghosts of the infidels who had worshipped in this place. Ghosts of those who had made their lives here.

At the western end of the great cliffs was a structure that could have held Mas'ud's entire home village, carved out entirely from the flaky, soft stone. In one of the caves, Mas'ud found a comb of white bone, in another a figure of a child made from cloth and fire-hardened wood. People had lived, many people over many years, in these caves. Perzo would not say anything about them. Mas'ud thought Perzo might share the heathen faith that these others must have held. Sometimes he spoke in his strange mountain language and the sounds were breathy and rhythmic like prayers to God.

And these constant reminders of those whose spirits hung on did nothing to help Mas'ud forget his own dead. They spoke to the boy's ghosts, kept them just out of touch but always in his mind. There were no other voices to hear in these haunted hills. Even when he was whipped through villages on his way from his ruined home to Bam-i-yan, the curses and beatings had been some kind of intercourse with living humans. He was a young man. Silence wore harder on him than all else. Perzo's silence. The silence of the caves and the forgotten places of worship. The silence of the hills themselves. And, perhaps most of all, the silence of the great stone men whose eyes were ever on him.

Mas'ud had seen them from the road when he first entered the valley, but he thought they must have been part of the fever dream he'd suffered. It wasn't till the third day with Perzo that they came upon them.

They were running with the dogs and, for the first time, Khwaga was openly playful. She nipped at Mas'ud's ankles and jumped back as he yelled and then chased her. The boy pelted along after her for a number of paces, flailing his arms to keep his balance. Breaking through the light feathery branches of a bush willow, he saw Kwaga ahead, laughing at him, standing on the edge of the stone that was a pediment for...for one of the giants Mas'ud had seen from the road. He forgot the dog and almost fell to his knees.

Had men made this or had Allah himself fashioned it? For what reason, he could not imagine. He had been right when he had seen it from afar. Surely, a hundred men could stand one on the other and not touch the top of its head. Perzo walked up behind and put his hand on Mas'ud's arm. Mas'ud turned to him.

Perzo looked up at the statue and spoke.

"Skyamun" the hillman said, "the Little Father."

LATER THAT DAY, their hunt brought Mas'ud to the larger statue, "the Great Teacher," as Perzo called it. It was, indeed, even larger than the Little Father. But, magnificent and mysterious as they were, the giant stone men were passive, still, never changing. They were not likely to hold a fifteen-year-old boy's interest for long.

What Mas'ud *never* tired of was watching and working with the dogs. As in so many other things, Perzo gently guided him as the boy became more deeply involved with the hounds and their world.

Khwaga came around quickly. It was not long before Mas'ud and the dog chased each other in mock hunt and battle for hours, usually until Mas'ud collapsed from exhaustion. But the great grey bitch Barsala continued to act as if Mas'ud did not exist. She would stroll off to sleep somewhere in the sun, hunt rabbits on her own, or pursue any number of other activities while Khwaga and Mas'ud cavorted around her. Mas'ud saved up meat when they had fresh kills and tried tempting her with sweet morsels. She accepted the food, but gave Mas'ud no more attention than if he'd been the bowl in which he placed her food.

After a week of total indifference, and many grumbles from Mas'ud, Perzo dropped the sharp stone he'd been using to strip a rabbit pelt, rose from his habitual squat and ambled over to Mas'ud.

Expecting to be scolded for his complaints, Mas'ud stared in surprise as Perzo pulled out a stitched rabbit-hide sphere from his bag and dropped it in Mas'ud's lap. Perzo cut his eyes toward the napping Barsala, then looked down at the ball and made a forward motion with his arm.

Mas'ud was completely confused. Did Perzo want him to fling the leather pouch at Barsala? Surely the dog disliked him adequately already.

Perzo sniffed—his sound of frustration—and plucked the ball back from the boy's lap.

"Barsala! Run, beauty!" Then he threw the bag thirty or forty paces away from the dog.

When Mas'ud glanced over to check the haughty dog's reaction, there was nothing to be seen until he looked in the direction of the pouch-ball. The silver flowing streak that was Barsala in full stride was already stooping her head to pick up the round hide. Not slowing in her dead run, she scooped it in her mouth, wheeled and then accelerated back to Perzo, dropping the ball at his feet and sitting. Her head swiveled up and down, from the ball to Perzo's face, the feathers of her long slender tail swished in the sand and gravel behind her.

Perzo exchanged a look with Mas'ud and then nodded at the ball.

Mas'ud had never thrown a ball, so Barsala's circuit from ball to thrower took even less time, but she just as dutifully returned it to the boy's feet as she had to Perzo's, and this time it was Mas'ud's face that enjoyed her undivided attention. Until he picked up and threw the ball again, when it was clear that her whole world focused on the pursuit of this whirling, flying object—this marvelous *prey* that *flew* and *rolled* and was brought back to life by the a human to fly and roll again and again—that she could catch perfectly and excellently. There was no purpose, no reason, no distraction or compulsion that could prevent her from her destiny—the destiny of prey chaser and retriever.

Mas'ud threw until his arm was sore. Then he switched arms. He could not throw as far or as straight with his other arm, but Barsala did not seem to mind.

The pouch, despite the dog's surprisingly gentle treatment, was a sloshing compressed mess by this time, and had Mas'ud not been so determined to win over the dog, he would long ago have quit from disgust. The ball hardly made twenty paces in the air now. Both Mas'ud's arms were burning with fatigue and strain. Barsala showed no sign of tiring.

As Mas'ud pulled back his arm to throw once more, Perzo made a loud clicking noise, a sound he used to call the dogs, who did indeed trot over to him, Khwaga jumping up from a nap and Barsala moving as if she had not been running full speed for a quarter of the day. He nodded for Mas'ud to come as well and when the boy ran over, he took the ball back, looked at its condition and smiled.

"She likes the ball." The hillman wiped the vigorously abused hide casing on his leather breeches and tossed it back into his bag.

THE MOON WAXED and waned seven times after Mas'ud fell on the road into Bam-i-yan. The baking heat of summer passed; the cold of the hills now rolled into the valley before nightfall. Farmers pulled or cut most of their crops, except for the sweet white turnips and the winter oats. The shepherds brought their flocks down from higher pastures into pens beside their homes. Mas'ud, Perzo, and the two dogs had been several days at Perzo's "farm," mending broken fences, cutting goat wool from shaggy nans, and fixing the holes in Perzo's roof.

On a chill bright morning, Perzo shook Mas'ud awake.

"Market, Malquin." The little hunter was already out the door before Mas'ud slid on his shoes (ones that Perzo had re-soled in goat leather).

"Where are the dogs, Akaa?" The boy asked when he emerged from the brick-and-straw hut.

Neither stopping or turning as he ran toward the middle of the valley, Perzo called over his shoulder, "Free today."

MAS'UD HAD BEEN BACK to the village three times since he began living with Perzo and the dogs. He stopped once at the mosque, but no one was there. This was only his second time to the market, though, and he was very excited.

They passed several slow wagons and carts as they made their way, most filled with the gourds and grain and fruits of the autumn harvest. In the largest wagon—painted with brilliant purple and red circles and pulled by an enormous yellow ox that chewed more quickly than it walked—rode dour farmer Izat and six of his children. These included a brown-haired, black-eyed girl of Mas'ud's age who smiled boldly at him as he and Perzo jogged by.

They did not slow their run, but when they'd passed the wagon a hundred paces, Perzo moved a step ahead and looked back at Mas'ud. He raised his brows, squinted his eyes, and pressed his lips together as he nodded back at Izat's wagon. Mas'ud felt heat rising to his face and looked down at his own feet lest they stumble.

HIS EXCITEMENT WAS REWARDED when they reached the village. It was changed like a dream. The dusty empty streets were full of the people of the valley. The cistern fountain-well in the middle of town shone in a dozen colors, flower garlands and parts of harvest plants tied together in colorful arrays festooned the rambling brick building that housed important visitors and the meetings of the town's elders. The market, which usually consisted of six or seven farmer's carts huddled around the fountain, spread out from this centerpoint of the village along the rays of the streets. Mas'ud had never seen so many people in one place (except on a morning that he wished to never remember).

"Blacksmith," Perzo held up his skinning knife for Mas'ud to see the nicks that scored the edge. Then he pointed at the sun, still rising in the sky overhead, and placed three flat fingers under his eyes.

"Yes, Akaa, I will meet you here then." Mas'ud said.

"Good boy," Perzo reached out for Mas'ud's hand, grasped it lightly, then ran off to the backside of the village where the smithy was to be found.

Mas'ud opened his palm and looked in wonder at the two bronze drachms that he held there.

. . .

BY THE TIME the sun reached the midpoint between noon and night, Mas'ud had seen a juggler spin pots on his head and hands, dancing women whose feet and bellies were bare, heard a tabla drummer who came from somewhere over the vast mountains to the south, and had filled his own belly with roasted, candied pheasant and juices from pomegranates and plums. He had one coin in his hand, but it was smaller and not as bright as the two Perzo had left him.

The sun was still warm and it had been hours since he drank the juices, so he made his way back to the well in the center of town to ladle some water. As he was taking his first sip, he felt a hand on his shoulder and then, to his greater surprise, someone spoke his name.

For the briefest of moments, Mas'ud thought someone else from his village had survived and had found him. Perhaps he was not alone!

He turned with a curious smile on his face and looked into the dark brown eyes and fierce black brows of the imam Abu Fadl.

"Greetings, my young Believer! Allah is kind that we should meet again."

"Greetings, grandfa...Abu Fadl," Mas'ud did not know what to call this man. In his village, elders had been called "Elder." Here, he called Perzo by his name or, as he often did now, "Akaa —Uncle." This great, tall man who had tended him so kindly but who had turned him out so quickly, what should he say to this man?

Abu Fadl did not remove his hand or his eye from Mas'ud. "Come with me, my son, to the house of Allah. I have things to tell you of which this street is not worthy."

Glancing at the sun's height, Mas'ud walked silently by the side of the old man.

. . .

INSIDE THE MOSQUE, in a room that Mas'ud had not seen before—smaller and not decorated like the great hall where he had awakened three seasons earlier—they sat on cushions and Abu Fadl spread his hands out before speaking.

"I am certain it is nothing less than the Grace of the Prophet that has brought you back at this time, young Mas'ud." Abu Fadl looked up at the boy and continued, "A great scholar and servant of Allah has come to us. One who has renounced the corrupting pleasures of Baghdad—all of which were his for the asking as he was born a prince—who has won many battles against the infidels, using words to confound their infernal philosophers and swords to quash their wavering spirits, revealing to them the bravery that fills the hearts of true believers." Abu Fadl raised his palms again, in benediction of the air that was made holy by the very mention of this nonpareil's exploits.

"Did he fight the Turks?" Mas'ud ventured, matching the old man's intensity with his own.

"He is a mighty arm of the One God. As the Turks are godless, he has fought them if they have been so foolish as to cross his path."

Pleased enough with Mas'ud's rapt attention, Abu Fadl continued, "His name is Bahram Wadi al-Shariff. He is a cousin of my grandfather's first wife and has come here as a courtesy to our families. He spoke yesterday after the *Salah* at dawn and will speak again today before he departs for the great mosque in Balkh, where his brother serves daily as muezzin."

Abu Fadl reached forward and placed a bony hand on the boy's knee.

"You must stay for prayer. My cousin will speak after *maghrib* and I am certain that the words of the Prophet followed by my cousin's entreaty will touch you keenly, wanderer Mas'ud. It is a rare opportunity for one such as you to be carried along the path of righteousness at so early an age by so puissant a man. But I see great deeds in you, Mas'ud. My heart, which beats but to please the One God, feels that you will be a powerful instrument and will bring many an infidel to His Justice. Perhaps even to the infidel Turks. Stay and listen to al-Shariff. It is the will of Allah."

As he spoke the name of the One God, Abu Fadl's eyes and chin rose toward the ceiling and he squeezed Mas'ud's knee with a warm confidence.

MAS'UD TAKHAR HAD FOUGHT against the sons of Sebuk Tigin, against Ghazni. He had not fought against the Seljuks when they descended upon and destroyed his village. He could not remember that night very well now, almost twenty years later, but he recalled the fires and screams...and the smells of burning roofs and bodies. But those sounds and smells blended with countless other similar sounds and smells that he had been a part of since. For the past decade, he had fought *for* Ghazni and for the Caliph Al-Mu'tamid's shadow, al-Muwaffaq,—so distant and sacred in a Baghdad he'd never seen—and for an almost countless number of clear-eyed, long-bearded interpreters of the word of the Prophet of Allah. He had traveled far, across the Kush, across the Pamir. He had seen and killed—for the glory of the One God—the infidels and heathens in the south, the east, and the west.

The Seljuk to the north—who had presided over the destruction of his village—they were now also followers of the One True Prophet, may his name be ever blessed. The Sultan had made peace with them, which was as it should be, but... well...these were the kinds of thoughts that had brought Mas'ud back here, to the fertile valley of Bam-i-yan. Away from the Sultans, the Caliphs, the atabegs, away from generals and bloody battlefields and crying soldiers, away from the temptations of the grand souks and the cities, and—yes, he had to admit it—away from the imams and holy men who always seemed to have a gleam in their eyes and bloodthirsty business in their beards.

Mas'ud Takhar had left all these things behind and come back to Bam-i-yan. Long a land of the infidels, there were still many here who did not follow the Word of the Prophet. True, most of the farmers bowed five times a day toward the southwest. But Mas'ud knew that was country prudence and force of habit. Their cycles—the cycles of the soil—were only interrupted when great events, meaning wars or battles, were fought in the valleys and on the hills that provided for them. Unlike in Balkh or even in Kabul, there were few here whose lives centered on the mosque. These farmers and shepherds lived for their land and their flocks. They left religion to God—whichever one they might pray to this year.

As a frightened and penniless youth, Mas'ud had stumbled into this pocket of the world and had left behind this green valley with the vast, cave-pocked sandstone escarpment that loomed over it, following the man who would become a veritable Sultan in Balkh. Now he returned to this land that he'd never forgotten. His long spears, his quiver of Djerid, his fine scaled armor, he left them all with his fellows, with Bahram Shah—to be used to cut down other infidels in other lands. There were always more lands and more infidels.

His eyes filled his heart with peace as they drank in the soft farms with their waist-high grain. It seemed every farmstead he passed had a goat or a sleepy cow. *Not like the deserts that man has created in every direction. Every direction that I have been. Deserts that I have made.*

The harsh cries he heard now were not from dying men or horses but from the crows and kites attending the last remnants of a dead animal under the dark purple leaves of a spreading smoke bush. Bam-i-yan was still as gentle and pleasant as his memory. He had spent three seasons learning the people and customs of this place. Would old Abu Fadl still be alive, or had he found his place in Heaven? And what of Perzo? A smile came to Mas'ud's lips when he thought of the short hillman who had taught him so much, so silently, in so little time.

Yes, he would seek out Perzo.

But first I stop in the mosque.

THERE WERE few in the valley that did not soon have word that a great chieftain in costly colored silks and turban had ridden up to the mosque and left his enormous grey Persian horse tied to the farm hoist next to the well. It was said that he bore a scimitar of gold and a hundred jewels in his turban and that he spoke only the language of the Emperor of the West.

Inside, Mas'ud Takhar was treated with great respect. It was clear to the caretakers that this was an honored warrior of Allah. His fine horse and his *saif*, distinctively forged of Damascene steel, were enough to show his position and past.

"No, Master Abu Fadl, after many years of service to this humble mosque and to the word of the Messenger of Allah blessings and peace be on him always, has joined his illustrious family in the heaven of the One God." The caretaker never raised his eyes above Mas'ud's navel and bowed three times as he related the fate of his old friend. "His bones are next to the shrine outside, facing the Stone and the Prophet. If you would like to make your honorable visit to him, there is rose-water by the grave." The near-toothless functionary spread his hands and bowed in expectation.

After breathing a silent *Allahu Akbar* benediction by the plain resting site of the old patriarch who'd set him on his path, Mas'ud began inquiries regarding Perzo.

The caretaker of the mosque was little help. He did not gladly mix with infidels.

Shabsan the blacksmith was more informative. This was Shabsan the younger. The older Shabsan rested in the ground with Abu Fadl now, though in a different patch of earth.

"I remember that old thief," the younger Shabsan said over the hiss as he doused a beaten iron ingot in a clay trough of murky water. "My *Plar*...my Father, patched his blades and they diced for pay. *Plar* almost always lost." The younger Shabsan snorted, then smiled. "But then he paid *Plar* half and they drank beer."

Still clutching his smoking ingot, the blacksmith turned back to his anvil, "I last mended his knife seven...eight winters back. No doubt the Gods...Allah...has taken him."

The elders insisted that Mas'ud stay in the building reserved for visiting dignitaries. It was an honor, but Mas'ud had not returned to be an exotic in a shabby rural mosque. He was trapped by courtesy: to these simple souls, to The Book, to his own image of himself. And so each day he asked after Perzo, asked about hunters in the hills, shared ritual meals with the town dignitaries and visitors, practiced his weapon-craft in the courtyard, and tended to his horse. The locals understood some of his court Farsi and, of course, some of the Prophet's tongue, and he slowly began speaking again their language, so similar to the parlance of his youth. When they heard him (outside the window or in the town square), the farmer's wives smiled behind their hands at his accent.

Days became weeks, and still he had not left the village and heard no further word about Perzo. Mas'ud always woke just before dawn for *Fajr*; it was the holiest time of the day for him. One morning, immediately after he moved his chin from his left shoulder, after calling down the blessings of God for the last time in this prayer, he was distracted by noises floating in through the window behind him. He stepped to the door and looked out at the central square. Farmers, their wives and children, and the local merchants were dressing the town center with sheaves of red poppy flowers and strewing the streets with bundles of pink and white blossoms, their fragrance strong enough to reach him as he leaned out. It was the first summer Market.

A small boy in deerskin splashed in the waters of the square's fountain and didn't notice the tall stranger everyone spoke about until Mas'ud's shadow loomed over him. Then he gulped loudly and started to dart away, but Mas'ud extended a hand and caught the boy's shoulder—just firmly enough to stop his flight.

Releasing the child, he asked, "A copper drachm for an answer, child."

The boy's fear faded at this offer and he turned solemn brown eyes on the Prophet's warrior. Sharp, thin eyebrows tilted upward in query.

"Do you know of the livestock protectors of the village, boy?" Mas'ud asked gently.

The boy shook his head and looked at his hide-covered feet.

"Do you know of hunters for the village?" Mas'ud added.

The child looked up, still serious as plague, and responded, "My wrawar kills rats."

Mas'ud smiled. "That's good. Your brother kills the rats in the grain?"

The boy inclined his head.

Mas'ud handed the child a coin.

As he turned to walk away, there was a tug on his pant leg.

"*Turh* Kurhat is going to town. He kills cats. I can't pet Shaperai." The boy continued.

"Who's Shaperai?" A warm current touched Mas'ud's belly in anticipation.

"She's his bitch."

"Whose bitch is that, boy?"

"My *Turh* Kurhat's. And...and his other dogs, too. He smells." The boy's nose wrinkled.

"So your uncle Kurhat has dogs and kills cats. Big cats? Is he coming to town here today?"

"Unh-unh. He's going to *town*. He's not coming here. He's *old*. My *Plar* says he's going to die, so he's going to *town*."

"Where's your *Plar*, boy? Where's your Father?" Mas'ud handed over another copper to the child as he asked.

The boy stared at the coin for a moment, then walked slowly away. He turned in a few steps and shouted, "You can follow me. I'm hungry."

TWO STREETS AWAY, Mas'ud found the boy's father by a cart of carrots and green onions. He learned from this voluble farmer that Kurhat—the best local hunter and livestock preserver—was getting old, that he had a son in far Ghazni who missed his aging father, and—most importantly—that he had a fine, mated pair of tribal dogs just coming into their prime.

"Take the morning sun's path from the village. The old hunter is an hour's walk on the river road," the farmer advised happily, his palm holding more of Mas'ud's coin.

WELL BEFORE HE reached Kurhat's home, Mas'ud knew where he was bound. He'd left his charger stabled—afraid a humble hunter might be overawed by the mount and trappings and so not talk openly. He walked along a familiar fence line, then passed under an arch that he had helped raise almost two decades ago.

A balding head with a long fringe of white hair tied to the side with a thong bobbed near a small cookfire outside Perzo's stone-and-timber home. Could it be? Why had he changed his name?

A lined—and entirely unfamiliar—face turned to meet Mas'ud.

"Greetings, stranger. What is your interest in this old one?"

Before Mas'ud could reply, two shaggy dogs—one gray, one mostly white—raced around the side of Perzo's old home. The gray dog stopped even with the old man. Teeth bared and a soft growl wafted toward Mas'ud.

The larger dog, the white, continued forward. Mas'ud stood his ground. The big animal charged at the soldier's feet, stopped abruptly, bent its front legs, and lowered its long, narrow head almost to the ground before the stranger. Its round black eyes never left Mas'ud's face and when the man smiled, the dog opened it's jaws wide and sounded a soft yowling yawn.

"That is Hakim. He approves of you, stranger."

Mas'ud squatted, as he'd seen Perzo do so many times in this place, and stroked Hakim's matted, fuzzy side.

They shared hunter's stew before the old man's fire. The other dog's name—the bitch dog—was Shaperai, as he'd been told by the boy in the village. The little hunter confided all his simple plans to the tall stranger. Needlessly, he explained that at his age he could no longer bear the harshness of the hunter's exposed life. And he was concerned that his dogs would not fit in well with the city life Kurhat would lead at his son's house.

As they banked the fire, Mas'ud asked the question that had been in his mind since he first saw the old man's weathered face, "Did you know the hunter Perzo?"

Kurhat did not pause in his close-of-day preparations as he replied. He was Perzo's distant cousin. Game had been overhunted in his own village and he'd heard that Perzo had disappeared from Bam-i-yan, where it was well known that many predators remained. Having visited his cousin once, he knew the location of his farm, so he came, found it empty, and took over the business. Did Mas'ud want the last of the stew?

MA'SUD STAYED THE NIGHT, then spent the next month travelling with Kurhat as he met with his clients, hunted in the hills, and worked with his dogs. When the next full moon rose, for a small handful of silver—enough to pay for the old man's trip to Ghazni—Mas'ud became the new hunter-preserver of Bam-i-yan, and the proud owner of the grey bitch Shaperai and her shaggy, stocky white mate, Hakim.

❋

IT WAS four years since he'd ridden his Arab *hisan harb* into the village, four years he'd run in these sandstone hills, hills that held innumerable caves and temples of the old heathen religion. Mas'ud rarely encountered now the small groups of men with flowing robes and shaven heads whom he knew were not People of the Book. Not that he minded them. Maybe that was a concern for Caliphs and prophets, but it was no longer an issue for Mas'ud. He and his dogs had their own business, which was the protection of the flatland dwellers below, particularly the protection of their flocks and livestock.

Three years earlier, Shaperai bore a three-whelp litter. Mas'ud still felt strangely timid about the powerful feelings he'd had that night, worrying about the health of his dog. But she had emerged from the ordeal with no evident damage. Within a week she was coursing the hills for game again, leaving all but the feeding of the small ones to her mate, Hakim.

Mas'ud exchanged two of the young dogs—all were male—for enough grain and sheep jerky to last him through the winter. The third and largest, Zwak, he kept to train.

The hills surrounding them were the Earth's final expression of the great Kush, the vast range of peaks that rose to the south and east of this valley. There were stories that high in those mountains lived dreadful beings, perhaps djinn, that could devour a man in one bite. Fortunately, such creatures did not descend to the level of *his* mountains. There were sufficient dangerous animals here. Some bear. And Mas'ud himself had driven a spear through a mangy lion only two seasons past. Where there was one, there were surely more. That's what he told the farmers. He carried part of the lion skin with him to show prospective customers. It always impressed the diggers of dirt.

But, as in the past with Perzo, their hunting was mostly wolves and pards. Shaperai, Hakim, and Zwak were all mountain-bred and so these tasks were for them as the breath that filled their breasts. Shaperai could run across slopes too shear for any man. Sometimes she was pursued, most often she was the pursuer. Despite Perzo's instruction and his own curiosity, Mas'ud himself never understood quite how the dogs' hunting game was played. He depended on his readings of their sounds and actions to know where he should best place himself to assist the kill.

For Mas'ud was *not* always in on the kill. He was, of course, the one who dressed the animal (there was no reason to bring an entire mountain cat down to the villagers; it was far too heavy and its meat was good for little), the one who brought evidence to his paying customers. He was the one known as "the Lion Killer of Bam-i-yan." But two times in five, Mas'ud did little but watch his dogs—the lithe, lightning-fast silver Shaperai, burly white Hakim, and the tall, thin, aloof Zwak. Zwak, whose eye-teeth were longer than those of the mountain pards he killed. Zwak, black as the dark pitch pools of Merv. Zwak, whom even now Mas'ud was not sure was *his* dog.

Mas'ud sat this day at the foot of Skyamun, the Little Father, and watched his dogs below him. Last night, one his best customers lost a goat—probably to a large cat. At first light, Mas'ud was awakened by the heavy breathing of Algaz's son outside Mas'ud's hut. The boy had brought a gourd of sheep's milk as payment in advance, with more to come when the hunter's trophy was shown to the client.

So, the hunter and his dogs searched for spoor throughout the morning. Now it appeared that old Hakim had a scent; he still had the keenest nose of the dogs. Yes, when he raised his tapered tail like that, he always had the trail of something. Zwak and Shaperai seemed to have noticed, too, and ran up the stony hillside, huffing and snorting. Perhaps talking tactics, Mas'ud speculated idly. How did these dogs make their game? For the thousandth time, he watched as they streaked uphill, running within a few feet of Mas'ud but granting him no sign of recognition, their full-tilt gait stretching out long legs, feathered with thick hair, almost to a straight line. Mas'ud knew better than to call to them.

Below, Hakim loped in the same direction the other two dogs ran—down valley, but he stayed on roughly the same horizontal parallel as his scent discovery.

Clearly the dogs had the day in hand and wanted no interference from him. Mas'ud moved back a few paces until his back was directly against the pedestal of the foot of the Little Father, and sat down in the deep shade.

PATH OF SAND...STONE...THORN...STONE—NO-ICE...
<in wider vision> *valley in greys below to my side, hill slanting down to it where I run, last of great stone rising on my strong side... there's a ground mouse—no time*
...sand...sand...around the bush...
<smell narrowing> *scent of the cat here...run...run...there...scent of dam down hill behind...scent of small prey—no time*
...stone...around tree...light grey ahead and around...
THERE—cat-scent stronger up...up

MA'SUD DROWSED at the foot of the soft stone colossus. It seemed he'd only shut his eyes when he awoke to find his dogs standing before him.

"Back from the hunt already, dogs?" Ma'sud began to rise, but found that he could not. It was as if his back had become part of the cool stone.

"Ho, what's this?" Ma'sud struggled. He was still a strong man, but it didn't take long to realize that he'd as soon lift the statue itself as break himself free from this mind thrall. "Ho, dogs, this is a strange fate that Allah has visited upon me." He said this, of course, mostly to himself.

"I'M SURE HE CAN'T UNDERSTAND," Zwak said in purest Farsi.

"I'M NOT SURE. HE'S ALWAYS MAKING THOSE NOISES WITH HIS MOUTH." Hakim answered, also in the Persian tongue. "SOMETIMES, THOUGH, I THINK HE'S TRYING TO SPEAK TO US WITH HIS HANDS—THE WAY HE WAVES THEM ABOUT."

"YOU ALWAYS MAKE HIM OUT AS MORE THAN HE IS." Shaperai

leaned her long muzzle against her mate. Hakim raised his forepaw and gently rubbed her jaw.

"He's been loyal to us. We should be patient with him."

"I suppose you're right." The grey dog answered and looked critically at Ma'sud, who was still stuck hard against the statue's base. Zwak had vanished.

Shaperai's grey then lightened and blended with the green and twilight background of the valley and Hakim's white body became almost transparent. Ma'sud could do nothing but sit and watch as his vision blurred to an empty wash.

WHEN MAS'UD WOKE THIS TIME, it was still afternoon. The sun had not set and he had not become part of the statue. Quickly—and a little suspiciously—Ma'sud jumped up from the stone pediment and ran his hands up-and-down his sides to see that his body parts were warm flesh and not cold stone. *What in the Prophet's name had happened to him?* It must have been a dream, but one such as he'd never had.

"I'll not sleep beneath that stone devil again," Ma'sud glanced quickly behind and up, and made an ancient tribal sign his mother had taught him against the Evil Eye. He began walking in the direction that his dogs had run earlier in the day. As he walked, he tried to remember all the passages from the Quran that dealt with dreams and the visitations of demons.

ZWAK RAN AHEAD of Hakim this day. His dam, Shaperai, ran below, following the older scent trail where the great cats had descended into the valley for easy prey.

Shaperai always smells of hunger when she nears the sheep.

Zwak did not long for sheep as she did. He yearned only for the run, the hunt, and the mountains.

Hakim smells strongest when the Puller is near. By the fire, when

the Puller gives us back our meat. When he strokes Shaperai and pulls briars from our coats. Hakim's belly is soft for the Puller.
Today, though, there is cat on the mountain.

"I'LL SPEND the night in Iblis' bed before I'll sleep 'neath those cursed statues again," Mas'ud muttered, all the time scanning ahead for sight of his dogs and to his right and up for a prospective camp site.

The hunter slowly picked his way across the face of the escarpment that rose above the valley. He was too far behind now to see the dogs, particularly the black streak of speed that was Zwak as he glided over stone and bush on the steep hillside above. Here, as in most places on this side of the cliffs, there were hundreds of caves. Wind and water had begun many, but all were modified in some way by human hands. Those hands were gone now.

"*Allahu Akbar...Allahu Akbar*...God has prevailed over the heathen. It is as it should be."

Mas'ud froze at the sound of a soft chuckle. His hand moved swiftly to his sash, where he'd so long worn his warrior's *saif*. It closed instead on the pommel of a much shorter *peshkabz*.

"I'm no army, soldier. Though I am one of your 'heathens.'"

Mas'ud squinted into the shade cast by the hill. There, twenty paces from him, in the mouth of one of the innumerable hollows, sat a lump of yellow rags that was probably human. His mind considered then skipped over the honored question, "Are you djinn or are you human?"

"Come, soldier. You can help me build a fire. I have *kviss* and dried apricots to share."

Willing his hand to slide down from the hilt of his knife, Mas'ud walked into the darkness and squatted.

"Thanks be to Allah, the all-Merciful, stranger. I will share your fire...and apricots. Also, I have cheese."

"Ah! Then thanks and praise to your God, indeed! Cheese is most welcome."

PATH OF STONE...SAND...STONE...BRUSH...PAWS *and legs straight in air. Small prey all around, but cat near.*

This day will be my kill.

<in wide hunter vision> *Hakim far behind...Dam just above and behind...flash now around and then up*

I will make the kill today. Dam will drive the cat to me. Hakim is too slow.

Zwak darted up slope in an impossible tack, sharp claws gaining just enough purchase as they scraped the ancient red stone. He was through a thin gap between two small natural pillars. He stopped abruptly, tongue hanging out to taste the air and cool his lungs.

This will be the killing spot. Dam will smell my route.

THE TWO MEN squatted on either side of the fire. The yellow-robed man's apricots were consumed and they both nibbled chunks of the hard white cheese Mas'ud had drawn from his side pouch. The day was fading. A steady breeze blew a soft susurration below them as thin-bladed willows swept the edges of stone.

After a long while, the stranger spoke.

"They are not idols, my friend."

Mas'ud's head bobbed up, but before he could respond, the other man continued, "Yes, I know. Yours is not the only faith that proscribes graven images." He unceremoniously and rigorously rubbed his own backside before going on, "It may have been in the minds of the makers to build giants that would impress, to build monuments that would themselves become as gods. But I do not think so."

Until now, the yellow-clothed man had been half-hidden in

the darkness of the cave mouth in which he squatted. Mas'ud had seen no part of him clearly except his knees and feet. Now he leaned forward. He wore a strange, ruffled cap that shaded his face, but which had no sides. His eyes bored out of the shadow and fixed Mas'ud in a strong and somehow familiar stare.

"All the Little Father and the Teacher have to say to you, hunter, and to me, and to all men, is that they exist. That they will continue to exist after our little lives and bodies and dreams turn back to mud. That they will tower over us and our world long after our plans and schemes and desires have blown away in the dust at their feet." The small stranger coughed and spit to clear his mouth and throat. "And finally, they tell us that someday *they* will not exist, either. *They* are on the Wheel as much as you or I. They do not ask for, they do not need, they do not acknowledge worship. And so, friend hunter, they are not idols—even though they were made by heathens." Yellow teeth shone out of the darkness underneath the cap.

"Who are you?" Mas'ud asked.

"An old man," the old man replied, "one who wishes you well, friend hunter."

"Have we met?"

"I think not. But then I'm often mistaken."

The little man stood. He had a long pole staff that Mas'ud had not seen before, but Mas'ud felt no threat.

Face still hidden by his odd cap, the robed stranger turned and walked away toward the village. Before he jumped down and out of sight, he turned and spoke once more, "Your life has been hard, hunter, but sometimes it is the soft that surprises us most."

Mas'ud rose soon after him. He had a little time before dark to find the dogs, or—failing that—a campsite where he could wait for them.

❅

ZWAK PACED THE CAT. He tracked the wind and it now blew into him, along with the cat's spoor, now mixed with his dam's.

She is driving it now.

This will be the killing spot.

Acid fear tang filled his quietly panting mouth like the sweetest meat. Zwak's body readied. He trembled in his strength, setting his paws to lunge.

MAS'UD CLIMBED SLOWLY. His legs and feet moved on their own as his mind filled with other thoughts than his search for the dogs. The giant men were not idols, the monk had said—for surely that was what the old yellow-robed man was, a heathen monk. If they were built to make man seem small, then they had been successful. Was humility triggered by a forbidden likeness an evil humility? What would Abu Fadl or the imams he had listened to from Balkh to Isfahan say? Mas'ud no longer thought often of The Book, much less of the Hadith. He seemed to recall that the Hadith was very clear about images. They were all the work of Iblis. They all eventually led a believer into a wrongful path and so they must be destroyed.

Where are the dogs?

It is becoming difficult to see.

Too late, he felt the soft rock of the thin stone bridge crumble beneath his feet. His shoulder and then his head struck unforgiving surfaces as he plunged into the crevasse that opened below him.

THE PARD ERUPTED through the little "gate" between the two pillars. The opening was small enough that it had no visual warning of the dog that waited on the other side. It was moving quickly enough, though, that Zwak almost missed the strike he'd been waiting to execute. A miss would mean his death, or —at the least—a horrible mauling by the bigger, stronger pard.

But this was his day.

This is my kill.

Fangs as long as a man's finger drove through the pard's sleek dark neck skin, past muscle, missing bone, then ripped outwards, savaging the pulsing artery that supplied life's blood to the powerful cat.

Within seconds, the mighty killer lay lifeless at the feet of the tall black dog.

Shaperai jumped lithely through the pillared opening and slid to a halt beside the dead pard and her victorious son. Her elegant silver head bowed and she delicately licked a drop of gore from the dead cat's throat. She sat, contented, at Zwak's feet and watched placidly as Hakim ran through the opening to join them.

MAS'UD TAKHAR LAY on his back at the bottom of a narrow gap between two sections of the escarpment. The sky above him was darkening. Tonight would be moonless; there would be little light when the sun fell. And even less warmth.

Not that anyone else was likely to venture into these hills in the dark. Mas'ud glimpsed another human once a fortnight when he was hunting with the dogs.

Though dazed, what confused him most was that there was little pain. He had fallen more than thirty feet and the surface below him was not smooth.

Carefully, he reached down and felt the stub of a branch underneath him. *Odd that he did not...By Allah..He could not feel his legs.*

He tried to move them and they did not respond.

With great effort, he used the still-responsive muscles of his chest and attempted to sit up.

He was able to raise his shoulders enough to see...to see...*Oh Sands of Shaitan*—the branch he'd felt with his hands protruded through his left thigh. *And he could not feel it.*

The discipline and experience of the battlefield cleared his mind. He stretched his left hand down to touch the leg and the protruding branch. His fingers registered a soft, warm, and steady pulsing of his life's fluid as it flowed out of his mangled leg.

He had seen such wounds on the plains before Talaqan, in the marshes of Sindh, and after the battle of the Iron Gate. He knew the inevitable result. Already, he felt the coldness of rapid exsanguination enclose him.

HAKIM NOSED the limp pard at his feet. It seemed much smaller in death. Then he looked up at his son, all blackness limned against the cream-red stone behind him. The scent of the pard's blood, of Zwak's triumph—the scent of the kill—drenched the dogs' senses. Hakim shuddered, whined, and shuffled back and forth between the dead cat and the opening in the stone through which it had last run.

Hakim wants the Puller. I feel that too. The Puller is at danger.

Long, tightly ringed curls gently slapped his cheeks as Zwak shook his shaggy head and snorted.

This is my kill. This is my day. The Puller is...

Momentarily confused, Zwak snorted again.

Hakim whined, then barked. He moved to Zwak and pressed against the taller dog with his side. He barked again.

Zwak stepped away from his father and turned his head from him.

Hakim shifted toward his mate, who was standing again now. He pressed his nose against her side and stood back.

Shaperai sniffed in the fallen pard's direction. She sniffed at her son, who stood with his back to her and Hakim.

Hakim straddled the space between the sandstone pillars. He looked back at his mate. After a long moment, Shaperai began to trot toward him, leaving Zwak with his kill. Hakim jumped through the gap, then ran along the ridge on the other side. He followed the distant scent of man and some other thing that he did not understand.

MAS'UD LOOKED up at the slit of black sky above him. He no longer had the strength to raise his head. Except for a dull ache in his side, he was not in pain.

It was a beautiful night. There were many stars that filled the gap above him. He could see the edge of what a mathematician in Khorasan had named the Water Pourer, a wash of light so thick it blurred the sky with a celestial milkiness.

But the stars, too, were cold. It seemed that was all there was for him now: coldness. Even his eyelids, barely open as they were, were cold.

As they closed, his last sight was of two streaks—one silver, one white—that flowed along the edge of the crack above him. The corners of his mouth curled up and his starved heart smiled at the beauty of their movement, as fresh with wonder as was that boy who stumbled on the road so many years ago.

ZABZI WATCHED her young twins pull the tails of the black and white pups.

"Out! Out of the turnip field! What do you think we will eat if you dig the roots up with your toes!" She shouted at the children and dogs, but there was no meanness in her tone.

Whether they responded to her admonitions or were merely moving on to new playgrounds, Izhat and Manso ran out from between the feathery tops of green, racing the two half-grown hounds toward the stone water trough.

Zabzi lifted her eyes from her children, scanned over the rough rows of crops, and regarded the sacred hills to the east. She squinted slightly, thinking of the handsome hunter who had been lost several years back now.

Some of the villagers thought he'd been eaten by a djinn, perhaps a demon in the form of a giant pard. Some of these same villagers thought that that was why there had been no further sightings of the great cats since that time. The warrior-hunter had slain or sacrificed himself to the djinn for the sake of the village. Someone had even slaughtered a young goat at the small shrine set up at the hunter's abandoned farm.

Zabzi did not think so. She thought the hunter had gone to dwell with the Little Father and the Great Teacher. He had been a good man, she was sure. There was a way he had that made her remember rain, good crops, and the clear sky. There was a way he had that made her remember her youth, when she rode on her father Izhat's brightly painted wagon to the grand Market and had not the cares of a mother and wife.

Zabzi closed her eyes.

A cry and a loud splash raised her eyelids and turned her around.

"Out of the trough! Get that hound off of there! Zat! Zat!"

Thoughts of hunters, pards, and Buddhas vanished as her goat-boots shuffled back toward her boys, the dogs, a full life.

3
HEALING ARTS

1209 CE – near the village of Montlaur, Carcassone département, Languedoc, France

LIE DOWN. SOFT HERE.
MUST RUN. OH, FEET HURT. LICK FEET.
BETTER.

WHAT'S THAT? MUST RUN. LITTLE MOUSE? CAN CATCH LITTLE MOUSE.

UP. OH. FEET HURT.

LIE DOWN. HEAR WATER?

UP. OH. WON'T RUN. WALK TO WATER.

The small russet-colored hound limped through the dry, scrubby underbrush toward the tiny stream, named a dozen names by the locals and therefore nameless. She bent her delicate, oblate head down and drank deeply of the clear water.

Before she had her fill, her ears pricked up.

HUMAN SOUNDS. RUN? HIDE IN LEAVES AND ROCKS? RUN?

FEET HURT.

The ravaged pads of her paws seeped pink fluid. The dog knew that she, who was so swift in her good days, might not outrun even a human now. Yet she was attracted to these voices. Particularly to one voice. Daintily, quietly lifting one bruised paw after the other, she stepped across the narrow stream and up an easy incline to peer through the trees that bounded a small open patch of short grass.

Two female humans stood a short run away. The brush was think and she could not tell them apart by sight. But when the breeze blew toward her—*oh*—such a difference as she had never sensed. One of the humans, the nearer one with back turned, smelled like a female. She would run if that one approached her. But the other, who faced her, the one with yellow hair. THAT ONE filled her nose with a world of promises and half-remembered odors. SO MANY SMELLS. There were whiffs and tangs of things that grew, flowers and trees. And other things, human things that she'd sensed before. Some were burned things, some were things she'd seen humans drink from their drink stones, and still other fragrances: some strong and some tantalizingly faint, whispers of flavors she'd never tasted.

There was something else about the yellow human. It wasn't just the color of her head hair. The human herself was yellow.

SHE WAS A LIGHT. The little hound heard herself whine softly as she lay down and watched the two females.

"THE CHARCOAL IS MOST WELCOME, *Madama* Mistral. It will save me much time and labor," said the yellow woman, standing just outside her small blue door.

"It is the least we could do, *Dama* Reymera, the very least. Premedeta is fine now. We were so afraid that she would not be able to see and where would that leave us? Two sons already gone in the wars, following the Comte de Montfort L'Amaury..." The older woman shifted foot-to-foot and squeezed one hand in the other. Anxiety shone through gratitude.

Rescuing her visitor from further obligation, the younger woman interrupted, "I know that your family has suffered, *Madama* Mistral. I hope that Fortune will soon shine on you and yours." Reymera rubbed her own slim hands together quickly and vigorously, half-turned toward her cottage, and added, "I have preparations on the fire, *Madama*, and I must attend them. Of course, if you'd like to come in and have some wine with me after I'm through, you are most welcome." Her eyes opened to *Madama* Mistral with a clear clean smile.

"Oh, no, *Dama*. No, not at all. I, too, have many chores waiting at home. Now that Premedeta is up and working, I never know what that girl will be into. The wine is most kind, but I *must* be going. Thank you, thank you again. Our family is far indebted to you." *Madama* Mistral bowed and backed away from Reymera, as if from a dozing serpent.

Reymera waved *adieu*, turned, and stepped into her house.

As soon as the door closed, *Madama* Mistral picked up her skirts and joggled away—as quickly as she'd run since her childhood.

. . .

THE LITTLE RUST-HUED hound lay in the grass at the edge of Reymera's clearing, watching the now-closed door.

After only a few moments—long enough, Reymera judged, to allow *Madama* Mistral to make a complete escape from "the witch's glen"—Reymera walked outside. She wore a complicated apron with many pockets and around her neck was a cord with a pair of scissors attached.

The dog was puzzled by the change of this human's head. She had noticed other humans transformed this way sometimes. Their legs, feet, and the coverings on their bodies looked no different, but the tops of their heads took on strange shapes. She had even seen them take off parts of their heads and then put those parts back on. It scared her. But the beguiling odors that surrounded this female remained the same.

Caution rose easily in her heart, but she felt no threat from this human—not even with the strange head she now wore, which was shaped like the little ground fruits she knew not to eat, the soft white sticks with wide round tops.

She watched the female human walk up one way and down another, sometimes disappearing from sight, though her pleasant odor stayed strong in the little dog's nose. Always she returned into the glen, though. New smells clung around the human now and odd lumps bumped out of the covering she wore on her stomach.

On the human's last reappearance, she walked down the line of trees that marked the edge of the open space, the line of trees that hid the dog.

Quivering, the little hound stood ready to bolt as the human drew closer. She knew she could not run far or fast. As her muscles tensed, the human stopped ten feet away, bent down to the ground, and pulled at some plants at the base of a ground cedar.

"I know you're there, little girl. There's no need to be shy. I'll leave some cheese and water by the door and you can have it when you want." The dog knew these noises were meant for her.

Reymera walked back into her daubed stone cottage without looking behind her. A few heartbeats later, the door opened a crack. A pale hand appeared near the ground and set something on the threshold by the dimly shining door, which was already closing.

THE SMALL RED dog waited under cover of the trees until the sun went down. The air was chilling. NIGHTS ARE COLDER. IT IS THE TIME WHEN THE LEAVES OF THE TREES COVER THE FLOOR OF THE WOODS. She'd taken advantage of this blanket over the past several weeks, since she'd run away from the hunt. BUT THE NIGHTS ARE COLDER. The leaves helped, but she thought of the night coming and a shiver ran down her clearly visible spine.

She lifted her head and sniffed.

YES. FOOD AT HOUSE.

She wondered if the yellow human would try to catch her.

CATCH ME? BAD? NOT BAD?

She missed her littermates, most of whom were also in the hunt. When nights were cold, they slept close.

WARM TOGETHER.

She stood.

WALK. OH. FEET HURT.

She made her way very slowly across the springy green. Near the yellow female's cottage—far enough away she could easily have run before, but—she was afraid—too close to run now, she stopped.

She knew the smell of cheese. A few times, the Comte or one of his men had dropped crumbs of it before a hunt and she'd captured a bit.

Painfully, one foot moved forward with precision, then the next. She might not be able to run away, but she could *act* like she could.

BEND. TAKE FOOD. RUN.

She bent. She took the food. She did not run.

FEET HURT.

Stomach and chest resting on the ground, all four paws forward, sphinx-like, she quietly ate the cheese, drank a mouthful of water, then fell deeply asleep.

SHE WOKE with the leaves covering her.

LEAVES WARM.

WAIT! NO! UP!

FEET HURT. LEAVES...NO...HUMAN?...CLOTHES? FEET HURT. COLD.

"*Oh, ma petite Damaleta, ma petite.*" The human made soft, kind noises. She remembered this one from before she fell asleep.

THIS HUMAN BROUGHT FINE FOOD.

The dog stood and shivered. Slowly, smoothly, Reymera pulled the thin blanket from the ground where the dog had shrugged it off and slipped it over the little hound, all the time murmuring "*Damaleta, poudre Damaleta.*"

WARM.

The dog did not run.

When she had the dog covered with the blanket, Reymera reached slowly for one of her front paws. The dog offered it, looking into the woman's blue eyes with her own brown ones.

"Oh, you have a deep soul, my *poudre Damaleta*, a deep soul. You bring me memories of my sister, Jacqueline. She is not with me any more, but you have come to stay, I think. Let me look at this poor paw of yours." Reymera looked down, "Sssss...it is as I feared. You have run a long hard way, haven't you, little one? But I can fix this. Reymera can fix this for you."

Reymera got up and went back into her cottage.

The scruffy little dog's fears subsided under the blanket and her new name, *Damaleta* Jacqueline. She put her head between her paws, and unblinkingly watched the pale blue door of Reymera's cottage.

AUTUMN GENTLY TOOK hold on the north slopes of the hills. Leaves fell, wind blew. Inside the cottage of Reymera, first resort for many, last resort for some, the thin red hound grew well and strong again. Her frizzy, somewhat harsh coat became glossy. The prim, extreme tuck up that her stomach formed above her over-large rib cage became full and firm. The pads of her paws, ministered to by Reymera's salves of green and brown ("Do not lick the brown one, *ma petite*, or your little belly will empty all over my floor!"), followed in the last weeks by gentle massages, no longer oozed or bled. They were not as tough on the bottoms as when she'd run with the hunt, but she *knew* that she could run now as quickly as she ever had.

It rained for near a week and Reymera did not often go outside the cottage. *Damaleta*, not wanting to dirty her den, soon learned that when she wanted to go out, it only took a moment of standing by the door before Reymera would open it and go out with her. Outside, she thought of running. Not of running *away*, but of *running*. But she was afraid her paws would hurt as they did before and so when she was through relieving herself she bent her slim head down and slid back into the warmth of the cottage. And she had never liked running in the rain.

But this day, she felt a hunger for the run and also for something besides the food that her mistress, Reymera, provided for her. She would hunt and bring back food to share.

Jacqueline slipped out past Reymera when she next opened the cottage door.

GRASS WET. PAWS COLD. OH. THE AIR! THE AIR!

Weeks inside Reymera's fragrant cottage had overwhelmed the dog's sense of smell. It had not been unpleasant, but now the air outside was so clear after the rains. The fresh, pure smells of the earth, the woods, the creatures around her: these filled *Damaleta*'s heart and left no room for fear or even caution. She ran in figures of flowing design around the soft green in front of Reymera's cottage, darting to the left at a patch of clover, to the right at an orange stone, circling back to ring around the smiling Reymera, then creating a new pattern of steps and leaps. Part of what she wove was her speed, constantly accelerating or decelerating. The changes in her velocity were as much a part of her dance as the angles and curves she described with her movements. The longer she ran, the more she felt the grass and earth with her paws, the better she *understood* herself, her mistress, the smell of the world. Her life soared ever farther from fear and pain.

Then others joined her. They moved in the air as she moved on the grass. Not as quickly as her nimble feet bore her from side to side or back and forth, but magically they moved—like birds—up and down in the air. They were not birds, though. Even transported by her sublime exertion, she knew they were not birds. These partners in her dance were like her, like the mistress knew her to be. They were so rare and delicate that the air itself seemed likely to crush them, the sun dissolve them. But, like her, they knew nothing but the dance they danced with her. Around and over and down and up, in happy mindless endless figures of flashing light and color.

A sound joined the dance.

As Jacqueline pounced, pirouetted, and leapt with the bright fliers, Reymera sang wordlessly behind them, adding her joy to the air and light of the sun.

ONE MORNING, *Damaleta* Jacqueline heard a scraping coming toward their cottage. It was faint, but it grew closer, so she jumped to the door and told Reymera that someone or something approached. She couldn't tell who or what because the smell did not penetrate the cottage. Reymera had not had a visitor for several days, not since *Per* Raimundo had run up, unnoticed by Jacqueline because the rain washed the scent from the air and muffled the sounds of his footsteps. She liked the smell of *Per* Raimundo. His large hands held scents that *Damaleta* did not know, things beyond even the vastness of Reymera's wide universe of aromas. He also made human noises at Jacqueline and, though he did not shine like Reymera, his eyes were kind. *Per*haps it was the other human that came with *Per* Raimundo sometimes, the slow one who broke wood for the fire and who never looked directly at the mistress.

What she heard, though, was not the strong step of *Per* Raimundo or the heavy dragging walk of the other man, it was a lighter, quicker note. She tried to tell Reymera that, as well. Reymera understood so much, Jacqueline was sure that if she kept telling her these important things, then Reymera would come to understand.

Reymera patted *Damaleta* on her ears, which the dog knew meant that she should be quiet, and opened the door on the bright, sparkling December morning.

"Oh, *Dama* Reymera, *Dama* Reymera! I am so glad to find you here. There was talk in Montlaur that you had traveled to Toulouse." A young woman in a white dress with red and blue embroidery on the bodice carefully made her way up the stone path to Reymera's glen.

"Ahh... Nuèit la Mistraleta...it is very good to see you. How are your good parents?"

"*Madama* Mistral and *lo* Mistral are well, *Dama*. My mother has asked me to bring you this." Nuèit held out her white, long-fingered hand. In it was a silver thimble.

Reymera carefully lifted the thimble from Nuèit's palm and examined it in the morning light. It glittered and shone.

"This is a grand gift fit for a high lady. Why has your mother sent this to me, Nuèit?"

"She has done nothing but talk about the miraculous cure you effected for my sister, *Dama*." Nuèit spoke softly and raised her hand to her mouth, as if there were others nearby who might hear, "I believe she is embarrassed to have only given you coal for your payment."

Reymera quietly moved back a pace from Nuèit. *Damaleta* Jacqueline, who had remained on the cottage threshold, stepped forth to stand beside her mistress.

"The coal was gratefully received, Nuèit. There could have been no more thoughtful gift. I am sorry that your mother felt that payment for my help was necessary. I only did what I could for your sister, as I would within my power for any of God's creatures." Reymera glanced at the beautiful thimble and handed it back to Nuèit. "Here, please return this over-generous gift to *Madama* Mistral with my thanks. And tell her, too, that I am most happy to hear that Premedeta has recovered so completely."

Reymera did not turn, but it was clear that she intended to go back into her cottage.

Nuèit did not leave. Instead, she fell down on her knees at Reymera's feet and cried, "Oh, *Dama* Reymera. I did not come here for Mother or my sister. The thimble is from me. I thought it would be enough. I so need your help. Otherwise I will lose him."

Reymera put her hand on the sobbing girl's auburn head, but she looked at Jacqueline, who stood at her side. Not long ago the girl's outburst would have overwrought the dog and *Damaleta* would have had to find a quiet place to get away from such powerful emotions. Now she just looked up at her mistress, who smiled gently down at both her and the crying girl.

"Rise up, Nuèit, rise up. Do not let this sorrow of the heart overcome you so. See, you have not met my dog. Sweet *Damaleta* Jacqueline, be pleased to meet Nuèit Mistral."

Damaleta stood still and quiet as the weeping girl looked at her. A delicate sniff revealed a strong redolence of human sweat, sunshine, and some of the flowers that Jacqueline's mistress kept by her bed. It was not a bad smell. Her eyes were very ugly, though, with lines and spots and salty streaks around them. Not so ugly that *Damaleta* was afraid, so she looked up at her mistress, who nodded to her, then stepped forward and tasted the moisture around this human girl's eyes.

Nuèit made a quick movement with her arm and Jacqueline jumped back reflexively, but she saw then that the girl had not tried to hit her. Nuèit stood up and she and her mistress laughed. Jacqueline followed them into the cottage and lay by the low fire.

"SO YOU SEE, *Dama*, you are the *only* one who can help me. I *must* have a love philtre or else I will surely lose my Pierre." Nuèit seemed perilously close to weeping again, as she sat on the bench across from Reymera at the wise woman's tiny table.

Reymera resisted the impulse to suggest that this Pierre could not be borne away from an issue of the heart except by his own will. The girl was in need of comfort, not cold wisdom.

"It is very sad, Nuèit, very sad. But you would be robbing Pierre of his own will were you to use such a device on him. Surely your love, if true, is strong enough to endure without a potion?"

"But I have *told* you, *Dama* Reymera, our love *is* true. Here..." Nuèit looked around suspiciously in Reymera's cottage, then reached between her breasts and withdrew an object that she showed to the older woman. "This, *this* is how much he loves me."

Reymera leaned forward. The cottage light was strong enough for her to make out a shield design containing a blue bar of lapis lazuli and an elegant silver swan outlined by tiny rubies, all laid in gold on a brooch pin of considerable size and ornament—the crest of a noble.

"Pierre's father knows of this gift?" Reymera asked carefully.

"Pierre will be a Baron someday. Why should he have to ask his father for everything that will be his?"

Reymera suppressed a heavy sigh at the girl's foolishness.

Time to shine light on her wild imaginings and end this misfortune with as little destruction to Nuèit as possible.

"I do *not* make love philtres, Nuèit. I've told you that several times now…"

"But *Dama* Tomalu said that *Monsur* Tomalu…" Nuèit began.

"…I was able to help *Monsur* Tomalu, it is true. But that is a matter between *lo* Tomalu, *la* Tomalu, and me. It was *not* what you understand as a love philtre. Trust me, what I provided there is *not* something that your Pierre needs or that you would want him to have," Reymera explained, then felt a bit impatient with herself for revealing even this much of other's private matters. But it was enough to quiet Nuèit, at least for a moment, so Reymera continued, taking the girls' hands across the table, "Dear one, the best you can do is to put this behind you. I'm sure Pierre is a very good boy. I'm sure he loves you very much, as you, no doubt, have great feeling for him. But it is not a match that can be made. Perhaps some places, sometimes, with some people. But have you met his parents? You must understand that until your Pierre *is* a Baron, there is no possibility that his father —a great nobleman it would seem from this pin—would allow such a union. Think, *ma belle jeune fille*, if the son of the local Comte du Carcassonne loved you, would the Comte bless the marriage of his son to the daughter of a charcoal maker from the village Montlaur?"

"Pierre could come and work for my father. I'm sure he would allow it." Nuèit did not lift her head when she said this. Head resting on the cold hearth, *Damaleta* whined softly at the sorrow and dejection she felt emanating from the table.

Reymera squeezed Nuèit's hands, "And you must return to Pierre this pin that he has given you. It will mean nothing but trouble if his father finds that it is gone."

The girl and Jacqueline looked up with the same expression. The dog understood this kind of panic and fear, but it was Nuèit that spoke, "I cannot. He rides with the *Duc de* Montfort. I cannot see him again just to lose him. They travel soon to

Carcassonne and there is no place for me there. And if we are not to be together, then I cannot bear to see him."

Nuèit jumped up from the table, overturning the stool upon which she sat, and ran out of the cottage weeping.

Jacqueline watched her mistress. The other human female was very frightened and very sad. Her mistress was sad, too. Was something bad going to happen to the mistress?

The little dog put her head on Reymera's folded hands.

"You know that *poudre jeune fille* is in trouble, do you not, *Damaleta* Jacqueline? She has a heartache that only youth and first love knows. No plants or medicines can allay that pain. Let us pray for her, *dulcete chienne*. Let us pray for her."

THE WINDS BLEW. The rain fell. The light of the days became shorter and thinner. The rain softened to snow and the bright clear air of winter spread across the Aude. To the south, whiteness covered the slopes of the Pyrenees.

Damaleta walked beside her Mistress as they searched under hawthorn, cedar, and oak for roots and fungi.

As Reymera and her dog made the gentle descent into the flat that surrounded their cottage, *Damaleta*'s nose sensed an odor she'd not known for many months—the smell of fine horses and leathers.

WAS THE HUNT COME TO TAKE HER AND HER MISTRESS?

Jacqueline announced her fear to Reymera. She tried to tell Reymera to stop, to run, to hide. She did not want to return to the hunt. She did not want the hunt to find her mistress. There could be no good in that. She did not stop telling her mistress even when Reymera patted her ears.

Carrying her basket of mushrooms and leaving the little dog barking behind her, Reymera hurried down to meet the finely clad soldiers bustling together in front of her cottage.

Within moments, two of the mail-clad, orange-and-white

liveried men seized her, forcing her into the back of a rough cart. They wrapped a large chain tightly around her waist and fastened it to a board on the outside of the wagon.

"What is happening?" Reymera asked of the soldiers and of the other woman who sat chained next to her. The girl, for she was far younger—and dirtier—than Reymera, flashed the white frightened eyes of a cornered beast and said nothing.

One of the soldiers who had thrown her into the cart climbed onto the front of the wagon, the other circled behind and struck Reymera hard in the mouth with his rough gloved hand, "No talking." The girl shrank back as if struck herself.

The guards did not speak to each other, and so in human silence the ill-made tumbrel and its tender contents jostled up the rocky, rutted road to the west, to the high-walled city of Carcassonne. As they neared the castle and the town that surrounded it, the cart bumped over huge cobbles: stone below, on every side, and even arching over them as they climbed up into the vast fortress. Unchained, pulled down from the harsh conveyance, surrounded by heartless encompassing masonry, Reymera was led through endless grey granite passages, finally stumbling across a threshold into a darkness made complete when a heavy wooden door shut behind her. As she waited, unknowing and evidently unknown, hope and anger seeped away. Only cold and filth remained, and these eventually brought their companions to her: fear and despair.

Six times, a molded crust fell through a brass-bound slot in the door and onto the slimy floor of that vile, lightless place. Then the door opened and two black-and-white robed monks filled the gap. One beckoned wordlessly. Reymera stood and walked between them down one corridor after another. There was no natural light in the halls they trod. Reymera was thankful for the illumination of the many torches on the walls.

After bewildering turns and three iron gates, they came to the end of a passage. The leading monk opened the door in the wall and the small procession moved inside. The glow from the gigantic brazier in the center warmed and soothed the bone-deep chill that had overcome Reymera in her dungeon cell.

At the far end of the large room, a gray-cowled, white-robed person sat writing at a desk. Standing next to him was an odd man, also robed but with a bare head. Reymera could not prevent herself from some examination of this one. His face might once have been normal, but something had changed it. Or him. The muscles around his mouth were slack, creating a dark empty cavity in middle of his face. His cheeks sagged as if melting below an undiscoverable jawline. She was not close enough to make out the color of his eyes, but even from where she stood on the other side of the room, she could tell they saw nothing. It was not a blindness of the body, but a blindness of the soul, or of a mind that dwelt elsewhere. Wild shadows cast by the brazier danced on the wall behind both men, mixing with faint odors of fear and excrement.

The writer put down his quill and lifted his head. Shockingly beautiful green eyes looked into hers. He motioned with a hand and the two robed brothers who had brought her into the chamber released her arms.

"Reymera of Roquecave: You stand before a servant of the Vicar of Christ, accused of witchcraft most foul."

Reymera noticed, as she sank to her knees, just before the darkness of the faint overtook her, that the other man had closed his mouth.

THERE WAS FROST on the grass every morning now. *Damaleta* Jacqueline did not like the frost. It made it harder to find the mice and rabbits that she now took to fill her belly.

She shivered from the cold.

Lady does not kill food.

Lady is gone. She does not like this.

When she returns I will not kill food.

WHEN SHE RETURNS.

Sometimes the big man in brown came to the cottage. Once he brought a piece of cheese to her. He picked her up and carried her part way down the road, talking to her and stroking her as he walked.

When he set her down on the road, she'd licked his square, good-smelling hand, then ran back to her home in the glen.

That had been a cold night. The door to the cottage was closed and *Damaleta* waited untill the next evening when the brown man came and let her back in. She'd jumped onto their bed and slept until the sun filled the room the next day.

This morning the frost was even thicker. *Damaleta* Jacqueline had been sniffing and searching for prey a long time with no luck. The frost was not melting away, as it had done on other days.

A flush of heat rose through *Damaleta*'s cheeks. It was as if she'd eaten too much of the soup that Lady made, too soon off the fire.

RUN. MUST RUN.

Except the time the brown man had borne her down the road, Jacqueline had not ventured more than a hundred feet from Reymera's cottage since her mistress went away. Now she ran as she had when she chased the foxes in the hunts.

She hurried down the stony wash that led to their home. She turned away from the sun onto the high road, away from the village of Montlaur, and ran faster.

No merchants or farmers or workers, knights or peddlers were on the road this cold February morning. No one saw her race up the old way toward Carcassonne.

PER RAIMUNDO PULLED the leather rein and halted the church's decrepit hobble cart in front of the cottage. He stepped down from the low seat and moved quickly to the open-ended back, lifting out his load and carrying it into the daubed-wattle structure.

Jacqueline hopped down from the rear of the cart and followed him into her house.

The priest carefully picked up a tattered bundle from the back of the cart and carried it into the cottage. Old, dry rushes crackled under the slight weight of *Dama* Reymera as the clergyman laid her on her bed. He started a fire, left the room, and returned with water, pouring it into the iron kettle hung over the flames.

Then he moved back to the woman on the bed. Sitting on the edge of the frame, his large hands gently lifted one foot, then the other.

"Sweet Jesu, *Dama*. What have they done to you, child?" He muttered into the room.

"Not as much as they could have done, *Per*. Or so I was told," the woman on the bed replied.

Her voice was hoarse and cracked. It matched well the shock of matted white hair that covered her filthy head. Shadowed hints suggested new lines carved deeply in her face, but such detail was masked under dirt and caked stains. Her garments, though torn and tattered, still covered most of the thin, shaking body underneath them.

Per Raimundo had remarked not on these things, but on her feet, which were uncovered—except by blisters, scabs, mud, sores, and blood.

"How did you come...how did you come to the roadside there, daughter?" *Per* Raimundo's baritone voice quavered, as if in response to the chills that racked the young woman's broken body.

"I walked." The reedy voice that was now *Dama* Reymera's replied.

"Barefoot? In winter? From Carcassonne? That's thirty miles."

"My hosts did not provide a carriage."

Per Raimundo grimaced and turned to tend the kettle.

That was all the conversation exchanged that day.

Per Raimundo saved her feet ("I have not your gift, Lady, but I can at least cleanse and dress them," he'd said that first night). She directed him silently to the dried comfrey and lavender and other herbs on her shelves and the combination of these ministrations left her uncrippled.

"*Dom* Amalric assured me that I was treated with great forbearance." She cackled this confidence to him the second night he came to the cottage to dress her wounds.

"I believe he was speaking truth." A deadly rictus stretched her features, so unlike the clear honest smiles that shone from her face before her journey and her return.

Throughout the remainder of the winter and the cold spring that year, the priest visited the cottage of Reymera and Jacqueline twice per day: once after Morning Prayer and once before Vespers. On Sundays, he sent his ward, the simple Costigos, to stoke the fire, bring water, empty nightsoil, and chop wood.

One windy afternoon in early May, as *Per* Raimundo was leaving to read Vespers, Reymera asked him to stay.

Her voice no longer creaked like a crow's call, but it had not returned to its former sweet tone.

"The young lord Pierre asked that they not break my fingers," she held up her mangled, distorted hands, "and so Good Brother Gonsalvo only played with my thumbs." The dry cough of a laugh escaped her withered chest.

Per Raimundo willed himself not to shrink when she laid her thin, distorted hand on his shoulder.

"Of course, *Dama*." He pulled the stool near her bed and peered into her blue eyes.

"I will speak of this once, Father. Then we will never mention it again. I believe it is a story that you must hear. And it is a story that I must tell."

Per Raimundo raised his palm. Reymera grasped his wrist in a cold grip. At the foot of her bed, *Damaleta* whined.

A whisper of a smile curved Reymera's lips as she acknowledged the little dog's consternation. Slackening her hold on the priest's wrist, she shook her head in anticipation of his objection.

"No. It must be said. Once."

Reymera sat up on the bed, filled now with fresh, fragrant rushes. This much movement was still an effort for her, so she paused. After a moment, she began talking, never glancing at the priest that sat beside her.

"It is a simple story for a simple maid." She allowed herself a small sigh. "*Dom* Amalric, whom *Frere* Gonsalvo always referred to as Abbot, read me the charges—that I corrupted the local youth, that I was a witch, that I served Satan. Then they removed me back to my dungeon cell. I was there for days I could not count for there was no light. A hand's breadth runnel of water ran under one wall, across the floor, and under the opposing wall. That was my drink and where waste was carried out."

Per Raimundo's fingers gripped and wrinkled the folds of his cassock.

"At some time—two-three days, I think—they returned for me and took me back to the chamber where I had been accused. There, I was affixed to a heavy table in the center of the room. It stank of blood and the sweat of fear."

Reymera paused and gasped briefly for breath. Jacqueline rose from the end of the bed and put her head in Reymera's lap. Unconsciously, she stroked the dog's ears for a moment, then proceeded with her tale.

"*Dom* Amalric read the accusations against me again. He asked if I repented. When I began to explain that there was an error, the two gray-robed brothers who brought me in strapped my mouth closed with leather thongs. *Dom* Amalric told me that my voice could only be used to acknowledge that I recanted and that then he would hear my confession and I would be allowed to die in the bosom of Holy Mother Church."

Reymera filled her lungs with a deep breath.

"Then *Dom* Amalric motioned to *Frere* Gonsalvo, who had been standing motionless at his side. *Frere* Gonsalvo moved out of my sight for a moment and returned with a large, open wooden case.

"He held the case in front of me, so that I could clearly see its contents.

"Inside it were dozens of tools. Pincers, hammers, prongs and prods, stakes, knives and saws of all sizes and descriptions.

"One of the Brothers raised the back of the table I lay upon, so that I lay at a slant upright but could not move. My mouth remained strapped closed.

"As *Frere* Gonsalvo removed each instrument in turn from its brown-stained berth in the case and held it before me, *Dom* Amalric described the function of the device, in plain and simple detail: gouging, prying or holding open, slicing, severing, crushing, scooping.

"The first time the instruments were shown to me…"

Per Raimundo interrupted in a shaken voice, "…The *first* time?"

Reymera's eyes did not smile, but the edges of her mouth quirked up, "Yes, Father. This procedure was repeated daily."

Per Raimundo crossed himself. When he stretched his hand forth to exert benediction to Reymera, she darted her good fingers out and pressed his palm down to his own knee, shaking her head. *Per* Raimundo glanced at her, then lowered his eyes.

"There is not much more," Reymera continued.

"The first day they showed me the instruments of God's work, I swooned half-a-dozen times. As much from the uncanny thoughts that came to me as I looked on the unworldly mien of *Frere* Gonsalvo as from the unspeakable descriptions of torture that his master revealed to my innocent imagination."

Reymera started, surprised at her own passion—shocked by the memory of what she had lost. She stared at *Per* Raimundo in mute terror and rawest need, "By the Saints and any goodness there is in the world, Father, I never knew that man could dream such evil; I never dreamed that such hells could be brought into this world." Her fists dug into her eyes, dry of tears she could not shed.

Jacqueline placed her forepaws on her Lady's shoulder and delicately washed Reymera's ear with her narrow tongue.

Head still bowed, Reymera continued, "When the last of the instruments were shown, *Dom* Pierre came to stand before me." Reymera paused and gripped the priest's wrist, "He explained that he would know when I lied, and that even if he did not know, God would know. That I should speak only the truth and then I would be given the chance to recant my sins. Then my mouth was freed to let me speak and he would ask his first question. It was always the same."

"What did he say, my child?" *Per* Raimundo whispered.

"He would ask, 'When did you become a witch?'"

THEY SAT TOGETHER in silence by the dying fire. *Per* Raimundo missed Vespers that day.

WARMTH BLEW in from the east and the great sea, replacing the chill winds that rolled in from the mountains that rose in the south. Winter storms became cool and welcome breezes. Delicate pale flowers bloomed in the shade of the bushes and trees. Bolder blossoms covered the slopes of the Corbières as the Mediterranean summer circled Reymera's and *Damaleta*'s cottage.

Per Raimundo's visits were still frequent, and Costigos still chopped her wood and brought her water, but Reymera was no longer in immediate danger. She could walk. She could even bend and lift.

But she did not return to the glades and ravines and copses

and valleys to ply her craft. She did not plant or tend her roots or beans or grapes.

She prepared what was brought to her in thin soups. She fed her dog. And she sat on the stool by the side of her bed, a cold hearth behind her, an open empty door in front of her. She sat, smooth-faced, clear-eyed.

No villagers from Montlaur, Ribaute, or Lagrasse arrived for aid or friendship.

When Costigos came, she fed him her soup. He said her name and then his own several times. She thanked him simply and returned to her stool, blankly registering the "Chonk-Chonk-Chonk" of splitting wood outside. Then he was gone and she was alone again.

Except for *Damaleta* Jacqueline.

Mostly the little red dog lay at her feet, pressing her warm back against Reymera's bare toes.

For such a small animal, her dreams were mighty. She twitched and moaned, sometimes emitting short barks or other noises. The rhythm of her leg contractions clearly showed that she ran strong in the dreamland in which she slept.

And—often—she rose from her place and stood by Reymera, thrusting her scratchy soft wedge-shaped muzzle down onto her mistress' folded hands or lap. Sometimes she whined once or twice. Sometimes she looked up into Reymera's face, brown eyes soundlessly meeting blue ones.

Summer wore on. Earlier each day, the heat crept down the hill that shaded the cottage on the east and the cricket song grew louder in the night.

One morning, as Reymera sat on her stool and a hot wet wind curled around the hill behind the cottage, *Damaleta* Jacqueline's head jerked upright from her reclining position in front of her mistress. Just as swiftly she was on her feet and to the door.

Reymera's gaze drifted back from the gauzy nothingness with which she tried to fill her world. She looked over the barking dog, out the door and down the slope in front of her dwelling.

An undersized human figure stumbled up the stony wash. The top of the figure was covered in what once might have been a bright cerise shawl. Head down, every few steps it fell to the ground and lay still for several heartbeats. Then it rose and moved up the hill again.

Jacqueline stopped barking on her own, but remained standing in the doorway. She swiveled her head toward Reymera, then just as swiftly shifted her gaze forward.

Slowly, creakily, Reymera stood up from the stool and moved to the door, bracing herself on the frame.

"Who do you suppose..." she began.

Shy *Damaleta* Jacqueline bounded out the door and hurtled down at the struggling visitor.

"No, *Damaleta*! Stop!" Reymera found herself walking down the familiar path, a course she'd not trod since returning to the house months earlier.

The little red dog reached the invading presence. The pink-covered head looked up. Mud and tears obscured the retroussé nose and sweet features of a young girl.

"*Dama* Reymera. *Dama* Reymera." The girl moaned, filling her eyes as she willed herself up the hill a few more steps.

"Premedeta?" Reymera was almost to the girl now. Jacqueline stood unnoticed by the child's side. "What is it, *ma petite*? Where is your *Maire*?"

With a final effort, Premedeta Mistral drove herself into Reymera's thin, outstretched arms, sobbing, "They're gone, *Dama*, they're gone. *Maire*. *Paire*. Pierre. Nuèit. All gone. I didn't know where to go. They're dead. They're gone. Oh, *Dama* Reymera. They're gone."

Reymera's arms encircled heaving shoulders and the two figures sank to the ground. Ears pasted flat to her skull, Jacqueline's wet nose and tongue gently brushed the salty moisture that ran down their necks.

. . .

FOR THE NEXT FEW DAYS, Reymera sat and listened to the girl's near-incoherent grief. She made teas, which meant she had to gather plants—but only the ones nearest her cottage. She combed the child's hair; kissed her forehead; made her a pallet of rushes next to the fire. Her soup became thicker.

Time passed. Weeks. The hot wet breath of the Mediterranean, *Le Vent Marin*, faded with the late summer flowers. Together, *Per* Raimundo and his deacon, brown Costigos, built a second cot for young Premedeta Mistral. By the time the first cold wind blew down from the northwest, the girl's pretty round face was more often smiling than somber.

Reymera sat on her stool, face and heart as empty as the space in the open door she stared out of. Today was such a day, even though on this November morning, the air was bright and still, and the sun shone as warmly from the clear sky as if it remembered summer.

Premedeta had gone to gather fresh lavender for the floor; it kept some of the winter insects away and both women loved the smell. This would be the last harvest before winter. *Damaleta* had followed the girl outside. Reymera almost smiled at that thought. *Damaleta* had quickly extended her trust and Reymera's two charges were best of friends now.

I must live for this girl. She has no one else. There is no longer a life for me. Can I do this for this girl, this other's child, when I can do nothing for myself?

These thoughts and darker ones passed behind Reymera's eyes as she gazed down the sun-drenched hill that stretched below her.

"Reymera! Reymera! Come! You must see! Come quickly!" Premedeta's high voice drifted in. She was not far. It did not sound like a call of fear or danger, but Reymera struggled up and stiffly walked out the door with as much alacrity as she could muster.

"Here! Here!" The girl called, then loudly whispered, "Hush!"

Reymera hobbled in the direction of the voice. When she rounded the corner of the house, she could see Premedeta kneeling down with her arms around *petite Damaleta*. Whether she was restraining Jacqueline or comforting her was impossible to tell. A hundred feet above them—on the slope of the neighbor mountain that protected their cottage from the north and east—ranged a lanky black bear.

The bear did not pay any attention to the watchers below; he had a more important and immediate mission. Every few instants he became obscured by an intensely colorful mass that burst from the ground and then dispersed around him.

Reymera carefully stumbled forward until she stood next to Jacqueline and Premedeta. Now she could hear the bear's weird groans, sounds that indicated both deepest satiation and frustration. She could also see the bold splashes of orange amidst the displays of white explosions.

"*Le Papillon d'Adonis*—the blue butterflies of the Midi. It's late for them, but then the day is so warm." She answered the child's unasked question.

All six eyes of the spectators remained fixed on the bear and the butterflies. Premedeta whispered, "But what is the bearling doing, *Dama*? Is he playing with the butterflies?"

"No, *ma petite*, he is *eating* them."

After another half-dozen sprays of erupted color, Reymera put her hand on the girl's forearm, "I'm going back to the cottage. It's time to build the fire for the evening." Leaving the bear behind, Reymera turned back, followed immediately by the girl and the dog.

Before she'd gone half-way back, *Damaleta* sprinted ahead of her, capering and jumping across the strip of grass that softened the entryway to Reymera's home.

"She loves the warmth today," Premedeta explained.

But Jacqueline did not run for the door. She bolted by it,

then leapt in the air and twisted in such a way that she landed facing the way she'd come. She hopped a step, ran three paces, pivoted, jumped in the air, and then ran and leapt and ran and leapt in very small circles.

"Is something wrong with her, *Dama*?" Premedeta asked.

Reymera leaned against the beech tree that shaded her lower garden. Small flashes of blue, white, and orange flitted around *Damaleta* Jacqueline, wings filtering and reflecting the clear light of the sun.

"No, *ma petite*, there's nothing at all wrong with her."

Reymera stretched an arm out and Premedeta folded herself inside it. Reymera's chest trembled with a rusty remembered music.

"She dances for us. She dances for life."

4

INTERLUDE: FROM THE ROYAL POCKET

SHOREDITCH, London, England 1594 CE

Dramatis Canes (et Alia Animalia)
Jackanapes, Will Shakespeare's dog
Dunsey, scout for St. Leonard's pack
the Noble Hound, a great dog guarding a Great House
Crib, leader of the Bishopsgate pack
Harry Hunks, a Bear

Lady Alice, leader of St. Leonard's pack

JACKANAPES
I be what I am: Jackanapes, bosom brother of my sweet master Will Shakespeare, literally his dogsbody, and also his dog's head and dog's tail, for I am my dear departed dam and pater's mutt and a true Shoreditcher.
Day's light is short now. Master Will sets upon me many

tasks, not least to play in one of his wordy stagings this very afternoon as Memers, Turk Prince of Dogs. Should I fail, all his machinations and confibrilations would be undone—and thus Will himself may be undone as well, as, without doubt, would I.

"I," now that's a word to conjure with, ain't it?

But on this day, after certain misadventures occurring to me and Master Will, one exploit particular caused me to anger a great dog—Noble Hound I do call him—thrice my height and more times my weight. I thus find myself seeking urgent shelter in Bishopsgate, 'cross the bridge from home grounds, in lands most unknown to me.

Now, hereby, a high tenor bugle voice beckons beneath my feet from out the grate below:

O Great Sir Jack!
Below, Sir Jack! Down here!

A white, black, and brown splotched face peers up at me from the ungrated sewer drain.

I slither through the dank slit onto a ledge where sits a wee dog, so small his round head near scrapes the top of the sluice.

Resting on my haunches, I peruse my rescuer. 'Twere Lady Alice's little scape, Dunsey, often o'erlooked by Alice's St. Leonard's pack for his lack of brawn, but altogether my dealings with the atomy pup hast been strong and respectful. From his shoulder to the slimy ground is no more than two hands, yet there was a wondrous discrepancy tween 'height and heart, the latter far surpassing the former.

Today he appears to make this sewer his home: mud and bits of flotsam besmirch his sad, spotted coat. Stuck on his forelock is a broad leaf that, despite all his many stains, fits him with a glamour of derring-do.

Sepulchral growls roll from above me as the Noble Hound wedges muzzle through gutter gate, inches from our heads. But that very gap mayhap be salvation sure as that tosspot Will Kempe is fond of drink.

The Hound squeezes his nose into the rough space, trying to open his maw, but the gutter is too narrow and he can but insinuate the tip of his mighty jaw, uttering doggy remonstrances made less fearsome by this concrete constraint.

Dunsey harkens not to the threatening beast, but sits smiling, thin tail a-thump, watching me in the gloomy air.

LET US BE OFF, SIR JACK.

Whereupon he bows, turns and trots into the soily dankness. I jot close behind on the meager ledge. Sounds from the street fade, replaced by the tip-tap-scrapes of Dunsey's claws. The darkness grows as we pick our path until a flickering ahead pulls us on in hope. Neither of us speaks or makes alarum.

The glimmer becomes a glow, the ledge—green and brown with soft and vegetative growth. The same moist verdancy covers ceiling and walls. Besides this carpet, little else but leaves and the odd pile of offal are to be seen or smelled.

I tread quiet toward the increasing brightness, now limning an embowed opening close ahead. At the arch, Dunsey pauses and I sidle up to sit beside him. We gape together at a mad scene.

The span under which we sit is one of countless others, arranged in tiers around a broad circle. On every brim—around, above, and below—are rats. More rats than ere I'd seen e'en 'round the middens of slaughterhouses. They proceed about their ratly ways, nibbling tiny bits of ratly things—including their ratly brothers and sisters. Making ratly noises of "gleee," "scratchy-scratch," and "snip-snip-snippett."

A roiling cauldron of dark water squats below us. Wriggling dark water, a rat lake. For rats swim upon it and paddle about on demi-logs of ratly filth.

The ratty noises, sights, and smells are a horror the like of which I pray ne'er to perceive again. I step back apace into the shadow of the arch. Dunsey follows, but speaks boldly.

Per Mervailous, Sir Jack, we find
The Center of their fest.
Wouldst thou allow I take the lead
To vanquish Satan's Nest?

I near strike the tiny lad with my nose, so hard do I swivel to stare upon him. His tail thumps. His bulging black eyes shine. Now, my old Dad was known from Bow Bells to Cheapside for his verminous exterminating prowess, and his son was bred right enough to that. I'd broken more ratly backs than I could quick recall. (Will was not overfond of the creatures and generous in reward of their demise.) But the boldest general would not countenance these odds. Yet doughty Dunsey was hard denied; best not address such zesty virtue direct, methought.

Be there another path, Dunsey,
From out this dankest hole?

The wee scamp blinks from under his leafy cap.

You do not wish to charge?
We'd mete them reddest death in large.

A few inhabitants of the far ledge stop their endless scuttling and stare at our arch. More stop and chitter and gnash their protrusive ratly teeth.

We'd scuttle this rare scurvy lot
Together, yes, sans doute.
But, Dunsey bold, I've other plights
And other fights are due.

Growling low, I show clear what those "other" knaves can expect.
Facing me, Dunsey can not see the massing ratness now swirling around the ledges toward our opening in a vast ratly mass. His turnip-sized head lowers, letting the leafy twig cover one eye; he sighs and stolid marches past me up the path down whence we'd come.
Dunsey's gait is swift in this closed and noisome alley and I oft bow my head to miss hideous outcroppings of dripping stain.
In earnest flight we hurry. Still, true as he is, I know Dunsey's thought oft wavers as the twig upon his head might ride a slow stream, like to be caught up in nameless eddies or fallen bracken lurking near the bank. And so I deem it best to engage the

honest muttling in our purpose lest he wander or delay, so I aver:

How now our Lady Alice sends
You here so far afield?

The crook in his broken tail twitches; the tip curls and points downwards. This topic distresses my diminutive guide.

INTERLUDE: FROM THE ROYAL POCKET

My Lady will not let me guard
She thinks me slow and frail,
She brought me to this darksome place
And says "Mind thou this trail!"

Feeling rodent eyes seeking ever closer upon our rear, I ply my companion with hoary encouragement—so to focus and distract our doughty pupling.

How do her deeds upon thee act?
Good Dunsey, tell me more.

Then, as if I did plunge Dunsey's hat-twig into his nether parts, the mitey dog takes the bit and hurries to the race. I pull deep upon all resource to match his strides and recollections, his twists and turns and frantic reconnoitering.

You know my tale, Sir Jack,
as I was Queen Bess' table dog and how she fed us
and how upon her revels we
—my merry packmates and I, oh how I miss Little Cakes and
Red Gary and all those who shared my bed and board—
ran tilt and tail betwixt the dishes
and meats and plates and fowl and pasties and cock-
feathers
on HAMPTON courts damask-bedecked tables
and our good Queen chortled and purpled in her
merriment
and how her courtiers aghast watched as we her Royal
pocket beagles cleaned their leavings
and lapped their ports and sac and other bibulous rewards
and she regaled us with her mirth and ribbons and great
pats and strokings
and then slept upon her high bed on easterly silken pillows
soft as duckling down.

BUT THEN WAS I SNATCHED WHEN NIGHT NEARED MORN
WHILE MY GOOD QUEEN BESS ATTENDED TO HER CLOSET HEALTH
AND IN STEALTH WITH SONGS UPON THEIR BOAT, DRUNKEN LORDS TOSSED ME
IN THE BLACK RIVER TO DROWN
AND WATER-FILLED I SPIED THE GREAT DARK FORM
AND SMELLED THAT DEVIL STENCH OF THE RAT GRANDEE
—DIRECT FROM POPISH SPAIN—
BORNE FOR NAUGHT BUT ILL DEEDS,
UPON HIS RAT BOAT WITH RAT MINIONS AS OARS
AND I, SODDEN SOAKED AND IN LARGEST FEAR, SANK IN FINAL THRASHES STRIVING UPON THE MUDDY BANKS SLIPPING BACK SHOCKED WITH NO THOUGHT OR STRENGTH.
THEN LONDON'S BRAVEST AND MOST BEAUTEOUS BITCH
OUR INCOMPARABLE LADY ALICE
PULLED ME FORTH WITH HER LADY JAWS CLENCHED
UPON MY NECKING FOLDS WETTING MUDDY HER FINE FUR
AND THENCE AND EVER HAVE I DONE WHAT E'ER SHE BID
THOUGH SHE IS NO QUEEN BUT MY LADY
AND THOUGH I AM SMALL,
I'LL EVER SEEK THAT EVIL LORD OF FILTH TO PAY HIS DUE
BUT WHY DID DEAR QUEEN BESS FORSAKE ME SO?

At this end, he turns upon me eyes that course with pain. Above his head, like heaven's will, light shines that glistens on the splatters and leathern crusts patching his tiny hide. Good Dunsey has faithful and sure brought us to the opening and escape.

I jump upwards, finding purchase, and easily gain the street. Looking back into the sewer, Dunsey's dark stare pins me as if to ask should he forsake the deeps or turn and meet the host that follows. I yip in sharp command. Dunsey scrambles and somehow breaches the port, though it is several times his stature above the ledge below. With no further word, we run together under the warming rays of great London's winter sun.

INTERLUDE: FROM THE ROYAL POCKET

Up an unknown lane and then another we creep. Dunsey's nose ever wrinkles and my own catches no scent of home. The courtly houses no more line the streets, but I suss we are yet in Bishopsgate and so in my half-brother Crib's lordship and demesne. I have not forgotten his last portentous words, promising my slow, painful, and untimely demise should I be found within his province.

We keep to shadows as we can. Humans traffick on the wide paved streets, but as these are as well highways for Crib's lads, we edge into dirt lanes and alleys, ever narrower, dingier, and darker.

A mackerel man's cart has been o'ertopped with provender and I grab a scaly prize from off the ground. We scuttle up the way that leads behind him.

Wolfing sweet mackerel meat and oily skin ladled with the sweet relish of fear and stolen goods, I mistake the deep warfling at its first cry or three. But as the angry sound grows closer, I know the great beast of Bishopsgate, the Noble Hound, has somehow found my trail.

Innocent of the import of my pursuer's warning cries, Dunsey tears at the remains of our finny repast. And 'deed, I'd no reason to suspect the Behemoth on my tail would offer Wee Dunsey any hurt. Yet I can not leave him oblivious in harm's hard way.

BRAVE DUNSEY FRIEND, RETURN THEE HOME
THY MISTRESS NEEDS REPORT;
I'M FOR MY MASTER'S THEATRE.
I'D WELCOME HER ADDRESS
IF SHE WOULD HEAR MY ODDLING TALE,
FORSOOTH, I WOULD THERE TELL.

So I abandon my savior pup with the dregs of his repast and make away. The more steps 'tween us, the less risk my boonmate will share my mounting peril.

. . .

DUNSEY

Doing the duty bidden by Sir Jack, I stand postern gate sentry at "The Theatre," as humans do call it, the workplace of Master Sir Jackanapes, bravest and tricksiest of all cur-dogs in all England. And in the crossroads plain before *his* master's shrine, Sir Jack courts and cajoles My Lady Alice. So watching at my station, I wonder how I'll e'er find again that evil which befouls our London earth and water and, yea, even sewer and abattoir, the Rat Grandee, who makes the blood of all—rough or innocent—sour with well-considered terror. Who steals babies, eats grown dogs, keeps vilest snakes and slithering things as pets and playmates for his licentiousness, plots ruination on the living and sacrilege of the dead, invades dreams, poisons the air with its rotten vaprous breath and the waters with its waste, soulless, mindless though cunning beyond ken, traitorous to its parents, meting out vasty wickedness to all virtue. My pledge renews each morn and each night before slumber to rid our England of this monstrous iniquity and make what small gesture of righting the world that I may.

But here comes our Jack, quick as hair on felt, and presents to me:

HOLD FAST YOUR TONGUE, FRIEND DUNSEY TRUE,
YOUR COUNCIL HOLD, I PRAY.
I MUST UNSEEN, UNSMELT, PURSUE
MY MISSION ON THIS DAY.
WARD GATE AND MAN THE STANCHIONS WELL
'TILL DIREFUL CRIB DOTH STEAL THIS WAY.

And 'fore I can reply, he passes me sly as lice, slips 'tween groundling legs and through the gate.

But Milady Alice has bid me hold here.

And yet I drowse.

INTERLUDE: FROM THE ROYAL POCKET

In dreams of royal pillows, warm tummies of dearest packmates, with no...

Wait, Awake! There Lady Alice nods...To me! To me! Bully breeds—ours and foreign—surround her. There's Slim John snorting at some tawny muscled mass, Nosey and Rosey backing from a band of fierceling terriers, Jock-i-the-Water is down underneath a towering barbarous red fellow. Lady Alice herself backs into an enormous lout and...ahh me...'tis Crib's thugs from Bishopsgate. Did they follow me here? Gadzooks! Sir Jack said he bore close relation to Crib. How reconcile such a pair as brothers: one so knightly, the other equal knavely?

But this is great foolery! To my Lady!

With other-worldly senses that have served her oft and well, My Lady Alice shouts to me before I can reach her side:

FLY! DUNSEY, FLY! THY WORTH IS SPEED.
OUR FORM AND MANNER HOLDS THIS FRAY
FOR DEVIL'S HERE AND NOW
FIND JACK! RELATE! PREPARE.
JACK'S BROTHER'S WRATH IS QUICK AND DIRE.

My scent is high as is my nether fur. None threaten Milady Alice and avoid my consequence. Deepest growls stir my belly as I look up. And up. Before Milady is the monstrous Crib himself: six stone if an ounce of scars and old nippings, half an ear here, none there, a gash along one rib showing discolored bone. I have no afright, as Good Queen Bess might say, "Fear the one that gave those marks!" But Lady Alice kens my martial mood and bids me again, with no reserve in her flaying tongue:

AWAY, PIP. NOW AWAY!
WARD JACK OR ELSE WE LOSE THE DAY!

And so into the great box Theatre I go, past pile of roasted nut there, apple rind here, ahh...sausages today—there are not always sausages... a mince tart whole-but-a-bite—What would the baker say?...Bliss, say I. Where's Sir Jack?

Into the roiling sea of human legs and skirts and pantaloons on the tasty floor of this place where humans cast their eatings and rinds and bones of all manner and quantity that I wonder they have food upon their tables. I've often scamped between the pinches in the walls and shuffled through the mix, while costumed men cried and clamored and tread above me on what Sir Jackanapes calls "the boards" and do make repast fit for even my Queen Bess, bless her rosy soul, mayhaps not served so seemly well. Where be Sir Jackanapes?

Upon the stage there is bellowing and moving and steely sounds. Here's a broad belling dress where I can rest and reconnoiter. Ah me, Milady Alice no doubt wishes less discretion; I move on. Around. Through. Orange peels on my head, scent so strong I'm taken back to Christmas revels at Hampton. Our good Queen tickled Red Gary's belly with a stout feather and matched him laugh for howl. A merry night. As were they all. My business now, Milady's business.

JACKANAPES

A warm nose brushed my chin and I looked down at Dunsey's scarred and mottled brow.

OH MASTER JACKANAPES
OUR LADY IS TOO SOON BESET.
CRIB LOOMS WITH EYES OF JET.
SHE'LL NOT LIST ME BUT YOU SHE'LL KEN.
MY MESSAGE NOW BE SET.

The tiny hound rounded then, sure I'd follow. The clash of swords resumed onstage above.

As if in charm to small Dunsey's warn, my beefy brother

Crib swaggered bold into Will's play-yard, sixes of his bully lads behind.

Meanwhile betimes, the be-staffed and barge-sized human Bailiff Brig, clinging amidships to his master the Lord Mayor as barnacle to hull, spied our mitey dogling Dunsey at his feet and absently struck down with his hulking staff upon my boonmate's minikin nob.

I had no moment to check aught but for his breath, which came in strong returns, before my Master Will urgently beckoned me to tie the knot upon his Gordian bow, to execute the final turn in his great trick upon the princelings whose plans so doomfully entwined my Master's livelihood.* Whilst behind my errant brother bulldog, the groundling crowd swelled and parted, revealing upon the unwary Crib's heels, that greatest denizen of Queen Bess's Beargarden, none but the famously angry ursine Harry Hunks! Thy nemesis comes upon thee from the pit that ended our father, brother mine.

Doughty Dunsey! I will return!

DUNSEY

I awake. Humans around me and above shout and move more than is their wont. Recalling the great blow upon my head, there is no divot in the ground to mark where the bolt that struck me descended so I consider not my fate beyond the flashes that now course across my eyes. No mind, my nose intact survives and a trustier guide no dog can have.

A lively dance these humans make. Skirts around me fall away. Strong and mighty yowling proceedeth; the soul of a cowardly mongrel afeared for life and all that's dear. Certes, not our Jack. And the voice too deep, methinks. Where is brave Jack? I'm stag again.

What smells pour forth? Forest? Dark fears of ancient Fate? Musk and berries.

All 'round me trousers and draperies avert like a mighty tempest has pressed upon them. I stand at the edge of "the boards" above and just in time retire as down from these hurtles a great beast as from the fighters' pits: a bear, burly and immense. Upon his fall he snorts a mighty snarl. The crowd retreats and with dreadful speed he's off in chase of whate'er doomed wretch has raised his ire.

Wonders had but begun, for snap, more human commotion, then snap here plummets a fabulous dog's body, not near as great as the massive bearish form but large as any cousin of mine could be. Heeding not the dust or nut hulls or tasty bones upon which he lands, he hikes away, in bearish pursuit swift as the bony curs in betting races upon the green. Amazed, I am, and proud to share blood of kin with creature of such sport.

Whilst this cavort unfurls, cacophonies abound on my right, towards those "boards" of Sir Jack's Master. Crashings and creakings of broken wood. Flailings of human limbs.

'Twas then Master Sir Jack presses 'gainst my side.

JACKANAPES

Leaf-cap gone astray since Brig the Bailiff downed Dunsey with his damnable staff, our valiant mite sniffed and looked inquisical as I made my presence known.

OUR VILLAINS NOW ARE SEIZED, GOOD FRIEND.
MY WILL'S PROBATE EXTENDS.
LET'S LEARN WHAT ELSE OUR FATE PORTENDS
AND PROWL, MAKE GROUNDLINGS BEND.

So the bold, bitsy waif and I roamed all edges of my Master Will's Theatre. Liberty filled our nostrils, but earnest Dunsey's ever-furrowed brow announced a purpose and passion beyond my faith.

WHAT TROUBLES YOU, FRIEND D,

INTERLUDE: FROM THE ROYAL POCKET

BREATHE WHEN THERE'S BREATH, DON'T BORROW GRIEF.

No response from the minikin dab but quickened feet and there—behind an arras I'd passed a hundred times—Dunsey stood transfix'd before a hellish hole from whence emitted (for dog that I am this stench fair pinioned my heart) the noxion, the evilest smell I knew, a compounded ratness and signature devilish dessication that could be no other than the Rat Grandee himself.

A light shone behind the mighty pup's brown eyes, matching courageous intent with the foulness that poured from that dark afflicted void. The nonpareil pup nudged me gently aside and shared this thought.

PERFECT DOG, PEERLESS FRIEND,
THE RAT GRANDEE IS MINE TO END.

Dunsey leapt.
Straight into the gap behind the drape covering the outer wall that led to a Rending Pit for the abandoned slaughterhouse abutting Will's Theatre. Straight into that port: black as Hades, with smells to match Lucifer's beard, plummeted Queen Bess' Royal Pocket Beagle on a mission to stop fabulous evil, a mission he would never forsake.
The intensity of that vile miasma was made clear enow.
For as Dunsey dove, so also in self-same time did that Prince of Perdition himself—the Rat Grandee—leap from the vaporous opening and the two fated foes met, nose-to-nose. From their destined collision came an awful sound of flesh and bone pressed beyond limit, a squeal of profoundest dimension, but so high in pitch that none but my canine cousins could detect.
Both enemies fell to the ground before me. Having taken the braining direct upon his head-bone, Dunsey's wits slumbered soundly. I heard and smelled his breath strong and regular. The evil rat suffered greatly; it's wicked proboscis—half-as-long as

noble Dunsey—was fair split in two. It's wits were addled, it stumbled slow, but it was quick regaining control of its monstrous body.

Some of the ghosty rumors were correct. This rodent was beyond any in my much-experienced ken. Indeed, it were more near my size than the size of any ratling I'd encountered, perhaps twice the length and girth of my friend, its heroic adversary who lay now helpless at its twitching feet.

Nor was this all. Dunsey hath forgot that kings, grandees, and their ilk have hangers-on, courtiers, men-at-arms. Already twenty, perhaps fifty of such had emerged from the Pit and were stalking near their master, awaiting his dread command.

And there were sick red flashing glows of numberless ratty eyes in the black of that pitchy passage. Ready when battle commenced or when called by their evil lord.

There are times when what you are is all that fate demands.

And I, Jackanapes, was my honest Da's true terrier whelp, and bred a hundred generations to this game.

The Master Rat himself offered more challenge than I'd had aforetime. His mammoth height was such I had need to jump upon his greasy back to reach that ratty neck. I grant it was an ungainly trick and if Will had been timing me upon his clock, as he had sometimes done, I'd have winced at the rude wit he'd aim at my awkward sloth. Hop! Snap! I jumped off the stenchy beast and it jigged its final dance o' death.

I moved on to the pestilent Dukes and Duchesses of Filth and Mire that attended upon the soon-deceased Grandee. Most cowered and slunk. A few bunched ready for charge. The smartest darted under Will's stage. I let the latter go. The others, being of normal size, I dispatched snick-snack anon. Used to such displays, the remaining humans noticed nothing untoward.

"Jack! Jack Dog! Here! Anon!" Across the yard, my Master's voice.

. . .

INTERLUDE: FROM THE ROYAL POCKET

DUNSEY

Queen Bess sits on her bed propped by purple satin pillows, surrounded by my sisters and brothers and kin, Red Gary, Merry Pip, Little Cakes. And there he is below her feet, climbing up the covers, rising on hind legs to threaten my Queen.

I leap and...

I wake upon nut hulls and orange peels, staring up skirts. Unseen hammers striking my forehead, I sit and gaze. In Jack's Master's place. I am not within the maw of Hell where I went to match the Devil.

Jack? Where's Sir Jack?

There and there and there. Until this day, I'd heard but ne'er seen Sir Jack's prime renown. In faith, it's not to be believed ere one knows Sir Jack. As I spy him alongside that base nest of hindermost Hades, he ends thirty vermin lives 'fore Lady Alice could've raised her plumed tail.

And *there*. Not a pace away. Within a breath. *There* is *the thing*. If kind heart can yearn for evil—not to *be* it, but to *end* it—then this is my heart's desire. The giant rodent who's brought such suffering to our shores lies hard by. Catching his breath, plotting his rearward attack on the unwary Sir Jackanapes. It will not stand!

Unable to charge, I crawl.

His rodent body covered in blood, it flows over the encrusted decay which seems part of his very skin.

I rise upon my hind legs, striving to reach his throat.

A great shiver roars through his damnéd body and I am cast off. But he is on his belly now. I dart under his long, crimson-covered jaws and nip-slice through his underthroat with my finest, sharpest foreteeth.

Blood from this carcass of evil gushes upon me and this figure of incalculable calamity collapses.

I slide out from underneath and shake myself free of the worst.

The Rat Grandee is dead. Pups and babes in our stout land are safe from his knavery forevermore.

Sir Jackanapes looms, forepaws upon the fallen corpse of our demolished enemy.

JACKANAPES

Heyday, Stout Dunsey! Come Away!
My Master calls anon.
You've vanquished evil on this day
All England owes you praise.

But now I'm Prince in Will's fair play
And Princes need good Aid
I'll have with me but bravest lords
And thine's the surest blade.

EXEUNT JACKANAPES AND DUNSEY BACKSTAGE.

JACK STRUTS forth upon the stage beplummed and proud in Turkish livery, accompanied by the richly pantalooned Dunsey, whereupon they play-act their parts as Memers, Dog Prince of Constantinople and his attendant Lord, all for the panoply parade of Master Will's latest thespic effort.

*But this is fruit for another pie, baked within the doings of the dogly prince of Shoreditch & c. in "Jackanapes: A Will and A Dog."

5

JACKANAPES IN HEAVEN

AN AFTER-LIFE: costumes, settings, all—from England, c. 1610-1625 CE

SWEET CLOVER SCENT filled my nostrils as I woke. I raised my head to see 'cross the narrow brook the pale, stripéd canopy of my sweet (if barbed-tongued) amour, Lady Alice. Farther down the stream my other light of love, Mignonette, no doubt cavorted in her most lively encampment. With vigor I shook out the last effects of malmsey wine imbibed last even, ready to meet the pleasantries of the day's endeavors with the bold spirit I'd inherited from my Da—spritely lure dog of the Bear pits in Southwark that he was.

'Round her pink-and-purple pennoned pavilion rode my fair Lady Alice herself. Perched—standing, as was her wont—upon an ornately tooled Seville half-saddle, she meandered toward me on her dappled palfrey, Demoiselle. Walking on either side of her were two members of her Court, Count Respite and the Duke of Forays. I knew them here, but remembered them best as Brown Billy and Three-legged Jim from our lives in Shoreditch, when we were all but London curs, spying and scraping for a crust or a bit of bacon. Life after life was a wondrous thing, but it spun the senses like a mule's kick to the head.

MANY OF OUR crew resided now somewhere upon this great meadow. Besides myself, Alice, Billy, and Jim, Stink Foot, and Brick the Enforcer, many others of the Bishopsgate and Shoreditch packs had appeared. Close eyes for the sleep of night and when next awake, there stood an old chum. Churls and villains like Crib the Brawler (my half-brother and murderer of our own mother) ne'er showed. I wondered where Dunsey—my boon companion, the brave and midget beagle—had been taken, for not a hair of his tiny frame was to be sniffed. And surely the Noble Hound, who had chased and cornered infamous Harry Hunks himself, surely that unredoubted spirit would sometime (after his Earthly demise) be ensconced in his own caninous castle upon our great greensward?

"Hail, Alice." I cried.

"Nor will it so, little my love. Nor rain nor snow." The tip of her small rosy tongue dropped over perfect teeth in the middle of a dainty lower lip.

"Weather or not, dearest. Thy wit distresses in degrees made sunny by my regard for thee."

She closed her brown eyes in approval. "Enough enow, silly Jack. I've brought your mount—honest Devil—that we may take the air face-to-face and so continue our bantrous pleasantries. 'Tis unnatural to look down upon you as we converse."

Count Respite/Brown Billy dropped from his mouth the reins of "my" horse Devil—a fiend black as his name that would have killed me many times over had I not been already beyond the natural world. Having gifted me this demon, dear Alice ne'er tired of my pitiful, awkward equistrations or Devil's hellish prancings.

I sat upon my haunches, licked the brown spot on the white fur of my left side contemplatively. As a monk might lick or...well...as a monk might. Striking my proudest air: chin raised, ever-pricked right ear alert, ever-false-and-floppy left ear suggesting deep mystery, I replied: "Mistress of my soul: if time and art allowed, my every breath, all wrinkles in my brows, all sense that my strong nostrils ken would follow in thy walks and airs, be they 'bove the ground, below the salt, or e'en amidst the starry firmament wherein methinks we dwell. Yet as the sky is rent by Zephyr's hornéd blows, so am I sorry spent to split my self in factors not my own and so true enough, as duty builds the grit in oyster's shell, I go, I resolve, I serve, I unfurl. Yet all that is mine best is left behind with thee." I had no hat, but my bow made true my words.

Quickly here no less than on our mundane Earth—for that alacrity had won her many an unsuspected squabble—so Lady Alice catlike pounced down before me. In such proximity, I was afforded that treat which had, as much as her sword-sharp wit or shocking martial prowess, ensured her supremacy on London's muddy streets: her luscious, ineffable, doggy, female perfume. The sharp, tender smell of her tufted derriere, the nosegay of her luxuriant, flowing fur: she was personified the heaven of my body's love and we had oft made much of each other's delight.

Yet, as quippers, lovers, and playmates, we understood the shortcomings of our minds' accord. And so she said, as she paraded in full amorous array before me: "False Jack, 'split' your 'self' to that French fluff's powdered puffery, or 'serve' your poet. I know whose will is which. I do not abide." She preened and switched her tail and flashed me a glance of promise as she turned back to Demoiselle. A pink-and-yellow mounting block appeared from the substance 'round us; she scampered up and resumed her stance on the Spanish leather.

"But I do reside." She added as Demoiselle pranced away, returning toward her gay pavilions.

I felt as one near smothered who yet savors life more and in some part yearns for that sweet small love-death that he knows awaits him.

Of course she was not in error. I'd learned from my Master Will that well-wielded high-flown words could stun and conquer sure as bludgeon or pointed blade. And certes, parts of me remained with him and with sweet Mignonette, e'en though I stood before the ravishing Lady Alice. Such is the wayward land of thought, truth, and betrayal enmeshed in single form.

But these dreary musings did not befit the glorious day, nor my glad surroundings in a land unrivalled for the clemency of its weather or the freshness of its breezes and blooms: what gloom could prevail from such? Howso a surfeit of rich goodness might engender the whining of a triumphant pup? How should I choose among my joyous options: to sieze an hour with the incomparable Lady Alice, enjoy the robust athleticism of the incomparably beauteous Mignonette, or hold fast to the wit and priceless companionship of my Master?

Indeed, another day in paradise.

I'd cavort with the ladies hereafter. Instead, my gaze turned up river and rose. And rose. And rose. The spires of the Wilcester Minster (for so my Master called it) did not end in the clouds they pierced; they vanished in the perfect cerulean heavens somewhere beyond my sight. Like so much else in this kind afterland, I did not ken why Will Shakespeare lived in a church. In my years with him, I'd listened to his ecclesiastical declamations—play Bishop, play Priest, e'en play Pope and play parishioner—but these were his manikins, creations of his imagination; I'd never seen him stride on holy ground, much less pass under the arches of a House of God, e'en that well-attended one of nearby Shoreditch. Yet, Will waited there, *sans doute*.

I walked toward the hill-cloud-mountain-cathedral. The sensation—always uncanny, no matter how oft I made the trek—began as the earth rushed beside me, tilting upwards, moving higher and closer. I soon came to the majestic entry, many doors wide and open, and entered thereupon.

"Good morrow, Jack." To greet me, Will rose from his carved chair set square in that vasty stone-floored vestibule. Smells of candle wax, incense, and cheap wine wafted around him, palpable to me as the stones themselves.

"What wouldst thou make of the day?" he asked. "Fishing? 'Twas a merry caper when you toothed that trout! Or adventures i' the wood? Or chasing of the doughty mice in the field?" My Master beamed down upon me, ever kind and warm. His smile broadened to a leer, "Or p'raps a visit to the ladies holds your fancy? Be it the Gallic exquisite or your saucy English pudding?"

"Ah, me." Falling back, he collapsed into the chair, which

had changed to a velvet-cushioned campaign stool. Will's eyes darkened, his brow deep wrinkled.

"Ah, me, Jack." He sighed. "This high pile of sacred pebbles weighs heavy upon my spirit." He jumped up, embracing himself and then the air in wild wide waves. "My soul should rise in this endless vault, but instead I'm leveled, become dust below these starry reaches. No writs, no disarray, no jumble of liars and thieves: in brief, dear Jack, no humanity." A cockaded cap appeared in his hand as he gestured broadly, "Only these damn minstrels with their thrice-damned *Te Deums*."

Of course I knew of what he spoke. The sacred chanting of small male voices never quite faded wherever you stood inside Will's new home. We'd both hunted through every corner of the cathedral, across transepts from nave to chancel, even to the oddly empty choir stalls. The voices retreated from us, but were never entirely faded. Nor did the faint odor of charred frankincense.

I whimpered.

"Good Jackanapes, good fellow." Will squatted and ruffled the back of my neck. "'Tis not thy doing. Must be some curse I laid upon myself." A stained quill now hung thrust above his ear. "P'raps it was penning that damn'd mishap Andronicus. I should never have followed ol' Dick's advice...'the ground loves gore, Will, 20 pounds gate for Kit's Tamburlaine—and that was two fortnight's into the run. Go on the game, Will, that's a good scribbler.'" The quill vanished and a small dirk filled Will's hand. "Phaww. I know what I'd do with a bare bodkin, and the only breast it would maul is mine own." He paused, touching his lips with the blade. "Or Dick Burbage's." His usual smile returned, but his eye and odor retained their downcast turn. "Would the wretched blaggard were here." He collapsed onto the stool again, cupping his chin in his hands.

Above his head, outside the nearest Rose window grew a golden glow (there were more Rose windows than I could count in this blessed pile of stones where my Master resided: eternally, apparently, in these infinite grounds).

With mind only for his miseries, Master raised his head and struck a note I'd often heard him play, regarding the lines carved on his death stone: "Here I cannot write a new word--and if I did, who wouldst play it? While below that fool's stumbling verse mocks the air above my remains in Stratford. What witless tripe! I know 'twas Robert Smith's beardless son that penned it. He never wooed a maiden, drank a man's fill, or struck a man's blow but his father paid to have his chin or baubles wiped. If I knew the charm to haunt I'd visit myself upon them, by Jove's wayward beard."

Will shrank in my foreground, frozen in his petty sadness. But needs required I find the source of this illumination and it fell outside Will's cathedral.

Turning from my Will, I found myself outside the massive Minster, beyond the towering buttresses. The mountain-hill rolled down steeply beyond, scattered with the white blossoms of our own English daisies and honeyed clover.

But their shine was as outdone as a candle by the Sun, which was itself eclipsed in grandeur by the enormous floating apparition that hung before me. Numberless petals of white and gold surrounded—at their center—a dog. If dog he was, for such a being, such a creature was so beyond any I'd seen—breathing yet with life, or on the boards in Will's Theatre, or even in my dreams. In form it was clear he was my distant kin, but size he had, though no scale to which I could compare: p'raps elephanto, cathedral-like, or the Leviathan whose specter I'd heard sailors shiver from. He reclined on the petals, clothed with fur more luxuriant and reflective than Queen Bess' necklaces and adorned with a stately ruffled Raleigh collar of shiniest white round his godlike neck. But it was his mien, his bearing, all expresséd in eyes of amber that poured forth such tenderness as could not be borne by mortal soul. Of particulars a spirit so besmirched as mine.

Fixed by those eyes, images and smells and veritable lives passed through me: running rough by empty seasides, lain down in palaces and beside most rustic campfires, dancing in moonlight and butterflies, racing across moors and mountains, in moist youth and driest age. And always Master and Mistress in my heart: children, men, women—in regal, barbarous attire or peasant rags. Then there were looming threats and deprivations. Unbidden, my muscles tensed for a leap, my growl hung in my belly.

These impressions fell from me, replaced by prancing, proud Alice. By the acrobatics of little Mignonette: pirouetting, balancing on a rolling ball, vaulting through hoops. By luscious repasts of dormice, swan, glazed roasted sweetmeats, gooseliver, all manners of swine flesh, beef turns, beef steaks, beef ribs, beef chops.

My lips drooling, these phantom meals dissolved and I felt the kind hand of my Master stroking my head, scratching the top of my hips in that one place that only he knew transported me and that I could reach with neither my teeth nor claws, his butter-warm voice more dear than my dam's.

These visions, too, faded, and the eyes looked into, beyond, through me.

There seemed little effort to my choice, but as I slipped into the golden maelstrom of those even-more golden orbs that shone from the Great Dog, I pressed my mind to remembrances of Alice, Dunsey, Mignonette, and—Master Will. It was, therefore, to my great surprise that my last expression as Jackanapes was spoke aloud:

"Ah well it is; the Thames will boil 'fore I miss riding 'pon that demon-spawn Devil horse again."

THOUGH SMALLEST, pupling Alice pushed aside her brother Crib from my hindmost teat. Of course, there were more spigots ready on my belly, so it made less-than-little difference to that near-blind rapscallion as he latched upon the next available.

"Near time to wean that wriggling crew, eh, Annie girl?" My dear Master, the beanpole-tall actor "Short Tom" Staples, came through our wooden door, dropping parcels on the rickety table above me and my litter.

With annoyed affection, I gazed down at the band of nuzzling creatures attached to my stomach. Timely indeed was Master Tom's wisdom.

A sheet of foolscap teetered from the tabletop and sailed back-and-forth until it rested just below my blunt, ruddy nose. Before my first litter, I'd found to my great wonder that I could read the writing that my Master and all humans held in such great regard. This printed scribble was a playbill, announcing a new work soon to be produced—always a matter of importance for our household. Gazing upon it, my spine stiffened as if a great fight portended.

the TRAGEDY of
THE DEVIL'S LAW CASE

the latest Masterpiece
Written by the Renownéd Author of
The *Duchess* of *Malfye*: Mr. John Webster.

Presented publiquely at the Blackfriers
by
The Kings Majesties Servants.
Curtain Rise at 3 O'clock
on the first tuesday of june

WEBSTER? That rat-coddling, twisted shadow man? What had Will called him? "That humourless pen of dung and gore." Yet somewhere, as deep inside as the pool of love from whence came the mother's milk that now flowed from me, memories I'd not known returned. Oh, Master Will! The only tragedy herein is that thou canst no longer skewer-spit the mussell-brained vanities of such lesser lights. But your Jackanapes is here—again—and I vow will make as merry pranks wi'em as ere we played together.

END OF *GOLD DOG*: Volume 3 of *Tales of the Eternal Dog*

1

A YAQUI DOG

1825 - SAN MIGUEL DE URES, **Sonora, Mexico**

CARLOS PRESSED himself against the dark flaking wood of the beams that held up the *alcalde*'s veranda. The *alcalde* himself, Señor Mantecas de Bustamente, cousin of Lopez de Santa Anna himself, had just passed by in his Spanish carriage of gold and white, pulled by his fine matched horses from Mexico City. Carlos did not want the *alcalde*, or—even worse—any of his retainers to see him so near the residence of this great person.

He had only come here because he had been told the *alcalde*'s major domo sometimes gave a few *centavos* to orphans on the Sabbath. And Carlos, a boy of nine, was now alone. His mother had performed odd jobs for many of the government officials in San Miguel de Ures for as long as Carlos could remember. She usually took her son with her and left him outside the high walls of the *casas* and *haciendas* where she worked. When he was very small, she left a Yaqui blanket over his basket to keep the sun and the flies off of him. When he was too old for the basket, sometimes he would follow her into the *haciendas* and sit in the cool, shady corners of the plazas and patios of the great houses.

His mother, Sacramento Giquamea, usually worked indoors cleaning, sometimes outdoors doing laundry, but two days ago, she was asked to work in the stables of the grandee Señor Hortensio. But Sacramento had never worked with horses. Some of her people, Yaquis in the north, had horses they got from the Comanche, but Sacramento had not grown up with them and did not know their ways. So when she walked behind the fine black racing stallion of Señor Hortensio, she did not know the danger she risked. The doctor and the priest told Carlos that she had not suffered, that she was in the arms of Jesus, *Madre Maria*, and the saints before she knew she had left this Earth. Carlos did not say anything.

His mother told him once that his father was a famous scholar. Carlos was not sure what that was, but he thought maybe it was like a general. When his mother was alive, he sometimes thought he could become a soldier in the *federales* and one day meet his father. Carlos did not think that could happen now.

He had not eaten since yesterday, when his mother made some fine gruel of *masa* and the pork leavings she'd been given at Señor Hortensio's kitchen. His mother was—had been—a wonderful cook. Carlos could still taste her tortillas. But his stomach was not as satisfied with this memory as was his tongue.

It would be dark soon. He could return to the wooden plank bed he'd shared with his mother in the back of the oldest part of the mission. Surely, the Padre would still let him sleep there, even though his mother could no longer work in the mission fields or make tithes at Mass.

The coach was well past. There were no servants to be seen. Carlos decided to walk across town to the mission. Maybe someone would have a tortilla or an ear of corn they had not finished. He turned into the setting sun and walked up the street, cobbled here in front of the *alcalde*'s residence, but soon paved only in the hard-packed dust and sand of the Sonoran desert.

Carlos was lost in thought as he trudged back to the mission, wondering how and what he would eat today, tomorrow, and the next. So he did not notice at first when a spotted, soot-colored Indian dog started pacing ahead of him.

Big dogs made Carlos nervous. The only dogs at the mission were the tall Spanish guards the Padres kept by the pantry stores and no one went close to them except their two keepers. Carlos thought for a moment and realized he didn't know any dogs besides these. He'd seen some trotting in the distance in the desert, and he heard them sometimes fighting over scraps behind houses, but they were usually gone by the time he and his mother walked by.

This dog was not colossal like the Spanish dogs at the mission. He looked like he might weigh as much as a small sack of corn that Carlos could carry. And Carlos knew he was a Mexican dog, a Xolo, and not a Spanish dog. That made him feel a little better. And Carlos liked the way the dog looked, all sleek and trim. Carlos even smiled a little because the spots in one place on the dog's back looked a little like Padre Garcia's big nose and moustache.

Well, he thought, as long as I'm going the same direction as the dog, he can come along. The dusky Xolo and Carlos made their way through the dimming dirt streets, the sun in their eyes.

The old mission had been built when the priests first came to Ures, or so he had been told by lots of people. That was before his father's grandfather's time—farther back than Carlos could count.

Carlos did not know it, but the mission had grown larger every generation. The Church had been no weaker or less influential here, in far *Sonora y Sinaloa*, than it had been everywhere else in New Spain, or than it was now in the new *Estados Unidos Mexicanos*.

Carlos did vaguely understand that over two hundred *indios* and *mestizos* worked within the mission walls. For most, a place to sleep and two simple meals a day was a bearable exchange for a lifetime of hard labor. And when the priests were not angry, these workers were given a mouthful of meat on feast days, too. Of course, catechismal

instruction and the full lay ecclesiastical services of the Holy Mother Church were also provided. This was the nature of life within the bosom of the Holy Mother Church. Few of these men and women knew—and certainly Carlos did not—that they received these benefits from Franciscans who had taken over the complex of San Guadalupe de Sangre de Cristo from the original Jesuits.

Before entering the mission compound, Carlos stopped outside. The dog also stopped a few feet away in the road, tilted his head and looked at Carlos.

"I have no food, dog. I don't even know if I have a place to sleep. I'm sorry. You seem like a good dog."

Then Carlos stepped inside the thick-timbered mission gates and made his way toward the sleeping quarters of the workers, the home he had shared with his mother.

BEFORE HE'D GONE a dozen steps, a familiar voice called out at him, "¡*Oye!* Is that *your* dog, Carlito? You cannot leave him there. You cannot let him in. ¡*Bestia Soez!*" Consuela Varigosa the kitchen drudge spat three times into the dust at her feet.

Carlos stopped and looked back at the dog, who paid no attention to Consuela Varigosa or her spitting. "He is not my dog, Señora Varigosa."

"Well, he *looks* like *your* dog, Carlito. He looks like a Yaqui dog. A devil dog. ¡*Uno perro del Diablo!*" And she spit again, three more times.

Then she grabbed Carlos roughly by his shoulder and drug him to the rear of the kitchens. "Wait here, scarecrow." Opening a huge iron-bound door, she vanished inside.

Carlos glanced back toward the front of the mission grounds. He couldn't see the gate from here and he wondered whether the dog, the *perro del Diablo*, was still outside.

Carlos did not like Consuela Varigosa. But she had been kind to him and his mother since Consuela came to the mission from Hermosillo two years ago. She had slipped both of them extra portions once or twice a week, and once—when his mother was sick with the dry blood cough—she had sat by Sacramento Giquamea's bedside all night, giving her water, mopping her brow, and emptying her waste. Consuela always smelled of pork fat. But that was not her fault. It confused him that he did not like her, but his mother had taught him to be polite.

Very soon, Consuela Varigosa opened the large door again. She squinted slowly at Carlos, up and down. Then she licked her palm and brushed it roughly over his hair and then his cheeks.

"There," she said, "that will have to do. Come in here, Carlito, and behave like you are in the church." Carlos was glad she didn't drag him in by the shoulder.

Inside was the largest room he had seen except for in the church itself. There were ten, no maybe twenty, women working in different places. Two women were chopping the heads off chickens, then dipping them in water before defeathering them. Looking like dead soldiers, a dozen bald, headless chickens were already lined up on the table in front of them. There were four fireplaces with two women in front of each, stirring or moving or filling or emptying huge pots. There was a very strong young girl, Maria Vendamos—Carlos recognized her, carrying piñon wood and setting it next to the biggest fireplace. Women were chopping onions and garlic and dried peppers. Women were moving plates and platters and cups and dishes and knives and serving forks by the dozens from one side of the room to the other or onto tables. In the middle of the room was an enormous table. It was almost as big as the table the *alcalde* put together for the *Dia de Muertos* and for Easter in the plaza in the middle of town. At the end of the table, there stood Dominga Peligrosa, the Mistress of the Kitchen. She was a woman Carlos and his mother always avoided. Consuela Varigosa had made it very clear that if Dominga Peligrosa ever learned that scraps from *her* kitchen were being stolen for *mestizos* (much less *indios*), then the thief would have to answer to Padre Garcia *after* answering to Dominga Peligrosa herself.

Carlos did not know what that really meant, but he was sure he never wanted to find out.

When he saw her at the table, shouting orders and holding a

huge cleaver in her left hand, he tried to disappear into the many shadows that lurked around the enormous room.

"Consuela Varigosa! Bring that boy to me here! *Now*, by the breath of our Sweet Savior—not after these scrawny chickens sour! Who grew these worthless excuses? I want the hide of the *ladrón* that foisted this sorry meat off on *my* kitchen! Consuela! Now!"

Consuela Varigosa dutifully charged forward with Carlos in hand. When she reached the end of the table, she released Carlos and performed a very awkward curtsy. Dominga Peligrosa spared her only the briefest of scowls, then turned her withering eye directly on Carlos.

"Boy," Dominga Peligrosa made this word a terrible accusation. She waited a moment, perhaps Carlos would deny it. Carlos only stood there, wondering how long it would take to reach the door outside—and whether he'd be able to open it if he got that far without being caught.

"Boy," Dominga Peligrosa repeated, "Your mother is dead. I understand you do not have a father. Which is just as well, for I'm sure he would be worthless, too." Her left hand, which ended with sharp-pointed blackened fingernails, shot out quick as sin, and grabbed Carlos under his chin. She held his head very firmly so he could look nowhere but directly at Dominga Peligrosa's black eyes. "What are you going to do, boy?"

For several heartbeats, Carlos could not understand this question. The tiny punctures that two of her fingernail tips had created in his throat were the least of his discomfort. Perhaps even more powerful, deadly, and arresting than her dark gloomy stare was Dominga Peligrosa's breath. It smelled of old meat, peppers, onions, and—there was no other word for it—rot. Rot like Carlos knew from helping his mother clean the wounds of the animals that had been injured in the fields.

Carlos tried to breathe without smelling. He realized that Dominga Peligrosa was not going to let him go until he answered her. What was he going to do? He decided telling her he was going to sleep was not enough. Nor would she want to hear that he would be missing his mother. There was something else, something very specific that Dominga Peligrosa's sharp fingers, black eyes, and deadly breath were asking him.

Carlos swallowed and said, "I'm going to make my way in the world."

Dominga Peligrosa's eyes widened. She did not smile. It was hard to imagine her face had ever been surprised by such a soft expression. But she did *not* frown.

"Call Padre Garcia!" She said to the room. She continued staring at Carlos for a few more seconds, then released her grip on his chin, turned her head, and repeated—directly into the face of the hapless Consuela Varigosa, "Get Padre Garcia, lazy girl, then...then...clean the ash out of the meat fire." In panic or confusion, Consuela's feet were planted statue-like. "Oh," Dominga Peligrosa sighed, "He's in the Rectory. Tell him I've got his new worker." Looking back at Carlos, she continued: "Yes, boy, you heard right. Now stand over there out of the way and wait for the Padre. He'll instruct you further."

And with that, Dominga Peligrosa turned her dreadful attention away from Carlos and he was able, once again, to breathe.

He shuffled over to the side of the room in the direction he thought the Mistress of the Kitchen meant and stood with his back against the wall, watching the busy women go about their work.

He stood and watched the preparations for the evening meal completed, as they were put into the pots, onto the spits, into the ovens. Then he watched as they were taken out of the pots and ovens and off the spits. Then he watched as they were put on platters and dishes to be served to the abbot and the officials of the mission. Then he watched as they were likewise taken to the monks. Then he watched as these dishes were brought back into the kitchen and the scullery and washer boys were brought in from the yard to wash and scour the dishes and clean out the fires.

All this time, Carlos stood and watched.

Long after Dominga Peligrosa left the room—which was after the abbot was served—Consuela Vendamos walked by Carlos and handed him two tortillas behind her back. Carlos thought if she had not done this, maybe he would not have been able to stay standing as he had been told.

Carlos did not know how far the night had moved when the washer boys began carrying out the buckets of scraps to the livestock. He had never been awake this long in his life. His knees and his back hurt in ways they'd never hurt before. He'd worked in the corn and bean fields with his mother and that was hard, but it never made him hurt like standing in this corner did.

He wondered if he would have to sleep standing, and if he could, when he heard a familiar-but-unwelcome voice booming down the stairs where the kitchen abutted the rest of the main church building. The voice was shortly followed by the wide brown figure of Padre Garcia. Carlos did not understand how the Church ranked their Priests and Monks, their Fathers and Brothers, their Abbots and Bishops. He had heard many of these titles, but they were all the same to him. He did know that Padre Garcia was a powerful man in the mission of San Guadalupe. He knew Padre Garcia sometimes ordered people to leave the mission. He knew that sometimes Padre Garcia ordered people to be whipped in the courtyard of the mission. People like Carlos. People like his mother.

But the Mistress of the Kitchens had said Padre Garcia was coming to talk to Carlos. Perhaps that meant Carlos could talk to him, an action he would not normally consider. Carlos decided to step out of the shadows, which were now very dark, and ask Padre Garcia what work he had for him. Surely the Padre would not be too angry for this.

Carlos started to move his legs, but his feet had fallen asleep and his knees did not obey his mind, so he fell forwards in front of Padre Garcia.

The priest, startled and thinking he was being attacked by a vagrant—or even a demon that had emerged from the walls, crossed himself and let out a frightened squeak as he jumped backward involuntarily.

José Torres, the *mestizo* who crept behind Padre Garcia, who took care of the administrative directives the Padre decided upon, did not jump backwards in time and Padre Garcia's considerable weight came down concentrated upon the toes of José Torres' left foot. Carlos looked up from the floor and did not know what to make of the sight of the gnarled little man who ordered around everyone in the mission jumping up and down on one foot, shouting imprecations at saints that Carlos had never heard of. He was so absorbed by this that he didn't notice Padre Garcia's enormous hand descend upon him and pull him up by the scruff of his collar.

"What do we have *here*?" Father Garcia boomed into Carlos' face. His voice having fully regained its rumbling and intimidating tenor. "A thief?" He glanced back at the still hopping José Torres, then back at Carlos, "A devil?"

"Pa...pa...pa" Carlos began.

"*That* I most certainly am not, child." Padre Garcia breathed heavily and looked at Carlos with a hint of recognition. "Are you the whelp of that poor...ahh...yes...it comes back to me now. Señora Peligrosa told me about you, *niño*."

José Torres was standing, if tentatively, on both feet now and had the presence of mind to slide a heavy kitchen chair under the priest as Padre Garcia sat without looking behind him.

"Yes, yes. You are the child of..."

"Sacramento, the washer woman." Torres supplied quickly.

"My mother wasn't a washer woman." Carlos heard himself say.

The priest looked closely at Carlos. His expression was unreadable. "Oh wasn't she. What was she then, boy, Duenna to the Princess of Seville?" Padre Garcia's chuckle shook his chest. José Torres cackled lightly behind him.

Pleased he was able to invoke levity in the face of human

tragedy, the priest continued in a more serious tone, "Boy, the sadness of this veil of tears can only be overcome by doing our duty to the Holy Church of our Savior. Do you understand this, boy?"

The priest continued after glancing at the silent Carlos. "You are a fortunate boy…"

"Carlos, your Excellency." Torres filled in.

"I told you not to call me that, Torres." Then, "Carlos, you are very lucky. As it so happens, Isidro Valenzuela, our pig tender of many years is no longer able to continue doing *his* duty to our Holy Mother the Church. And, *you*, young Carlos are going to be given this important position." The priest flashed a look commanding silence at José Torres. "What do you think of that, boy?"

"You want me to tend the pigs?" Carlos asked quietly.

"That's right, boy. And you will *never* be hungry for meat again!" The priest rose from his chair, satisfied he'd swept down from the lofty heights of sacred privilege and saved another otherwise unworthy lost soul from certain perdition. "Torres, show him the pig-keeper's quarters and instruct him in his duties." José Torres, still favoring his left foot, blanched at this, but before he could speak, the priest added, "Tomorrow, man, tomorrow. Return to your old cot tonight, young Carlos. Glory awaits you *mañana!*"

The priest turned his back on Carlos. Padre Garcia's twisted little assistant looked at Carlos with a face Carlos did not entirely understand, but he could see that José Torres was not completely in agreement with his master's decision.

Carlos paid them no more attention, though. He had been given permission to sleep one more night where he had always slept and he made his way—as quickly and quietly as he could —to the tiny cell at the back of the mission where he and his mother had a wooden bunk, fresh straw, and the few items they called their own.

He fell onto his hard bed without even removing the stiff

black mission sandals that hurt his feet. In the few moments before his mind went blank to the everyday world, he thought of his Mother, her warmth and her smile, how she was gone forever; he thought of the endless work and harsh treatment his mother had lived with at the mission; he thought of Padre Garcia's new job for him as pig-tender; he even thought of the Xolo dog—the Yaqui dog, as Consuela had called him—that had come to the mission with him this evening. All of these things he thought in the few seconds before sleep.

CARLOS WOKE ABRUPTLY. He was still very tired. It was dark, but that was not unusual. Someone was washing his face with a small rough cloth. *That* was unusual. His eyes quickly accustomed to the darkness in his cell and he saw it was the Xolo dog standing over him on the bed, licking his face.

Carlos found it very strange that he was not afraid of this dog. He had never been licked by a dog before. He certainly had never been awakened by a dog in his bed, much less one that stood over him and licked his face.

The dog stopped licking and jumped down before Carlos could say anything.

"I cannot let you stay here, dog. I have an important new job—pig-tender. I cannot let you get me in trouble with the Padre." When he said "Padre," Carlos thought of Dominga Peligrosa's deep pits of eyes and her horrible breath. The giant priest was nothing to worry about compared with her.

"I guess I had better get you out of here, dog. If Señora Peligrosa catches you, you might be in tomorrow's tortillas." The spotted Xolo dog did not seem moved by this speculation.

Carlos stopped and looked around the room. It was a rare night when the cracked, unfinished ceiling—their "window," his Mother had called it—let in enough moonlight to make out any details, but this was one of those nights. Sitting on an adobe ledge above the bed was a small corn-doll his mother had made for him and that she still gave him when he was not feeling well. Suspended from a wooden dowel on the wall was a blanket she had woven from soft wool a visiting nun had foolishly left in the waste area, dyed with plants his mother had gathered in her few spare moments. And a small ceramic water jug that she had always had, complete with a rare bit of cork to stopper it. He wedged the clay jug under his rope belt. He would fill it in the trough outside. For reasons he could not explain, he wrapped the doll in the blanket and slung it over his shoulder as he left his room.

The empty courtyard was heavy in its stillness. Staying on the trampled grass near the edges, Carlos circled the inner compound; the dog stayed at his heels, silent as the moonlight. Carlos paused to fill his jug, then quietly shuffled toward the thick timbered gates that locked away the outside world.

When he reached them, he realized he couldn't get out. There would be a guard or two, probably asleep outside, or maybe in the cantina across the plaza. But the gate doors were wide as two wagons and thick as a man's hand from wrist to fingertip.

"What are we going to do, Yaqui dog?" Carlos didn't look down as he whispered into the empty night. "If they catch me outside, they're sure to think I'm stealing food from the kitchen." Now he did look down at the dog. "What have you got me into?"

The dog sat in the dirt before the gate. His tongue, only slightly lighter than his dark skin, hung over one side of his mouth.

Carlos folded his arms, "I could climb the wall by the women's rooms. I've done that before. But I cannot carry you with me."

As if in answer, the dog stood, walked to the middle of the gate, and vanished.

The moon's light was blocked by the wall that held the gate, so the shadows there were deep, but Carlos found that he'd crossed himself even before he knelt down to see what had become of his strange new friend. His hand met soft dirt, not the hardpack he'd expected where countless carts and horses trod. Eyes quickly adjusting to the blackness, he saw a freshly dug trench under the gate. Not very wide. Not very deep. But enough for the skinny Yaqui dog. And almost enough for the equally slender Carlos Giquamea.

CARLOS DIDN'T NOTICE the sun rising until his shadow overtook and ran ahead of him. Since they'd left the packed dirt streets of San Miguel de Ures and headed off into the scrubby hills that surrounded the town like tired relatives at a funeral, the darkly mottled, hairless dog ran ahead or on either side of him, appearing and disappearing in the risky light of dawn.

"We must find some food, Yaqui dog. And some water." Carlos patted the little jug at his belt. He hadn't resorted to it yet, but he knew it would not last long after the sun rose above his head.

The rough mission shoes hurt his feet more with every step. When his path lay through deeper sand, he couldn't keep the dry soil out from under his feet and sharp bits of gravel slipped between his foot and the hard wooden sandal. At each footfall, these small rocks tried to pierce the tough skin of his soles. Trekking up a short hill in the deep sand, Carlos pulled his right foot up; it had been buried to the ankle in the sand and grit. As he raised it, the leather straps broke from the weight and pressure and the shoe was left sticking up out of the sand like a discarded toy.

"Oh, *Madre Maria*. I cannot walk without my shoes."

Carlos sat on the sand and tried for several minutes to repair the shoe. But he had no cord or leather or even string, so he picked up the useless thing and started hobbling forward again: one shoe in hand and one on his foot.

On the other side of the hill, he realized his shoeless foot hurt less than the one that was still shod. He pulled the good sandal off and tossed one, then the other, at a cactus that looked a little like José Torres. After pitching the shoes, he looked up; the black dog was seated in front of him. When he took off again, the dog fell into step by his side.

Carlos found that he was now walking faster. His weight shifted easily and the feel of the warm sand comforted him as it filled the gaps between his toes.

"You probably wonder where we're going, Yaqui dog." Carlos didn't pause or look at the dog as he talked.

"My mother told me her *abuelo* lives in the north and the west, near Cabroc...Carboc...some place up there. She said it had taken her five days riding in a cart to get to Ures from where he lives and that the sun was in her eyes every morning of her trip."

"I don't remember if he is the father of my mother's mother's or of my father's father, but we will find my *bisabuelo*. I can walk faster than a cart rolls."

Carlos snatched a quick glance at the dog beside him. Neither of them broke their stride.

"We will work for him. He will have a place for the son of his granddaughter."

A few paces later, he added, "I hope he does not keep pigs."

WHEN THE SUN stood almost above his head, Carlos found a ravine that slid under a small grove of wind-shattered oak trees. First he found a willow stick and, standing with the sun behind him, drew a line up from his right shoulder, pointing to the northwest. Then, after checking for hidden dens of snakes, he stretched out between the extra shelter offered by two boulders. He pulled the cork from his as-yet untouched water bottle and drank two short draughts, the second longer than the first. Cupping his hands, he held two palmfulls of the precious water for the eager tongue of his companion. The boy closed his eyes and sleep came hard and swift.

Carlos woke as the air cooled around him. The sun was going down. He took another sip from his jug, then stoppered it. He stood up, looked down at the arrow he'd drawn in the dirt, and headed out. The dog was nowhere to be seen.

The night sky was lustrous and the boy had no problems dodging cactus and stones and briars as he walked-then-ran under the stars. He strained his eyes many times at shadows, thinking the dog might be just at the edge of his vision.

When the sun rose, he sought shelter again, knowing he'd have to stop before the middle of the day or his head would boil like the *menudo* in one of Señora Varigosa's pots. Just before midday, he came upon a rocky stream bed. He had to pick his way in his bare feet—no more running—and it led too much to the west, but he would have to find water again soon and this seemed his best choice.

Around midday, the dry bed bent sharply north between two hills. Mesquite trees sprawled on each side. This was as much cover as Carlos had seen all day, so he drew his arrow sign in the side of the west bank and lay down to rest.

His belly hurt. It had been more than a day since Consuela Varigosa slipped him the tortillas. He frowned as he poured almost the last of his water. What had he been thinking, running away from the mission? Following a black Yaqui dog. To where? And the dog had left him as suddenly as he had appeared. The boy folded his arms over his eyes and collapsed into the sleep of exhaustion and hunger.

Carlos dreamed of the great feast of the Ascension and the roast pig he'd tasted there. His whole face was greasy from the juice of the meat. Moaning with pleasure, he opened his eyes and realized where he was. He was not in Ures. He was lying in a dry river bed in the chilly grey darkness of early nighttime. He had no water, no roast pig—no food at all. His mother was dead. He was alone. His eyes began to swell with moisture.

He jumped involuntarily as the charcoal black river rock in front of him shifted. *Madre de Dios, what was it?* The rock split and white teeth showed inside. Quickly adjusting to the light, Carlos' eyes recognized the Yaqui dog sitting in front of him, mouth slightly open and panting.

"Now you come back? What do you want? You led me out here, you *perro del Diablo*. Señora Varigosa was right! You are of the devil. Go away! ¡*Vete!*" Carlos reached down at his feet for the long rock that lay there. He would have no more of this. Maybe he could find his way back to Ures before he died of hunger or thirst.

His hand closed on the rock. It was not hard.

He picked it up. It was leathery, yet squishy, very rough on the top.

It was a fat lizard, what the old cook at the mission called a *chacahuala*. There were two dark red punctures just behind its frightening head.

Carlos looked at the lizard. Then he squinted at the Devil Dog that sat at his feet. He looked at the *chacahuala* again. He laughed. In his dry mouth and throat, the laugh sounded thin.

"We might as well drink the rest of the water before we feast, eh, Yaqui dog?" Carlos pulled out his canteen, carefully filling his palm and offering it to the quiet dog. He drained the last of the fluid into his own parched mouth.

"Ah. Now I can at least swallow. Let's have some lizard."

After a few minutes of searching in the light of the rising moon Carlos found two stones, one very hard and square, the other round and not quite so hard. He struck the square one repeatedly against the round one until it broke almost precisely in half, leaving a jagged, sharp edge.

It took him quite a while to get the tough skin off the *chacahuala*, but there was plenty of tender meat inside when he did. Soft and juicy meat. For every two bites he took, he gave one to the black dog.

"It is not roast pig, Yaqui, but it is very filling." Tossing the bones into the darkness, Carlos leaned down and stroked the sleek head of the dog, "Thank you, my friend. Now we must be on our way."

THEY FOLLOWED the stream bed all night and near dawn were rewarded by a rock-lined, sandy pool of water that sheltered in the lee of a cliff-face looming over the pond like a protective mother. Carlos and the dog lay at the edge and drank their fill, then Carlos thrust his face into the warm water, cleansing away worries and the dust of the past two days.

Much refreshed and encouraged by this find, and by the change in the river bed they moved along—the rocks had become fewer and farther apart, replaced by soft, gravelly sand that made for easy running—Carlos decided to press on till midday.

But as the sun rose overhead, then passed midpoint and began falling toward the horizon, Carlos found no shelter. The land was flattening out, even as the dry river obligingly angled a little more north than west. Fewer and fewer hills or trees were to be seen anywhere: the bright desert flowers, the portly barrel cactus, the inedible black bushes that stank of oil, and the tall cactus that looked like three-fingered giant's hands took over the landscape. Sometime around the middle of the night, Carlos fell, almost without intending to, onto a soft sandbank and was asleep before his eyes closed.

The next morning, the boy woke to find another offering at his feet. The spotted Xolo had killed another one of the big lizards. This one had an orange belly. With more urgency now than happiness, Carlos repeated the same procedure he'd gone through the day before. Though the orange *chacahuala* was tough and vile-tasting, it stopped the pain that grew in his belly. After this unpleasant-but-necessary meal, the boy found a muddy trench near where he'd fallen. He and the dog drank and then he filled his bottle with the brown, gritty water.

Carlos did not have the energy to run this day.

At noon, he and the Xolo stopped in the slight shade of the biggest "giant's hand" cactus Carlos had ever seen.

"We must turn north, Yaqui dog. *Mi bisabuelo* is that direction." Carlos pointed to the right of the river bed, which now fell away down a slope to the southwest. "We must pray *a Dios* that we will reach him before we need water. This is a very dry place and I do not think I can swallow lizard again."

They rested until sundown, but Carlos was not able to sleep in the brightness of the day, even though his exhaustion seemed to melt through his bones. When the sun rested, he and the dog rose and headed north, away from the stream.

They walked all night between the cactus and bright flowers of purple, green, yellow, blue, red, and white. Some of the flowers seemed to grow from nothing out of the sand, others even more weirdly perched on the cactus, as if they themselves were surprised at their resting places. Carlos heard, but did not see, the scuttling of life around him. Would the dog be able to catch them another lizard? A desert mouse? Could he swallow such a thing without *agua*, without the moisture in his mouth and throat that began to seem like a memory? It was morning and the canteen was nearly empty again.

Long before midday, Carlos lay down, this time in an indentation on the desert floor with only a few gangling reddish gray bushes to shade him. He was too tired to move. His body felt as it did the day after Padre Garcia had him beaten for stealing honey. There were no sharp pains, but every part of him was sore, throbbing and aching in protest. After an endless time of staring at the blank sand beneath him, he fell asleep.

CARLOS DIDN'T KNOW whether he was awake or asleep when got up in the darkness. The only constant now was the dull pulsing pain radiating out from his bones. His head throbbed. His tongue was stiff. His lips bled from cracks. He shared the last few drops of water with the dog, who lapped patiently at Carlos's trembling fingers.

"You should go, dog. I am dead. You can find water for yourself. Go." Carlos rasped half-heartedly. The dog did not move, but looked into Carlos' eyes: black into black. Carlos reached out again and stroked his companion's bony head, for only the second time. Then he got up and trudged forward in the gloom in the direction he thought was northwest.

CARLOS HADN'T SEEN the dog for a long time. But he did not feel abandoned; the thought that the dog might escape this waterless hell brought the boy some peace. That was some kind of triumph, even if a strange and remote one.

He stumbled forward. Memories of his mother, of working in the fields—happy times, but mostly thoughts of meals and feasts drifted through him. He remembered the Christmas feast where he'd first tasted wine—he had not liked it at all. And there had been yams dripping with butter and *nopalitos* and...

Carlos stopped. *Nopalitos*. They were not his favorite dish, yes, but that hardly mattered. They were food. And they were wet—the cooks complained how they spit at them when they were grilled. And they were cactus. They were all around him. He would not die. He would eat cactus and then he would find his *bisabuelo*.

He looked at the round barrel cacti that were near. He was sure these would hold water, but they were formidable; he was frightened by the long needles that covered the plants.

Next he looked at the closest "giant-finger" cactus. It was over twice his height. The closer he came, the more imposing were the needles that ran up and down the cactus in long lines. High above his head, there were white flowers that smelled sweet and delicious, but they might as well have been back in Ures. There was no way Carlos could reach them and the cacti's size and weapons were too much for his young hands.

Carlos sat heavily on the ground before the giant fingers.

"Owww." He cried. He'd sat on a broad shelf of stone that he'd not noticed. Now his backside was bruised, too. He leaned forward, about to put his head in his hands, and saw the low round mounds of cactus covering the ground a few feet away from him. They grew like tiny pies in the gravel, several with single beautiful pink flowers growing up from their centers.

Carlos crawled forward in happy anticipation. There were dozens of them. Like a nestling family of cacti. No terrifying thorns to be seen, nothing to climb. He was saved.

He pulled four or five of the smaller globes from the rocky soil and brushed them clean on his pants. Before eating the first one, he looked around again for the dog, and sighed when he realized he was still alone.

"I don't know whether you would eat cactus, Yaqui, but I will share these with you if you come back." Then he bit into one of the blue-green globes.

He almost spat it out; it was so sour. Yes, there was water and juice, but the taste made his lips curl and his empty stomach tightened.

He must eat these, he thought. It did not matter that they tasted bad. He took another bite. The bitter pulp moistened his chapped, broken lips.

He managed to chew and swallow three of the little round cacti. He didn't think he could swallow any more or he would bring up what was on his stomach and then there would've been no reason to eat them in the first place. He stuffed half-a-dozen more in his blanket, next to his corn doll, hoping he would not have to eat them.

Despite the taste, the water and flesh from the small buds revived Carlos, in spirit and body, and he plunged into the sweet-smelling desert night, certain now he would find his grandfather.

. . .

CARLOS STOPPED every few minutes and bent over to keep from spitting up the cactus in his belly. He had never heard of poison cactus, so he decided it was his empty stomach that had forgotten how to take food. He would be all right.

When the shadows began to walk with him, he no longer noticed his stomach's pangs.

"Yaqui! Yaqui dog! ¡*Vete aquí!* Come Here!" Carlos called. What else could be walking out here, just ahead and side-by-side with him?

The shadows from the bushes and the cacti were all moving now. And they whispered as they walked.

La luz es peligrosa. The light is dangerous.

CARLOS STOPPED and watched one of the wicked barrel cacti. It swelled and shrank, its needles stretching toward him, then turning back in on themselves. The voices kept up their whispering:

Mariposas: ¡Mira el bigote! Butterflies! Watch the mustache!

From the corner of his eye—he saw the spotted black dog leaping. He turned his head in time to see the dog—or the shadow of the dog—jumping from the top of one of the giant cactus hands to the top of another one, then vanishing behind it.

He started walking again. When his foot fell on the scratchy sand, the warmth of the day wound up his leg to his knee. The sand wanted him to walk on it. The cacti shadows that stretched out all around him were the souls of these great plants. They did not threaten him, they only told him that they were there, and that he was both separate from and part of them.

Tears moistened his cheeks as he felt that separation: from the cacti, from the beautiful flowers all around him, from the air. Only the sand was his friend.

Then he looked up.

The sky was blackness and lightness. The sky was all, everything, and everything in between. Shadow-black-nothing and white-everythingness. All of it met and was still separate. Carlos did not breathe. The beauty was like his mother's touch. His shoulders and his chest vibrated to this beauty and the sobs of joy that filled him.

There! There in the middle of the sky-milk was a gathering darkness. Unconsciously, his neck craned. Slowly, a shape came together of blackness, vibrant, radiating stillness. As he watched, Carlos' body lost its weight. Why did he not float? He still stood on his friend, the sand, but he was like the air. He could make out the black shape in the sky now. This perfect grey-blackness of stars and pure night had four legs and a thin tail, and a bright cluster of stars on its side that Carlos thought he should recognize. The black-grey animal of the sky swelled and breathed. Carlos felt his belly settle, as if he had eaten a wonderful meal. His weight returned and the warm sand welcomed his feet. The cracks in his lips spoke to him with their rawness, the pain in them a celebration of feeling. He walked forward on his new bare feet, every step a blessing from his earth-brother, the sand.

Carlos walked through the night and the great dark dog of the sky above faded. So, too, did the speech of the plants of the desert, and the bond with the sand on which he walked. When the sun rose to his right, its colors and power dissolved the friendly guiding darkness that spread above him and its heat slowly melted the night's power that carried the boy forward.

The land was changing again, too. Piled outcroppings of red stone littered the horizon on his right. If anything, the air and soil seemed even drier. Carlos' body moved on without his will. He was empty and soon, he knew, he would stop for a last time.

Carlos stumbled after Yaqui and toward the end of the world.

So it appeared to Carlos. He saw the dog limned on the horizon—or what seemed like the dog. He'd called to him, but the distance was far.

The blue of the sky rose, flawless above the vast rolling

desert, except straight ahead it looked like the world stopped, like it wasn't finished, and the deep violet vaulted above the ground with nothing to support its immensity.

His eyesight was becoming blurry.

A few more yards and Carlos stopped and looked down, down where he thought the world had ended.

It was a small valley. More a crease in the desert. There was no noticeable river or water source, but there was more green than he'd seen since leaving Ures. Even some scrubby grass next to a *choza*, a little hut.

A *choza*! Someone lived here. Had lived here.

Carlos tried to call out, but his tongue was so dry it almost filled his mouth and only a muted grunt emerged from it.

With fresh energy he didn't know he had, Carlos ran down the gentle slope toward the little dwelling—a sort of stick house, now that he could see it closely.

He tripped and fell over the gaunt body of an old man that lay on the ground, tumbling to the other side. As he struck the ground, trials and exhaustion washed over him; he passed senseless into sleep.

"HOW ARE THE FLOWERS?"

"*¿Qué, señor?*" Carlos raised his head from the leather-covered stone on which it had rested. He sat up. His back was against the inside of a wide ring of flat stones, just a few feet from the stick house he'd seen before he fell. There were three other rings of stones inside this big one. Suspended inside each of these stone rings was an iron pot. Next to the smallest of these pots—the only one that hung over a fire—was a slim old man with long grey hair. He was stirring the pot with a mesquite twig. "What flower, *señor*?" Carlos asked.

The old man continued stirring for a moment, then he turned. Carlos' palms hit the ground at his sides, he tensed, and pushed himself more upright. The old man's face was like the wilderness, lines upon lines. Carlos had never seen a face like this before.

"Eh? You've been to the flower world, *niño*. I'm not so blind I can't see that. It is beautiful, is it not?" The old man stood up and slowly limped toward Carlos. "And very dangerous. One so young should not go to such places." He squatted down nimbly by the boy and held out the doll from Carlos' blanket: "Where did you get this, *niño*?"

"It was my mother's. She made it for me." Carlos tried to back up again, but his spine was solid against the stone circle. "She is dead."

The old man held the doll gently, turning it over in his fingers, "What was your mother's name, *niño*?"

"Sacramento...Sacramento Giquamea." Carlos whispered, head down.

"Ehhhhh." The old man released a heavy sigh and stood. He walked back to the iron pot, bent over it. A tin dish and a spoon appeared from somewhere, which he filled from the pot and brought back to Carlos, handing it down to him. "*Muunim, niño.*"

"Are you my *bisabuelo*?" Carlos said around a mouth full of the most wonderful beans he'd ever tasted. There were bits of meat with them, too.

"*Abuelo*? No, *niño*, your mother was my brother's son's daughter. I am your *jaabi*, your uncle."

The old man stood patiently over Carlos while he finished the beans. Carlos set down the dish and stood up to face his uncle, "Do you have work for me here? I can work hard and will not eat very much."

"What's your name, *niño*? I can't keep calling you *niño*."

"Carlos...uncle."

"I am Juan Mateo, Carlos. Juan Mateo Giquamea. You can call me '*Jaabi*' or '*Jaabi Juan*.'" Juan Mateo walked back to the pot and began stirring the beans again. "What sort of work do you do, Carlos? Besides fainting over old men and eating *muunim*?" He asked without looking up.

When Carlos stood, his head felt like it would keep moving up into the clouds. He almost sat down again, but steadied himself, walked over and squatted by his uncle.

"I can cut corn and I can hoe weeds and I can carry water and I..."

"...Ehhhh, *Jakara* Carlito. You can do many things. You have been to the flower world and you came out of the desert world." Juan Carlos turned his ancient face to Carlos and cupped the boy's chin in his square hand, "And I think you have even seen into the world of the spirits." He let go Carlos' chin and returned to bean stirring, "We are not so busy around here."

Carlos did not want to leave this place, so he thought hard and added, "And I am good with animals."

As the boy spoke these words, he noticed a small, hairless blue-grey dog sitting just outside the big stone circle.

Juan Mateo caught Carlos' stare and looked himself.

"Ehhhhh! Where have you been, *Bebeje'eri*? Come back for Old Juan's *muunim*?" he shouted at the dog, who ignored him as it scratched an ear with a back leg.

"Bring me your dish, Carlos. That worthless *chuu'u* looks like he hasn't eaten in a week. That's about how long he's been gone. Missed the hunt that put the antelope in this pot."

Carlos scrambled over to get his dish and brought it to his uncle, who filled the rough bowl with steaming beans and antelope meat. Juan Mateo held the bowl up and blew over the dish toward the dog.

"Yes, *Diablito*, this is for you." He set the bowl down on the ground.

Finally taking notice, the scruffy little dog trotted over and gobbled the hot food, shaking its head after each bite.

Eyes stuck to the dog, Carlos asked, "His name is *Beebee jeebree*?"

The old man laughed. "His name is *Teta*—stone." Juan

Mateo reached down and tapped the eating dog's head. The dog did not respond in any way. "Like his head."

"But I think sometimes he is a *bebeje'eri*—a devil." Juan Mateo smiled at his nephew, "That is the way of *Xolo* dogs, Carlito. They all live here in our *ania*, in our world, and also in the spirit world."

The old man narrowed his eyes at the boy and his Xolo. "He's no good, my Teta. But he's a good dog."

Finished now with his last bit of antelope gristle, the little Yaqui dog turned and trotted back toward the stick hut. On his right side was a long looped gray-and-white marking that looked like stars in the night.

Carlos was sure he had seen that pattern before.

2

TICKLE 'EM JOCK

1909 — Leadenhall Market in the City of London, England

IT WAS love at first sight.

The blue eyes under the boy's plaid cap connected to the string of brown sausages as if they were part of Ned Joster's soul. With a practiced snapping glance at the aproned shopkeeper, young Ned snatched his toothsome prize and bolted for the exit from William Bidsley, Purveyor of Meat.

MEAT

CHASE

Halfway to his escape, a black square of fur skittled across the tiles. White teeth flashed as Ned's already bedraggled pant hem was snatched. Ned kicked away. The little dog pulled and grrred, releasing and gripping in lightning bites, moving up the pant leg toward Ned's calf.

"'ere...'oww...Get 'em hoff 'a me." Ned yowled, shaking his leg.

"Tickle 'em, Jock," the heavyset man behind the counter urged, turning from the shelf where he'd been stacking tins of liver. He slowly wiped his hands on his wool pants. A slight crooked smile curled his lips as he circled around the counter, the boy, and the dog. Bending down, he poked the black terrier's side briskly with one finger, simultaneously taking Ned's elbow in a not-very-gentle fist. "That'll do, Jock."

STOP

Jock released the leg, but continued growling at the boy.

"'ee's a monster 'ee is...a bleedin' monster..." Ned whined and looked up at the butcher.

Still holding the boy's bony elbow, Angus MacKenzie put a thick finger to his lips, "Enough of that, lad. Wee Jock is doin' his job, as you ought ta be doin' yours." Angus took the sausages from the boy's other hand. "And what would ya be sayin' aboot this? For your poor dyin' Mother, is it?"

Jock stopped his low rumble, sat at the duo's feet, black eyes following every undulation of the string of sausages in the butcher's hand.

MEAT

"I don't know where me Mum is. The bangers is for me brothers and sisters."

"Och, brothers and sisters be it," Angus snorted. He glanced down at the mesmerized Scottie dog, then back at the muck-smeared face of Ned. He released his hold on the boy's arm. "Off wi' ye."

Requiring no further invitation, Ned Joster sprinted for the door. Before he was out it, the butcher shouted him down again, "Wait, lad."

To the surprise of both parties, Ned halted in the doorway and looked back, eyes open wide.

Angus snapped the end sausage from the link and tossed half to the boy, "For your sisters." Not waiting to see if the catch was made, the butcher squatted down by the little dog. "You'll no be heisting victuals from Angus MacKenzie without a wee scrap from my Jock." He ruffled the terrier's stiff curls and handed him the smaller half of the sausage.

MEAT

RAT

"Hesh now, Jock, ye'll scare the custom. Sit your seat and quiet."

Angus MacKenzie absentmindedly smoothed his generous handlebar mustache, then patted the single long lock on his otherwise bald head. It was hair in which he must have felt considerable pride as it was pasted down flat and true from the edge of his crown to just above his right ear. He held an enormous meat cleaver in his left fist, which he waved listlessly at two women dressed in the downstairs dove greys of a great household.

"I'm only saying, Mr. MacKenzie, what Lady Ashcroft has directed us to tell you. She was not pleased at all with the lamb we purchased here Friday last."

"It ended in a stew for the gardener," offered the other woman, thin lips squeezed into a disapproving pout.

RAT RAT RAT

The small, dense black dog exploded from around the glass and wood counter, barking ferociously. Scuttling everywhere: under the counter, circling the ladies in grey, around the counter, *under* the ladies, thus eliciting hearty squeals and grey-gloved hands thrown into the air.

"Really, Mr. MacKenzie! Please control your...your..."

"...dog." Mr. MacKenzie supplied, accompanied by a weak grin.

"...hairy little *beast*."

MacKenzie laid aside his cleaver, reached down and picked up the squirming terrier, "Jock, that'll be enough, lad."

STOP

The dog subsided, but the women glared at the butcher and his dog and flounced out the open door and down the wide hall, primly marching in the general direction of London Bridge.

"Now you've done us, Jock, taken th' food out o' both our mouths." Angus MacKenzie stroked the bristly pointed ears and looked into Jock's half-hidden black eyes. "What am I gonna do wi' ye?" He added.

The butcher sighed, set the dog down with a final wag of his finger, wiped his hands on his pants, and repaired behind the counter to address the large side of beef that waited there for his ministrations.

WAIT

Just as MacKenzie began the trickiest part of this chore—separating the neck—he heard Jock's feet scrabbling on the hard tiles again. He cursed lightly, not willing to stop in the midst of this process, and finished cutting around the neck bones, removing the ring and tossing it into the trim pile. He looked up to see a gentleman in a three-piece blue suit, cream-colored spats, and a Top Rim Bowler hat holding Jock in his arms and scratching the dog's chin.

"I see ye met ma wee watchdoggie." MacKenzie ventured freely with this new customer; Jock had clearly vetted him.

"He's a friendly little fella, all right."

"Not for everyone, t'isn't, and that's a fact. American are ye, sir?"

"Yes, I am. Is it that obvious?" The gentleman flashed a thin smile and set Jock down. The dog made a slow circuit around this new customer, nosing up and down his shoes and ankles.

"Well, sir, ye doan't look to be from around the City."

"And you, Mr...ahhh..." The American looked at the sign riveted to the wrought-iron railing in front of the counter, "...Bidsley? You don't sound much like the Londoners I've been dealing with."

"Got it in one, sir. But the name's MacKenzie, from 'round the Firth o' Clyde. Scottish by birth, Londoner by trade and necessity. Bidsley'd be the pro-prie-tor, sir. What you Yanks would call the boss. *Sir* William Bidsley, he is, sir, OBE. I'm just the butcher here."

"Ahh," said the American, "Go where the work is, eh, Mr. MacKenzie? And Sir William is..."

"...at his lodge in the Cotswolds, I'd wager, sir. It's the way o' the world." MacKenzie put up his knife while talking to the American gentleman. Brushing his hands down on his apron, he asked, "Now what could I get for you, sir?"

"Well, I'm staying at the Dorchester." The American hesitated.

"Very fine hotel, sir."

"Yes, yes it is. And I don't suppose they are interested in me bringing back my own brisket for lunch would you think?"

MacKenzie barked a short laugh, "No, sir, I doan't imagine they would."

"I'll tell you, Mr. MacKenzie. I'm here on your side of the drink on business. And business can be, well, pretty darn tiresome if you get my drift?" The American gentleman winked one eye at the ever-more confused butcher.

"Yes, sir, I s'pose business is much the same on your side of... the drink" MacKenzie smiled self-consciously at this familiarity, "as on ours. But I doan't see what this has to do with buying ma meat." Then he added, "Not to be disrespectful, sir."

"Albright, Mr. MacKenzie, call me Albright—and I can call you...?" Albright thrust out his right hand to MacKenzie.

The Scottish butcher blinked twice at the proffered hand, wiped his own again on his apron and then shook. He was surprised to find Albright's grip as firm as his own, "errr...just MacKenzie, then, Mr....errr...Albright."

"That's fine, MacKenzie. Pleased to meet you." Albright pumped MacKenzie's hand for several seconds.

Before the ensuing silence became too awkward, Albright continued, "I'm a dog man, MacKenzie. It's what I do to blow off steam."

MacKenzie scratched his chin contemplatively, "Right. I understood they're using steam for pretty much everything in Amerikay."

"You have no idea, MacKenzie, no idea." Albright took out a silver-chased cigar case from his coat pocket, opened it, and offered one to the Scot.

"Don't mind if I do, sir. I like a good smoke."

"Cuban cheroots, MacKenzie, pure bliss."

The two men progressed through the intricate bonding process of cigar smoking for the next few minutes: rolling, tapping, cutting, smelling, and—finally—lighting and inhaling. MacKenzie ignored the glares from Wilford Abercrombie, the soft fruit seller across the row, as billows of heavy white smoke drifted out the store. Unnoticed by either man, Jock sneezed repeatedly into the sawdust on the floor behind the counter.

STINK

"So, MacKenzie—what do you say? How much you want for that little nipper there?"

The butcher dropped his expensive cheroot, quickly retrieving it and cleaning the end on his shirt sleeve. Albright's question seemed as if it were expressed in an unknown language, the sense of it was so unexpected. He upbraided himself silently.

Awkwardness such as this is what comes of allowing pleasantries in the workplace. The butcher mused to himself.

"Beg your pardon, sir?" Was the best the Scotsman could manage, struggling to regain the comfort of formality.

"Your dog, MacKenzie, 'wee Jock.' How much do you want for him?"

MacKenzie started to tell Albright Jock was not for sale.

He'd never heard of such. People didna go buyin' other people's pets in a butcher shop. Jock was a wee 'tinker for sure he was, but he was a bra little tyke and a cheerful laddie. And, well...

"I'm sorry, sir, but he's nae for sale." Angus said quietly, then added, "Meanin' no disrespect, sir." The faces of the two serving women from Lady Ashcroft sprouted in his imagination like worms from discarded meat.

They weren't the first had been startled by poor wee Jock.

Jock the Terror, he sometimes thought he should've called him.

"None, taken, MacKenzie. None taken." The American took a deep pull on his tobacco. "I'll ask one more time, then I'll let it lie."

The muscles in MacKenzie's broad neck tightened as he looked down at the now-quiet little Scottie. He cleared his throat and spoke softly, not glancing directly at Albright, "He is...was...

ma brother Jamie's dog, you see, sir. Jamie was muster'n outta tha Queen's own Fusiliers, he was. Coming home from Bombee —the Empire, y'know, sir. I got 'im Jock there as he and our gaffer loved the wee black dogs. A great coil o' jute fell from shipboard onta 'im. Crushed 'im sure as sure. Never knew it, his Color Sergeant told it. Never saw wee Jock there, neither. So, you see, Mr. Albright, sir" MacKenzie looked up now at his listener, "the wee dog is not mine ta dispose of and he's, well..."

The tall American stepped over to the smaller man and clenched his shoulder in a strong fist, "I understand, Mr. MacKenzie. Your brother's dog." Albright waited until MacKenzie looked him in the face again, "You honor your brother, MacKenzie. That's a fine thing. But I can take the dog and give him a great life. And you can let this pass."

MacKenzie's watery grey eyes peered into and past Albright's dark blue pupils.

Surely, now, this American can give Jock a world I couldna e'en dream of. He'd be the first Scots terrier to eat off gold plate and smoke Cuban cigars. Probably have his own house in Amerikay, just down the brick lane from Mr. Albright. I can hear Jamie roarin' from on high at that.

"Two pounds." MacKenzie stared up squarely at Albright, as if he were selling a crown rib roast to the Queen's agent himself.

It was Albright's turn to be taken aback. But not for long. "Two pounds. Hmm...that's...umm...about ten dollars, I think." Albright reached into the side pocket of his coat, then stopped. "I don't suppose he's got any papers, does he? I mean, he wouldn't have an actual pedigree?" Albright cocked his head to the side.

"Why, of course he does, Mr. Albright. Jock's a fine wee pedigreed Scot's Terrier, as right and proper as the Stone of Scone. Brought 'im down from Dumfries."

Albright almost sat on the floor in surprise. "Why, that's stupendous news, MacKenzie, stupendous! What do you say over here?—'top drawer!'"

"I doan't keep his papers at the business, Mr. Albright, ye'll have to come back for 'em tomorra."

Albright shrugged. "Not a problem at all, MacKenzie, not a problem at all." The American held out his hand, palm up, "Here's two pounds for the dog. I'll give you another when I pick him up and you bring his papers." Albright ducked his head back of the counter and grinned at Jock, who stood quietly by the chopping block. "And I'll see you tomorrow, boy. You're going to be an American dog very soon." With that, he raised his hand in farewell and left the butcher and his dog alone in the shop.

After the American was out of sight, MacKenzie knelt by Jock. The dog looked up at him, tail straight in the air. "Oh, my wee Jock, your goan to have a fine time in Amerikay. Land o' milk and honey. Or for Scottie dogs, p'raps mutton and milk." He gave the dog a rough brush over his shaggy black ears and looked up at the bright green tin ceiling, "You survived the bloody flux in the Transvaal, brother, and the mutiny in the Punjab, but ye were done in by a bit o' twine. Well, bless yer wee dog now. He's off ta the New World."

MASTER

18 MONTHS LATER: February 15th, 1911, Madison Square Garden, New York; the 35th Annual Westminster Kennel Club Dog Show

"JUDGING BEST IN SHOW, in the center pavilion, H. Hildebrand Wilson of the King of Prussia Gun and Turf Club," the high tenor of the Master of Ceremonies loudly proclaimed.

H. Hildebrand Wilson, a short, wide gentleman in a top hat and blue frock coat, sporting luxurious white moustaches and peppermint-schnapps-flavored breath, strode resolutely to the center of the roped-off display run. He was no stranger to prestige in the dog ring. His own Airedale terrier, Hildebrand's Prince of York, was benching for a special conformation cup on the other side of the exhibition this very afternoon. And he'd personally handled and judged many Best of Breed and Show in various venues of the East Coast dog world.

He gazed down the lineup of the dogs today, all Best of Group, of course.

The Deerhound moved well, but then they always did at this level. Damn scruffy dogs when they're not running. Must check those teeth.

Strong showing from the Toys—an impressive Pom from Mrs. Thomas' Endcliffe line. Endcliffe Raven, wasn't it? Bit of a set-to in the crowd when old Gerry Blenheim's Peke didn't make the cut.

That collie's gait is off-center. Looks thin, too. Have to check his eyes and coat when I'm close.

Did Miss Bullock bat those long lashes at the Working judge? Arvin Genuleas was a notorious womanizer, or wanted to be.

Now what is that?

It took him some effort to retain his judgely reserve and aplomb.

A Scottie or a dark Cairn? Never seen one quite like that little fellow. Does it conform? Surely Menard wouldn't pass over all the terriers if it didn't, they were always a competitive Group. Look at that strut! Well handled. That dog's already won in its mind.

Wilson felt a small upward tug at the corners of his mouth.

If only my Airedale had such confidence.

Wilson's slight smile faded as he looked at the last entrant in the waiting line.

My God, he thought, another of Gloria's Saints. What's this one's name? Atlas? Prometheus? The woman has no shame. Well, at least he's a fit-looking giant, not like that ton of blubber she had up two years ago.

Despite his initial misgivings and ruminations, the judging proceeded quickly (though while attending to business, Wilson couldn't get the simultaneous trial of his young Airedale out of his mind). Once Wilson assured himself that the Scottie, who was definitely unusual in his coat, fell within breed guidelines, it was clearly a choice between the little terrier and the enormous St. Bernard.

Finally, he benched the two together on the conveniently long pine show plinth, the sort of dais upon which the winner would eventually be crowned.

Wilson noted that the terrier was being manfully restrained by his young handler. The dog kept eyeing his huge, but somnolent opponent. The Scottie was anything but intimidated. Standing back a few feet and taking a last look, Wilson fingered his chin and made his decision.

BIG

He walked over to the Master of Ceremonies, informed him of his choice.

"Ladies and Gentlemen," the high, carrying voice called out, "the Best in Show at the 35th Westminster Kennel Club Dog Show is the Scottish Terrier, Albright's Tickle 'em Jock."

Wilson took the leather-strung blue ribbon he held and placed it on the podium next to the Scottie, between the little terrier and the giant Saint Bernard.

MINE

The spectators reacted rambunctiously, with as many catcalls as cheers. The judge had expected more than the usual din after the announcement of his choice.

That little black fellow's not one of the anointed. Oh, everyone knows Albright, and he's acceptable, but everyone's also heard that scandalous story of the Scottie's purchase. Or rumors thereof.

Wilson himself had heard—from a rival terrier breeder—that Albright had rescued the dog from an abattoir, where the small gent had only survived by imbibing bloody castoff remnants.

Preposterous!

But the furor that susurrated through the audience was louder and more continuous than he'd anticipated.

Best mark the book and be on my way, Wilson decided. He turned around ceremoniously and began walking across the show area to sign the official record with the winner's name—his last certifying act as a judge in the event.

The sound of a great crash blanketed the turbulent voices of the audience. Wilson looked up from the signing table and to his horror saw that a large pavilion tent in the back of the venue was collapsed. Shouts from that direction drifted across the hall's expanse.

Heavens! He thought, that's the Airedale show pen.

Book and personal dignity forgotten, H. Hildebrand Wilson pulled up the fashionably long hems of his morning pants and dove into the crowd to find his dog.

IN THE HOUR of his absence, the Center Ring audience moved through a range of emotions. Outrage and jubilation had equally divided the onlookers when Judge Wilson chose the feisty little Scottie as the show's top dog, but this was quickly replaced by alarm and consternation when the tent pole came down in the back of the hall.

The garbled intelligence of crowds dribbled in slowly as the gathered fanciers waited for the official culmination of the judge's choice.

"There's a police raid. Some dognappers were foiled trying to steal the Belray Harriers" shouted a young fellow in a straw boater as he jogged behind the Best in Show crowd.

"I understand it's a hoax. All set up by rapscallion newspapermen wanting a bit of adventure to raise circulation rates." A lady seated in the middle bench shared on either side of her.

"It's a fracas with the custodians. The Garden's refused to pay them anything but passes into the next shows and they've sabotaged one of the tents." A front-row gentleman with grizzled mutton chops and a stylish striped three-piece suit muttered after waiting over half-an-hour.

None of the many tales that circulated through the progressively more restive crowd neared the truth of the matter. The episode began when Mr. Rupert von Nilsberger secured House Wallenstein's Ensign Piltdown, his strapping young Bullmastiff, to the base of the center pole of the far pavilion.

Mr. von Nilsberger then became involved in a heated argument with one of the many Guggenheim brothers in attendance about whether President Taft's Dollar Diplomacy had enabled or impeded trade with Central America. Mr. von Nilsberger held a good deal of stock in a mining concern with operations in Mexico and Honduras and this was a matter of considerable interest to him. Unfortunately, Mr. von Nilsberger had not noticed that the pole to which he'd attached his vigorous canine was surrounded by a number of cages that contained the only female dogs at the Westminster show.

However, Ensign Piltdown *did* notice the bitch in the nearest cage, Caractacus' Sunny Brunhilde, a Pointer in excellent condition. He began wooing her with low vocalizations of a most seductive timbre. When Sunny Brunhilde joined her imposing suitor in a mellifluous duet, the Bullmastiff knew it was in his best interests to more closely approach the object of his desire. Not until that point had Ensign Piltdown realized the constraint under which he'd been put. Spurred on by both the beautiful, beckoning Pointer and the insult of the leather strap, Ensign Piltdown set his massive paws against the boards. His strenuous heaving, jerking, and tugging honored his proud heritage. A slight imperfection in the wood of the tent pole cracked and the canopy collapsed, to the dismay of all—including the besotted Bullmastiff himself who was now caught in several folds of heavy canvas, hopes fading of a *pas de deux* with his prospective lady love.

When Judge H. Hildebrand Wilson reached the downed canopy, he found the groundskeepers already rolling up the somewhat unnecessary tent. He didn't notice the purpling complexion of Mr. von Nilsberger, still trying to extricate his dog from the largest rolls of the canvas, shouting ungentlemanly imprecations at his hapless canine Romeo. It took Judge Wilson a quarter-of-an-hour to find his handler and his Airedale, another quarter-of-an-hour to ascertain no harm had come to the Prince of York, and yet another fifteen minutes to plow his way back to the Center Pavilion through the excited throngs of humans and their dogs.

TICKLE 'EM JOCK, soon to be officially Champion Tickle 'em Jock, sat on the polished wooden plinth staring forward. His handler stood a pace behind him, holding Jock's lead in a loose hand. Perched on the bench three feet to his left loomed the white, brown, and black behemoth Vandermilch's Orion of Hercuveen. The St. Bernard was so large that his head sprouted well above the level of the head of his handler, who also stood behind the bench.

WAIT

Between the two dogs, a few inches closer to Jock than to Orion, lay the Best in Show emblem, the blue silk medallion sewn onto a background of multi-colored ribbons, threaded through by a densely embossed leather thong.

MINE

Judge Wilson had been gone almost an hour, and the crowd's attention had shifted away from the kerfuffle in the back of the hall. A few disappointed patrons left, but most shuffled around, impatient, uncertain, and increasingly unhappy. Not many eyes were on the podium when Orion of Hercuveen bent down his lordly head—almost the size and weight of the terrier next to him—and took the leather thong of the prize between his wet jowls.

MINE

Jock reacted instantly. He chomped down on the other end of the thong and held true. Nor did the Saint release his hold.

Judge Wilson pushed through the foxhounds of the Middlesex Hunt and the beagles of J. J. Raymond Belmont's Harriers of Hempstead who milled and waited at the ring's periphery, and re-entered the Center Pavilion. He was greeted with this tableaux: at each end of a twenty-foot chain of man and dog and leather were the handlers of the top two dogs, leashes extended taut. The Scottie was suspended in mid-air. His body and rear legs dangled, but his teeth solidly held the leather thong and so his head was on a level with Orion's, who effortlessly gripped the other end of the prize.

"Here, here, my man. Release your dog!" Judge Wilson cried to Jock's handler, "You'll strangle him!"

Already dismayed and embarrassed, both handlers swiveled their heads at the Judge's authoritative tone and let go their leads simultaneously.

The Saint, who had been restrained hardly at all by the relatively flimsy lead, did not move an inch. However, Jock's body immediately swung into the giant dog's chest. Jock lost no time transferring his attack from the thong to the perpetrator of the theft and wrapped his mouth around the upper part of Orion's front left leg.

Judge Wilson was not far behind. "Heavens!" he cried, and bravely—if foolishly—waded in and grasped the doughty terrier in both hands and pulled him free from the confused Saint Bernard.

MINE

BITE

Jock's teeth snapped and closed on the Judge's wrist.

Audible gasps escaped from the handlers. Responsibility

quickly replaced shock and Jock's handler stepped forward and snatched the end of Jock's dangling lead, preventing the dropped terrier from reattaching himself to the Saint. Judge Wilson nodded approval as he wrapped his bleeding wrist in a white linen handkerchief. Silence reigned over the audience. A collective breath was held.

Nothing for it but to sign the damn book, Wilson thought, once again walking to the award bench.

Wilson had been bitten before by dogs—his own and others, but never by one he'd just named to the highest honor in dogdom. Taking the pen held out by the slack-jawed secretary seated at the table, the Grand Judge dipped the pen and unenthusiastically entered "Champion Tickle 'em Jock" under Champion Sabine Rarebit, last year's winner, then signed his own name.

That's done, he thought.

Remembering his place, he smiled to the crowd, holding his bandaged hand behind.

Home and a stiff whiskey. Let Ronson deal with the damn Airedales. No, make that two whiskeys.

Ker-Flop. A strange, moist popping sound came from his left side, toward the middle of the ring. *Ker-Flop...Ker-Flop...Ker-Flop*. Wilson turned his head in time to see three dirty grey-furred creatures drop from the air and land, stunned or dead, in the middle of the red carpet.

Before the Judge could further react, four small grey beasts —each roughly the size of the terrier on the podium, but with long, hairless tails—twitched alive. Round, frightened black eyes darted behind comically pointed noses. Then they were off, in four different directions.

For Wellington, Somerset, and the other foxhounds of the Middlesex Hunt, who had been restlessly waiting at the edge of the ring for over an hour, this was more than they could ignore, a clear call to the hunt. The pack tore through the ceremonial barricades, knocking over chairs, tables, and the occasional human attendee, pulling their hunting pink-clad master behind them.

Not far in arrears were the beagle packs: the Belray Harriers of Hempstead, complete with a cursing, stumbling J. J. Raymond Belmont, Master Harrier, wearing the traditional green harrier coat, then the Somerset Beagle Hunt Pack, and finally the Monmouth Beagles of Mr. George R. Preston.

RAT RAT RAT

Forgotten now was the altercation about thong and ribbons. Jock, the newly crowned King of the Dog world, surged toward the nearest of the hapless opossums. Overtaxed by previous strain, his leash snapped, and certain of his greatest ratting adventure, King Jock charged forth.

BIG RAT

But by the time his short legs took him to the edge of the ring, the scuttling, frightened animals had disappeared into a sea of wool pants, flowing dresses, overturned tables, and excited dogs.

It seemed that all dogs at the show were now participating in the grand hunt. A few, still constrained by leashes or pens, merely added their voices as encouragement. But many had broken free of their owners and handlers and were pelting hither and yon, up and down the aisles and benches, sometimes engaging in conversations with each other, sometimes in arguments.

The noise and the chaos broke Jock from his own hunting reverie. There was something else near, something of considerable interest.

MEAT

Just ahead of him was a ribbon barricade that miraculously had not yet been knocked down. It towered over Jock's head and he hardly noticed it as he trotted toward his nose's target. Several tables were set up here, though all but one was on its side.

Jock's nose led him to leap onto a chair that stood in front of the table, then onto the table itself.

MEAT

MINE

With good spirit and a well-earned appetite, the latest champion of Westminster set to on the remains of a fine plate of roast lamb, buttered peas, and scalloped potatoes *à florentine*. Jock swallowed the last morsel, then dipped his small red tongue into the edge of the glass of milk that leaned against the side of the show patron's abandoned plate.

THREE THOUSAND MILES away on the subsequent weekend, Angus MacKenzie opened the bright red door of 13C Brideswell, just off Charing Cross Road, stepped onto his stoop and picked up the Sunday *Times*. He looped one thumb absently through a gallus strap, flipped the paper open and, scanning the lead lines, turned and trudged back upstairs to his morning coffee—a luxury he allowed himself on Sundays. Before he reentered his parlor, he stopped. His eyes ran across the story on page five, a smile ever broadening across his mouth. "Bit tha judge, did ye, Jock? That's ma wee doggie, fer certain." The paper drooped slackly in his hand and he peered through the lace curtains at the grey-slabbed London sky, "Ee's yer laddie, 'ee is, Jamie, ma boy. Ee's yer laddie."

3

HEROES OF PASSCHENDAELE

OCTOBER, 1918 — World War I, near Ypres in Belgium: the British front lines

THE BRINDLE BULL terrier did not slow his pace or flinch at the screaming buzz that hurtled over his head and the head of Private Leftelle-Smithers. They were both well trained not to move, except when commanded. Jack the dog and his masters, Leftelle-Smithers and Corporal Pensance, were specialists. They lived in these forward trenches and holes and makeshift wooden caves, sending Jack with oil-skin wrapped packets back-and-forth between the two men. All three were small, fast, and hard to hit. Pensance and Leftelle-Smithers weighed in at less than eight stone each, and Jack was, well Jack was a "bullie." Solid as a shell from a Stokes gun—and roughly shaped like one—he stayed low, a tough target for even the most accomplished Jerry sniper.

Jack'd left Pensance in Ypres two days ago, walking wounded. The young corporal had lost his thumb and a couple of fingers on his right hand, but he—and his immediate commander—

considered that "cost of doing business, old chap" and Corporal Pensance remained in active duty.

A gentle whir passed over them and then a soft "thup" as the shell plopped almost soundlessly into the mud plain thirty yards to their left. An obscene belch followed its final descent; a few thin streams of iridescent smoke curled from the pocked earth.

"That couldn't have been larger than an eight-point-five, Jack old fellow," Leftelle-Smithers commented to his dog and moved ahead in a practiced "trench-trot"—head down, wide quick steps. "Jerry must be on a budget."

Today's mission was a cakewalk, a routine mail drop to a rowdy bunch from Leftelle-Smithers' own 91st Brigade, a group that hadn't had word from home since the shells began falling heavily in midsummer. As Jack and his master descended into the hollow that was their destination, the familiar distant "Huff" of a discharging Minenwerfer mortar rolled over the edge of the trench. In the lead, Jack's blunt nose twitched at the powerful odors rising from the canvas-covered "home" of the ten soldiers who'd been living on rat and dirty water stew these past months. Nothing Jack wasn't used to.

The direct hit of the twelve-centimeter round collapsed the timber-reinforced roof, then the explosion festooned the air with mud and flesh, blood and metal. The shockwave blast tossed Jack backwards only a foot— he was solidly built. Miraculously, no shrapnel touched him.

Living up to his moniker, "Lucky Lefty" Leftelle-Smithers stood up from the planks he'd fallen onto and moved down into the smoking hole gaping below him.

Jack stood at the edge of the new shell pit, staring forward, wheezing a soft penetrating sound.

Below, the private rummaged patiently through the body parts of the 22nd Battalion of the Manchester Regiment, looking for important papers and identifications. All ten men had died instantly. That was the good news. No lingering bleed-outs, lives ruined by lost limbs, lost hopes, the growing impatience and bitterness of caregivers, or decades of incessant pain.

Lefty crawled out of the hole. Under his arm was a shredded knapsack containing a handful of orders, a few IDs, and a pocketful of silver. Preoccupied with the gruesome and solemn details he'd ruffled through in the shell pit, the soldier mumbled to himself and Jack as they stumbled back toward the forward HQ from whence he and Jack had left that morning.

"Bloody Beggars. Lucky hit." The man and dog proceeded a few steps in silence.

"Bloody lucky hit. Probably just 'closing the circle' on their bloody T-map."

Jack followed dutifully at the private's heels. He continued to emit the low whining sound he'd begun making at the pit edge. Leftelle-Smithers stopped, squatted in front of the dog, and held Jack's head between his two grimy hands.

"What's this, Jacko-boy? Fright got into Stone Jack? Now that's hard to believe."

The terrier's broad pink tongue slid out the edge of his mouth and laved Leftelle-Smithers' palm. The soft, heart-wrenching sound did not cease.

The soldier stood up, palm open and forward to Jack, indicating that the dog should stay, then walked around behind him —careful to stay on the boards. Five feet back, he called softly, "Jack."

The dog remained still.

Leftelle-Smithers shook his head, patting the dog as he walked by him again, and continued on toward HQ, taking advantage of cover from every hillock and barren, twisted stem that rose in the grey-brown landscape.

AN HOUR LATER, Lefty stopped just shy of the HQ encampment, knelt down, and looked Jack in the eye. He held up his hand again. "Stay and wait," he mouthed, then he turned and ran on, leaving the terrier in a formal sit, panting softly, tongue hanging down over the edge of his jaw.

"LEAVE HIM, SOLDIER!"

The private hardly moved as the brevet captain in the spotless khaki Service Dress barked at him. The private's reactions matched his uniform, the landscape, and his spirit—tired, ill-defined, murky shades of brown, variations of the mud he lived in. But he pulled his hand back from the head of the little dog that sat hock deep in the mush covering the boardwalk.

With a mild snort, the improbably clean captain turned south down the trench, striding purposefully toward the command post just over the horizon.

The private stood next to the dog. He looked down, then at the retreating back of the captain. Anxiety etched a line in the filth that caked his forehead.

Like a monster from a world of mud, an enormous slab of slosh emerged from the side of the hill and spoke to the unresponsive private, "Tykes ain't to respond to nowt but thar gaffers, Private. Men as not ta be fraternizin and molly-coddlin em er else they could get compromised er ruint," the mud with sergeant's stripes explained.

Baffled by the non-com's quiet authority or his fantastic camouflage, the private grunted an assent. He looked down at the little dog, who also had not moved during this exchange, picked up his soggy pack, and trudged down the boards endlessly stretching before and behind.

Now that he was "in the open," that is, no longer pasted against the side of the indentation where he had secreted himself, the sergeant looked down at the dog himself.

"Why, yer just the lahlest o' tykes, ain't ya, me li'l mucker?"

A whip tail, still with noticeable traces of white and brindle under deep grime, fanned side-to-side and the bullet head looked up at the tall man.

"I kin where yer gaffer be, fella. Tha' should be back lowsin' time now. An'..." the giant Yorkshireman knelt on the sodden duckboards and looked slyly around the blasted environs for a few moments. He saw a broad brown plain stamped with shallow gray valleys, creased and crisscrossed by lines of darker brown and grey—trenches and wire fences. The river Lisl churned not too far away, but there was no evidence of it here. He knew that this had once been fine farmland—better than any he or his family near Housesteads had ever tilled. And he knew a step he took off the wooden planks might land him in a muckhole that could release poison that would burn out his eyes and sear his skin like the flesh of a pig on a roasting spit. He'd seen it dozens of times. He'd smelled it. His own brother, not two days earlier, drowned standing up in the juices from his own burning lungs. *Yeh, he knew this place where he knelt by the wee dog.*

"...an'..." he looked around once more, his responsibility as a non-commissioned officer and soldier of the Crown not something he took lightly—*never knew where those flippin' Huns might be hidin'*—and he leaned down by the bull terrier's tan-and-pink shell of an ear, and finished in a soft conspiratorial whisper, "...an' as I 'ear it, yer gaffer might just ave to take a ver-y im-por-tunt missive back to Gen'ral 'Aig hissen. And *that* means, boyo, that the two o' thee would be makin' fer Bond Street back where the 'igh Comman keeps issen. An' good fer you, I sez, good fer you."

Careful not to actually touch the dog through this entire explanation—no fraternizin' or molly-coddlyin' from this upstanding soldier—the sergeant rose, ready to move on to the travel trench a few yards back of the front.

A fierce high whistle descended in the air, followed promptly by a ground-moving basso thump-thump. The titan of a sergeant toppled like a chopped pine on his family's farm. His head, the side that remained, fell inches from the little bull terrier. His end had come so quickly that his face did not even register the grimace of surprise and dismay so many who died by powder and steel displayed. His mouth, intact across his face, showed only the same slow, gentle smile he had worn when he spoke to the terrier Jack and the young private who had recently vacated this killing ground for another.

Jack staggered from the shell's concussion that took the

sergeant's life and half his face, but he didn't fall into the mire. Stone Jack, he stood.

The torn body of the sergeant stretched across the walk beside him. He nuzzled the rough cheek with his smooth muzzle. His pink tongue flicked out, a brief lick of remembrance and recognition of death, a state Jack knew well.

What Jack didn't understand was what he couldn't hear now. He had been taught to listen carefully in that camp in Scotland. He never won the games held for the smell dogs while he was there, but he'd done all right with the seeing games, and he had been close to the top of the class in the hearing games. After Korpralpinsins had partnered with him, he'd given Jack sweet biscuits and praise when they won some of those games.

Now, though, he could only hear himself.

Should he break Leftee's orders and search for his masters? No. Leftee said to stay and wait. He would stay and wait.

Night fell. He stood six hours by the body of the dead sergeant, then Jack lay down and went to sleep, not the first time he'd slept by the dead.

THE SUN HID from the war. Wispy grey and white fog, mist, and smoke hung almost constantly in the air and colored the sky from before dawn through twilight. Incessant high-volume shelling of the sodden earth created a special—more palpable—fog, a muck fog that clung to the wizened sticks that had once been trees, to the canvas tents and uniforms of the men who lived in this oozy soup, to the men themselves and to everything they touched. If the shelling was recent and clean-up had not arrived, the coppery smell of blood mixed with the sweet scent of acetone from expended cordite.

The most reliable sign that time flowed the same in this violent, drab world as it did in the homes, offices, factories, and stores of Paris or London was the gradual return of warmth two or three hours after the day began, and the retraction of that warmth after the almost-forgotten sun set.

Jack felt the day's heat rising and awoke next to the remnants of the now very cold sergeant.

Something was wrong. He still could only hear himself. And there was no sign of Korpralpinsins or Leftee. He was hungry, very hungry. He could remember times when his masters gave him their food when he was hungry, but he was not as hungry then as he was now.

He would look for them.

They would be where their masters lived. Jack knew where that was. It was near.

He trotted in that direction. Something in his stomach that wasn't hunger began to gnaw at him. By the time he reached the still-smoking hole that had been forward HQ, this new feeling was stronger than his hunger. He may not have won the smell games in Scotland, but Jack *knew* that Leftee was in the mess of dead human meat that lay in the pits before him.

Delicately, as he had seen other soldiers do, he stepped into the pit to begin the search for his master, to find him—dead or alive. He planted one paw on solid-looking sludge, then he stepped down with his other front paw and crept into the sad morass. When all his weight shifted onto his front paws, his footing went out from under him and he tumbled into the pile of rubble and dead bodies oozing congealed liquids. Somewhere on the way down, his powerful, hard little head smashed against the map-covered operations table and Jack's silent world merged with blackness and oblivion.

JACK WOKE in a new place with strange smells. He lay on his side on a human bed. He stood up. Everything shook. He lay back down and the shaking ended.

Some of the dogs at the camp in Scotland were always frightened. Some were afraid sometimes. When dogs were most afraid, Jack knew not to go close to them. He could see fear when they shivered, or when their eyes were different, or even in how they held their mouths and bodies. Jack saw and smelled that fear, but Jack never felt that way. Now, when he stood up on this strange human bed, not able to hear, remembering the dead meat smell of his master Leftee, and finding that his world—that he—was shaking like a cold wet pup, Jack understood what those frightened dogs felt.

A small human about the size of Leftee entered and sat down next to him on the bed. He put his cold hand on Jack's head, then took his fingers and scratched lightly around one of Jack's ears.

Jack looked up at this new human. He had a thin face and dark eyes. Jack liked that he had some fur below his nose like Korpralpinsins and the dead sergeant. He did not easily trust humans with furless faces.

He saw that the human was making human noises. His lips folded and came together strangely. He looked at Jack with his round eyes and they were like Korpralpinsin's eyes when Korpralpinsin looked at Jack. Jack's back and chest relaxed. The human held his hand under Jack's nose; Jack licked it to know who this human was. He tasted like carrots and sour cabbage, which was better than the fire-smoke that Leftee—and so many humans—tasted like. Jack thought of Leftee, then, pulled away from this human, put his head between his paws, turned his eyes down toward the dried mud floor and sighed.

JACK WOKE AGAIN in the human bed. This time, the new human was asleep in it, too. He didn't mind that the human was cold and went back to sleep.

The next time he woke, the new human lifted him down from the bed. There were sausages there in a cup, and water—lots of water. Jack was so thirsty, he thought he would never stop drinking. He drank and then he made water, then he looked at the new human who was watching Jack and who was baring his flat human teeth.

Despite this strange new place and despite his losses, Jack felt good. His world was not shaking now that he was not on the new human's bed. *There were many new smells and he would find them all. He could run up and down the plank-covered trenches and find Korpralpinsins.*

When he walked into the open, onto the boards, the new human reached down and picked him up and put him back inside the place where they had slept. Jack did not know if it was time for a mission and so he stayed and waited in this place—even though Korpralpinsins hadn't told him. *Maybe this new human would tell him when there was a mission and he would run again on the wood roads.*

How would he know if he could not hear the new human? He ate the last sausage and started smelling all the new things in the tent.

AFTER SLEEPING AGAIN, the new human put the long leather on him and they walked out on the boards. Jack wanted to run, but he didn't know how to tell this to the new human. He stopped some places and smelled for other dogs and he could not smell any. Jack and Korpralpinsins came here with three other dogs. Jack knew two of them from the Scottish training place. One of them had been Leftee's dog, but he didn't come back one day and, since Privitansun died, too, Leftee started working with Jack and Korpralpinsins.

Jack wondered if the new human would find Korpralpinsins and they would have a mission soon.

DAYS AND NIGHTS PASSED. Jack liked the new human. They had sausages every day and they went for slow walks on the wood roads, but Korpralpinsins was not there. Jack was beginning to forget what Korpralpinsins looked like now, but he remembered his smell. And he still had not been on any missions or runs with the new human. One day, they went down into a trench hole like Jack had never seen before. His new master had to carry him down a long ladder. There were many good smells there and rats. His new master let him chase the rats, but he didn't catch any.

A few days later, Jack woke up next to his new master and he could hear the thud thud of the big air and ground-shaking death stones. Even when he couldn't hear anything, he had been able to feel when the death stones hit the mud around them, but now he could hear them in the air. After his next sleep, he could tell when his new master was making human noises, but he could not understand them yet, not even Food or Stay. He liked looking at his new master's face when he made the noises, though, and when his master noticed Jack's attention, he scratched Jack's ears.

Jack could smell when they walked together that the other humans did not like his new master. They did not make human noises to him until after he walked away. This worried Jack and made him sad.

Excited now that he could hear, Jack listened for Korpralpinsins name on their next walk on the boards. His new master was taking him on a new route and maybe they would see Korpralpinsins. Jack ran forwards and backwards while his master held the long leather and made strange human noises.

Then Jack heard the last thing he had ever wanted to hear again. It was the thump thump and the high whine of the air death. He barked at his new master and pulled at him to go back to where they slept, or—even better—back to that trench hole with the ladder and the rats. But his master only ducked down and looked at the sky.

Thump! Thump! Jack saw two of the air death stones strike the ground only a short run away from them. And now his master was making loud human noises. He bent down and pushed Jack hard toward their sleeping place, then he kicked him! He made loud human noises again, something like Fooksul! Fooksul! Green air came fast from the death stones. Jack ran like he had been taught, as his new master shouted. He ran as fast as he could. He ran and he looked back and saw that his new master was still on his feet in the green air, although his hands were at this eyes and his throat. He was putting on the skin that humans put on their heads and faces sometimes. But Jack knew his job was to run, as fast as he could.

WHEN HE GOT to where the other humans were, one of them waved his arms at Jack, bared his teeth, and made the noise his master had made, Fooksul! Fooksul! He bent down to pick Jack up, but Jack barked and ran back toward his master. Then he stopped and barked again. Now the human was following him and Jack ran back to his new master, who was not very far away. He was lying on the wood road. Jack could smell that he was alive, but Jack could also smell the air death and knew he could not go to his master to help him or he would die, too.

The human who came back with him made noises and put on his head-and-face skin and walked over to Jack's new master and pulled on him until he lay next to Jack. Jack jumped around his master, pushing on his legs and his body to get him to rise and run from the air death. But he only moaned. Jack didn't mind as this meant that the air death stones had not killed him.

The other human ran back to the den and left Jack with his master. Jack stood there. Waiting. He was good at waiting.

Soon, the human brought other humans with a thin human bed. They put his master on the bed and carried him away, leaving Jack alone on the boardwalk.

Jack stood watch until the darkness, then he walked back to his new master's den. His master was not there. He jumped on their bed and fell asleep.

. . .

IN THE BUNKER 100 yards to the north, Unteroffizier Hitler was delivered to the medics, suffering from severe gas inhalation. Despite his protestations about his duty and a dog, the decision was made to remove him from the front.

THE NEXT MORNING, Jack's new master was still not there. And there were no sausages. There was water left over from the day before.

He would find his new master and Korpralpinsins today. Now that there was not a long leather on him, he could run. Jack walked out onto the wood roads and plunged into the muddy grey mist.

4

STAR LOST

1957 – Zvyozdny gorodok (Star City), "closed military townlet No. 1," USSR

THE COUNTRY WAS COLD, but the food was fresh.

Outside, by the woods, I and my littermates—my *odnopometnitsa*—ran around the lake many times, smelling the mud and the frogs that tasted like old sour meat, and the ducks. Ah, the ducks. How we chased the ducks and the squirrels! That was the country.

This was before the hard streets of Moskva, before life in these wire-and-concrete dens, before the white-suited men began taking my Laika away for days at a time.

Our den is cold now, like in the country, but that is because she is not here.

The masters in the white suits took her and I wait. They have always returned her. If I wait, they will bring her back.

The white-suited masters frighten the other dogs. I see their tails fall in the sign of fear. I smell them. I see their ears flatten.

When the black suits come they bring food and drink. They move their fingers through our fur. All except Mad Boris and

Crazy Ilenka know the black suits are good to us. Sometimes they come and talk. Sometimes they come to let us run in the stone yard.

The white suits do not come to make us happy. I think Mad Boris can't tell between the white and the black. He acts like all the humans are the same.

I NEVER KNOW what the white suits will do. Sometimes a white suit takes me and pokes me with small sharp sticks. Sometimes a white suit takes me and puts me in human clothing. Sometimes he puts me in a small den where I cannot turn around or stand and leaves me there until I make water. Sometimes I lie in a bed that makes me sit on my tail. The bed shakes or drops or moves until I am sick and fall asleep. That is the worst thing the white-suited humans do. The dropping bed.

My Laika is their prize. They take her and Crazy Ilenka more than they take me. They leave Mad Boris alone most days.

When they came for Laika this time, even the white-suited humans bared their teeth and said her name again and again when they took her. My Laika did not shiver her beautiful white sides. I am proud of her, that she did not make water when the white-suited humans took her. Only I could smell her fear as she left the den.

I lie here and wait until they bring her back. The food sits under my nose and I do not hunger or thirst.

MY LAIKA HAS NOT RETURNED. The white suits came today and I thought they would take me, but they did not. They took her food bowl. I will share mine when she comes home.

Later, the black suit called Dmitri tried to raise me from my den. Dmitri has stroked many of the dogs (even Crazy Ilenka, but not Mad Boris) and brought sweet food cakes to us. I did not rise from my cage. I do not know if I can. I miss my Laika and her warmth by my side. I am not hungry, even for the sweet food cake Dmitri brought to me. I did lick his hand to show I knew the cake was good.

AT FIRST LIGHT, the white suits took me from our den and stuck me with their sharp sticks. I did not have to wear human clothes. I was so relieved they did not put me on the dropping bed or in the tiny den that I made water. I do not relieve myself except when I am full, but I think I have changed because my Laika is not with me now.

After they stuck me with their sticks, they put me in a new

place. It is very quiet. It is cold because my Laika is not here, but it is quiet. There are few dens and only one other dog that I can smell. I am no longer near Crazy Ilenka or Mad Boris. I am no longer where I denned with my Laika. When she comes back, will they know where our new den is and how to put her here? I am not hungry, but today I did drink.

DMITRI

"I have told you, Dmitri, we cannot afford to train the dogs the same as the bitches. The suits do not fit. Someday, perhaps, this will be done. For now, the dogs are reserve and second priority. We will conduct all the same preliminary tests that do not require suits, but it stops there."

"But Pushok is a very bright dog. He wants to work. I am sure…"

"I am sure he is a fine dog, Dmitri, but this is the last we will discuss this matter. Decisions have been made and we will execute them as is our duty."

Dmitri Sergeyovich began to speak, but the Chief Administrator of the People's Department of Canine Cosmological Engineering, Anton Krazelopov, held up his stark white palm and Dmitri gave up the fight.

For now. He knew the dog Pushok, "Zhok" as he called him, would die if he didn't find a new reason to live. He'd seen it in the dogs at his father's household plot in the Caucasus. Sometimes mate bonding was as strong as with any human couple. He remembered his Granpapa, so hearty and powerful, who could lift the hindquarters of a mule on his back when he was young. And when his Strelsi, his wife—Dmitri's Granmama—died in the bitter winter of 1951, Granpapa had withered and faded so quickly, changing from a proud, almost frightening, patriarch to a thin, broken shadow man. He was gone before the first snow fell the next year. Until then, Granpapa had never been sick a day in his life, as far as Dmitri knew.

He saw his Granpapa's change in Zhok, after the brave Laika died.

Surely Zhok must know that she is dead, that she is not coming back.

Would it make a difference to Zhok if Dmitri could explain that Laika was a great hero to the Soviet peoples—no, to all humanity! The first creature from the planet to ride into space! This humble, unexceptional dog—Dmitri had never understood the name *tovarisch* Alexsei and some of the other Maintenance Comrades gave her—Barking Dog, indeed! Laika, or as he thought of her, Zhuchka—Little Bug was a gentle little mongrel who never offered any harm. It was a great sadness she could not enjoy the triumph of her accomplishment.

No, Dmitri thought, it makes no difference to Zhok what wonderful, amazing things his shy, delicate mate had performed. He only knew she no longer shared his kennel or his life.

The Comrade Scientists had taken Zhok away from the puppies and from their old kennel, and they were giving him sustenance and drugs to keep him alive, but Dmitri had no confidence either in the constancy of their good will, or of the likelihood that Zhok would change his behavior—behavior that would end his life as surely as Laika's had ended somewhere in the airless space above the Earth. Unless Dmitri could think of something that would bring Zhok new purpose.

ZHOK

I hear men and women—in white and black suits—say Russia has the smartest, the strongest, and the best: people, dogs, drink, everything important. All the women and men say this. But my Laika, my *lyubovsh*, my little love: she was the gentlest and loveliest of creatures.

It is not that her strength was not Russian, but that her strength was less than her loveliness. It was clear to me from the first day we met that her beauty and grace were no match for the envy and cruelty of our world.

That day, that first day. Anton was the black coat that lifted me down from a truck. I was on the streets of Moskva since my dear mother, Nonna, froze on the banks of the Yauza. It was a blessing to be picked up and brought to this home. But I was full of the spirit of the street. I did not understand the world I was in. How could I? There were many dogs, but it was not a dog's world. It was a world of strange comings and goings. A world of cages and thin sharp sticks. But also a world of warmth and food that did not make us sick. Clean water, and—once the world was understood—there was *nemnogo dobroty,* a little kindness, companionship, and even love for some of us.

My first day they unloaded me and Laika into the open yard at the same time. She was so fair and so small. She could not have lived on the street as I did.

I stood stiff legged when they released us: smelling, looking at the other dogs. I would find the largest. I knew there must be a fight. It was best to have it now, while I was still strong, for I knew not what would come.

But none of the dogs came at me. They all seemed smaller, lighter. I relaxed.

This is not what happened for Laika. Two dogs—I was to learn they were Znachitz and Gottke—immediately ran at Laika. Malyshka snarled at her, saying terrible things. Laika, always agreeable, lowered her beautiful eyes and bowed, hoping submission would deflect this attack. As she did this, Gottke circled her and roughly mounted her from the side.

Dogs must mate. This is often a matter of convenience or an act driven by a madness that overcomes us. But Laika was not in her season. And, as a dog with some experience of the world, I smelled that Gottke did not plan to mate with Laika. His was the rude gesture of a brutalizer preying on the weak.

I did not rescue Laika that day. She was not yet my *lyubovsh*.

I was fresh from the lessons of the street, where no dog saves a tail he doesn't wag.

As I watched and rated my rivals, the black suit Anton returned and shooed Gottke away from the little white dog who shuddered beneath him; Znachitz had already lost interest and was across the yard, worrying an old bone shard. The man bent and ran his fingers over Laika's shivering sides, handed her a cake from his pocket, stood, then left the yard.

I never saw a dog so *lakomstvo*...so...dainty. If a black-suit man gave such a cake to Gottke or Malyshka or—yes—to me, it would be a quick snap and an instant's pleasure. Not Laika. I watched her, fascinated as she took tiny bites of the small cake. Each time her jaws met, her brown eyes closed and a small shiver moved across her ribs. After her last bite, she swallowed, then raised her eyes and met mine. My world changed. She was my Laika and I was hers.

DMITRI COMES to my cage every day. Each time he says, "Our Laika is a hero, Zhok. She is the People's hero. She is the greatest Russian dog that has ever lived...no...she is the greatest *dog* that has ever lived. Her heart is in the stars above, Zhok. It is greater than you or me." Then he reaches his hand through the cage and rub mys head.

Some days, I hear our pups crying for milk or for their mother or, perhaps, even for me. Dmitri brought young Strelka to share my pen. She had lost her pups and would now feed Laika's. She would keep them safe. But I can not care for them. Not as a father should, for my heart is stiff as stone. I hear their cries and it is as the sound of the wind in winter. I know it means life, not death, but those two are the same for me now.

AFTER MANY DAYS, I moved out to the yard where Laika and I and the others ran, where we scampered in our youth. Dmitri brought me the fat from a goose and I ate it. I saw the growing pups of my Laika—my pups, though I had no sense that they were mine. I had been right; Strelka was a good mother. Pushinka and little Mushka were the strongest.

From that day onward, I walked in the pen and ate some food that Dmitri brought me. But when I lay my head upon my front legs and closed my eyes, I did not know why I should do these things.

One day a small man in a uniform accompanied Dmitri. He knelt before me.

"Zhok. Zhok." Dmitri called softly, extending his hand and squatting beside the younger man, "This is Lieutenant Gagarin. He has come to see you."

I raised my head and sniffed. This other man smelled better than either the black or white coat humans. He smelled...like the night.

Dmitri unlatched my cage. I did not move out. It was not time for my walk in the pen.

But the stranger slowly put his hand into my den. He turned the back of his hand to me and held his wrist close to my nose.

"My grandfather was a watchmaker." He told me in a rumbling human voice. I did not know what his words meant.

He twisted his wrist gently in front of my nose. "Do you see that, Zhok? Is there anything you recognize?"

His wrist was almost touching me now. I sniffed it. And whined. There *was* something. How could it be? How could this human smell of my Laika, my *lyubovsh*? It was not quite her. It was the scent of her and metal, a very faint scent of her.

"This is the buckle of her collar, *tovarisch*. It now holds my timepiece to my arm." The stranger explained. Again, though I knew not what he said, my heart swelled.

Dmitri's kind hand stroked behind my ears. "Comrade Senior Lieutenant Gagarin is going into space, Zhok. He will be like Laika. As she was the first dog, he will be the first man to leave our Earth."

"Comrade Dmitri has told me how you pine for our little Laika. I trained with her, you know, *tovarisch*." Lieutenant Gagarin's hand—much harder than Dmitri's, but still gentle—touched my other ear. "She was a great hero. I thought I should take something of her with me. Without her sacrifice, my mission would be far less likely to succeed."

He looked down at me, and I gazed up at him. The uncovered lights above shone into my eyes and I could not see him clearly, as if he also shone too brightly to be seen. I licked his wrist and laid my nose on the back of his hard hand.

A moment later, Dmitri softly pulled my head away. Comrade Senior Lieutenant Gagarin rose and I was put back in my cage.

As the two men walked away, I raised my head and looked at those bright lights. I thought of my Laika. They had sent her up to those lights in the great roaring iron. Her body had returned. Her spirit remains above. In the deep sky.

JUNE, 1961, United Nations Building Main Hall, New York City, USA

"THEY'VE FINISHED INTRODUCING the Soviet Premier, Mr. President." Whispered the man in the thin-lapelled black suit and dark glasses.

"Ummm...thanks, Chet." President John Kennedy muttered, eyes fixed on the scribbled notes he held in his hands. Then he looked up at the Secret Service agent, flashed his famous smile, and added, "Time to beard the lion in his den, eh, Chet?"

"Yes, sir, Mr. President." The agent paused, then added, "We've swept the area, sir, and there are...ah...no problems. Would you like some assistance up the back way?"

Kennedy shot a glance at the agent, who'd been with him for quite a while. *Is that the hint of a smile on that professionally immobile countenance?* More darkly he wondered: *Does he know how much pain I'm in?* Maintaining his own grin, Kennedy curtly shook his head "no" and walked around and up the podium.

The New York crowd was welcoming.

Good Democrats, he thought.

And there's that old fox, Nikita. No, make it bear—a wily little old bear. Suits. You'd think we were on the campaign trail together, the way he's leering. What's the bastard got up his sleeve today, I wonder?

Kennedy strode to the center of the stage, his attention partly on Khrushchev's expression, which remained suspiciously pleasant, partly on the crowd, and partly—as was always true these days—on the pain in his back. When he reached the Soviet Premier, he extended his hand and the two men vigorously exchanged a greeting. Then he turned to the audience, and raised his hands for quiet.

"It's always a pleasure to follow a great warm-up act." Appreciative laughter and applause rippled through the crowd. Kennedy glanced back at Khrushchev, who had what now seemed an almost vacuous smile pasted on his face.

"Thank you, my friends. I'm here today at the United Nations for all the celebrations, but I'm here particularly because Mr. Nikita Khrushchev, Premier of the U.S.S.R., has informed me that he has a special presentation to make to me and to the American people. So, with no further ado, it's your show, Mr. Khrushchev." With a magnanimous wave backward to the other waiting head of state, Kennedy backed away from the podium.

Never shy, Khrushchev stepped to the microphone and spoke briefly in forceful Russian, gesticulating effusively with both hands. The English interpreter who stood by his side leaned forward and translated, "Thank you very much, Mr. President. I, too, am pleased to share the stage with so accomplished an actor. The Peoples of the Soviet Socialist Republic, in honor of the toil and accomplishments of all working peoples everywhere—including, of course, the United States of America—and in the spirit of continuing peace and cooperation would like to make this gift to your household, Mr. President." Khrushchev turned away from the podium and gestured to one of his assistants, who in turn bent down to a large black box that Kennedy had not noticed. The short, solid Soviet Premier picked up something floppy from inside the box and held the object above the podium for the crowd to see and appreciate.

It was a small white dog.

The audience reaction was complex. Some were struck to silence. What did this mean? What was the right response? Was this a Soviet trick? There were some oohs and aahs. This *was* a young dog and some responded with unfettered feelings. There was some laughter, both nervous and approving.

As much a showman as any American politician, Khrushchev gave the audience time to express themselves and then, as soon as the sound and emotion began to waiver, he raised the squirming puppy in one meaty hand and cupped the microphone, speaking briefly but enthusiastically. A slim, dark man leaned forward over Premier Khrushchev's broad shoulder and translated: "To honor you and your country, President Kennedy, the Soviet Socialist Peoples gift you this dog—born of our People's Hero, the brave dog Laika—that you and America can be a part of our great adventures in the skies above this planet."

Lowering the little dog from on high, Khrushchev decorously and melodramatically handed him to President Kennedy, who had stepped back up to the podium, not to be upstaged.

Kennedy held the puppy snugly under one arm, stretched his other hand out to Khrushchev and shook hands again, leaning down to the microphone and saying simply, "Thank you, Mr. Khrushchev. I thank you, and the American people thank you." Then, as an apparent afterthought, holding the dog up in the air now with both hands, he added, "And this American dog thanks you."

The audience exploded in laughter and applause and both heads of state smiled their best violin smiles and waved widely.

LATE THAT EVENING, the White House, Washington, D.C.

"AN OLD BEAR handing a young dog to a crippled eagle. Humphh...that bastard is about as clever as they come. I wonder if he's as sentimental as he thinks I am?" Kennedy smiled wanly—not the broad, well-known public grin. "I think maybe he is," the President said as he absentmindedly stroked the small dog's coarse fur.

Bending with a grimace, he picked up the puppy and looked into his solemn fuzzy face, "You've quite a look there, pooch. What've you seen in your few months that could bring that kind of sadness into those eyes?"

"Well, never mind, when Caroline and John-John get you to Squaw Island, you'll have lots of pals to play with."

The President leaned back in his rocking chair, steepled his fingers, and sighed, "I just hope to God the kids don't decide to call you Jack."

5

THIS IS MY YARD

1995 COMMON ERA, **15 miles west of Harrison, Arkansas, USA**

WHAT'S THAT?

It's a rat.

There it is.

No. Not a rat. It's...it's...it's not a rat.

Run. I'm running, running to it. I'll catch it. Catch it.

There it is. Almost there. Near the fence. It's running for the fence. I'll catch it. I'll catch it. I'll...

...Up a tree.

I can't climb a tree.

I can jump and bite it.

Jump. Jump. I'll jump.

THERE, I say.

THERE. COME BACK DOWN.

It's gone. I'll smell around and see what it is.

Nope. Not a rat. Something No-Master said—'possum'? Right. Possum. That's what it is.

COME BACK DOWN, POSSUM. I'LL BITE YOU AND I'LL EAT YOU. COME ON.

I'll look around the yard. Time for that.

What's that? In the house? Miss Kitty barking. She's still in the house. Good thing. And there's Jennifer's whine. She wants into the yard. Molly's quiet. Big surprise. Is that food noise dropping into the bowls? That's okay. Miss Kitty knows better than to touch mine, that's for sure.

Patrol. Time to patrol.

There's Kevieboy and Gorp. Kevieboy's ears are high. He saw the possum. If I can't catch it, he sure can't. His tail's down now that he's seen me. Hah, Kevieboy. You have to catch something before you can bite it with that big mouth of yours.

HAH, SMELL ME AND PUT YOUR TAIL DOWN, KEVIEBOY. I tell him as I run around him and he stands still.

Gorp smells me behind. I turn quick,

HAH! SMELL ME AND PUT YOUR TAIL DOWN, GORP.

Gorp backs up a step, but he is Gorp. Bigger than me or Kevieboy, he's just Gorp. He tried to mount Jennifer one time and I had to nip him, but he's just Gorp, so I leave him and go back to patrol.

I run between the side of No-Master's house and the bathtub that Max and Trog drink out of sometimes because they are the only ones tall enough to get their heads in it. Somebody's been chewing on the corner of the house again. Could be Gorp or Trog. LD? No, LD can't reach above the hard bottom of the house. Never know about those three.

What's that—back behind there? Just in front of my old nest. Run.

Oh. LD and BD rolling their log. Pushing it and gnawing on it. They're doing something different. What are they doing?

WHAT ARE YOU DOING? I bark at them.

LD's pushing his nose into their log. BD's biting one of the knobs on the log and pulling. There's a hole in front of my nest and they can't get their log out of there. Haha. BD and LD and their log.

WHOA!

Here comes Whirlaway. Whoa!

Not gonna chase him. Haha. Maybe I will. Run.

SEE, WHIRLAWAY, I RUN, TOO. I say as I run around next to Whirlaway in his endless circles.

Whoa. No wonder he's skinnier than Willie or Valentino. That's a lot of running. Even for me.

GO, WHIRLAWAY.

I encourage him, then head back on patrol.

I stop in front of my old nest. BD and LD don't look up. I don't need them to. Those two are—well, that log is all they pay attention to. Except No-Master, of course.

The door is open to my old nest, and I jump around them and go inside, smelling the smells where I lived when No-Master brought me here. There's old smell of me here.

So small. Brothers, sisters, mother milk. Little bites. Warm wire mother home.

At the end of my old nest is my hole. I dug it and I can fit through it. LD is little and can fit through it, too, but all he does is bite his log.

What's that? Door squeak from No-Master's house. He's coming into the yard. I run to the house. Now I'll patrol our yard with No-Master.

I run back past LD and BD, Gorp and Kevieboy. Jeff's standing up by the front gate. As I round the corner of the house, Miss Kitty's out in front of No-Master—like she doesn't think I'll be there. And Jennifer is still on the porch, pretending nothing is important.

I'M HERE. I'M HERE. GET BACK, MISS KITTY.

I tell her and No-Master. Jennifer hears me, too, but she's on the porch. She doesn't care anyway.

Miss Kitty unfluffs her white tail and steps back behind No-Master. He has his two extra stick arm-legs today that make holes in the ground. I run up to his feet and smell his shoes. I like to smell his shoes.

"So, Dax—you keepin' the cows out of the corn?"

No-Master doesn't have any cows. I don't like corn.

"Miss Kitty and I are headin' out back. Gotta check on Miss Jojo. Haven't seen her around."

No-Master walks slowly past the house on his four legs. I'm in front. Miss Kitty is beside No-Master. Jennifer, Kevieboy, and Jeff come after her.

What's that? Behind us all, past the front gate, fast approaching. I run past No-Master, Miss Kitty, Jeff, and the others.

WATCH OUT!

WATCH OUT!

HE'S BACK!

I know this sound.

HE'S BACK.

I warn them all.

I'm to the front gate now and there he is, stepping out of his box car. Round thing on his head. Bag on his back to catch us all and take us away.

BACK!

I shout.

BACK! GET AWAY! STAY AWAY! THIS IS MY PLACE!

Outside. My nose in the white cold. Brothers, sisters, mother milk. Hands pull me away. Mother home gone. Brothers, sisters gone. Small hands squeeze me.

I shout.

GO AWAY! GO AWAY!

The human does not come inside the gate. He sticks papers in the box high above and then gets back in his car and rolls away. I have beaten him again. I have saved No-Master and all my dogs again.

What's that? Something on the window. My head's up and so

am I. No-Master makes loud sleep noises. Molly's on No-Master's bed, near his head. Jennifer is down by his feet. Jennifer looks at me, then closes her eyes. She doesn't care.

I run between the tall piles of papers on No-Master's nest floor. I know my way and I never knock them over like Miss Kitty does sometimes. I jump into the chair under the window.

The yard's empty. Everyone's asleep except Crackers. He's standing in the yard, looking up.

A CAR IS COMING up the road. I do not run. I do not make any noise. I am ready. This could be the time. It's a big box car with bright lights. It could hold a big wire nest.

World moves. Wire nest not home. No brothers, no sisters. Sick. Spit. Choke. World moves.

The car passes. I jump down quiet from the chair and lie down by the door. They will have to get through me.

I sleep.

BEFORE NO-MASTER WAKES, I run out my little door at the bottom of No-Master's door. Time to see Solly. And maybe bite that possum.

I run to the back, where Willie, Wilson, Jojo, and Solly sleep. Trog and Crackers are digging by the dirt pile. The white part of Crackers' face is as black as the top of his head. I run to them.

WHAT ARE YOU DOING?"

They don't stop.

WHAT ARE YOU DOING?

I ask again, because they should tell me. Trog stops and looks at me. Crackers keeps digging. He digs fast and there's a big hole now. Maybe I should dig, too.

I start to dig, then Trog hears something and runs toward the front fence. I don't hear anything and I leave Crackers to his digging. Crackers is crazy anyway.

I run past the dirt pile—that's the hill where we all poop and where it rolls down and mounds up against the fence. Sometimes LD goes down there, if his log rolls that way, but nobody else ever does. There are a lot of flies that bite you there. Chasing flies is fun, but it's not that much fun.

Many things sit between the dirt pile and the back: empty old nests without doors, big faces of humans that are not real, other big things that do not move and are hard and that smell like humans. One of the humans that is not a human is small with a cat.

Small hands pull. Different nest. Mother home gone. Brothers, sisters gone. Cry. Cold. Ground hard, cold, slick hard taste. Cry.

Wilson sits in front of the big nest where he sleeps with Jojo. He is round and he sneezes if he runs. I don't smell his behind and he keeps sitting when I run up. Just after that, I pass Willie's nest. She is somewhere else. And past her is where Solly sleeps.

Solly is old. He wears white on his mouth and the rest of him is black. He's pretty big. Not as big as Max, maybe not as tall as Jeff or Trog or Willie, but he is big. He smells old. He smells like the wet food that No-Master gives Molly and Miss Kitty sometimes.

I sit in front of Solly. He is the only dog I sit with. He lies with his head on his legs. I put my head on my legs, too, and look at him. Solly is sad.

That's enough sitting.

I jump up in front of Solly.

WHY ARE YOU SAD, SOLLY?

I ask Solly this a lot.

Solly doesn't say anything.

I'M GOING, SOLLY.

DON'T BE SAD.

I hop backwards and run into Jeff, who stumbles a little.

HEY, JEFF.

BETTER WATCH OUT.

I'm not mad at Jeff. Jeff is sad like Solly. He sleeps in the back, too. His nest leans against No-Master's porch and faces Willie's nest across the back yard. A tree with food was there but it doesn't have any food or leaves anymore. Jeff watches Willie all the time. Some days he walks behind her.

I don't see Willie. I raise my head and smell for her.

Uh-oh. That's a mate smell. Trouble. I'll stop trouble. This is my yard.

I run for the front, to find who has the mate smell. If it's Molly, No-Master keeps her in the house. If it's Jennifer, then I will bite Bildad or Kevieboy again if he tries to mount her, or Valentino or Yellow Dog if they come out from under the house. If it is Willie's smell, though, that is trouble. Jeff is here. He runs behind me. Where is Max?

There is Willie. She is by the front gate. Where is Max?

I run to Willie. It is her mate smell. Jeff runs behind me.

WILLIE!

I shout.

WILLIE!

WILLIE! GO BACK TO YOUR NEST! YOU CAUSE TROUBLE! GO BACK!

Right after I tell her what she should do, Jeff starts calling to her.

Solly makes me sit—just because he is Solly. No-Master makes me full—just because he is No-Master. When Jeff calls to Willie, I stop where I am. Jeff's call is sadder than Solly and fuller than No-Master. I do not jump. I do not shout.

Willie lifts her long head and looks at Jeff as he sings to her. Jeff's head is high in his call, though, and he does not see this.

What's that? A loud banging noise from back behind the house, getting closer fast.

There's Max! He is running and there's a bucket around his leg. It's crashing into nests and the old bathtub and sticks in the ground. Max does not care. He smells Willie's mate smell. This makes Max not listen to me. This is trouble.

BACK, MAX!

I bend my front legs down and shout sharp at him, showing that I'm ready to jump any way I need to and that I mean business. My tail is straight up in the air. I will not have trouble here.

BACK, MAX—I MEAN IT!

I tell him again. And I mean it.

Max still runs toward Willie. Willie does not move. Jeff is not calling anymore.

Jeff adds:

BACK, MAX—I MEAN IT!

This should make me mad, but I am not mad at Jeff.

I agree, shouting with Jeff.

BACK, MAX.

Max is almost to Willie and I prepare to bite his leg. I will not have this trouble in my yard.

Now Bildad and Kevieboy and even Crazy Crackers are shouting with me and Jeff:

STOP, MAX! STOP!

No-Master's door squeaks open and No-Master steps out on his porch. I can see Valentino's sharp black nose sticking out from under one end of the porch, Yellow Dog's wide muzzle pokes out of the other.

No-Master blows his red whistle.

Everybody's shouting so loud that they keep shouting.

No-Master blows his red whistle again and stomps his foot on the porch.

Everybody stops shouting and looks up at No-Master.

Everybody except Max. His eyes are almost closed and the wrinkles on his head have their own wrinkles. He's smelling Willie's behind and now he's rubbing against her.

No-Master blows his red whistle one more time, then he shouts, "NO, MAX, NO!"

That stops him. Even I stop when No-Master says that.

Cry. Big boxes pile high next to nest. Humans take human things in and out of boxes. Sharp hard smell. Cry. Boxes move. Boxes fall loud. Cry.

No-Master has a leash-lead and puts it on Max. No-Master takes Max to the other side of the house where there is no sun and where nobody goes except Whirlaway. Max's head is down as he walks with No-Master.

GO WITH NO-MASTER, MAX. LISTEN TO ME.

I tell Max as he walks away.

That's good enough. I stopped that trouble.

Small hands grab. Little arms hold, bend my leg, my tail. Scratch, run. Get away. Little human cries. Run. Big human shouts, hits me with tube.

I HOP from my nest below No-Master's bed and run through my door. Something's wrong in my yard.

Trog is sleeping standing up, leaning his long body against the wall of No-Master's house. I leave him alone.

BD and LD are asleep with their heads on each end of their log. I leave them alone, too.

I can still smell the sharp wet smell of Willie's mate scent. It is strong from the back where No-Master put her. And I can smell something else coming from the back. It is bad. Something is wrong in my yard. I run to the back, not stopping to say anything to Whirlaway who's walking slowly around in circles with his tail in his mouth or Kevieboy or Gorp or Bildad who are all waking up sniffing the air.

Wilson is sitting outside the nest he shares with Jojo. He's looking into the dark of their nest; his head is on his front paws and short sounds puff out of his round body every time he wheezes a breath.

WHUFFF.

I sneeze. There is a very big smell coming from their nest. It is like when the rats died in the poop pile. It's dead, but I don't want to touch it.

NO-MASTER!

I call.

NO-MASTER! COME AND SEE JOJO. SHE IS DEAD.

Bildad and Kevieboy and Gorp are behind me and they sing for No-Master, too. And they sing for Jojo. Then Solly joins in from the next nest. Wilson just lies there looking and he doesn't sing at all.

New nest, no wire. No brothers, sisters, no mother milk. Hot place with soft hairy ground. Wet food. Pee on hairy ground. Human cries. Hits with tube.

No-Master pushes a wire cart to his car. Jojo smells dead, but she's inside the cart. Now she is inside the car.
WHERE ARE YOU GOING, NO-MASTER? WHERE ARE YOU GOING?
No-Master is taking Jojo away but this seems like trouble to me. No-Master cannot make trouble.
WHAT IS THIS?
I ask at his feet.
WHAT IS THIS?
No-Master stops after putting Jojo in the back of his truck. "Gotta taker her in, fella. Damn Health Department all over me last time I buried one of you out here." No-Master leans down and pats my head. I do not like pats on my head, but I do not shout at No-Master and I never bite him.

Small human grabs. Small hands hard on my head.

"You take care of things till I get back, Dax." No-Master opens the front gate and drives through. Whirlaway runs out right behind No-Master's truck.
GET BACK HERE, WHIRLAWAY.
I shout and run outside my yard. I catch Whirlaway—who is running in a circle—and bite his tail. Just a little nip.
YOU GO BACK INSIDE, WHIRLAWAY.
Whirlaway does not stop but he stays away from me and runs back inside the yard. No-Master gets out of his truck and closes the front gate as I run back in.
"That's a good boy, Dax. I knew I could count on you."

GORP! STOP EATING THE HOUSE.

It is Gorp that's eating the house. I should know. That Gorp!

GORP! STOP IT OR I'LL BITE YOU.

I run at Gorp and just before I bite him he jumps away from the house. That Gorp.

No-Master is still gone. I will patrol. No-Master is not here. I will patrol.

It is very hot in my yard. I hear Yellow Dog under the porch scratching hard. Yellow Dog had many fleas. No fleas now, but he scratches them anyway. I don't like fleas.

I run past the porch. Valentino's black nose sticks out from under the step. I do not stop. I run by Gorp and Crackers and Max all lying in the shade of the house. They are panting. I run by BD and LD and their log. It is not in the hole in front of my old pen, but it is close to the edge of it. I run by the dirt pile. There are many flies and I try to catch one. I don't. I run by the big human box things and the humans that are not humans. Trog is behind one of these.

WHAT ARE YOU DOING, TROG?

YOU ARE NOT A HUMAN. YOU SHOULD GET AWAY.

Trog looks at me like he is Trog. He sits and pants, then scratches his long white nose with his paw.

OKAY, TROG. YOU SIT THERE.

I run on to the back to see Solly.

Small human gone. Jump! Jump on soft human nests. Jump on soft hairy ground. Chew hairy boxes. Humans gone. Brothers, sisters, mother milk gone. Where is small human? Pee on small human nest. Run. Chew tubes. Chew hairy ground.

Solly is outside his nest, in the sun.

WHAT ARE YOU DOING, SOLLY? GET OUT OF THE SUN! IT'S HOT!

Solly raises his head and looks at me, then puts it back down on his paws.

GET UP, SOLLY, GET UP!

I shout. This is trouble. Solly is smart. Solly does not lie in the hot sun. I push my nose against his side, then shout at him again.

Solly groans and stands up. He is a big dog. I hop around him until he moves to the side of his nest where there is shade. Wilson is already there, asleep.

Solly turns around and surprises me. His big tongue wipes across my nose. It smells bad. But it smells like Solly. And it makes my face cool. Then Solly flops down hard on the ground and groans again.

THAT'S GOOD, SOLLY.

I sit with Solly and listen to the noises of the trees above us.

WHAT'S THAT?

I shout and jump up. But I know what it is. No-Master is back in his truck. Patrol is over. I must take him into our house. I run back to the front.

NO-MASTER IS out of his truck. He waves to me and I run around him as we go into our house.

Jennifer is sniffing around No-Master's piles of paper. She does that. Miss Kitty jumps down from No-Master's chair and runs to him—on the other side from me and shouts, HELLO like she does. She doesn't look at me. Molly is asleep on No-Master's bed. Big surprise. But she wakes up.

No-Master smells old. There is a smell like the color he puts on our house walls. I sneeze.

"Okay, Miss Kitty. Out on the porch. You, too, Jennie."

No-Master waves an arm at Miss Kitty and at Jennifer and they start for the door. I go first and start to run ahead.

"No, Dax—you stay. Stay, Dax."

I stop running. This is No-Master. Miss Kitty and Jennifer are through the door and No-Master leans down to face me. I sit.

"Think it's best you stay inside for a little while, boy. Just till we get all settled down. I know you run things around here, but that could be trouble—if you know what I mean." No-Master looks sad at me. His eyes look like Solly's. I swallow hard.

No-Master goes to the door and opens it, then looks back at me as he slides the wood cover down over my door—the one that we use in the winter to keep the cold out. "Miss Kitty'll know what to do with this new fella. She can break him in for you, Dax, then everything will be just fine."

No-Master closes the door.

I run and jump into the chair by the window. Molly lies back down on No-Master's bed. Big surprise.

Humans shout. Small human cries. Hits me with tube. Nest on hard cold ground with scary boxes. Back in car. Small human cries. Car gone. New nest. No brothers, sisters, no mother milk. No small human.

No-Master walks on two legs to the truck. He walks slowly. No-Master takes the back of the truck down and pulls a blanket off the nest in the truck. No-Master opens the nest and reaches in with his leash-lead.

A big dog with brown and black hair jumps down beside No-Master. Inside No-Master's nest, I cannot smell this dog. He has high ears and a bushy tail like Crackers. His nose is pointy, but not as pointy as Valentino's or Trog's. He is almost as big as Max.

BE CAREFUL, NO-MASTER!

I shout through the window. No-Master does not hear me.

BE CAREFUL, WILLIE!

I add, then I warn Kevieboy and Jeff and Bildad and Gorp. I do not know if they can hear me.

The big new dog walks quiet by No-Master's side, like he belongs there.

YOU DO NOT BELONG THERE, NEW DOG.

I shout, then I shout that again.

No-Master puts his hand to his mouth and blows his red whistle two times. That means that everyone should listen. Crackers and Max and Trog and Jeff and Kevieboy and Willie and Bildad and Gorp and Jennifer all come close to No-Master and the new dog. I open my eyes wide as BD comes, too. Whirl-away runs by them all and I cannot see him until he runs back around them. Last, Miss Kitty trots up, fluffing her tail and standing on the other side of No-Master from the new dog. I growl. Miss Kitty!

No-Master is talking. The big new dog keeps his ears up like Crackers. His tail is as high as Miss Kitty's.

I shout at the window.

LOWER YOUR TAIL WHEN NO-MASTER TALKS, NEW DOG!

No-Master walks forward, Miss Kitty on one side, the new dog on his other side. The new dog's mouth is open. He is laughing or he is hot. I do not know. Miss Kitty's tail moves down.

I shout.

WHAT'S WRONG WITH YOU, MISS KITTY? RAISE YOUR TAIL!

But her tail is down now. Everyone in the yard except Max and Crackers lowers their tails. Crackers is crazy. He walks away with Jennifer. Max's hair is rising. His tail is straight. I can see his teeth.

GO, MAX!

I shout. I do not like this new dog.

GO, BIG MAX!

But the new dog does not jump or move at Max. He wags his big black and brown tail and then sits next to No-Master. No-Master puts his hand on the new dog's head and pats him. No-Master pats him! Then No-Master takes the leash-lead off the new dog, turns around, and gets back in the truck.

There is trouble in my yard. I shout.

TROUBLE! TROUBLE!

I keep shouting.

I cannot see No-Master because he is in the truck. But I can see the new dog. His tail is straight now.

Fast as a fly, the new dog runs at Max and bites him. Through my window I hear Max cry and fall forward. The big dog bit his leg and Max falls. Now the big dog is standing over Max. Max rolls on his back. There is blood on him and on the ground. I cannot smell the blood. The fight is over.

Where is No-Master?

NO-MASTER.

I shout again and again. I press my head against the window but it is hard and does not move.

Now I see No-Master again. He walks slowly, and he has his two leg-sticks. Even through the window I can hear him shout, "NO."

The big new dog steps away from Max, who tries to get up but cannot and just lies there. The new dog turns toward No-Master. Miss Kitty runs in around the new dog—not too close—and shouts at him.

GOOD FOR YOU, MISS KITTY.

I shout at her.

TELL HIM HE IS A BAD DOG!

Miss Kitty and No-Master will stop this trouble.

The new dog does not try to catch Miss Kitty. He leaps forward instead—at No-Master.

Before I jump down from the chair, Miss Kitty runs after the new dog from behind.

The board that covers my door—scratch it down. Scratch. Fast as I can, I scratch. No sounds from No-Master in the yard. Bite the board. High scream of death pierces through the door into the house. I bite and bite and bite the board.

Bottom of the board moves up and I claw. Board moves and I push my nose through and up. Splinters and my blood in my nose. Scratch and claw and the board moves up and I am out the door and fall on the porch.

Jump over the steps and land in my yard.

No-Master is there. He is on the ground. He does not move. Miss Kitty lies by him, red blood all over her orange hair. I smell her dead.

THIS IS MY YARD

WHERE IS THE NEW DOG? Bite him. Stop him. Where is No-Master?

Many dogs, but no brothers or sisters. Hard, cold ground. No nest. No food. Hungry. Hungry.

No-Master comes. Smell shoes. Lick hand.

New dog is chasing Willie.

Run by Max on ground. Willie runs this way. Runs to me. I'll fix this trouble. Jeff runs behind. New dog stops, turns on Jeff. Jeff stops and new dog bites at Jeff. Jeff shouts, but it is a shout of being scared. I do not smell Jeff's blood. New dog is smart. Smart as Solly.

Willie is behind me now. Her tail is down and she still smells like mate smell some.

Jeff rolls over on his back and the new dog makes killing biting sounds. But he does not bite at Jeff again and turns.

But I am faster. This is my yard. I stop trouble here. Without No-Master.

I am behind the new dog before he turns and I bite his back leg. He turns quick. He is surprised and angry. I jump over Jeff and run behind the bathtub that Trog and Max drink out of. The new dog runs after me—quick, but not as quick. I run between the tub and the house and he cannot fit there.

Now I run to the porch and jump on the steps. I am bigger than the new dog now.

He is close and when he jumps for the steps, I dive under him and bite his leg, holding on this time. He hits the stepside with his head. His yell is loud. Hah. Stupid new dog.

We fall to the ground. His leg is between my teeth and I bite hard. The new dog yells again, but he is strong and turns. I let go. Run.

He is slower now, but he is still fast.

Run around corner to old nest. Big new dog runs behind. Jump on empty nest next to my old nest. Leave new dog in corner. Jump. Hah new dog! You have to run around and I'll bite you again.

Jump. Unh! Crackers on top of nest! Front legs land on Crackers. Crackers stands. Back legs on nothing. Fall. Unhh.

Growl is behind me. Push hard and whirl. New dog's teeth are long. Back. Down in front of old nest. Back. Inside.

BACK! BACK, YOU BAD DOG!

But the new dog comes forward.

YOU HURT NO-MASTER! BACK!

I shout, but I go back, into the dark of my old nest with my old smells.

The new dog has stiff legs.

DIE.

He says.

YOU DIE.

Head down, teeth wet, he stalks into my old nest.

YOU DIE.

I say.

YOU ARE BAD. YOU ARE TROUBLE.

But I do not fight.

The new dog is inside my old nest now with me. We are very close.

I stop trouble in my yard. I help No-Master. I do not jump yet. Eye? Leg? Throat? New dog is big, strong.

What's that? The door to my old nest clangs shut behind the new dog. Trog's long white nose is behind it.

The new dog turns to the door.

Clang. BD and LD are outside now, in the hole in front of the door. Their log is against the door. That BD and LD.

LD tries to pull the log out. BD stands behind his brother. Trog stands next to him. They are panting.

I start to bite the new dog's leg.

I stop. I don't bite.

My hole. I dive for my hole in the back of my old nest. I push hard and I pull hard with my front claws. My back claws strike hair and teeth. I am out.

The new dog's teeth are in my hole and flash at me. He tries to shout something, but his mouth is in the hole and it is too small. Hah! Stupid new dog!

YOU CANNOT GET OUT, STUPID NEW DOG. STAY IN THERE.

YOU STAY, BAD DOG.

I run for the front to help No-Master.

NO-MASTER IS STILL on the ground, Miss Kitty next to him.

Bildad with his big mouth, Kevieboy, black-and-white Gorp, tall Trog, Crackers with his high ears like the new bad dog—all sit around No-Master. Max limps up and lies down by No-Master's good-smelling shoe. Willie lies down next to No-Master's head on one side. Jeff sits next to her. Jennifer lays her head on No-Master's other shoe. What a surprise. Jennifer.

Valentino crawls out from under the porch. Valentino is skinny and black. Yellow Dog comes out, too. They sit next to Jennifer.

The new dog shouts from my old nest.

I WILL KILL YOU. I WILL BITE YOU.

I look back at him. Wilson and BD trot around the side of the house. Solly is behind them.

SOLLY.

I say once.

BD and Wilson sit next to Gorp and Trog. Solly limps up to me and we go to No-Master.

I push on No-Master's head with my nose.

No-Master is always cold, but he is colder now. No-Master is dead. I don't push again.

Solly licks No-Master behind his ear. Then he lays his head on No-Master's neck.

Jeff stands up. He sings.

Max is next. He does not stand up, but he raises his head and sings louder than Jeff.

I cannot hear the new dog shouting anymore now. Everybody is singing, singing about No-Master. No-Master is dead. We love No-Master.

Solly does not sing. His head is on No-Master's neck and he does not move.

THE GMC STRETCH van jerks up the rocky drive, avoiding getting centered on the large stones that litter the "driveway."

"I'm not going in there. Last time somebody bothered Old Judge Jones, they got a load of salt in their britches."

"Well, Mary Lou called his number about a zillion times and nobody answered. The Gordons and the McNairs both called the Sheriff about the dogs howlin' and..." The younger of the two men in worn brown coveralls replies.

"...Yeah, yeah. The Sheriff gets the calls and we're the one's gotta clean up the mess. Typical. Okay. You go knock on his door, then. I got no mind to pick buckshot out of my backside, Milton."

The truck pulls up to the closed, mesh-covered horse gate and Milton—the young blond-headed driver—gets out. Billy Shanford, his partner, watches him pick his way up to the gate and look over it. After a few seconds, he waves to Billy to get out of the truck.

Milton's expression told Billy that something is very wrong.

THEY DON'T EVEN TRY to catch the little brown-and-white Jack Russell. First, he runs at them, trying to keep them away from the old man's still body. He bites at their shoes. He jumps up and tries to nip their hands. He barks and barks, as if saying "Stay away." Or "This is our place. Leave us alone."

The men pay little attention to him. They shoo away the other dogs. Except the big red Setter who just sits near the body, her black eyes staring straight ahead. And the ancient grey-muzzled black Lab, who doesn't move until the blond man bends down and gently lifts the dog's head off the corpse.

Milton doesn't seem to notice that the Jack Russell stops barking after he lifts the dog's grizzled head off the dead man. He doesn't notice that the little terrier lays down and looks across the fallen man at the Lab. He doesn't notice that the old Lab's eyes don't look back, that they remain fixed on the dead body.

A deep, ringing bark challenges from the back of the yard. The heavy-set man tucking a blue plastic tarp over the body on the ground looks up.

"I know that one," Billy Shanford says. "He's trouble." The two men walk back to their truck and come out with a stick and loop net, a large chain, and a thick muzzle. Soon they're dragging a big, angry German Shepherd and loading him into a heavy wire cage in the back. The bigger man takes the driver's seat and the blond goes back in the yard. Returning to the truck, Milton closes the gate, then drops the dead white Pomeranian in a garbage bag and seals it with a red twist-tie. He climbs into the truck and the two men bump down the drive.

LIGHTS SHINE up the drive and through the front gate. The van is back and another longer car is behind it. Both pull into the yard.

The men from the new car take the tarp off the old man on the ground and load him into the back of their car. They drive away.

The men from the van step into the yard, each with a hoop leash in his hands. Billy Shanford loops a medium-sized charcoal-colored Pit Bull first and puts him into the truck. Milton moves his hoop toward an impossibly round Pug-Beagle, who waddles up to him, tongue lolling to the side. Milton drops his leash, picks up the dog and loads him in with the Pit. Added to the group are an odd-looking spotted dog with blue eyes and shaggy ears.

"Looks like a Catahoula-Cocker mix, I swear." Milton says as he pulls the sad-looking mutt along.

"Wonder if he can hunt?" Billy Shanford grunts.

Next taken is a small terrier-Chihuahua female, then a big Husky-looking dog with one blue eye and one brown. After these are loaded, both men nod at each other and move from different directions toward the gray-and-white Whippet that has been constantly running back and forth across the yard as they rounded up the other dogs. Chasing the skinny looping runner, Billy Shanford stubs his toe on an old root and curses. Hoop leash outstretched—Milton falls in the dust as he dives for the fast-moving hound. As they're about to give up and target a different dog, the Whippet stops in one place, pirouetting on his hind legs. Hunching down conspiratorially, they creep forward and dash their hoops down. The butterfly that had captured the dog's attention slips through the hoops and disappears into the blue sky. The Whippet does not struggle. Then Milton crawls under the house and comes out with a long, sleek, pointed-nosed and hairless black dog. He goes under the steps again and brings out a medium-sized yellow Lab mix.

Silently, the men agree to leave the old Lab alone that had been lying beside the dead body. They don't notice the little Pug-Dachshund that's worrying away at a flanged metal pipe stuck between two stumps, forgetting that they'd tossed that pipe there when they'd had to remove it to open the cage and get to the big, mean German Shepherd on their first trip.

They also ignore the Jack Russell that had bothered them so much when they first came into the yard. He was staying close to the borders of the yard as he ran. "Must be looking for a bone." Billy Shanford said.

"That's all we can take this load, Billy. The rest can wait till tomorrow. There's plenty of food and water."

"Tomorrow's Sunday, Milton, and Monday's the 4th. I'm going fishing up to my in-law's for the weekend."

Milton looks worried and unconvinced.

"They're fine, Milt. There's a open food sack 'round the back and water in the tank. Mary Lou said the Judge had a granddaughter wanted to see the place anyways. We'll head back up on Tuesday."

By the time the sound of the van faded, the sun was down and the hard heat of the day began to ease.

I HOP from my nest below New Master's bed and run to the chair under the window. There are no paper hills to run between now. New-Master sleeps quiet, but Molly makes sleep noises. Big surprise.

Whoa! What's in my yard? Is it a possum? Shaking leaves in New-Master's new trees?

I'LL GET YOU, POSSUM.

YOU WAIT RIGHT THERE.

I jump down to run through my door.

"Dax." New-Master speaks soft. I stop.

"Hush, Dax. Stay."

New-Master gets up and puts on her shoes.

I jump and shout.

IT'S A POSSUM! A POSSUM!

I WILL BITE IT! COME! COME!

New-Master is faster than Old Master, but she cannot catch a possum like this.

"Okay, Dax—you run on ahead. I'll be out in a minute."

I run through my door. That possum will be sorry.

WATCH OUT, POSSUM. I'M COMING!

I shout as I run.

New Master's new trees are where the dirt pile was. New Master put Solly under the dirt where the trees are.

Where's the possum? There it is! There it is! That little tree is moving.

WATCH OUT, POSSUM.

YOU RUN. I'LL BITE YOU.

I run at the tree.

Trog steps out from behind the tree. He has white flowers in his hair. They smell like New-Master's water bath. These are the flowers from New-Master's new trees. That Trog.

WHAT ARE YOU DOING, TROG?

YOU ARE NOT NEW-MASTER'S TREE.

Hah. That Trog.

The door to New-Master's house slams. New-Master is in the yard. She will need my help.

COME ON, TROG.

WE'LL GO HELP NEW-MASTER.

I run for the house.

New-Master holds Molly in her arms. Big surprise. I run up to New-Master and smell her shoes. I sneeze. They don't smell like No-Master's shoes. They smell like corn. She leans down and rubs my head. Her hands smell like No-Master.

"Let's go check on our new parents, Dax." New-Master walks toward the back, where Jeff and Willie have their pups—all smaller than Molly.

Trog does not follow, but I walk beside New-Master, ready for trouble.

What's that? Behind us all, past the front gate, fast approaching. I run past New-Master, Molly, and Trog.

WATCH OUT!

WATCH OUT! HE'S BACK!

I know this sound.

HE'S BACK.

I warn them all.

There he is, stepping out of his box car. Round thing on his head. Bag on his back to catch us all and take us away.

BACK!

I shout.

GET AWAY! STAY AWAY! THIS IS MY YARD!

YOU CANNOT HAVE MY BROTHERS OR SISTERS.

GO AWAY! GO AWAY!

The human does not come inside the gate. He sticks papers in the box high above and then gets back in his car and rolls away. I have beaten him again. I have saved New-Master and all my dogs again.

6

THE LONG CONTRACT

2008 CE, Coquitlam, British Columbia, 30 miles east of Vancouver

THE OLD DOG sprawled on the too-small sleeping platform. The amber-and-gray head dropped over the side of the white tubular bed frame. Extending well past the other end, tail and one leg touched the concrete floor.

"THAT'S MY DOG. I want my dog," a small boy's voice piped. Narrow shoulders poked through his oversized red-striped rugby shirt. Solemn blue eyes stared past slender fingers that gripped the chain-link caging.

"Corbin, honey, that's a very nice dog, but he's too big. Wouldn't you like a happy, new puppy?" Giving up on the tugging stratagem—she'd lost that battle too many times—Philippa Chatterjee squatted down beside her son and gently patted his forearm.

The dog did not move. Dark eyes, the color of ancient bronze, fixed on empty space. On the floor two feet away, a bowl of untouched dry food sat next to another half-full of water.

Sporadic shrill yips ricocheted down the concrete and wire hall of the Wemberly Humane Society kennel, mixing with the pungent smells of dish soap and canine waste.

"I want *my* dog." One hand clinging to the cage, blond head bobbing rhythmically from side-to-side, Corbin pointed through the fence wire.

"Come look at this doggie, Corbin. Look! He's standing on his back legs! Come look, Corbin."

"His name is Jack and he's my dog," Corbin announced.

Restraining a huff, Philippa moved away from the tri-color spotted Papillon mix and looked over her son's swaying head at the large animal on the plastic mesh bed.

The label on the gate read *Mary: Gold Ret., Age 11+, arthritis, dysplasia...* "Her name's not Jack, Corbin. She's a very old dog. She's sick and she would not be able to play very much." Having reinforced herself with these facts and sure of eventual triumph, Philippa reached down, took her son's hand, and gently pulled him toward the fluffy, excited Papillon.

Corbin's feet and the grip of his other hand held firm. His eyes remained on Mary. Finally, he said, "He's a *girl* dog?"

"Yes, honey, she's a girl dog. An *old* girl dog." Philippa squatted down, released her son's hand, and paused long enough to let this damning data sink in. "Now let's go look at those puppies."

Corbin's head movements halted. He raised his free hand and rubbed his sharp chin, "I guess her name could be Jackie."

"Yes, Mary. You're a good girl. Let's have a sweet biscuit now, the both of us."
Mary's tail thumped hard against Agnes Throckmorton's thin, chenille-covered thigh.
"Now, now, girl. Such a strong girl. When my Bill was still with us, he said you'd the makings of a longshoreman yourself. He was the key to my heart, was my Bill."

The old woman knelt down and handed Mary one of the two biscuits from the tin.
"It's just us two now, dearie. Now you're my key, Mary; you're my key."

"Jac-Kie...Jac-Kie...Jac-Kie... Jac-Kie!" Corbin yelled through the wire.

Mary-Jackie's head stirred from the plastic and she focused, for the first time aware of the little person on the other side of the gate that defined her noisy new world. She stood up slowly, shook herself, walked to the wire, and pressed her dry nose against the pudgy fingers that stuck through the openings in the diagonal mesh.

If she could only smell as she once had. Still, the stories that this skin told her were strong and different. Her warm tongue flicked out to increase her reading of this strange young one.

"He licked me! He licked me! He *loves* me! I told you he was my dog! Good boy, Jackie! Good boy!" Corbin made a valiant effort to stick his fist through the fence, so that he could pat *his* dog.

Half his hand still crammed through the gate, Corbin turned and looked up at his mother.

"Please, Momma? *Please*? Jackie's a *really* good dog. I *know* he is. He's the goodest dog."

His mother's sigh was so palpable that the Yorkshire Terrier, the black Lab mix, and the Sheltie suddenly ceased the barking contest they'd engaged in since the Chatterjees arrived.

"Stay here with...Jackie, Corbin. I'll go up front and start the paperwork."

As she opened the door out of the kennel, Philippa looked back at her eight-year-old kneeling on the hard floor, face and hands pressed against the fence. Framing him was the hairy outline of the yellow-russet dog that pressed hard against the other side of the wire.

"Oh, well," she whispered to herself, "That's done. Maybe

Miss Therapist Emily Jones is right. I just hope this huge old mutt doesn't scare Lisa."

"Wait, Corbin! Corbin!"

Too late, the boy opened the back door of the Subaru and slid out, Jackie-the-dog not far behind him. Through the window, Philippa watched three-year-old Lisa squeal as she jumped off the swing to meet the new canine playmate.

"So much for being frightened." Philippa smiled softly and got out of the car.

Over the next few weeks, the dog paid little attention to Philippa's youngest child. The old retriever occasionally delivered an arm or face lick; Philippa noticed these ministrations as Lisa always giggled when "Jackie kisses me." From the beginning, though, Jackie stuck close to Corbin as he made his rounds—running frantically inside and out, the dog patiently trailing along behind him. Lisa, on the other hand, usually played by herself in her room when she wasn't outside with the family.

Sometimes Philippa noticed Jackie limping, and that she often groaned when she rose from a nap—not that Corbin's activities left the retriever a lot of nap time. Usually, she trotted after the boy as he pelted hither and yon, a wordless but constant companion. When Corbin crashed, when his seemingly limitless energies depleted themselves and he collapsed in a heap on the sofa or under the birch trees at the edge of the yard, Jackie could always be found resting her head on his leg or arm. Slowly, almost imperceptibly, Philippa noticed that her son's manic energy levels were subsiding, regularizing or regulating. Small frustrations that had led to his violent outbursts of non-verbal activity now triggered instead questions and articulate pleadings.

FOGGY FROM A LATE night at the clinic where she worked, Philippa stumbled through the house in the soft dawnlight. She stood in Corbin's open doorway for a moment, looking at her sleeping son. The boy splayed across his low futon in the far corner of the room. His mouth was open and his right hand lightly clenched a fistful of the thick golden fur on Jackie's back.

Philippa crept toward her son, walking heel-to-toe so as not to awaken any creaks from the old pine floorboards.

"Damn!" she squeaked as something small and sharp bit into the sole of her foot.

Jackie's head rose from between her paws and watched as Philippa stood one-legged and removed the offending, embedded blue plastic from the bottom of her foot.

"I hate Legos," she muttered, glancing anxiously at her still-sleeping child.

She looked down. Red and blue and yellow-nippled boxes and rectangles randomly covered much of the floor. A half-finished castle lay in ruins in front of Corbin's desk. Between her and the bed, a collection of two- and four-wheeled axles were parked haphazardly inside a block-plastic corral.

Philippa folded her arms and a broad smile crept over her face. She focused her attention on the dog, who had not closed her eyes but had settled her head back down on top of her outstretched legs.

"Good girl, Jackie," Philippa whispered, turned, and left the bedroom.

"THAT'S RIGHT, Hari. *All over* the floor." Holding the phone to her face an hour later, Philippa was still smiling.

As she listened to her husband's reply, Corbin ran through the living room in his bright Yu-Gi-Oh! PJs. Jackie trotted right behind him.

"No. It couldn't have been Lisa. She never plays in Corbin's room—you know that."

The screen door in the kitchen slammed.

"Put your shoes on if you're going outside, Corbin." Philippa tilted the phone away from her mouth as she yelled through the wall in her son's general direction, then raised the receiver to her ear again. "Sorry, dear. Yes, that's what I'm telling you. No more 'military formations.' Everything was all over the room in a… well…in a mess—a glorious mess."

"I know, I know. But the last week has been amazing. I can't wait to tell Emily at the next session." Philippa paused, listening.

"It seems like a month. Can't you push through tonight? Kamloops is not that far." Gravity tugged down her brow and the corners of her mouth. "Tomorrow, then. Love you, too. Be safe. Bye."

Philippa punched her phone off and headed for the sink of dirty breakfast dishes.

SHE FINISHED CLEANING the egg pan and began wiping the counters. Jackie was barking outside. A pleasant homey sound, Philippa thought; Jackie's barks always sounded like talking.

The screen door banged again. As she wiped the dark-green tiles at the back of the countertop, Philippa felt the slight warmth of her son at her side, just before he spoke to her.

"Mama?"

"Yes, Corbin?" Philippa pulled a copper-bottomed saucepan from the rinse water and started drying it.

"Mama?" The pitch of Corbin's voice rose a third.

"What is it, dear?" She reached down into the sudsy water, searching for the tongs she'd used to turn the bacon that morning.

"Mama—I'm really sorry. I won't do it again."

Philippa turned to the side and looked down at her son. His dark green eyes were open wide, and he was holding his right wrist up to her.

Taking Corbin's arm in her wet hands, it was impossible to miss the angry red dot in the middle of a puff of swelling on his forearm. "What happened, Corbin?"

"I'm sorry, Mama. I know it scares you. I didn't mean to." The boy was beginning to hyperventilate. Jackie appeared behind him and pressed up against his leg. He caught his breath, "A bee stung me. It hurts a lot."

The color drained from Philippa Chatterjee's already pale

face. Nasty reactions to mild insect bites and stings ran in her family. A cousin had died from just such a sting. And Corbin—along with all his other challenges—had inherited this problem in spades.

Quickly and carefully, she examined the bump for residues of the insect's stinger. Nothing. Already down on her knees at his level, she held her son's face between her two palms, kissed his forehead, and spoke softly and urgently to him.

"It's okay, honey. It's okay. You didn't do anything wrong. Don't cry." She kissed him again and wiped his eyes with her fingers. Straightening up, she grabbed the Benadryl from the back of the counter, pulled a spoon from a drawer, and poured the cap full of the red liquid.

Wordlessly, Corbin downed the medicine.

"Now you go out and get in the car right now, dear. We have to take you to the doctor."

"All right, Mama." Corbin ran for the door, but holding it open he called back, "Can Jackie come, too?"

"No, honey, Jackie has to stay here and watch the house for us. Now get in the car and buckle up." As she talked, Philippa rummaged through the third drawer under the silverware, looking for the case where they kept the Epi-pen. She might not need it if she could get to the doctor. There it was, under the rolling pin—she grabbed the tin box and ran out the door, letting it swing closed behind her.

Ten miles, she thought, *maybe half-an-hour.* Coquitlam Clinic was in the center of town. For the thousandth time, she wondered what they were doing staying out here in the boonies with small children. She firmly pulled the Subaru into gear and backed out, resolving to have a talk with Hari again when he returned. A fierce calm settled over her as she sped down the two-lane blacktop toward the saving graces of civilization.

JACKIE

Where did they go? Corbin is hurt. Mama helps him. They go in the car. Mama's smell is sharp with fear. I will wait.

There's sun-warmth in the yard. Corbin is hurt but he is with Mama. I will sit and wait.

My back legs hurt. The floor is cold. The sun is warm and stops the hurt. I will wait for Corbin.

A squirrel! At the edge of the yard, a squirrel! The door is closed. My legs hurt. I will wait.

A car comes. Corbin and Mama are here. We'll play in the warm sun. I will catch that squirrel. Corbin will laugh.

Another car. Not Mama's car. It stops.

Woman-person-I-know smell. Lisa. Lisa is here. She is not hurt.

HELLO, WOMAN-PERSON-I-KNOW.

I bark.

HELLO, LISA. CORBIN IS HURT.

Woman-person-I-know opens the door, barks into the house.

Smell Lisa. She is happy. Smell woman-person-I-know; she is—afraid? Tired? She is tired. She barks into the house again.

I tell her again:

CORBIN IS HURT, WOMAN-PERSON I KNOW.

She hits my head softly. She does not understand me.

Lisa comes home.

HELLO, LISA, I kiss her. Lisa laughs.

Woman-person leaves. She closes door.

Lisa runs. I run after her.

She barks little noises. She runs and holds her hands in front of her. I run behind her. My legs hurt to run on the floor, but Lisa laughs and runs.

Lisa opens the door and we run outside. It is warm. My legs and feet do not hurt so much in the warmth and on the grass. Around and around we run.

We are under the big tree at the edge of the yard. The squirrel is in this tree. I don't see him, but I smell for him. Yes, he is here. I do not smell all the things I once smelled, but I know squirrel smell.

We go up the hill into the woods. It is not as warm here. We run and run. I smell new things all around as we run. I am strong from the new smells and I run like I am young.

"HORSE PUCKY," Philippa muttered quietly, sitting in the beige-and-white examining room, waiting for the doctor, "I must've left my cell at home or...oh my god, I left my purse in the car."

The thick oak-and-metal door opened and a woman about Philippa's age and size, dressed in purple scrubs, backed into the room.

"Hi, Philippa." The newcomer smiled at both the other occupants, "Hi, Corbin."

"Oh, Gwen. I'm glad they sent you in. Corbin's been stung."

"Did you pen him, yet?" Juliet tucked an unruly strand of straw-colored hair under her matching purple scrub cap.

"No, he hasn't shown many symptoms except the swelling."

Dr. Gwendolyn Stonely turned to Corbin and broadened her smile. She took his right wrist in her left hand, simultaneously checking his pulse and examining the swollen forearm, "How are you feeling, Corbin?"

"The stinger hurts a lot." Corbin's face twisted between recognition and upset. "Mama said we had to leave Jackie at home."

"I bet it does. We'll take care of that right away, dear." She checked her watch, released Corbin's arm, and folded her arms. "I'll need to take him back for some bloodwork, Philippa, then we'll watch him for about half-a-day. He's going to be fine, I'm sure." The ginger-haired doctor reached forward, gripping and releasing Philippa's elbow.

"Will you stay with him, Gwen? I've got to call Hari and I left my phone in the car."

Dr. Stonely's face blanked for an instant, then her lips straightened into a thin smile, "Sure, Philippa. I'll stay with him till you get back. Come on, big boy, I've got a piece of chocolate down the hall with your name on it."

"Dr. Stonely will stay with you, Corbin. I'll be right back. I've got to call your Dad." Philippa pecked a kiss on the top of her son's head as he slid off the examining bench. "Back in a minute—I promise. Thanks, Gwen."

"No problem. We'll be in the Green Recovery next to Radiology."

JACKIE

It is colder now. The ground is soft and smells alive. Lisa sits. I sit next to her. Home is far down the hill now. I cannot smell home.

Many new scents here. Squirrel and skunk—I know skunk—and deer and rabbit. Other things I do not know. Between the trees in the sun is sweet grass. I am too tired to run to it. Lisa's hands are cold on my ears. She barks my name softly.

Little blue flyer moves in the air in front of me. Lisa jumps up and runs. She wants to catch the flyer. I stand. Ohhh. My hips. They shake when I stand. I start to fall. I cannot run after her and the flyer.

STOP, LISA. STOP. DON'T RUN. WE ARE TOO FAR FROM HOME. IT IS COLD.

But Lisa does not stop. The smells are so strong all around me. Lisa will not like skunks. And it is cold now. I must bring her home.

I stand now without shaking. Run to Lisa.

COME WITH ME, LISA. WE GO HOME NOW. IT IS COLD. YOU WILL NOT LIKE SKUNKS.

I bark in front of her. The blue flyer is gone and so is the sun warmth. Lisa walks down the hill away from home.

NO, LISA. NO. COME WITH ME TO HOME. THAT IS THE WRONG WAY.

Lisa does not stop and walks faster. I must run. Ohh. Every step makes hot hard pain in my hips. I am in front of Lisa now. I take her hand in my mouth.

Lisa pulls away and makes the very bad hurt sound. She sits and makes the sound louder. Water comes from her eyes. When I lick her face, she hits me. Her eye water tastes like soup. I sit beside her. She pushes me and gets up and runs. She runs badly and falls down the hill. She rolls and hits a tree. I must run to her. She is hurt. I run and hurt. I cannot fall. I must help Lisa.

THE GREEN SUBARU waited at the edge of the lot accusingly. Quickstepping across the concrete, thoughts ricocheted through Philippa's mind: *I couldn't have locked it; the keys are in my bag. Oh my god, if they're gone, Hari will never let me live this down. I've got to get back to Corbin. What if he's really not all right? What if Gwen doesn't stay with him—I could tell she wasn't happy. What are we doing living in the wilderness when we've got a boy like Corbin? Where is Hari? Why is he never here when these things happen? If my cell is gone, I'll never remember everyone's numbers.*

She lurched the last few feet to the passenger-side door and yanked it open. Her purse leaned, half-open, against the center console. Philippa snatched it up, then slammed and locked the doors.

"No problem," she said out loud, allowing herself the slightest of smiles and a little sigh. "Oh, Canada. Good thing we're not in Seattle!"

"We Are The Champions" cascaded out of her purse. She had a text message. *Okay, Okay— Gwen could wait another minute or two. And I need to call Hari anyway.* Philippa dug out her phone and navigated to Messages:

```
Mellie got 2go 2 th DDS, bringing Lisa home
early. CU, Kate.
```

The time was almost an hour ago.

For an instant, Philippa stared at the phone and the message. Her hands, her feet, even her chest seemed unable to move. Then she punched Redial. Two rings later, Kate answered—loud television gunfire almost drowning out her familiar contralto.

"Heya, J. In the middle of getting supper down for the boys. What ya doing?"

Philippa controlled her voice, asking simply, "Is Lisa with you, Kate?"

The reply came with no hesitation, "Whaddyamean, dearie? I left her with you about an hour ago."

"You left her at the house?" Philippa strangled the words out of her tightening throat.

"Well...yeah. Jackie greeted us proper. I called for you and Corbie, but you must've been in the back, eh?" Kate's cheerful tone wavered.

"I wasn't there, Kate. I'm in Coquitlam with Corbin. We're at the Clinic. No one was there, Kate."

"Oh My Stars, Philippa! I didn't know! I'm on my way."

"No. Call 911 for me first. I've got to check on Corbin before I get out of here to my baby."

Snapping off the phone, Philippa ran back through the clinic doors.

JACKIE

Lisa is cold. She wets her eyes and I kiss her face. She sleeps and it is cold. My back and my legs and my hips and my feet hurt. I will make Lisa warm. Circle her and make her warm. She sleeps.

The sun and its warmth are gone. I will sleep.

What is that? Above us. Smell. New smell. Bad smell. I am afraid.

Lisa does not smell this thing. If she smells this she would not sleep.

Ohh. I cannot run. I hurt and I must stop this. It smells like an eater. I must stop this eater. But I cannot run. I will climb to the top so the eater cannot jump down on Lisa.

ANGRY SWELLING and pain stiffened every movement of the old golden retriever as she rose from her encirclement of the drowsing little girl. Head down, she pushed through brakes of salal, brushing past tall ferns that grew around the bases of the tall cedars and Doug firs that covered the mountainside. Her nostrils were full of the scent of a powerful carnivore, its smell drifting with the night air that slipped over the crest of this foothill. Jackie didn't know what this creature was, but she knew it was coming closer and that it ate meat. She must climb to its level, maybe distract it. If it fell from above on the little girl, the end would be quick and certain.

The shooting stabbing pains in her joints and back lessened some as she climbed—the natural lubricant of movement combined with adrenalin anesthetic. Now she was at the top of the hill that Lisa had fallen from. The smell was not as strong, but Jackie felt something, something she didn't understand. It was like fear, but it moved her heart; it did not freeze it. She knew this thing. She had never smelled it before, but she *knew* it.

A scream rips across the chill mountain air, tearing through Jackie's heightened senses. She raises her head and it—the source of the smell and the scream—crouches in front of her, thirty feet away. She turns to run from this terrifying monster of death.

"Jackie?" Lisa's small voice, made thinner by the filter of the forest, floats up from the dark below, "Jackie?" The faint voice repeats.

The mountain cat swivels its head downhill; the small threat of the dog forgotten with the promise of an easier meal.

Jackie's vision blurs, but it's not the blurring of age or illness.

Standing still for this long moment, the tawny cat in front of her grows larger. Its teeth extend beyond its jaws to become something impossible, nightmarish. And as this horrible transformation occurs, Jackie feels her own body changing. She is no longer an arthritic fifteen-year-old house-dwelling golden retriever. She is the protector. She is the guardian in the dark. She is the friend to the hopeless, savior of the helpless. She is dog.

Jackie roars forward in anger and defiance. Surprised by its prey's aggression, the cougar pauses long enough for the dog to close the distance. Jackie hurtles into the shocked beast. Though less than half the predator's mass, she knocks it sideways into a thick stand of bearberry.

Dog and cougar rise together, inches apart.

Now cautious, the great cat cringes and growls.

BACK AWAY, BAD THING, BACK AWAY!

Jackie shouts hoarsely:

LEAVE US ALONE! GO AWAY! I WILL BITE YOU!

The cougar screams in Jackie's face and tears at her muzzle with a harsh-tipped paw.

The sharp talons rake down Jackie's throat, leaving dripping red streaks on her yellow fur.

The blood smell of prey emboldens the puma. It coils its haunches for a final attack. Forgotten instincts fill the old dog. Muzzle wide, Jackie charges again, stretching for the cougar's heavily muscled throat.

Used to mortal struggles, the cat twists before the dog's jaws close and Jackie's pointed canines close through the puma's tufted right ear.

The dog clamps and holds.

Though far from life-threatening, the dog's ear-grip causes the cougar enormous pain. The cat flails, striking this crazy prey again and again with its deadly, claws-out paws. It rolls, managing to bite down again on the dog's shoulder, but then releasing to concentrate on batting away its antagonist's head.

One of Jackie's teeth loosens and breaks off in the cat's mangled ear. At the same time, the cougar pulls away at an angle that pushes the dog backwards. The cat's ear rips, the dog falls away, snarling.

Confused and rumpled, the puma turns and runs into the wilderness night.

Bleeding from a dozen wounds, energy drained beyond reserves, adrenalin flushed, Jackie collapses where she stands. After she falls, she moves in and out of darkness. Each time she wakens, she creeps a few inches down the hill toward the little girl who still calls for her.

"Let's all of us have a sweet biscuit now."
Jackie's tail thumps hard against Agnes Throckmorton's bony knee.
"Now, now, girl. I know how strong you are. Isn't that right, Lisa?"
Lisa, dressed in a yellow pony suit, nods as she eats her cookie.
"And my Corbin says you've the makings of a longshoreman yourself."
Corbin and the old woman and Lisa all kneel down in front of Jackie.
Everyone has a biscuit. Agnes' frail hand holds one out to her dog.
"It's just us now, dearie. And you're my key, Jackie. You're my key."

"Oh. Jackie. Jackie." Lisa puts her arms around most of the big dog's blood-matted chest. Human sounds roll down from the hill above and Jackie's ears prick up as she recognizes Philippa Chatterjee's voice among them. Rising from the soft grass, Jackie feels no pain. In wonder and joy, she lifts her golden head to the blue, empty sky.

7

PURELAND BARDO OF THE ETERNAL DOG

SWEET RABBIT SCENT filled his nostrils. He was running. No, now he lapped cool water from a stone pool under a jewel-blue sky. No. He lay by the fire with his mate and his master, belly full of deer. No, He dug—fast and faster—closing on his prey's nest. No, he ran. Through mist and grass and stream. His brothers and sisters coursed next to him. He stood still and alert on a windy hill, watching sheep eddy and flow around him. He licked the hand of a dying child; her touch soft as snow on his brow.

Short, long, tall, heavy, frail: with coat gold, brown, black, white, Jack stepped through dense rising fog, climbing a hill of bright, long-bladed grass. The air cleared as he rounded the top. He stopped, looking ahead.

A great crowd of familiar humans waited. The grey, bent head of Dre-khe-mosul, scribe and embalmer of the 18th Dynasty of Egypt's pharaohs. Proud Fu Hou, dressed in her fine silks and towering helmet, stern as always, but with the corners of her mouth turned up in the tiniest of smiles. A teenager in furs holding a stone spear. A bald, middle-aged man in hose and an open collar, ink-stained feather stuck over his ear and an unreadable expression on his face. A small boy and his parents, all in white tunics: standing, laughing quietly. The soft brown eyes of a serape-clad young man, the anxious ice-blues of Dmitri Sergeyovich in his crisp black smock, the watery gaze of an old man in worn blue-jean overalls: all smiled their own smiles at Jack. As did many, many others.

Jack knew each of them: the positions of their feet, the angles of their eyes and bodies, the lines in their brows and cheeks, the movements of their hands and fingers. A lifted eyebrow from Korpralpinsins, the drooping shoulders of Reymera sang full tales to Jack.

Their smells: pungent dungy odors of sheep and cattle, the rich well-remembered aromas of cloth and wood and leather, the sharp smack of copper and iron. More powerful than all these were the scents of the humans themselves, sweats of a hundred varieties—all with vast and complete stories telling him of fear and love and kindness, of ownership and care. These smells sang the loudest, longest songs to Jack.

Jack moved forward to meet these humans—his humans.

But their smiles and gestures did not beckon him to come.

Something in Carlos Giquamea's chocolate eyes made Jack feel as he did when he watched Flower Nose nurse their first litter, cleaning the birth sacs from their children, then giving them nourishment from her body. In those young brown eyes he saw himself for what he was.

THEY ARE HERE BECAUSE OF YOU, JACK. ALL BECAUSE OF YOU.

THEY MADE NO SOUNDS, yet the deep warmth that pulsed inside him grew into this meaning, as surely as if his humans made their noises at him. And as the heat within him grew, the recognition of what he was to these humans and what they were to him, they shimmered and faded into the greens of the grass and the blues of the sky. Last to fade was the boy in furs who held the stone-tipped spear. Sad green eyes locked with Jack's and he raised his spear in salute, then lowered his head as he merged with the air and the earth.

There was no sun in the clear sky, so Jack did not know how long he stood there, his body pulsing with the heat of who he was. He was not surprised when he looked down at his feet to find they were golden and they no longer touched the soft grass of the hilltop.

He looked further out now, across the plain of endless grass. Another dog was running toward him. Wide, square jaw, brindle coat. As the bully breed approached, Jack could see a still-bleeding hole in her side. She ran toward him, but stopped when she realized Jack's feet did not touch the ground. She looked up, then down, and moaned a faint whimper.

The smell of this dog rose to Jack—not just into his nostrils, but flowing through his entire being. Pain, hopelessness, betrayal, brutal mating, an unexpected tenderness of motherhood, and guardianship of the innocent. Jack knew these things as he knew red meat and clear water. He imagined from these a place of security and joy. Happy humans with soft hands and shining faces who threw balls and brought toys to pull and hide and bury. Soft, warm nests and birthing places hidden in cozy boxes, on and under plush couches and beds, behind dog-sized doors in snug closets and rooms. Bowls of treats—some soft, some crunchy—filled with flavors and scents of every description. Other dogs, small and large: playful, respectful. Dogs that lounged and slept near, bringing warmth and companionship for this tired spirit, whose energy would be endless when this young one was ready again to play and romp.

As Jack imagined these things, he watched the cowering young dog below him. He opened his mouth to encourage her and a bright path flowed from him along a ridgetop that led to a new hill, a new place where his imaginings took form.

The shy pit bull mother raised her head to look at Jack. Her long mottled tongue swiped across her lips, brown eyes blinked. Her tail uncurled from beneath her and began wild helicopter swings. Eyes clear now, she stood for an instant on her back legs, barking acknowledgment and acceptance. Then she ran down Jack's pureland path and into his waiting vision.

After Jack lost sight of the other dog, he noticed her worn, studded collar had fallen off and now lay below. Something about this collar held his attention and he found himself descending to it.

He put his nose to it. He sneezed. Anger, fear, desperation: he had expected those. But there was more. He took the collar between his jaws. The tastes were so strong. His path was clear. Closing his eyes, Jack imagined again. He imagined not what he did not know, but what he did know. He would return to where he should be. Jack was coming back.

DELCO JONES IGNORED the faint tang of sulfur and smoke that curled by him in the cold Detroit morning and pushed open the broken oak door with his size 12 Air Jordan.

The stucco walls around him were scarred and gashed open, all remnants of copper removed. Most of the floor of the coved-ceiling living room was piled with stinking trash bags and mounds of unbagged waste.

Stopping in front of a quaint mosaic tile fireplace from another century, he looked down and called out, "Get over here, homey."

The shattered mirror over the green stone mantelpiece showed an unmoving dark brindle figure, outlined against the clear light jabbing in from broken windows. In a moment, a second person appeared in the reflection and stood beside Delco.

"You shot that mother dog, Chunlee."

"What you sayin'? She was divin' for my nads."

"Yeah. Well, you killed it. Big man."

Between two twisted floor lamps and a discarded microwave,

an ancient plaid sofa squatted in the middle of the trash bags. At one end of the couch, surrounded by a heap of unmatched cushions, was a ragged foam-edged hole. In the middle of that hole were three young pups: two brindle and one black. They made the squeak-toy sounds universal to all canid offspring of such an age, occasionally nibbling on their siblings or even on themselves with sharp but ineffective milk teeth.

Chunlee stuffed a still-warm Cobra .380 into the waistband of his shiny red slip-pants, and picked up a brindle in each long-fingered, coffee-colored hand. The pups mewled, but no louder than before.

"Yo, brutha. Got some gaming meat here. Six months and five pounds of Mickey D and we got ourselves some In-Come!" Chunlee tossed the squirming pups back into the nest with their littermate, then picked up the nearest trash bag and dumped its clattering contents on the hard red pine floor. He picked one of the brindles up by the scruff of its neck and dropped it into the bag, then repeated this with the matching puppy. When he reached for the black pup, another hand grabbed his wrist.

"Leave that black one, bro." Delco Jones' voice was soft.

Chunlee pulled away and stepped back from the dog nest. He held up his hands, palms facing out, "Chill, my man. It's all good. You saw 'em; you pick. We straight?" Chunlee's feet slid backwards half-a-step as he spoke.

Delco Jones did not reply. His hands hung at his sides. He was looking down at the last pup in the nest. He didn't notice when Chunlee picked up the plastic bag that held the two mewling pups and slipped away. He just stood in the empty house, watching the random movements of the little dog in the hole in the sofa.

For some reason, he was thinking of his grandfather, who died when Delco Jones was ten. The old man's deep rich voice rolled over him like syrup over pancakes, "Del, my boy, you gotta take care of yourself. You gotta take care of your sisters."

Remembering then that Gramps had said the same thing to his sisters, a thin line of bright teeth flashed across his young face.

He focused on the baby pit again. The dog had stopped wriggling and was watching him, too. Sober brown eyes looked up into his.

"You a serious lil' devil, blackie. What I gonna do with you?"

Delco Jones' lips curled on one side. Reaching into the cushion nest, he gently picked up the little pup and cradled it in his large hands. It nipped him mercilessly and ineffectually.

His shoulders hunched as he gently corralled the puppy, but his head was upright when he walked out of the abandoned house. He hadn't seen his sister Agatha in a year. She could use a good dog to keep her safe. And this, Delco Jones was certain, was a good dog.

END OF *STEEL DOG*: Volume 4 of *Tales of the Eternal Dog*

DEDICATION

To my canine teachers & friends, in order of appearance:

Tinker: a dipsophiliac Chihuahua
Castor and Pollux: ill-fated sibling Weimaraners
Cleo: Gladys & Mack's Bassett Hound
Slippers: foundling Border Collie/'56 Ford cross
Rosemary: a *real* Cocker Spaniel, Slippers' best friend
Pepé: a thoroughly *au naturel* standard Poodle
Dog: aprobablykindof Beagle owned by Slippers
?: an anti-bicyclist Chow on the corner of Bolivar & Taliaferro
Greta: an overprotective German Shepherd Dog
Sweet Pea: an undocked Dobie sweetheart
Josephine: Aussie Shepherd/coyote—one of the three smartest canines I've met
Softie: older (& smarter) half-brother of Jake
Jake: Monster (& Star) of Gribble Springs, omnivorous Bobtail/Golden Retriever
??: Irish Wolfhound assiduously & gentilely guarding the NTSU Graduate apartments at 1 am
Fergus: Irish Terrier afraid of naught but pillows

Zanzibar: Australian Cattle Dog; brightest & homeliest pooch south of Canada
Dudley: Schipperke bearing a strong similarity to my beard
Katie: Welsh Pembroke Corgi who, like all her breed, knew her own mind
Friday: bravest coward, little Lab "and something"
Fabio: aka Mr. Fabinus, a magnificent Cavalier King Charles companion & jester

And most particularly to
Golly St. Nicholas Chompsky...Nick: our "biddable" Rough Collie/Malamute/Lab/German Shepherd/etc. goof dog beyond alpha or beta

ACKNOWLEDGMENTS

Highly recommended (mostly non-fiction) books that greatly informed my understanding of dogs and dog-human relationships:

A Dog's History of America: How Our Best Friend Explored, Conquered, and Settled a Continent by Mark Derr

Always Faithful: A Memoir of the Marine Dogs of WWII by Captain William W. Putney D.V.M., U.S.M.C.

Animals in Translation: Using the Mysteries of Autism to Decode Animal Behavior by Temple Grandin (and Catherine Johnson)

City by Clifford D. Simak

The Genius of Dogs: How Dogs are Smarter Than You Think by Brian Hare and Vanessa Woods

The Hidden Life of Dogs by Elizabeth Marshall Thomas

How Dogs Think: Understanding the Canine Mind
The Intelligence of Dogs
The Modern Dog
The Pawprints of History
Understanding Your Dog for DUMMIES
Why Does My Dog Act That Way
by Stanley Coren

In the Shadow of a Rainbow: *The True Story of a Friendship between Man and Wolf* by Robert Franklin Leslie

Last Dog on the Hill: *The Extraordinary Life of Lou* by Steve Duno

Merle's Door: *Lessons from a Freethinking Dog* by Ted Kerasote

Paws & Effect: *The Healing Power of Dogs* by Sharon Sakson

The Right Dog for You: *Choosing a Breed that Matches Your Personality, Family and Lifestyle* by Daniel F. Tortora, Ph.D.

Through a Dog's Eyes: *Understanding How They See the World* by Jennifer Arnold

Wild Animals I Have Known by Ernest Thompson Seton

ABOUT THE AUTHOR

Alec enjoys the bumblebees & the swiftly flowing streams of the Pacific Northwest. He's married (has been but once), is deeply attached to herb & vegetable gardening, reading history & philosophy, pre-punk Japanese culture (especially Akira Kurosawa's films and Ichiro Honda's Mothra & Godzilla), live acoustic music and the accurate reproduction thereof. He plans to continue writing about his (spousily shared) Sixer Diaspora Universe (and dogs) until he's crated up and shipped away. He's seldom right about anything and almost never wrong about everything.

Telling Jack's stories has been my privilege, but if you'd like to keep up with future developments, check out my media links (listed below).
And if you enjoyed reading about Jack, please leave a review of this book on Amazon.

https://www.amazon.com/author/alecrowell
http://www.soundvolumes.com
http://www.facebook.com/alecrowellauthor

Milton Keynes UK
Ingram Content Group UK Ltd.
UKHW040659050124
435493UK00001B/70